SWIFT AS WIND

EARTH STONES TRILOGY BOOK TWO

SWIFT AS WIND

LISA CRAM

THUNDER ROAD PUBLISHING

SWIFT AS WIND

Copyright © 2024 by Lisa Cram
All rights reserved.

Published by Thunder Road Publishing LLC

Cover design by Rick Holland at myvisionpress.com
Cover illustration by Dana Cram
Maps and chapter symbols by Lynn Nansen-Dale

ISBN-13: 979-8-9917887-2-4 (Paperback)
ISBN-13: 979-8-9917887-3-1 (Ebook)

First Edition

This is a work of fiction. All names, characters, places and incidents are either the product of the author's imagination or are used fictitiously, and any resemblance to actual persons, dead or alive, business establishments, events or locales, is purely coincidental...

Or more simply stated, I made everything up purely for your entertainment which entailed stretching science and technology to fit the story, ignoring inconvenient real life world events, and distorting what might be construed as everyday reality.

No AI was used in the writing of this book.

www.lisacram.com

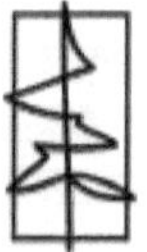

For Mom and Dad
I would not be the person I am today
without your love and encouragement.

N
Sea
of
Meura
Winterlands
(Arctakai)
City of Ice
Desertlands
(Seakai)
Forestlands
(Terrakai)
Inception
Great
Ocean

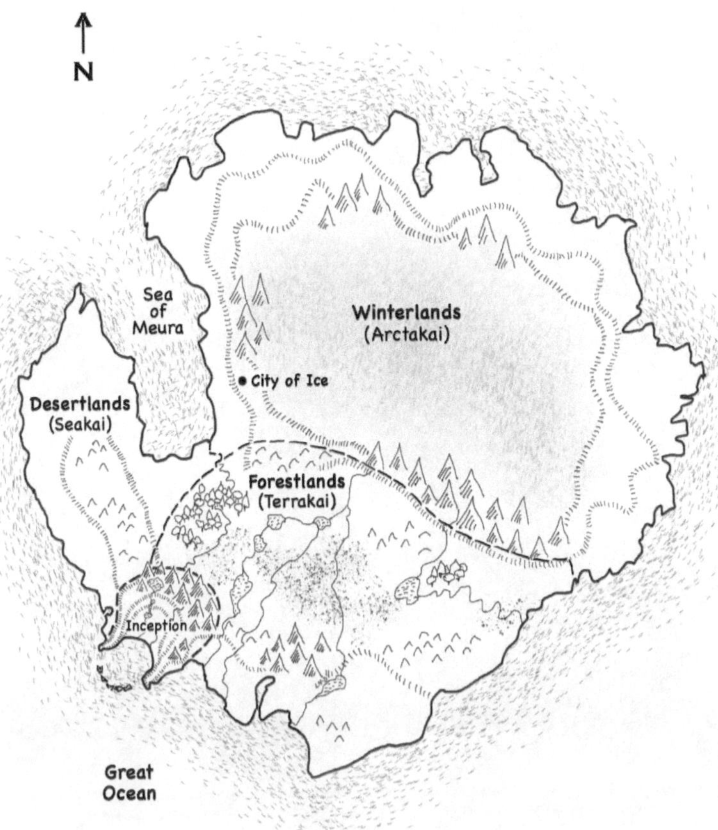

MERLUMA

N
The Ruins
Black Mountains
Deep Lake
Labyrinth
Great Ocean

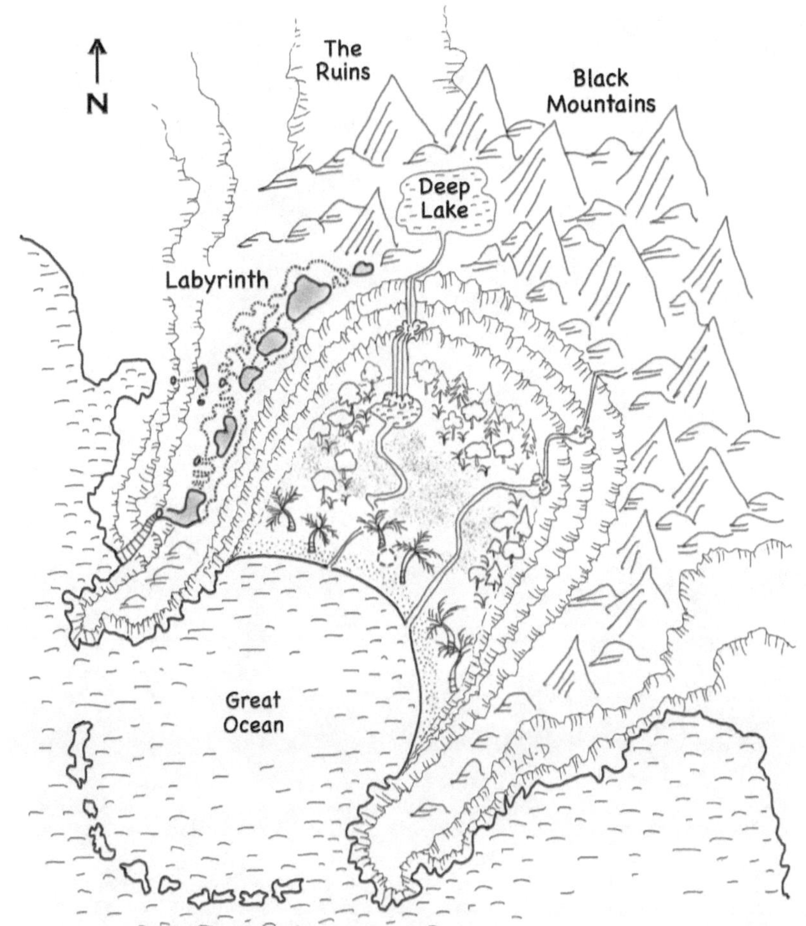

INCEPTION

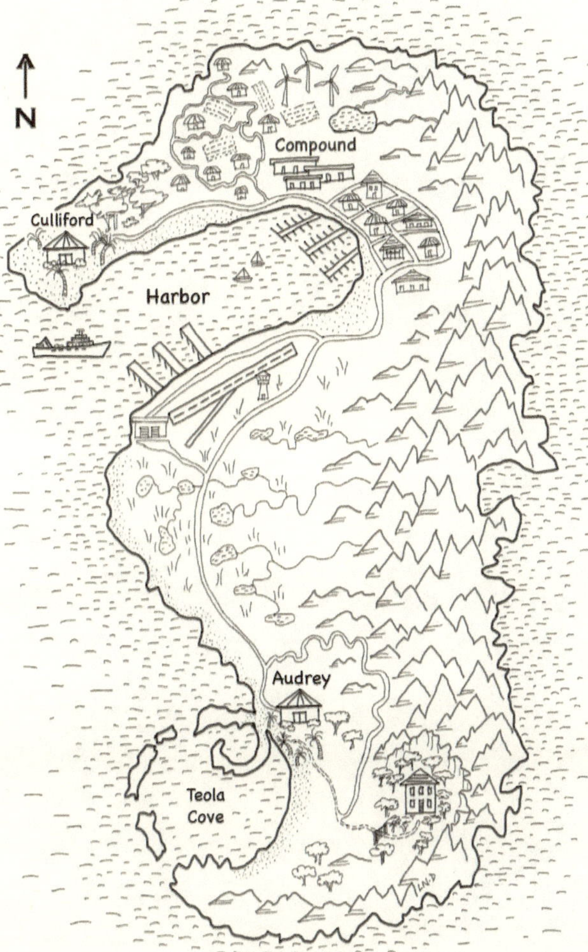

ISLA SALVACIÓN

PART ONE

1

Bring Out The Dead

IT WAS STRANGE BEING dead. The freedom to do as one pleases, go where you want, when you want. To move through the world like a shadow of your former self, pretending to be who you are not. Ever cognizant of your carefully crafted disguise, and in Sinto's case, by the use of camouflage like that of a cephalopod of the sea. An innate trick of illusion, like applying makeup to change one's skin color and texture, or employing hair dye to darken one's golden hair to a nondescript brown, or drawing a cloaked curtain over ever-glowing green eyes.

And as Sinto recently learned, how easily one could let that disguise slip and potentially invite catastrophe to a carefully laid plan.

An Earth month had passed since the day he officially died, but he could wait no longer. He had yet to fully heal and was not quite feeling like his old self. His mentor and healer, Wantemo, said it could take months. Time Sinto didn't have. He had vowed to himself, and his mother—before his faked death—that he would search for his missing father.

He returned to Merluma with hopes of shortcutting his journey. His plan was to slip through the portal in Deep Lake that led directly to the Terrakai City of Green located in the great waters on Earth. The climb to Deep Lake would be arduous. But starting on the opposite side of the Terrakai settlements and working his way through the jungle and foothills of Inception to the Black Mountains was the best way to avoid detection.

The sun was readying to rise, casting the sky and reflective sea a soothing pink. He extinguished the coals from last night's fire with sand, then called for his bird Scout, Moonstone.

It took a couple of tries to roust him, but Moonstone finally swooped down from his sleeping nest in the leaf node of a nearby palmamide tree.

Moonstone was a large black bird; a cross between Earth's raven and an eagle with a touch of red flair. His crown of spiky red feathers was skewed. If a bird could yawn, then that's what he did, after casting Sinto a stink eye and sharing images of unspeakable acts that his wicked talons could do to Sinto's eyes for waking him before the sun rose.

"*Save it for the enemy,*" Sinto responded in mind-speak, a telepathic form of communication the Merahvu had perfected between themselves and most other creatures. His words translated into a language of images and senses Moonstone would readily understand.

Moonstone shared back, "I *did.*"

Sinto gave him a dirty look. "*Your attempt at humor could use some work.*"

Moonstone replied with an image of Sinto sleeping and Moonstone swooping over and relieving himself directly into Sinto's eye.

Sinto smiled. "*Better than a sharp talon.*"

Moonstone squawked, *hah-hah-hah,* then took off down the well-trodden game trail cut through the jungle that led to the foothills of the mountains.

Sinto followed Moonstone, who scouted ahead for others. He carried and wore nothing, choosing to travel fully camouflaged, mimicking the shadows and greenery of the awakening jungle. It was warm here, but that would change once they reached higher elevations. Regardless, the cold would do him good. His body could handle freezing temperatures, though it would be unpleasant. He needed a jolt after lazy days recovering on the warm beach after his recent trip to Earth that he took shortly after he was healed. A trip that exhausted him more than he expected.

Sinto's thoughts drifted back to that day on the northern shore of the Sapien island of Oahu, a beach filled with Sapien surfers who stood upon pointy boards and competed to be the one to ride the longest inside the tube of a wave. Pipeline. Wantemo sent Sinto there for his last, and most important, test under his tutelage. Anger and distrust were wicked emotions that Sinto had recently gained, which Sinto had to choose whether to diffuse or let guide him. The test was to reveal Sinto's true nature—which path he would travel into the unfolding and unknown future.

Sinto chose to stop the tsunami born from the destruction of his underwater city—Tallamure. If he hadn't stopped it, many innocent Sapiens on the beach would have died, and everything beyond the shore would have been swept away. He chose the brighter path. And intoxicated by the power that filled him from that decision, he impulsively dropped his disguise to show the Sapiens what he really was. To declare that he was real—human like them—not some mythical fantasy.

After the impassioned excitement faded, he remembered that Sapiens shared stories electronically—stories that could span the globe in a nanosecond, including pictures taken with cell phones. He didn't recall seeing anyone documenting his "revealing" but, if they did, he had given them every opportunity to capture him in his full natural glory on their tiny cell phone screens: the green fire burning in his eyes; the unique swirled and dotted markings adorning his spine and buttocks, encircling his hips, and merging in an especially artistic expression across the protective sack of flesh covering his groin; how his fluked tail seamlessly nestled against his spine and across his shoulders, and—subsequently demonstrated with dramatic flair—how easily it unfurled with a loud *whomp* when its mighty fluke landed on the damp sand.

It had seemed like a good idea at the time, but now he wondered if Merahvu Scouts, who secretly roamed the Sapien world, would learn of his recent escapade on Oahu and discover he was not as dead as everyone was led to believe, but alive and well enough to put on such a show.

Complication was something he needed to avoid. Searching for the truth of what happened to his father could be treacherous. Something that required poking around in places where someone like him should not be poking around. His likelihood of success would be greater if he sought his father's fate while pretending to be someone who was not the son of Queen Ianthe or the brother of the future queen, his younger sister, Naiada. Sinto feared his father's fate might be tied to the very real, and growing, threat of a Terrakai rebellion against his queen mother and the Circle of tribal members who governed the Merahvu people—Seakai, Arctakai, and Terrakai alike—as a unified and peaceful society.

And the role his father might be playing within the rebellion, if he were not indeed dead, was a deeply troubling worry occupying Sinto's mind.

Sinto paused at the base of a cliff and asked Moonstone to run a full sweep beyond the ridge above. Sinto sat, hoping Moonstone would take his time, cognizant of Sinto's need to rest.

While his body was weary his mind was not, and another ever-more-present and acute worry persisted.

Audrey Grey and the fiery Mark she had invoked. He traced the hardened symbol buried in the crook of his right forearm; the swirl, the circle, and the line connecting them. As he had many times, he pondered its meaning. The swirl he believed represented himself, the circle Audrey, and the line the ever-present connection between them. Like Merahvu to Sapien, Merluma to Earth; connections dependent on the other.

It was a mystery as to how Audrey was able to invoke the Mark. It was thought to be rare between Merahvu, reserved for the chosen and powerful, such as the one binding his mother and father. But that turned out to be a farce. *Faked*, his mother recently confessed.

But his Mark wasn't a farce. Audrey Marked him—for real. Sinto didn't feel special as if chosen by some divine entity, but special because *she* chose him to be her mate, and her his. All they had was the Mark; not a material token such as a ring. Nor had there been a special ceremony with friends and family, such as a wedding—common things that Sapiens associated with formally coupled pairings. Audrey had drawn upon a deeper and more mysterious connection. The Mark was bound to the kernel of one's being, the *essence*—or soul, the Sapiens call it—and was linked to the mysteries of the universe and its vast number of connections. The Mark was a blessing or a curse—depending on how you looked at it—that lasted a lifetime.

Sinto believed the die was cast when he met Audrey a decade ago while on a special month-long assignment with his father. At the time they were both ten years old. But their budding friendship ended suddenly and grievously when Audrey's mother drowned. She had become ensnared in a fishnet in what looked like a tragic accident.

Sinto later learned it was his father who intentionally wrapped the net around her and tangled it amongst coral on a shallow reef. Sinto had found her struggling and tried to free her, unaware of his father's secret plan: to take vengeance against Audrey's father, Robert Culliford, who had a long-running affair with Sinto's mother.

It wasn't the first time his father sought vengeance against Culliford. The first time was nearly three hundred years ago when he wrongly believed Culliford and his crew of pirates had killed Sinto's older sister, Leela. Enraged, Ramasis led a team of Terrakai who chased them down in the Pacific as they fled and killed all but six of Culliford's crew. Those who survived were alive to this day, and ageless, thanks to his mother, who shared the secret to the Merahvu's elixir of life, sucuvita. They called themselves "Larkians" and over the years had grown increasingly dangerous and very wise.

The Larkians bided their time, awaiting the day when technology would enable them to hunt down the Merahvu and take their revenge. But as the years passed so did their fury; still bitter, but resolved to live comfortable lives as they grew quite wealthy and successful—thanks again to his mother, who shared visionary tidbits about the future that they readily exploited for the past three hundred years.

All was good until his father decided to murder Culliford's new wife ten years ago, stirring up the Larkians' dormant fury. But this time was different. Now the Larkians had the knowledge and the technology to hunt down the Merahvu and wield their vengeful wrath.

Sinto's fingers found the puckered scar near his heart. The pain he felt when Culliford yanked the knife from Sinto's chest was still vivid and raw. A reminder of how the path before him would be difficult and fraught with danger.

Sinto's mother had foreseen a great conflict brewing and sought to end it before it began. Last year, she sent Sinto's sister, Naiada, and his father, Ramasis, to deliver a message to Culliford, requesting a truce. She hoped their grievances could be aired and mitigated without further bloodshed. But Culliford poisoned Naiada and Ramasis before they could deliver the message. His sister grew deathly ill. After his father delivered his ill sister to Tallamure, he disappeared. As time passed, Naiada clawed back from near-certain death.

His mother decided to try a new tactic; to gain the trust of Culliford's daughter, to make her an ally, empathetic to the many troubles the Merahvu faced and how it affected her own world. Eliminating the threat Culliford posed was vitally important to tackling the growing discontent among the Merahvu, in particular the Terrakai. With Culliford's grievances resolved peacefully, she would be free to address the rebellion, perhaps with Culliford's aid. It was a long shot with little possibility of success. But his mother was desperate and Sinto agreed to her quest.

But things went horribly awry. Once Culliford arrived in Tallamure to meet with Sinto's mother, he demanded retribution for the death of his wife, Teola. But Sinto knew the truth—one that would destroy the fragile hold on peace between the three tribes of Merahvu that Ianthe, along with the governing Circle, fought to maintain—of his mother's deception and his father's violent response. So Sinto confessed to playing a part in Teola's death—which was *technically* true since he failed to save her—and sacrificed himself to placate Culliford and protect Ianthe. Shortly after, Culliford's knife found its way into Sinto's chest.

But that was not where it ended. Sinto's sacrifice did nothing to stop what happened next.

Terrakai rebels attacked Culliford's ship and he bombed Tallamure in retaliation. Their enduring symbol of peace was destroyed as was the alliance that created a unified Merahvu.

In one swift moment, Culliford crushed the city and scattered the Merahvu, shattering the peace established between the tribes three hundred years ago. Wantemo told Sinto afterward that the Terrakai rebels celebrated the fall of Tallamure, marking its destruction as a sign of better things to come—one that did not include the governing Circle or his mother's guidance, but the guidance of a new leader. A leader whose secret identity was yet to be revealed.

~ ~ ~

Moonstone returned to Sinto with good news. He encountered no one, neither bird Scouts nor Terrakai, and... the late-blooming suka trees in the meadow were bursting with ripe fruit! Good news, indeed. Sinto was hungry. Stomach rumbling, he scaled the ridge and swiftly passed through the grove of barren aspenian trees, the last of their white leaves crunching underfoot. Once in the meadow, Moonstone bathed in the pond while Sinto ate his fill of suka. After a brief dip in the restorative pond waters and munching down a troutfish, Sinto continued his trek onward.

At this point, he requested Moonstone stay close by, especially as they neared the base of the mountains. Sinto would be forced to slow down and be tested physically on this last part of their journey, and the possibility of encountering roving Terrakai this close to the mountains was more likely. An encounter Sinto hoped to avoid at all costs. He couldn't afford for the Terrakai, or anyone else, to discover his death was a ruse.

Wantemo was the only person who knew Sinto was alive. He had whisked Sinto from the city before it imploded and nursed him back to life on Merluma. Audrey most certainly believed him dead, a fact confirmed by the Mark lying dormant in his arm. But Sinto did not believe that would remain true forever. The Mark would one day awaken with a progressive and determined simmer, potentially alerting Audrey that he was still alive. The Mark would hound Sinto to seek her out and complete its unfinished business: the Joining, an intimate ceremony of binding their essences; two halves made whole, where their shared and vitally important purpose would be revealed. A rare and irrevocable cast of fate, binding two humans together until one of them died. *Real* death, not fake.

It was Wantemo who suggested Sinto stay dead, for which Sinto was eternally grateful. With Audrey believing him dead, he was given reprieve from the Mark and its unfinished business, a distraction Sinto didn't need right now. But, more importantly, he could be far more dangerous to unsuspecting enemies if they believed he was gone.

If only Sinto knew who his true enemies were, learning the fate of his missing father would be a far easier task.

Or so he thought.

2

Newborn

THE COOL THIN MOUNTAINOUS air clouded with Sinto's breath. His heart pounded more than usual and he wondered if he had pushed too hard, too fast. Wantemo had warned about overexerting himself before he was strong enough. But life didn't always allow for following good common sense. Instead, Sinto found himself here, perched on a narrow shelf with his back pressed against a wall of obsidian, fighting off a sudden bout of dizziness. Below was a steep drop-off and he had no intention of finding out just how deadly it might be should he fall.

He fired up his merlux. The electricity flowing through his body helped to clear his head.

Dark clouds stacked up against the soaring peaks of the Black Mountains. The temperature plummeted the higher he climbed. A persistent moist wind swooped up the horseshoe-shaped valley from where he came, colliding with icy mountain air. Snow threatened. He had a few hundred feet left to go until he reached the upper plateau where Deep Lake lay. The thermal layer of dense fat beneath his thick rubbery skin did little to ward off the damp chill. He shivered with each breath and cursed his weakness.

He began to question his decision to climb this side of the mountains, rarely used because of obvious obstacles, like sheer cliff walls and narrow footholds above deadly drop-offs. But berating himself at this point would be fruitless. It was the right decision, as challenging as it may be. A well-trodden game trail could be heavily surveilled by Scouts, especially now.

The Terrakai were fiercely protective of their lands, even during times of peace. Anyone should be able to freely roam across them, not just Terrakai. But that was before the collapse of Tallamure—one Earth month ago, but nearly two years in the accelerated Merluma time scale. Because of that, he was certain the Terrakai would be more prepared and aggressive about protecting their original territory, questioning anyone not of their tribe making passage. And bird Scouts, like Moonstone, were frequently used to monitor the comings and goings in and out of the Terrakai territory. Deep Lake was claimed by the Terrakai during the Forever War so Sinto was taking every precaution to avoid discovery. They wouldn't hesitate to reclaim it as their own, especially now.

He gritted his teeth against the cold and adjusted his camouflage to reflect the shiny black glass and rubble making up the bulk of the mountainside.

A large dark shadow shot overhead. Moonstone landed on the shelf at Sinto's feet, his sharp talons slipping on the slick obsidian ledge. He splayed his red mohawk of thin-shafted fan-topped feathers at the crown of his head, prompting for Sinto's next request.

His blue-and-white eyes flashed with each of his characteristic twitchy head movements; hence his name, Moonstone. Sinto had originally named him Rave, but Audrey didn't know that when Rave made her his new best friend. She was the one to call him Moonstone, because of his eyes. He liked his new name—and Audrey—so much that he no longer responded when Sinto called him by his old one.

Sinto had recently sat Moonstone down to explain his current predicament and found it rather daunting to translate the concept into Moonstone's limited language and avian understanding: that Sinto was pretending to be dead, and at times would pretend to be someone other than himself, and Moonstone would need to play along whenever Sinto may be forced to improvise. After Sinto ran through several scenarios of the concept *improvisation*, Moonstone politely reminded Sinto that he understood what improvising meant, citing most of the recent encounters involving Audrey. Especially how Moonstone had to *improvise* after all of Sinto's many blunders. Much to Sinto's chagrin the lesson quickly ended after being rightfully schooled by his feathered Scout.

Moonstone shared with Sinto images of what he saw at the top of the ridge: rocky cliffs pocked with cave openings, sheltering hibernating creatures and painted with the guano of snowbat; thick forests of sentinel pine and roughy fir; a desert of mountain scruff and patches of ice and snow, surrounding the wind-rippled surface of the icy gray waters of Deep Lake. The scene Moonstone shared was barren of intelligent life, Terrakai or otherwise.

At this point, Sinto thought it best to be seen as one of the Terrakai, not someone intentionally hiding should he be discovered scaling the mountain. He switched his masking camouflage to reflect him as a Terrakai; bronze skin and coppery hair. Sinto's father was a Terrakai and his facial features mirrored those of his father's—upward slant of eye and angular jaw, strong cheekbone and nose to match. Sinto also had inherited his father's emerald-green eyes, which were a rarity among the Terrakai so he colored them amber. His mother was a Seakai. His golden hair and naturally fair-colored skin were distinctly Seakai.

While those colorings were easy to change, his tail was another story. Merahvu tails were unique to the tribe from which they were born. Seakai tails were horizontally fluked like that of a whale. Arctakai tails were fluked like his but with sharp tips, like that of a shark. The Terrakai tail was the most unique of all, delicate and lacy like that of a goldfish. Try as he might with shading and contouring of his camouflage, he could not replicate a believable version of a lacy multi-finned tail.

He decided to keep his tail tucked along his spine at all times, even when entering the lake's water, but that, and the task of securing his Terrakai coloring, would require a great deal of concentration. A task that would hum in the background of his consciousness no matter what distractions he may face. A slow burn of precious reserves he needed to preserve in his less-than-desired physical state should he encounter a confrontation and be forced to flee or fight.

Moonstone took off and disappeared beyond the ridge. Sinto forged upward along the steep narrow ledge, zigzagging up the ridge until the ledge ended at a sheer rock wall. There he stopped to catch his breath. He would need it. He had only fifty feet to climb to reach the top. This last leg was the most treacherous, but would be worth it. The lake offered a shortcut to his first destination in what might become a long journey.

Deep Lake was formed when a massive mountain collapsed during the Great Upheaval that ripped open a new portal between Earth and Merluma long ago. The lake was thousands of feet deep. At the bottom was the portal to the City of Green, which lay at the bottom of Lake Superior in North America. The City of Green sheltered a large community of Terrakai. The first city established by his kind on Earth. A city his father helped expand and develop into a robust and thriving community once peace was established following the Forever War. It was there that Sinto hoped to find answers about what happened to his father.

Sinto found it odd that Moonstone had observed no one roaming the shores of the lake or occupying the Forestlands on the other side of the mountains. Those lands were typically inhabited by great numbers of Terrakai. A perplexing concern; where had they all gone?

Sinto gazed up at the vertical face of obsidian, fifty feet of smooth black glass with a large crack running through it. The crack was narrower at the bottom but grew wider as it stretched toward the top. About halfway up, it would be wide enough to slip his body completely inside. It was getting to that point that was the most precarious, as well as at the top where the crack yawned just shy of his total height. In addition, obsidian was either smooth and slick or rough and sharp depending on the state of it, and the face had few protrusions to cling to. One slip and he risked bouncing off the ledge and down the steep barren hillside with no means to stop until he reached the distant line of trees at the bottom. A potentially fatal fall.

Once he started up, there would be no turning back.

There is only up. If I don't look down, then the danger doesn't exist...

Sinto reached up and planted his fingers in the narrow crack, curled his toes around a small protrusion of slick glass, and pulled himself up. He repeated the movement, fingers in the crack, toes gripping the next protrusion. Slowly he rose, setting finger and toe. A slow, grinding process that took great patience and physical stamina, both of which were in short supply. The crack widened and as it did, he worked more of his body inside, a shoulder and hip wedged half in and half out. Another shimmy upwards, and the crack accommodated his whole body.

Halfway there.

A new challenge, and change of positioning was required. He broke his earlier rule and carefully unfurled his tail. He planted his fluke on the opposite side of the crack and shifted his weight, enough to free his legs. With his back and fluke leveraged he curled his knees up and planted his feet opposite his chest. He made slight adjustments until he was in a secure and comfortable crouched position with his back and feet wedged within the crack; a good place to pause and rest.

Don't look down.

Giant snowflakes began falling from the sky, silent and wet, clinging to his eyelashes and beading on his shoulders and knees. The snow introduced a new and troubling problem. Moisture would make the smooth parts of the crack very slick.

Best to hurry.

He clenched his teeth and soldiered on, ignoring the throbbing ache in his chest from his recent wound. The smooth glass walls of the crack in which he was wedged grew slicker with each passing second. Warmed by what little sun had poked through the clouds earlier, the dark glass transformed the snow to liquid instantaneously. Rivulets of melting snow trickled down from the crack's opening above.

Don't look down.

He focused on the snowflakes twirling down from the sky and repeated a pattern of upwardly movement: planting of feet, hands, and shoulder, a press of his fluke, then an upward drive and shimmy. The higher he climbed, the wider the crack grew until he had an important decision to make. The leverage he came to depend on would no longer work to his advantage. The bulk of his weight was pulling him down the farther apart his shoulders and feet became. The only way to continue would be to spin around with his buttocks elevated and body positioned in an upside-down V.

He took a moment to rally his confidence. A major shift of body weight and a realignment in position against a slick surface would be rather tricky. Not only that—it meant looking *down*. He wrestled with the physical and mental challenge before making this next, critical move.

He channeled one of Wantemo's many wise lessons: *Don't think, do.*

He used his fluke to his advantage again, leveraging it as a pivot point. In one continuous movement, he spun on shoulder and foot, shot his hands out as a brace, coiled his body, and raised his butt and tail to the air. Water ran down his cheeks, dripped from his nose, and fell into the abyss. His body quivered from the effort. From this point forward he would have to rely on pure muscular strength. He could no longer see the top, only *down*.

He feared if he twisted his head to see where he was going, he would slip and fall. He closed his eyes and began a determined blind march upward, feeling ahead with his fluke.

An eternity of time passed. The snow was thicker now, stacking up on his backside and melting fast. Rivulets of water ran off his body, disappearing to that place where he dared not look. *Down*.

The tip of his fluke rounded the top and he felt flat ground. Hopeful, he marched, hand and foot, butt up and core coiled, inching his fluke until it was fully flattened on horizontal rock. Upward he rose, butt cresting the top, then shoulder and knee. His whole body quivered, awkwardly stuck at the crest of the crack. Another critical move.

Don't look down!

Sinto planted his fluke on a larger patch of solid ground. Then he marched upward with hands and feet, muscles screaming, until his fingers crested the top of the crack. He pushed with what little strength he had left and rolled. He lay on solid ground, gasping for breath. Snow landed in his eyes and his opened mouth, and once his heart calmed and breath slowed, he sat up. He surveyed his surroundings, arms hugging chest, shivering.

Deep Lake stretched before him, the far shore erased by the snow storm. Standing between him and its rocky edge were two figures bundled in fur cloaks as if they had been expecting his arrival. Their amber eyes glowed from behind furry hoods. They pulled the hoods from their heads. A man and a woman, seasoned but still youthful.

"Who are you?" the woman asked, not in the Terrakai native tongue, but English, as spoken in the Sapien world.

The man beside her stepped forward and lifted a lock of Sinto's hair with a walking stick. "Gold hair, green eyes. Huh, Seakai." Then he fell to a knee getting a closer look at Sinto's face. "By the shape of his eyes I'd say he's got some Terrakai blood in him." The man's gaze drifted to Sinto's tail. He stood, looked at the woman. "Dual-breed. Is that what they're doing now? Mixin' 'em up?"

The woman shrugged her shoulders. "Hard to keep up with all the goings-on." She nudged Sinto with a booted foot. "You lost, *Newborn?*"

3

Deviant Scouts

THE TERRAKAI WOMAN ASKED, "Cat got your tongue, *Newborn?*"

Dumbfounded by their presence and overpowered between the two of them, Sinto decided to keep his mouth shut. He questioningly cocked his head. And silently kicked himself for letting his camouflage slip during the arduous climb.

The woman rolled her eyes and launched into a diatribe about breeders and shepherds and their carelessness. Then she bent over and gazed deeply into Sinto's eyes. "His eyes are still green but he appears old enough. Strange, he hasn't been initiated yet." She stepped back. "Figures. I knew they were getting careless." She laughed. "Maybe he's dumb as a doorbell and they found no need to bother, like them nursery maids. But with those golden locks of his, he's cute enough to pass for one."

The man grabbed Sinto under the arms and lifted him to his feet. "Let's get you by a fire and something to eat, then return you to your flock."

Sinto surreptitiously scanned for Moonstone, disappointed he had failed to warn Sinto about the couple. It was difficult to see anything through the snow. Perhaps that was the reason Moonstone hadn't spotted them on one of his many sweeps.

Sinto debated if he should flee the way he came or sprint for the lake in hopes he could slip through the portal before they caught him. But innate senses warned that might be a bad idea under the current circumstances. For one, he was thoroughly exhausted and needed time to rest and think.

Sinto decided to play along. The beginning of his journey. Time to be spontaneous and to practice his improvisation. He tried to put a positive spin on the situation. Perhaps he would learn something vital to his quest. He was most curious what they meant by *newborn* and *breeders*, *shepherds* and *nursery maids*. Besides, he was starving and numb from the cold and weak from the thin mountain air. Food and warmth would give him the boost his body was craving.

The man and woman moved with strength and purpose toward a set of cliffs. Next to them Sinto felt meek and helpless, lacking energy and thick furs. The ground was slick with ice and snow and he struggled to keep up, slipping every other step.

The man stopped and prompted Sinto to follow the woman through a small cave opening cut into the side of the mountain. Inside a fire crackled. Smoke gathered on the ceiling before being sucked out a hole carved into the top of the cave. The air was scented by sap and rosemary and the tantalizing smell of roasted meat. Sinto's stomach rumbled.

The woman pointed toward several large rocks set in a circle around the fire. Sinto sat on the one closest to the cave opening. The walls were dark and slick with moisture, gobbling up every ray of light cast by the flames.

The man laid a white bear fur across Sinto's shoulders, secured it around his waist with a leather belt, and sat down on the opposite side of the fire. The woman sat next to the man. Together they regarded Sinto.

The woman said, "If it hasn't been initiated then it doesn't have a name, right? So what should we call it?"

The man laughed, "Goldilocks."

"And we're Momma and Poppa bear!" The woman leaned over howling.

Sinto was taken aback by his captors. *They must be Scouts*, he thought, because of their use of the Sapien language, reference to a popular Sapien fairytale, and by the way they looked and carried themselves. The woman's hair was black and sharply cut along her chin line and across her forehead; her ears were pierced multiple times with varying-sized rings. The man's hair was closely cropped along the sides but longer on top, which he frequently flipped to keep out of his eyes; he kept his natural bronze coloring.

Scouts were recruited by the Circle's tribal leaders to maintain a pulse on what was happening in the Sapien world, to report new information to the Circle, and to share memories and experiences with others for education and entertainment. Being a Scout was a lifetime commitment, an honor if asked; one that required them to be keenly observant and adaptive. To naturally blend into the Sapien world, to learn their various cultures and languages. Essentially, to become *Sapien*.

Scouts were the Merahvu's most trusted soldiers, devoted to their queen and the Circle. Most Scouts were either Seakai or Terrakai since their natural coloring blended more readily into the Sapien world. Arctakai Scouts were rare, mostly because of their distinctly pale colorings requiring them to maintain a constant disguise. With silver hair and colorless skin they stood out the most of the three tribes among Sapiens. Sinto had new respect for Scouts, especially after attempting—and failing—to secure his disguise even for a short time.

Sinto wanted to ask, among other things, what these Scouts were doing on Merluma in a cave beside Deep Lake, far from the Sapien world. He wanted to learn what they had heard about the collapse of Tallamure, if they were still devoted to the queen and the Circle. But as his limbs warmed and his mind cleared he realized there was much he didn't know of the Terrakai rebellion: how far it had spread and the number of recruits, and if those recruits might include Scouts such as those staring back at him.

Sinto had yet to mutter a word and decided it might be best to keep it that way. The less they knew about him the better. They believed him to be a newborn—whatever that meant—and of simple mind. So he sat staring back, slack-faced and stupid.

The woman gestured toward a mountain weeble—a large rabbit that only lived in the Black Mountains—roasting over the fire. "Help yourself, Goldie."

Sinto didn't move, pretended not to understand.

She rolled her eyes and stood up. She pulled the rabbit from the spit and sliced off a hunk of its hind leg with an obsidian knife she hid in her furs. She held out a chunk of meat for him. "You do know how to eat, don't you?"

Sinto took the meat and heartily began to eat as a savagely hungry and simple-minded newborn might do.

"Poor thing's starving," the man said.

"How can you feel sorry for it?" the woman said, "Dumb as a rock and acting like an animal."

Sinto stopped eating. Grease dripped from his chin.

She stood and approached Sinto. She yanked the fur from his shoulders, studying his physique, and zipped a finger across the markings along his spine. "You must admit, this one's extraordinary. Look at these markings, not bland and uninspired like the others." She tugged his ear. "He seems so *real*."

"They *are* real," the man said.

"Maybe, but they're not natural," she said. "What they do to 'em—" She shook her head. "It's cruel and not how nature intended." She pulled the fur up around Sinto's shoulders, gave him a sympathetic pat on the head.

"Better them than us." The man pointed to the rabbit. "I'll take some of that."

The woman pulled the knife from her furs and cut several slices off the breast of the rabbit. They sat eating, staring across the flames at Sinto as if he was some kind of alien.

Sinto ate, giving the meat between his fingers his utmost attention, acting as if he didn't understand a thing they said, showing no reaction to their words, eagerly absorbing new facts spilling from their private exchange.

The Scouts grumbled about guarding the portal and missing the old days when all that was required of them was to roam the Sapien world, gathering information and experiences to share. From what Sinto gleaned, those who could pass through the portal were subjected to a strict screening process, but it was unclear what it was they were being screened for. Then they bitterly complained about resorting to eating wild rabbit because of all the newborns and the strain on Merluma's resources of all those extra mouths to feed. But in the end they agreed those small sacrifices were worth it. To topple Queen Ianthe and the Circle, especially after the catastrophic failure to save Tallamure from the wrath of Culliford and his men.

Once a boney carcass was all that remained of the rabbit, the woman stood. "Go ahead. I'll return Goldilocks then join you at the portal. Make sure Raye stays until I return. Don't want any unexpected visitors accidentally slipping through without a fight. You remember what happened last time."

The man winced and a funny sound came from his mouth.

She looped her arm through Sinto's. "This way, handsome; time to take you home."

She led Sinto deeper into the darkness of the cave.

Sinto stole a glance back. The man had stripped off his furs and extinguished the fire. A fiery glow radiated from a ball of electrical fire hovering above his head, painting the walls of the small cave a gold patina.

Sinto's decision to keep his mouth shut paid off. Sinto got his answers and more, and believed he was about to learn more than he could have ever expected.

4

Cave Of Horrors

THE WOMAN YAWNED. SINTO noted the wish for sleep reflected in her eyes and the pinkish tint coloring her aura; the fatty meat in her stomach most likely drawing energy from her reactionary senses. Her pace had slowed and her demeanor was relaxed and off-guard, like the conversation he just overheard between her and the other Scout while believing him ignorant.

The fact the portal was guarded was alarming but not surprising. The Terrakai always felt the Deep Lake portal was strictly for passage between their own lands on Merluma and their city in Lake Superior. But most alarming was the total disregard for his queen mother and the Circle by Scouts they had individually vetted; Scouts who had sworn to honor the peace accord and everything the Circle represented: a unified governance of the tribes.

The cave narrowed and the ceiling dropped lower, and Sinto and the woman Scout could no longer walk side-by-side. She grunted and took the lead. Sinto was much taller and had to bend over to avoid bumping his head. Unable to see his feet in the growing darkness, he shuffled.

The woman snapped her fingers. A ball of amber fire sprang from her fingers and hovered in the palm of her hand. Well-timed, as the floor began to slant downward and was uneven, then transitioned into steps carved into the gray stone.

The stairs grew steeper and narrower, his toes extending beyond each one. They were concave and heavily worn from many footfalls. Sinto wondered if the stairway they were descending was carved by the original Homo-Sapiens who had slipped through a land portal after Earth splintered and Merluma was born. Certainly they were not carved by Merahvu, whose feet were much larger than a typical Sapien.

It was awkward descending the stairs with most of his weight upon his heels, slowing their progress but serving a useful purpose. He scanned for possible detours—of which there were none—but most importantly he counted each step, calculating how far they had descended from the Deep Lake plateau into the bowels of the mountain. He guessed they had descended hundreds of feet, and based on the location of the cave from which they started, believed they were heading westward, toward the Forestlands; a possible shortcut from Deep Lake to the Terrakai territory.

Is that where the woman is taking me?

Sinto grew uneasy. He was being led farther from his goal of reaching the portal at the bottom of Deep Lake. A portal he now knew was heavily guarded. The stairway carved into the mountainside offered only two options; up and out, or down to some unknown destination.

He cursed Moonstone for failing to warn him, then cursed himself for blaming Moonstone for his predicament. He was the one who chose to come to Deep Lake and to play along with his captors and whatever fate may await him.

He channeled the fear blooming in his chest into something purposeful; to focus on the first opportunity to gain control, to make use of whatever situation may present itself. But other than shoving the woman down the stairs and potentially awakening her from her state of digestive stupor he saw no other possibilities. Plus, she had a knife hidden somewhere in her furs. He had no doubt she would know how to use it, effectively and efficiently, after watching how deftly she cut up that rabbit.

The stairway ended and the floor leveled. The air grew warmer and the smell of sulfur wafted from the direction they were heading. He estimated they were well below the upper ridgeline and somewhere equivalent to the elevation of the Forestlands and parts of Inception—like the meadow where he rested on his way here—that were thick with hot springs from the ever-present geological activity in this part of Merluma.

A glow of light pierced the darkness ahead, as did soft voices speaking in the native Terrakai tongue. There were Sapien-like pronunciations accentuated by high-pitched squeals and peppered with ticks and guttural barks, like the intelligent creatures that lived in the sea. A different smell joined the sulfur: a sweet and pleasant one. It was familiar, but the memory of what it could be lingered outside his grasp.

The light and voices ahead grew brighter and louder. Sinto needed to act, and now, if he was to escape being discovered by others. At Sinto's feet was a puddle of water on the smooth obsidian floor. He pretended to slip, grabbing the woman by the arm and throwing her off-balance. She yelped when Sinto kicked her feet out from under her and she fell to her back and smacked her head.

The voices he heard silenced.

Sinto fired his merlux and gave the dazed woman a mighty shock before she could arm her own electrical defenses. She gasped before her eyes rolled back in her head, then her lids slid solidly shut. Sinto checked her vitals. Her heart beat and lungs drew breath. Alive and unconscious but for how long Sinto did not know.

He rummaged through her furs, found the knife, and took it.

He heard movement and tossed his fur and leather belt next to the woman. Pressed his naked back to the gray stone wall, camouflaged to blend in seamlessly. He held the hilt of the knife in his fist with the blade vertically hidden behind his wrist, shielded from sight by his gray-mottled camouflage.

A woman ran down the narrow passage from the direction of light. She dropped to her knees next to the fallen woman and yelled for help. Another woman came to her aid. Together they lifted the unconscious Scout by her feet and shoulders and carried her back through the passage they came from.

Sinto turned to run back up the stairs, but hesitated. The sweet smell was strong and piqued his curiosity. It was the smell of humanity, but not an unpleasant smell like when too many people were trapped in a tight confined space or of the aged. This was a smell of something new. Something untainted and sweet.

The smell of the newly born.

Newborn.

He remained camouflaged and moved slowly against the wall toward the light. He abruptly stopped when he heard the sudden eruption of a baby's cry, a youngling's sob, then more distant, a woman's blood-curdling scream. Not born of joy and pleasure but of pain and suffering. It was in that moment he realized the cries were coming from more than one baby, youngling, or woman; they were many voices in a shared chorus of suffering.

He quickened his pace to the end of the passageway and stole a peek around the corner into a giant cavern, soaring far beyond the hovering balls of fiery light scattered throughout. Multi-colored stalactites stretched from the darkness above, reaching for sprouting stalagmites from the cavern floor. Water moistened distant walls and the echo of running water persisted.

Thousands of babies and younglings lay in nests of animal skins and furs spread across the vast floor. Beyond were other passageways like the one he came through; the source of women screaming.

Like women in labor...

The Scout who Sinto rendered unconscious lay on the floor not far from the passageway opening, abandoned by those who found her. The women who came to help were nowhere to be seen.

He crawled to the nearest nest where a baby wailed and looked inside. He gasped in horror. Tears streamed down the infant boy's face. His body was a blur of movement: swinging arms, thrashing legs, spine arching. His lungs worked, hyperventilating between bouts of crying. Multiple scars covered his body at each of his joints, as if a sharp object had punctured the skin repeatedly. A bladder of orange liquid hung above the nest. A tube extended from the bladder and was plugged directly into a vein in his neck.

After several agonizing moments, the baby stilled, arms and legs splayed. Exhausted, his eyes rolled shut, the child reduced to sputtering twitches and moans. Sinto gazed in disbelief. In that brief moment of frantic movement the child grew at least an inch in length. The muscle along his limbs appeared thicker, his facial features more defined, his skull slightly larger.

He went to the next nest. Inside lay a female youngling. He guessed her to be four or five years old. She lay in a fetal position, eyes wide and unseeing. She panted like an overheated wolf, pink tongue spilling from her mouth. She had the same bladder of orange liquid feeding directly into her bloodstream. Her gaze found Sinto's face. She moaned. Her scarred hand reached for him. She said something he couldn't decipher, but her eyes screamed, "*Help me.*"

He heard a baby begin to wail and ducked down. A young Terrakai woman with a swollen belly—a child barely old enough to bear her own—was bent over a nearby nest. Her flawless face was emotionless as she stabbed a sharp needle into the baby's body, ignoring its screams. When she was done, she placed her fingers to the crown of its head and coaxed the child asleep with her mind. Its wailing sputtered, then fell utterly silent. She replenished the bladder of orange liquid from a large cauldron set atop her push cart. Mindlessly, she moved to the next nest in line.

From deeper in the cave Sinto heard screaming, not babies, nor women in labor, but older younglings screaming for their tormentors to stop. The more vocal voices were abruptly cut short.

The horror of what he witnessed sank in. The vastness of this first cave, the spawn of multiple passages leading to more cavernous spaces that glowed in the distance, the hum of torture bleeding from places beyond. What he witnessed was the acceleration of life, unnatural and forced; an unfathomable suffering of the weak and the innocent. Thousands of newborns grew before his eyes, babies to younglings, younglings to young adult; women in labor produced more. Nursery maids barely past puberty, gestating the next generation.

The Terrakai were breeding as fast as they could by feeding the newly born an elixir of some sort, inflicting injuries, and triggering their minds to rapidly heal their tortured bodies.

Forced cellular acceleration.

A breeding factory.

But why and for what purpose?

His heart skipped a beat when the obvious answer struck him.

The Terrakai are breeding an army.

The woman lying on the floor stirred and her eyes opened. She gazed at the ceiling dazed. Sinto held his breath and froze, his skin mimicking the outline of the nest where he crouched. She started to get up, but faltered. He had seconds before she would realize what had happened, that he had tripped her and shocked her unconscious. That he had stolen her knife.

He bolted for the stairway, scaling multiple steps at a time.

He heard a shout and the clamor of others in pursuit.

He didn't look back.

His heart thundered and lungs burned by the time he reached the top. He didn't stop and ran into the cave where the Scouts had offered him temporary shelter and food. Smoke still smoldered from coals where the picked-over carcass of the mountain weeble dangled on the spit.

He ran to the cave entrance and pressed against the wall, stealing a peek outside. No one on guard. The only movement the swirl of snowflakes falling from a purple sky and blanketing the ground. His footprints from earlier were erased by snow.

Poised to flee, he heard a strange noise. He froze and pressed his back to the wall, melding into it. He heard it again, strangled and desperate, coming from the dark opposite of him and near the cave entrance. He fired his merlux and set his eyes aglow, sought its source.

Moonstone!

Moonstone's feathers were soaked from melting snow raining down from a crack in the ceiling. Someone had bound his beak with a leather string and his wings with a leather band. The band was secured to a heavy rock to keep Moonstone from escaping. Sinto used the stolen knife to cut him free.

Moonstone shared in Sinto's mind what had happened. He stomped, frantic and anxious, as he recited his story. He was attacked by two other birds of his same species and captured by the male Scout who had discovered Sinto. He thanked Sinto for wisely removing the chain clipped around his neck before they headed for the mountains—a chain that indicated he was claimed by another master. So Moonstone pretended to be wild and unclaimed. They had tied him up and spoke of their plan to train him as a Scout and employ him to carry out whatever nefarious acts they saw fit.

More voices rose from the stairway passage; one became many, in pursuit.

"Flee!" Sinto told Moonstone. "*Hide in the meadow. Trust no one! I bid you farewell my friend with hopes we may meet again. Now go!*"

Moonstone took flight. Sinto camouflaged and followed, running to the crack in the cliff he had climbed earlier.

He clamped the knife between his teeth, laid on his belly, and dropped his legs down the crack. He shimmied down until he was clinging to the ledge by his fingers. He extended his tail and feet for the opposite wall. In one swift move he twisted and swung his arms down and behind him. He hung for a beat, butt down with his shoulders over-extended and screaming in pain. He had to move else something would fail and he would fall. He slowly shimmied until gravity took him and he slipped. He came to a sudden and crumpled stop with his knees driving into his chest and butt and tail wedged below in the narrow crack. He took a few well-needed breaths to calm, then he worked his way up until he was able to free his tail and drop his feet. Once vertical, he slid down faster than he expected. He extracted himself from the crack and jumped the last several feet to the narrow ledge.

He looked up, heard voices growing closer. He looked down. He had no other choice.

He slipped from the ledge to the steeply canted slope below, landing feet first and butt to ground, and slid. He quickly gained momentum. Using his hands and elbows, he managed to keep his feet below him, skiing on loose dirt and gravel. He grabbed at mountain scrub and bounced off randomly placed boulders to slow himself down and help direct his descent. Barbs cut into his palms and rock chafed his feet and arms. Once he reached the forest at the bottom, he ran blind, crashing through fern and bush, around pine and fir, until he reached the great river and a massive waterfall.

A large dark bird circled. A bird like Moonstone but not Moonstone; a Terrakai Scout.

He looked back. Two Terrakai males were in pursuit, no doubt guided by their bird Scout. They tore down the river toward Sinto, teetering at the edge of a seventy-foot waterfall.

Sinto jumped, plunging into a deep well carved by continuously churning water, the knife slipping from his teeth from the jarring landing. He popped to the surface flailing and was sucked downstream by whirlpools, bashing into rock, sucked into churning waters beneath dams of fallen logs. He fought to break free only to be sucked into another further downstream. He finally gained control, pointing his feet downstream and riding the tongue of the current. The river rushed and meandered through forest.

Sinto slipped over another waterfall, then another, riding the river through the jungle to the beach where he was spit into the Great Ocean. The Terrakai Scouts were hot on his tail.

Two more Terrakai Scouts joined the others from the beach jungle and dove in after Sinto.

Sinto fired his Merlux and cut a vortex in the sea, destination unknown, and dove inside. Sinto disappeared in a flash of roiling bubbles and green sparks.

A vortex tunneled through the water behind him, then another and another, occupied by his pursuers. He swerved and dipped his vortex through the dark deep sea, stopped and cut a new one, traveling in a different direction. Once, twice, thrice, he changed course, not knowing where he was traveling, how far, or what deadly obstacles he may encounter. He feared slamming into an underwater mountain in his frantic haste to escape.

The effort drew on Sinto's reserves, as surely it would on his pursuers'. At least that was what he hoped when he sputtered to a stop in the dark depths to catch his breath. A risk he had no choice but to take. He had no idea where he was or if one of his pursers would suddenly find him, but knew he should not linger.

A faint glow caught his eye. A crack in the seabed. Firelight from Merluma's core, and that meant a possible portal to Earth.

He dove down. The light in the seabed grew brighter, as did his hopes.

The portal lay before him. Its gossamer seal stretched across the crack in the spheres encapsulating the hearts of Merluma and Earth. He slipped through the seal, to what the Merahvu call the *between*, with no idea where it would lead him on the other side.

First came the heat and fire from Merluma's core—her heart, the Merahvu called it. Spinning beside it, the heart of Earth. Both beating with vitality, closely aligned but not touching, floating in a shared pool of molten lava, orbiting around each other.

Merluma's heart was the smaller of the two. Fiery balls of energy, beating to different rhythms: Merluma's beat fast and fleeting like a hummingbird; Earth's beat slow and thundering like a great bear.

As he slipped passed the circling hearts, he was assaulted by their ever-present and persistent struggle to become free from the other. His eardrums thrummed, the synovial fluid in his joints swelled, pockets of fat cradling his internal organs contracted before expanding. Then came the flattening, as if his entire body had been pressed between layers of rock. Every cell stretched, contracted, then bounced back as he passed through the space-time continuum, knotted by two unnaturally bound worlds.

He was spit out on the other side, achy but whole.

5

TMFS

THE DAY BROKE DARK and gloomy. Rain drummed the copper roof and a waterfall spilled over the gutter outside Audrey's bedroom window, clogged by needles and prickly cones shed by Douglas firs growing too close to the house. Late November. Seattle. Typical.

She missed hanging out with Blake and Ryan at the Labs on San Juan Island, grinding away on their research project, analyzing the resident orca language, and breathing the scent of the Salish Sea. A previous life she could never return to. Not now, not ever.

Since the incident in Tallamure, one day blended into another; another week would pass. How long since she dropped out of school at the Labs? How long since she had talked to her best friend Ryan? How long had it been since Audrey held the knife that ended Sinto's life? A week? A month? Did it matter?

Every day felt the same. Hollow as her heart and meaningless as her life.

Shortly after surviving the implosion of Sinto's underwater city, Tallamure, and the near-fatal ascent to the surface in her father's high-tech submarine, Audrey felt fortunate and lucky. Now she wasn't so sure. How does one keep living knowing you helped destroy a young and promising life? Sinto was dead and she was alive.

Guilt was a wicked thing that ate your soul a little bit every day. Some days she wished it was her who had died. How do the living endure a lifetime of guilt's sting?

She fingered the Mark buried in her right forearm. The thick coiled flesh felt cold. Like it did yesterday, and the day before. And like yesterday, and the day before, she traced the lines of the symbol forged by hardened flesh representing two worlds connected. Hers and Sinto's. A Mark symbolizing an irrevocable bond between the two of them. It was Audrey who initiated this bond by choosing Sinto to be her lifelong mate, though she had no idea how, just that she did. Sinto said what she had done was impossible, her being a Sapien, and the Mark—and what it entailed—a rare thing even between two Merahvu. But it happened. She had no regrets. Her heart and soul pined for him, more so even, just as it had the moment she Marked him.

Sinto revealed they never got the chance to finish the next most crucial step, an intimate ritual called the Joining. He never got the chance to tell Audrey exactly what the Joining entailed but she imagined it not much different than what happened on one's wedding night, with one exception. A consummation including not only the joining of body, but also of mind and soul. A joining of *essences* that ran deeper than the physical or heartfelt love for another; lifelong companions bound with a shared and profound purpose.

She wondered how long the Mark would live in her flesh. Sinto had told her their bond was forever, until one of them died. With Sinto dead and gone would the Mark buried in her arm eventually fade away, like the crystal-clear image of his dead gaze and the cloud of blood swirling around his broken body? Would another fill the hole blown open in her heart?

Could that other be Blake?

Blake had been respectful, patient and understanding of the post-traumatic stress disorder Dr. Wickman diagnosed her with, and that she was wrestling with every day since the *incident*. Dr. Wickman reminded her, frequently, that Blake had been a victim too. Locked away in a watery prison for weeks, unaware of his plight. His life reduced to a thing of barter by Sinto's mother, Ianthe, queen of the Merahvu.

Ianthe had used Blake as a pawn to force Audrey to convince her father to meet with her so they could resolve their escalating differences peacefully. A game in which Sinto played a big part, where he twisted the truth, carefully presenting facts in that slippery way the Merahvu used to manipulate one's mind. But Audrey eventually learned the truth—witnessed it—when Ianthe forced her to relive Sinto's memory of his role in planning and directing orcas in the Salish Sea to attack and cripple the boat Audrey and Blake had borrowed for research. Afterward, with the assistance of his mentor, he kidnapped them both.

Needless to say, Sinto screwed with her mind and emotions. Looking back now—why he twisted the truth, manipulated her memories, and did the things he did—made total sense. He too had been used by his mother.

Even in death, Audrey loved Sinto greater with each passing day. A moment didn't pass without her thinking of him and what could have been. She never had the chance to forgive him. But if she had, would it have made a difference? Would he still be alive?

Yow. There it goes again! Guilt. And the *chomp-chomp* of its needling teeth, munching on her battered heart and soul.

Audrey had also learned that her father was a pirate well over three hundred years old who had an affair with Ianthe long before he met Audrey's mother, and long before Audrey and Sinto were born. Ianthe had bestowed on her father the secret source of an elixir, called sucuvita, that prolonged life. The way Sinto explained it, it worked by halting the biological process that triggers aging, something to do with chromosomes and the length of telomeres.

As long as you possessed and ingested it, you remained essentially ageless, which meant you could live forever if you wanted to.

Audrey wasn't sure that was such a great thing. Living forever with the guilt and hollowness she felt would be a nightmare.

She also learned that her mother's death ten years ago was intentional, not an accident—another secret that Sinto confessed to. But because of the Mark and the emotional connection between them, she sensed he was lying to protect someone. Enough to take the blame for her mother's murder, sacrifice his own life, and leave her hollow and emotionally broken. As noble as his sacrifice seemed, she had no idea why he did it.

People of the sea. A three-hundred-year-old pirate father who was still quite alive and kicking. A parallel world called Merluma where mythical things like faery-butterflies and great-horned unicorns existed. Mind manipulation. Life-prolonging elixir. Marks and irrevocable Joinings. Some pretty heavy shit that could drive someone to believe they had gone mad. Dr. Wickman called it PTSD. Audrey called it TMFS, *Total Mind Fuck Syndrome.*

And here she lay in her bed, watching a spider spinning its web between the wooden rafters crisscrossing the vaulted ceiling of her top-floor bedroom; living in an over-sized, stone-and-cedar historic mansion on the shores of Puget Sound, in a prestigious gated neighborhood north of downtown Seattle, wondering what a spider thought about its seriously mental roommate lying below. *Friend or foe?* If Sinto was here he could mind-meld with the arachnid and easily give her the answer.

A tear slipped down her cheek. Oh, how she missed him.

The only person giving her answers, or rather suggestions, was Dr. Wickman. Audrey was able to confide some of her most intimate feelings and thoughts, and he was helping her cope, like the days following her mother's death. It was Dr. Wickman who came to her aid, then and now—not her father. *Daddy* or *Father*, she would call him, depending on her mood and the character he currently occupied: modern-day father or swashbuckling pirate born in the seventeenth century. Dr. Wickman, in contrast, was a stabilizing influence in life.

Add on top of that, her father had a whole other set of psychological issues he was dealing with. And naturally they had everything to do with her.

Not. Going. There. Yet.

But, Dr. Wickman insisted: *Soon. He will be ready. And so will you.*

She didn't share his enthusiasm and was far from ready to step into the quagmire of her and her father's rocky relationship.

Dr. Wickman was one of her father's original crew from his pirating days and also over three hundred years old. That's a long time to learn things, and he was very, very wise and helpful. He was originally signed on as ship doctor for her father's pirating crew, and over the years he had gained a deep knowledge of the life sciences, psychology, and other mental health issues. He also dabbled with technology and organic matter and how they could be integrated.

She found it ironic that Dr. Wickman was the one helping her deal with her issues when he himself was part of the problem. She was told he looked exactly like his thirty-something-before-elixir pirate self, like the others who were part of her father's original crew. As a budding young scientist, it blew her mind that human cells could remain the same with no consequence over an unnatural span of time.

Newsflash! The fabled fountain of youth is real!

Not only did she have to deal with her own PTSD—oops, scratch that—TMFS, she had been enlisted to help her father recall his lost memories. It all came back to the incident in Tallamure when he ordered his crew to blow up the city, a retaliation provoked by an attack on his ship by a band of Terrakai rebels he mistakenly thought were sent by Ianthe. He suffered a traumatic head injury when the shock wave from the city's collapse struck their submarine. In truth, Ianthe had nothing to do with the attack. She said so and her father refused to believe her. The way Audrey saw it, his injury was self-inflicted and rightly deserved. Killing Sinto wasn't enough to satisfy a decade of mind-eating grief and blind rage. Audrey tried to stop him, but he was driven by the need to inflict pain and destroy everything Ianthe had accomplished, as if killing her son wasn't enough.

If only Dr. Wickman had been brave enough to put him on the couch ten years ago, maybe none of this would have happened.

Wishful thinking.

While Audrey wallowed in her present-day guilt, her father lived in the past; in that past, Audrey's mother, Teola, was alive and the Merahvu were a distant memory. And when Dr. Wickman told him she was gone and ten years had passed, he started making up fantastical stories of what happened between then and now, none of it attached to reality. Something Dr. Wickman called confabulation. An aliment related to amnesia that can occur with the type of injury her father had endured. He didn't remember a thing that happened in Tallamure.

If only I'd been so lucky.

Audrey wasn't convinced it was helping her overcome her Total Mind Fuck Syndrome having to relive the moments leading up to Sinto's death for her father's benefit. But Dr. Wickman insisted it was beneficial for her too, and that he believed she's making progress. Something about helping her move on.

Yeah, right, like helping me move onto the train tracks running along the shore below my bedroom window and stepping in front of a speeding train. How's that for progress?

A hint of daylight.

Seven AM.

Dr. Wickman would be raring to go in an hour for her daily counseling session. He would ask questions, some seeming more random than others. She would talk. He would listen, nodding once in a while, then taking a note. Then, he would take a short break to meet with her father. After, he would sit with her for lunch, pretending it was off the record, so to speak. Audrey knew better;

just another psycho-wily technique he employed to extract and twist some hidden secret. Then dinner, maybe some card games or a movie—strictly with no violence—then off to bed. Lather, rinse, repeat. This house felt more like a mental asylum than a place she could call home.

Audrey cast aside her covers and swung her feet to the cold, dark, hardwood floor. Slipped her toes into a pair of woolly slippers, shuffled to the adjoining bathroom, and hopped in the shower.

6

Referral

Dr. Wickman met Audrey at the bottom of the main stairway that spilled into the foyer beside a conference room that once served as her father's office. It was there they met every morning for her therapy session.

Dr. Wickman looked like he did every day, like a thirty-something Englishman. He wore the same tweedy flat cap with his trim, sandy-colored hair tucked beneath. His pale blue eyes sparkled with vitality behind a pair of round glasses. He was lithe and lean and favored daily runs to clear his head.

He slipped on the navy pea coat he held in his hands. "Let's take a walk today."

Audrey grabbed her favorite gray hoodie lined with sheepskin, green Wellingtons, and a black watchman's cap from the mud room off the kitchen. In the kitchen, she poured coffee into an insulated mug, then followed Dr. Wickman outside through French doors leading to an outside patio.

The rain had stopped but the ground was soggy. Swollen dark clouds moved swiftly to the north, a stiff breeze pushing them from the south. Wind whipped strands of hair and lashed at her cheeks;

her nose instantly began to run. Audrey was glad she had grabbed her hat, and pulled it low over her head.

Rays of sunlight cut through a break to the east, offering a brief glimpse of sunlight between the march of storms passing through. She missed year-round sun; the warmth and golden sunsets that were a daily part of her childhood. It had been too long since she'd been back to the tropical island where she was born. Never, in fact. Not since her mother's death.

They strolled to the west-facing side of the house with a large wrap-around covered deck overlooking the wind-whipped waters of Puget Sound. Officially, it was the front side of the house, though Audrey always thought it was backwards. That the front of the house should be oriented toward the road, facing the driveway. But her father said it depended on your perspective. He wanted the front of the house to face the view. In addition, he built the house in the eighteen-nineties before he owned his first automobile. He said back then it made more sense to keep the horses and their accompanying smells away from the most prominent side of the house and closer to the stables on the back side of the house, near the road.

Built from old-growth cedar logs and river stone, the house had stood the test of time. It was renovated and modernized after her father met her mother and shortly before she was born. Walls were removed and rooms combined into seven bedroom suites, a library, a conference room, a media room, and a grand room with soaring ceilings and living and dining spaces connected to an open kitchen with a separate pantry for food prep and a mud room for stomping Pacific Northwest mud off your boots. The only part of the house he left unchanged was the grand stone turret. The small circular space had a creaky stairway and drafty leaded-glass windows facing every direction. An ideal place for quiet introspection or picking off enemies with a sniper rifle.

Her Polynesian-born mother hated the house. She felt that an over-sized, cobweb-riddled mansion was no place to raise a family.

And she couldn't understand the logic of placing train tracks along the shore at the foot of the bluff, cutting off the natural flow of access to the water for animals and humans. Shortly after it was renovated, the house was boarded up and Audrey spent her early years growing up in a modest two-bedroom house set by the sea on a quiet island west of Kauai.

Audrey couldn't agree more with her mother. It felt like she lived in a historic museum, complete with living ghosts from the past wandering its halls. It boggled her mind that her father, Dr. Wickman, and the rest of his original crew members had it bested in age by over a hundred years.

Audrey and Dr. Wickman followed a paved pathway to the bluff, facing west. The bluff was fifty feet off the water with a bushy drop-off ending at the train tracks; the main BNSF Railway route running north and south at water's edge.

"How are you feeling today?" he asked.

She rolled her eyes and wiped her nose on her sleeve. He always started their sessions with the same question. She decided to be honest. "Cold."

He smiled. "I was thinking, emotionally."

She gazed up to a patch of blue sky about to be consumed by hungry bruised clouds. "Honestly? Like I should lie on the tracks and let the next train take me."

He stopped walking. "How will that solve anything?"

She fought back tears. "I don't know. I—I—feel alone. Hollow."

"Like when your mother died?"

"Like that, but worse. I mean, I was a kid and had no idea she was in danger. I don't know what I could have done to stop it. But now—"

"You feel like you are responsible."

"Yes."

"For what exactly."

"I don't know—all of it?"

"Are you talking about what happened in Tallamure?"

She nodded. "Mostly."

"What do you think would have happened if you weren't there?"

"I had to be there. Remember, I was the key! I was how we were able to pass through the city's protective dome, to get inside the city so my father could meet Ianthe. The whole reason Blake was kidnapped."

"How can you be so certain? Stokes said your father was—how did he put it?—*snatched and yanked* inside while you idly stood by. Is that how you remember it?"

"Yes, but—

"It seems to me from what I knew of the plan it was your father Ianthe wanted to see, not you. Is that not true?"

She paused a beat, then, reluctantly agreed. "Yesss."

"And was Blake returned to the ship once your father entered the city's dome, before you both entered the tower and he met with Ianthe?"

She took a sip from her coffee. "Yes."

"So it is possible that the events that happened could easily have happened regardless of your participation?"

Audrey nibbled the inside of her cheek. She always replayed the day's events as they happened, with her as a key player. She never considered what would have happened if she hadn't been there.

"From what we've covered in previous discussions it was you who tried to stop your father from killing Sinto. You at least tried. Your father intended to kill him and there was nothing you could have done or said to change his mind. Sinto was the one to accept his fate, whether or not it was justified. It was Sinto's decision. Not yours. And it was you who acted as Stokes' hands on the submarine to fill the ballast tanks with air. If you hadn't been there, both Stokes and your father would have been lost."

"True…" She had been the one to step up and take charge. Stokes had several cracked ribs, a broken arm, and cracked clavicle. Her father had a spear in his shoulder, was pinned to his seat, and was acting weird from a blow to the head. The submarine was off-line and sinking. If she hadn't blown the last of the air reserves into the ballast tank they would have ended up on the bottom of the North Pacific, entombed forever. As it was, they barely made it to the surface before they sipped the last of the air remaining in the cabin. Pure luck played a big role, but luck she bought by being there and acting fast.

"There is nothing you can do to change the past or the role you played, good or bad. The guilt you feel is your subconscious telling you something. A powerful lesson. One that is painful and necessary. Life is painful and filled with lessons. Some more powerful than others. It is what shapes you, helps you grow. Helps you to be a better person. Learn from it."

Tears blurred her vision. "I should have been able to stop my father from killing Sinto. I fought him for the knife, just as he taught me, but he—he—tricked me. My hand was on that knife when it cut through Sinto's chest. He put Sinto's blood on my hands. I hate him for that. That's what I learned."

"What you are feeling is perfectly natural."

"What? Are you saying I should hate him forever?"

"You experienced a violent act perpetrated by your father against someone you cared about. I suggest you accept these feelings. It is the only way you will be able to heal. Maybe someday you will forgive him."

She took a long draw from her mug of coffee. It suddenly tasted bitter. "Not sure I can go there. It hurts all over, has for a long time. Like after one of his *training* sessions. I never understood why he fought back so hard. Like I was the enemy, not his student."

"Because he loves you more deeply than you can imagine."

She scoffed. "Right. I've seen what he does in the name of love. If that's what he calls it, I don't want his love anymore."

"Maybe not now, but I suggest you reconsider forgiving him. Maybe not today, but sometime in the future. Feeling anger and guilt makes you human. You love therefore you feel. Find that part of him you still love. These feelings are persistent and manifest in different ways, physically and emotionally. Yes, it is painful, and the negative feelings may not stop for a long time, if ever. I'm trying to help you accept that truth."

"I'm trying. It's hard."

"I know, and you *are* making progress."

He wiped a tear from her cheek with his finger.

"I have a favor to ask of you. I want you to imagine that *you* were the one who died, not Sinto—that in your struggle for the knife with your father the knife ended up in *your* chest, and Sinto lived to witness it. How would Sinto feel, knowing it was him who should have died?"

A train's horn blared, making her jump. The ground beneath her feet rumbled when it passed by. The noise was mind-numbingly unnatural, flaring that primal part of the brain that imminent danger was near. Minutes ticked by as train cars whipped by below the rise where they stood. Audrey pondered Dr. Wickman's suggestion in silence, the roar of the train making it impossible for her to answer right away. The air swirled with the smell of diesel, creosote, and low tide. Then finally silence.

Dr. Wickman quirked a brow, encouraging her to answer.

"I'd feel like me. Shit."

"How would Blake feel?"

"Blake?"

"Yes, Blake. He played a part in all this too. Even though he doesn't remember anything, was he not the reason you felt strongly compelled to accompany your father to Tallamure? Were you not trying to save him?"

"Yes." Her stomach burned with fresh guilt.

"How would *he* feel if it was you who died?"

She had been avoiding Blake ever since they were reunited after the Tallamure incident. He told her he didn't care what she had done since he'd last seen her, that he forgave her for everything. He said he loved her no matter what. He asked if she still felt the same for him and would be willing to pick up where they left off:

before the orca attack; before she Marked Sinto; before her world exploded. She told him too much had happened to go back to the way things were before and wasn't sure she would ever be able. But he persisted; told her he would wait and asked her to consider trying. She agreed, but ever since…

"Why have you refused to see him?"

She instinctively reached for her arm where the Mark lay hidden.

"I don't know."

"Have you considered giving him a chance to reconnect with you?"

"Honestly?" She frowned. "No. I really haven't thought about him at all."

"Could you?"

"I guess…"

"Just an observation, but I think it could be beneficial for both of you."

7

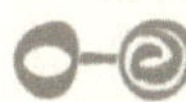

Larkian Mission

WHEN AUDREY AND DR. Wickman returned to the house, Captain Stokes and Alvarez were seated in the conference room.

Stokes was a true thirty-something in age, and of Polynesian descent, like her. He was usually involved in discussions when it came to dealing with the Merahvu, and was privy to her father's and his original crew's true history.

His arm was still in a sling from the injuries sustained when the shock wave struck their submarine after the collapse of Tallamure. It was clear he was relegated to breathing shallowly because of his cracked ribs. His upper body was just as broad as ever, as was his commanding presence. He had shaved his head and it glistened like a polished coconut. He had grown facial hair around his mouth and chin which was impeccably trimmed, like his dark arched brows. He was much less threatening than when she first met him. She valued him more than as a crew member, but as a friend. He flashed her a great white smile. She flashed him one in return.

Alvarez looked exactly like the day she met him, weaselly and oil slick. A late seventeenth-century-born Spaniard with black ringlet hair, pale skin, large hooked nose, and a slightly too-large head for his five-foot two-inch wiry frame. His glasses were smudged with greasy fingerprints, like always. Audrey wondered if he preferred seeing the world through a fogged lens.

Audrey recently learned her father and his original crew called themselves Larkians, a name referring to their original ship *Sea Lark*. Over the years, it naturally stuck. Since then, everything associated with them was "Larkian;" their ships, their technology, their rules... everything. And because of her association, as daughter of their original captain, she was deemed a Larkian too.

"I was unaware of a meeting," Dr. Wickman said.

"Because we hadn't called one, until now. Sit." Alvarez gestured to a pair of empty chairs at the table big enough to seat ten. Alvarez was the strategist for the Larkians. His laptop was open and ready to strategize. "You too Audrey."

Her face and fingers tingled from the sudden change in temperature. She pulled off her cap and hoodie and wrapped her long braid across her shoulder before sitting down. The tip of her nose burned from the heat.

Leonard popped through the doorway with a pot of freshly brewed coffee and a platter of fresh-baked croissants, a slab of butter, and a jar of raspberry jam.

"May I join ya?" He winked at Audrey. "I bring bribes."

Seeing Leonard brightened Audrey's mood, which needed an uplift after her thought-provoking and emotion-churning session with Dr. Wickman. Leonard was the chef on the *Sea Lark*, and was one of the original Larkians. Google "old pirate" and that would be Leonard: wild bright eyes; bushy white beard; plump, vein-reddened cheeks; and a nose that had been broken many times over the course of his three hundred or so years. He was a big man with a rounded belly who wore drawstring pants, billowy white shirts, and leather vests. He wore suede moccasins on his feet and colorful bandannas around his head to tame his wild hair. Today, he chose purple.

Her father met Leonard in a prison in India during his pirating days and after they escaped, invited him to join his budding new crew. As ship's chef he honed his cooking and baking skills over the years and everything that came out of his galley—he called every kitchen whether on land or sea a galley—was mouth-watering perfection. Leonard was staying in the suite off of the kitchen, and she must have gained five pounds since coming home.

Audrey grabbed a steaming croissant from his proffered bribe. She took a bite and smiled. "I certainly won't object."

He set the coffee and croissants on the table and settled his wide girth into a chair next to Dr. Wickman.

Alvarez jumped right in. "Something strange is happening in the North Pacific. We've picked up unusual reports from vessels collecting plastic garbage in the North Pacific Gyre."

"What kind of reports?" Audrey asked.

"That's just it. Most report nothing at all. There's *nothing* to collect. It's spotless. Just six months ago the ratio of particles collected in that area was seventy percent man-made to thirty percent organic. The reports last week revealed that what they did find, if anything at all, was mostly organic."

Stokes asked, "Is it possible the patch shifted its location, maybe a slight change in current?"

"They considered that and ran tests. They dropped dye and hundreds of rubber ducks in the water; the currents took them on the expected path. The scientists were dumbfounded but ecstatic. Except for one more-recent report, which caught my attention: it mentioned collecting some plastic, but what they did collect was coated in an orange slime they couldn't identify."

Alvarez sat back, drumming his chin with his long, bony fingers.

Audrey sat forward. "Why is that a problem?"

"Because that's the last anyone has heard from them."

"How long ago?" asked Stokes.

"Approximately forty-eight hours."

"That's not unusual, maybe their satellite link went down," said Stokes.

Alvarez pursed his lips. "True, but this wasn't a usual report."

Audrey sat back and calculated how long it had been since the day Sinto took her for a wild tunnel ride from the Salish Sea to the garbage patch in the North Pacific. That was while she was back at school, well over a month ago. There had been plenty of plastic on the surface and peppered below several meters from the surface. Sinto took her there, not to see what she already knew about the growing accumulation of plastic, but to see something else happening on the ocean floor.

"There's something I need to tell you." She put down what was left of her croissant and brushed crumbs from her fingers. "Before," she glanced over at Dr. Wickman, "all of you—*Larkians*—got involved, Sinto showed me what was happening below the garbage patch where, as I understand it, most of the clean-up efforts have been taking place.

"Growing on the ocean floor was a highly active orange fungus stretching as far as the eye could see. It fed on chunks of plastic drifting down from the surface. I watched as it peeled away all organic matter growing on their surfaces before consuming it. The Merahvu call it *Orange*. This Orange is smothering whatever sea life gets in its way, impacting the local food web in that part of the ocean. It radiates heat, warming the water well above normal. Orange has been killing off life in that part of the ocean for the past six months, maybe longer. Sinto said they didn't know where it came from, only that it feeds on petroleum-based polymers; mostly common plastic collected in the gyres... but they have observed more, meaning anything petroleum-based. They believe Orange was benign originally, but mutated radically, possibly from exposure to radiation leaking into the Pacific from the Far East.

"Maybe Orange is the reason they hadn't found any plastic," Audrey concluded.

"Maybe tis wormed its way up, ya know, ter the surface," Leonard added.

"Consumes anything *petroleum-based*?" Stokes said. "That could include fiberglass, circuit boards, fuel—many critical components on a ship."

"Has the Coast Guard been dispatched?" Dr. Wickman said.

"First, let me clarify." Alvarez raised two fingers. "Two ships are missing. They were working together. Second, our tech team intercepted this notice before it reached the authorities. Normally, a rescue ship would be sent only after confirmation that it is missing. It's too early to know for sure, but I'm sitting on it. So no, the Coast Guard is not aware. I wanted to discuss this with all of you first."

He stopped, tapped something on his keyboard, slid and clicked his mouse. "And from what Audrey just told us, I'm inclined to suggest we might want to look into it immediately."

He spun his laptop around so all could see the screen. "Not a prominent part of their report, but here, near the end. This is what caught my eye." He pointed. "The mention of, and I quote, 'an unidentified orange-colored slime coating the last haul dumped from the retention zone'. From what I can glean, this retention zone is where plastic collected in nets strung between two vessels is funneled as it sifts through the top two meters of the ocean waters.

"Now look at this." The four of them leaned closer to read what Alvarez highlighted on the screen. It read, "Some of the crew have reported rashes and are showing signs of agitation and restlessness on both ships. They have been isolated and are being monitored."

Audrey gasped. "Sinto said the Merahvu were alarmed by Orange, its aggressive nature and the danger it posed. What if that aggressive nature infects whatever organic matter it comes in contact with?"

Dr. Wickman stood up. "We need a sample." Then he swung his gaze toward Audrey. "And I'll need help analyzing it."

Audrey caught his gist. A challenge to get her out of her head space and a lifeline to get her out of this insane asylum of a house. "Count me in."

Dr. Wickman raised a brow. Then it dawned on her; Dr. Wickman meant something more. A way to reconnect with Blake. She had also blown off her best friend Ryan. For that she felt doubly shitty.

"Plus, I know a couple of guys who might be interested," she added.

That made Dr. Wickman smile.

"So are we in agreement?" Alvarez asked.

"Aye," everyone said in unison.

"Then I'll put out the call, dispatch the jets, and gather the crew. Stokes, you up to the task of captaining a ship?"

"Maybe no diving or heroics from me, but with a crew, I can captain the ship."

Alvarez shut his laptop and stood, stole a glance at his watch. It was one of those with four time zones. "Forty-eight hours, *maximum*, till cast off. I'll ready the ship."

Audrey looked at Stokes, questioningly. "Wait, what ship? I thought the *Requiem Sea* was scrapped?"

Stokes grinned. "The Larkians have more than one ship."

8

Reconciliation

AFTER THE IMPROMPTU VOTE to investigate the missing vessels in the North Pacific Gyre, Audrey headed up to her room. She sat on her unmade bed, gazing out the rain-splattered windows. She cradled her phone in her hands, waffling between dread and remorse. She had been putting this moment off for weeks.

While she had enthusiastically offered Ryan's help in their mission, she wondered if she had the guts to ask him if he was interested. In normal circumstances, Ryan would see it for what it was; an amazing offer. But it wasn't normal circumstances and she wrestled with how to begin. And what she would say if he refused to talk to her ever again.

Ryan became her best friend after they met at the University of Washington two and half years ago. The two of them, along with Blake, had been working on a research project at the Labs in Friday Harbor when the whole situation with the Merahvu ignited and Blake disappeared.

After Blake's disappearance, Audrey basically shut Ryan out. She blew off his suggestions to seek help once Blake was presumed dead and expected Ryan to faithfully jump to her aid with no questions asked. And he did, like a true friend would. He agreed to help her capture Sinto, and only then did she confide in him that Blake was still alive. She left out many, if not most, of the details of the precarious situation she was drawing Ryan into, unknowingly.

But the plan unraveled. One in which she had asked Ryan for help. Sinto escaped and she nearly drowned. At that point she dropped off the radar. Whisked away by her father and his merry band of modern-day pirates, to the North Pacific and Sinto's city of Tallamure where Blake was being held captive.

Audrey never called Ryan to tell him that she was okay and on her way to save their good friend, Blake. She left Ryan hanging, to fret and wonder. She had been consumed by a single purpose; to get Blake back from his underwater prison. It didn't help that she was suddenly thrust into a side of her father's life she never knew existed; learning the history of his pirating ways and of his original crew, aiding in his obsession to destroy Ianthe and everything important to her. And how could she forget that brief stroll at the bottom of the ocean, between the submarine and Sinto's underwater city, Tallamure, breathing oxygenated Liquid—a sensation akin to drowning. And after, participating in Sinto's death.

But none of that mattered. She *could* have reached out, but didn't. Instead, she used Ryan, crushed him under foot, and never looked back.

After the destruction of Tallamure, she called him, and he hung up on her. She tried several times after, each time he blocked her calls. And she didn't blame him. He had every right to feel used and betrayed. It wasn't until two weeks ago that he answered. Normally, he was full of support and advice, but he merely listened when she told him she had dropped out school and withdrawn from the research project that she, Blake, and Ryan were awarded. He merely replied, *I already know*, then hung up without saying goodbye.

Dr. Wickman helped her confront this guilt in one of their earlier sessions. She knew what she had to do, but it didn't make it any easier. The knowing was easy. It was the doing where she was stuck.

The meeting and her suggestion to enlist Ryan to help meant she could procrastinate no longer.

Her heart pounded. She swiped the screen of her phone, entered her passcode, and pulled up Ryan's phone number. Her finger shook as it hovered over the call button. She pressed it.

Ryan's phone rang, once, twice—then it cut off. Call dismissed. Rejected.

She fought back tears, her phone crushed in her hand. Then—

A ping. Text message, from Ryan. *Not able to talk just yet.*

Audrey typed, *How I've treated you was wrong in so many ways.*

No response.

She kept going, *I was thinking only of myself. I should have reached out to you. I failed to consider your feelings.*

No response.

Audrey stifled a sob. She had waited too long, lost him for good. She thought of all the sessions with Dr. Wickman, imagined what he might say if he were here at this moment: *Be patient. You can't eat a whole elephant in one sitting. Little gains add up. Don't give up.*

She raised the phone, tapped out another message. *I miss you... terribly. Please tell me what I need to do to fix this.*

No response.

Ry? You still there?

Ryan's typing bubble went active. She sat up, held her breath.

I thought you were dead. Do you know what that feels like?

Her heart trembled. She knew exactly what it felt like, all too much, so she tried one of Dr. Wickman's suggestions for dealing with her father—empathy.

She typed, *I do, and knowing that, it was incredibly irresponsible and insensitive on my part, not to mention extremely selfish.*

Another long pause. She waited, patiently. Like with her own sessions, there were times it was too painful to move on. She was slowly coming to realize time was a great healer. So she waited, giving it in spades to Ryan. He deserved that much, and more.

More typing on Ryan's end. *Never do that to me again. Ever.*

I promise, it will never happen again. Forgive me?

She waited, and waited, chewing her thumbnail till it bled, then—

Forgiveness is hard coming, Aud.

A cold chill settled in her stomach. Would he ever forgive her? That too she understood all too well. She was still struggling to forgive her father, and might not ever as Dr. Wickman had warned her. But that didn't mean she shouldn't try. She would crawl back to Friday Harbor on her hands and knees to regain Ryan's trust and friendship.

A tear slipped down her cheek. She typed. *Please, help me find a way back to you. What more can I say or do, if anything? I'm lost without our friendship. I've had to deal with things that reopened old wounds, deep and painful ones. I know that's a poor excuse for not reaching out sooner. I should have. I should have thought of nothing but contacting you after I crashed Roy's boat. I've made some pretty serious mistakes. Ones that I regret deeper than you can possibly know. But one of the biggest was disrespecting you. I'll understand if you never want to see me again. All I can do is ask you to forgive me, to give me another chance.* Audrey's fingers shook, she had to know, no matter how painful his answer may be.

She asked, *Will you give me another chance?*

Five minutes passed, and she got no response. She checked her signal, her phone's charge, all good. She tapped her phone against her head, believing no response was just that. That no, he would not give her another chance. She jumped when her phone pinged.

Clean slate?

Audrey burst into tears, joyful ones. When Audrey met Ryan they agreed to never hold a grudge. True friends worked things out, no matter how bad. Once they agreed the slate was clean, they agreed to only look forward.

Her fingers shook so much she had to try three times to type three simple words: *Yes, clean slate.*

Her phone rang. It was Ryan. She answered on the first ring.

"Ry!"

"Don't say anything. I'm gonna talk and you're gonna listen."

There was the sound of his phone being muffled. Audrey bit her tongue and nodded, mostly to herself.

After an agonizing pause, Ryan finally said, "I have never felt so helpless in my life." His voice was subdued and wound tight. "I knew you shouldn't have gone alone, felt it deep in my bones the morning you left, then—*Bam!*" She jumped at the sudden rise in his voice. He quieted, and said in a tight shaky voice. "You were gone, not a word, nothing. Roy and I—" He sucked a noisy breath. "We—we scoured the waters between Friday Harbor and Andrews Island, called in the Coast Guard to help. At first, we only found a couple cushions washed ashore on Jones Island. Then we found Roy's boat, sunken, just off Center Reef—hull ripped out, forward hatch missing, metal barbed darts littering the decks. No body, not a shred of clothing, not even a clue as to what happened to you." He was gasping at his point, went silent, then burst out, "It was as if you had been abducted by fucking aliens!"

He broke down after that, muffled sobs leaking through his muffled phone.

It broke Audrey's heart, imagining what Ryan and Roy went through, sick with worry, the not knowing, the hollowness, that gnawing ache that never went away, even in slumber. Feeling that way for *days*. More than a week had passed before Ryan and Roy learned that she had survived and moved back to Seattle to be with her father; that she indeed had not been abducted by aliens, but was alive and safe. As was Blake. Ryan had no idea of the untold risks she took to save Blake in the North Pacific. She wanted to gush, to tell Ryan everything, to justify the why—

But she bit back the burning need to say something. Ryan asked her to listen, so she was going to listen. She gave him the time he needed to compose himself.

Then he continued, "Roy aged ten years and that's a lot for someone his age. How could you do that to such a compassionate and caring man? *Selfish* doesn't begin to describe what you did. My stomach turned inside out. I couldn't eat or sleep or go to class... I almost chewed a hole in my fucking cheek anguishing over what happened to you!"

He stopped, took a couple of shaky breaths. When he continued his voice was so tight she could barely hear him. "And then I learned that all that time you were *safe*, that you had access to the Internet—and a satellite phone?" His voice rose on that last part. "Did you even think for one second I might have been dying here?" A pause. "After I learned you were okay, I hated you, I loved you, I—I never wanted to hit something as much as I did then. Especially once I realized you failed to consider, for one second, what I must have been going through—you put me through hell, drowned me in an emotional stew that ate me alive. Jesus, Audrey!"

He choked down a sob. Her heart ached. She never wanted to hurt Ryan but she had, in a deep and profound way. It would take another round with Dr. Wickman to unpack the guilt wiggling to the surface after hearing the hell she put Ryan through. And Roy too. Her reconciliation list was growing longer.

Audrey's heart settled in her throat like a hard stone. She knew she had to say something or else risk losing his friendship forever.

"Can I—talk?"

A pause. "Yeah. Shoot."

"I know I can say it a thousand times and maybe it will have no meaning. But hear me now, I am so sorry. Sorry, from the depths of my core. I truly fucked up. I am ashamed and horrified at what I put you, and Roy, through. No one deserves what I did to you, especially you. You are my rock and I don't know what I would do without you as my friend, my confidant, the brother I never had. I love you, Ryan, more than you could ever know."

She heard a gasp, a muffled sob. Her heart raced waiting to hear his response. She was uncertain what more she could say that would matter. She waited patiently for him to calm, if he ever would. She drew comfort from the fact he had not hung up on her. She gripped her phone with white knuckles and bated breath.

A minute passed. She could tell Ryan was dealing with his own swirling emotions. She waited, heart awash in shame but feeling a tiny bit hopeful.

He said, "It starts now—we look forward, clean slate. But before we do, I have one more thing to say. I never had a true family. My mom, she was flawed, so I can't really blame her. My dad, well you know about that, never met him. I never understood what it was like to have family, to know someone cared about me, *included* me, until I met you and Blake. I love you, Aud, like a sister. I hope you never forget that."

She wanted to reply but her throat was tamped shut.

"Damn," he said, sounding a lot more like himself, "I feel much lighter. Dizzy in fact. Woo! I am seeing other colors besides red. Damn, that slate was awfully grimy. I never thought I could get all of that off my chest in one sitting. Sorry if it was a bit raw, but I couldn't help myself." He paused. "Hey, you still there? That was a dump-load of shit I just dropped on your head. You okay?"

"I'm here," she squeaked. "Yes, and thank you."

"Thank me?"

"I deserved that." She faltered on the rock stuck in her throat. "I needed to hear the truth. I needed to know how much I hurt you. I lied and treated you unfairly. I would understand if you never trusted me again."

"Wow, are you the same Audrey Grey who pranced into my dorm room a month ago acting all wily and secretive about kidnapping your water-loving friend?"

"That was a lifetime ago."

"Hmm. Trust you? Hmm. And you're truly sorry?"

"I don't know any other way to say it, but yes. Yes. YES. I am sorry."

"Prove it."

"I've got something that might interest you."

"Is it related to that situation you and Blake got tangled up in?"

"Yes." She held her breath.

"Huh. Hate to be the third wheel, but I'm tired of missing out on all the fun."

"It might be a tiny bit dangerous..."

He fluttered his lips. "Ha, I'm learning everything about you is more than a tiny bit dangerous. Spill."

"You sitting down? Cause I've got a story that will rock your world. The truth. All of it."

9

Violent Cleansing

AUDREY FELT EXHILARATED AFTER her call with Ryan. He readily accepted her offer to join her father's crew to learn what may have happened to the missing ships in the Pacific.

One reconciliation down, one to go. Blake.

But first, she needed time to recharge and sort through the stew of emotions dredged up after talking to Ryan. While it felt good, she realized it was more akin to peeling an onion, with new challenges surfacing with every layer. She was emotionally exhausted but physically restless. Filled with pent-up energy, she needed to get outside and move. Yesterday her life was going nowhere. Now it was careening forward at mach speed. A vigorous run would help her decompress and blow off new emotional steam.

She dug out a pair of leggings and a fleece pullover from the antique dresser next to her bed, changed, and tossed her clothes aside. Her gaze drifted to her phone lying on her pillow, the dark screen beckoning.

Text Blake now or after I return?

Her heart beat faster, debating. *If I don't do it now then I'll find an excuse...*

She grabbed her phone before she could chicken out and typed a message to Blake. It surprised her how easily the words flowed.

Sorry if this is coming out of the blue but I need to talk to you, soon. Actually, today, if possible. An immediate situation has come up and I'm hoping you could join me and Ryan on an urgent mission with my father's crew. I've been working through a sea of emotions and dealing with the consequences from my past actions since I last saw you. I know that's a poor excuse for me ignoring you. For that I am truly sorry, but I need to formally apologize. I think this mission would be a good opportunity for me to tell you, in person, that I am sorry, and for you to vent the many ways I have hurt you. Dr. Wickman said it's the only way I can heal. Anyway, I hope you might be interested.

She hit send, but she wasn't finished, and struggled to find the right words to say what she needed to say.

One more thing... I was thinking that maybe we could start over, void of previous promises. A reset of some sort. What do you think?

She tossed her phone on the bed and didn't look back. She padded down the stairs in stocking feet to the mud room off of the kitchen. She laced on her running shoes and slipped out the back door.

She felt raw with a new flavor of guilt to deal with: breaking the promise she made to Blake and how easily she cast him from her heart after reuniting with Sinto. And that was just her own shit she had to deal with. She couldn't imagine how Blake might feel and what she must do to earn back his trust and friendship.

A gentle mist floated down from a cloud-swollen sky, moistening her face and fogging her breath. She shivered in the cold but once she started running her body quickly warmed. She followed the same path she strolled earlier with Dr. Wickman, paralleling the shore and the now-quiet railroad tracks below. She felt like a different person from earlier. In the few short hours since their discussion she had regained a friend and opened the door to another.

She quickly fell into a rhythm. The trail that carved through the twenty acres of woods surrounding the house was deeply ingrained in her memory. She could run it blindfolded. Various pathways veered off from the main trail to cleared training circles in the woods, where she had spent hours wielding modernized ancient weapons, training for warfare. A few months ago she shunned such training, but after the Larkians destroyed the Merahvu's city of Tallamure, she found merit in resuming the disciplined training her father had, quite literally, beat into her over the years.

She veered off the path to one of those cleared circles, where practice staffs leaned against a tree and a circle of rubbery dummies had been staged—upright or crouched—to mimic live enemies. Several body-sized sand bags lay on the ground to mimic the dead or the injured. She grabbed a staff without missing a step and pranced stealthy around the circle of dummies, twirling it in her hands, getting the feel of the hard resin against her palms, and the weight and length of it as she swung it side to side as if fending off an imaginary attacker. Wielding a staff was a whole-body affair, engaging multiple muscle groups, requiring a lot of bending and twisting with sure footing.

Past lessons came flooding back. She spun and struck a dummy atop the head, swung behind her to take down an attack from the rear. She pranced around the circle, surging forward to strike and back to block imaginary strikes to her head, feet solidly planted in classic warrior postures. Her breath flowed as did her mind-state and body. The air fogged from her effort.

Once she tired of pummeling dummies, she struck sand bags lying on the ground, raising the staff directly over her head, hyper-extending her body from head to toe, then coiling into a deep squat and whipping the staff overhead to strike the bag at her feet. The movement was sudden and aggressive, requiring every ounce of strength she could muster. The staff reverberated violently with each strike, tearing away built-up callouses and raising blisters in their place. She ignored the pain blooming in her hands and struck repeatedly. A repressed vent opened and the deep-seated anger she felt poured out—for failing to stop Sinto's senseless death and Tallamure from being blown to smithereens. She swung and pummeled bags and dummies until her hands grew numb and she was gasping for breath.

She tossed the staff aside and bent to catch her breath. Tears ran from her eyes and she found herself sobbing uncontrollably, from the sudden eruption of violence and outpouring of emotion. Once she composed herself, she looked around the circle, shocked. Sand leaked from split bags, and every dummy was missing its head and most of their limbs. She wondered if Dr. Wickman would approve of her method. She found the violent outburst surprisingly soul-cleansing.

She returned to the trail and resumed running, much lighter on her feet and springy as a doe. The trail ran along the eight-foot-high wall surrounding the property. Mounted atop were cameras and motion sensors recording her every move. Then the trail swerved into the woods, zigzagging around glacial erratics, rotten stumps of old-growth fir and cedar, and moss-covered tree trunks. She vaulted over and veered around these obstacles, and headed back toward the house.

She felt that old quiver of dread as she passed the outdoor saltwater pool and the original stables her father had converted into a training center shortly after her mother died. The scene of much agony and abuse. It was where he taught her to fight to survive, on land and in the water, using weapons like the staff she wielded earlier. Not the type of weapons and tools you might think to use in the twenty-first century. Her father wasn't a bullets-and-gun guy. He preferred to strike stealthily, up close and personal. She now knew why. Bullets were too slow underwater and they made too much noise. The Larkians preferred weapons from the past, updated and high-tech. Cross-bows for long-range targets and short-length spear-guns for close encounters, both with rapid-firing, multi-spear barrels that could quickly and easily be replaced. The spears were designed with a specialized star-shaped tip that sprung open after burying in flesh, shredding it. They were especially deadly when buried in a vital organ. Darts were useful for injecting debilitating drugs or poisoning intended targets and could be shot from a dart gun, rifle, or multi-barrel gatling-like gun.

In addition to the staff, she had trained with metal pipes, steel mace, spears, knives, rope, and anything else one might find at the ready to use as a weapon if attacked unexpectantly.

Lastly, and most often, her father taught her how to maim and kill with her bare hands, pointing out each and every vulnerable spot on the human body, which he often demonstrated on her. In particular, he made sure she understood which you strike to maim versus which you strike to kill. He taught her to never contemplate, always commit. At the time she didn't take it seriously. She now understood the reason for his obsession.

She veered off the trail and onto a shortcut she made for herself long ago. It had since been adopted by local deer who scaled the bluff next to the train tracks and sneaked past her father's defenses.

She burst out of the woods and onto the paved pathway that meandered around the house, and skidded to a sudden stop.

Blake stood twenty feet away, hands tucked in his pants pockets, pensively staring up at the sky. He turned and stunned her with his cerulean-colored eyes. He looked exactly the same as the last time she saw him: ivy-league prep-boy with his perfectly clipped hair and award-winning smile. Today he chose to wear a pair of mustard-colored chinos with a butter-soft gray leather jacket. His signature cashmere sweater and collared shirt peeked out from underneath.

Blake smiled and walked toward her. She felt self-conscious, sweating and gasping for air. The fog of her breath swirled between them. She wiped her nose on her sleeve and tucked loose strands of hair that had escaped her braid behind her ears. Thankfully, she had brushed her teeth.

"Hi," he said.

"Hi."

"Got your text." He laughed. "I can't believe you thought you needed to ask. Of course I'm interested."

She swallowed. "Which part?"

He gave her a lopsided grin, one that melted her heart. "All of it." A beat. "Ryan filled me in with what he knows."

"How did you get here so fast?"

"I was in town, not far from here."

A trickle of sweat ran down her cheek. "I'm a sweaty mess."

"Then take a shower. I'll wait."

They lazily strolled to the house, her falling into Blake's calm and reassuring pace.

"How's your dad?"

"Um, Dr. Wickman says he's getting better, but every time I'm asked to help with his memories he still thinks I'm my mom. It makes me uncomfortable to be around him. Dr. Wickman said not to worry. It might take a while till he acknowledges that she's gone and I'm his daughter, not his wife. He's getting help from the others to rebuild his memories. Slowly, he's coming around. I guess he took quite a hit to the head and Dr. Wickman doesn't know yet if the damage will be permanent. The good news is he's finally clearheaded and self-sufficient. He's just stuck in a time warp from the past."

They entered the house through the mud room and kicked off their shoes. Blake hung his jacket on a hook next to her hoodie. Audrey pointed to a communal basket filled with various-sized slippers. "Help yourself. The house feels especially drafty on days like today."

They wandered into the kitchen in slippered feet. "Make yourself at home: tea, coffee, ice cream… whatever you want."

He asked, "Are you hungry?"

She nodded. "Famished. Took quite a run, among other things…"

He opened the fridge and dug around. "I'll make us some sandwiches."

"That's it? Make us some sandwiches?"

"What do you mean?"

"I thought you'd be upset. Ryan sure was."

"I think you've said enough. Between your message and what you're going through with your father. Maybe I'm a little simpler than Ryan that way."

"Ryan deserved to be pissed." She rolled her eyes. "What a bitch I've been."

He pulled some cheese and meat from the fridge, set them on the counter, and gently closed the door. He leaned against the counter and regarded her.

She held her breath expecting damnation. Instead, he said, "I don't think you've been a bitch at all. I think you've been incredibly brave. Life is messy, requiring difficult choices. I believe you did what you needed to do. Sure, you hurt Ryan, but you called him, didn't you? You made the attempt to make amends. That's not what bitches do. That's what true friends do."

She gazed back in amazement. Tears threatened to spill. "I guess they do."

He made a face and sniffed. "Didn't you say something about a shower?"

She laughed. "Yeah, I did." She paused in the doorway, fixed him with her best rendition of a businesslike gaze. "One other thing. When I return, I'll be expecting a killer sandwich."

He smiled. "Of course."

10

Reset

AUDREY SMILED. BLAKE'S SANDWICHES were as put together as he was. He had cut off the crusts and cut them into triangles, revealing even layers of mayo, turkey, ham, provolone, sliced pickle, lettuce, and Dijon mustard. An origami folded rose was balanced on top of a toothpick and stuck into one of Audrey's triangles.

They sat at the kitchen counter on a pair of padded stools.

She poked the rose. "I should take a picture of this, send it to Ryan."

Blake laughed. "Don't bother, I already did."

She wrinkled her nose. "Really?"

"Na. I doubt he'd be as excited about it as you are."

She spun the plate. "It's too pretty to eat."

He picked up one of her triangles, held it to her mouth. "Open wide."

She took a bite. It tasted as wonderful as it looked.

"See, that was easy."

"That's weird."

"What?"

"Easy. Nothing about my life has been easy."

"What do you mean?" He looked around the kitchen. "Look around you. A refrigerator to keep food fresh, a stove that gets hot with the spin of a dial, abundant hot and cold running water. *That's* easy. Could I have made you that sandwich three hundred years ago?"

"That's weird."

"What?"

"Three hundred years? Seems to be a common theme around here."

He blinked. "I don't understand. It's just a random number I pulled from the top of my head. How about one hundred ninety-eight?"

"Nevermind." She took another bite. "Thanks for the killer sandwich."

They ate in silence trading awkward glances as if there was something that urgently needed to be said but neither wanted to be the one to say it.

Audrey cleared their plates and put them in the dishwasher. She turned toward Blake sitting at the counter, watching. She chuckled as she closed the dishwasher, imagining Leonard hand-washing every dish after serving a full complement of Larkian crew three squares a day. "I think you might have a point. My life has many things about it that're easy. Maybe I'm looking at everything all wrong, my perspective is wacky."

"Could be." He stood up. "Want to go somewhere?"

Blake drove. He still had the Pathfinder, the one Audrey had borrowed from time to time when he was missing. They took I-5 south to downtown Seattle and veered off toward the waterfront and touristy part of the city. Blake parked in a lot across from Pier 62 and turned off the engine.

"When was the last time you went to the Aquarium?"

"Wow, like in—forever."

"Figured it might be good place to, you know, reset."

The Aquarium was located on a pier along Puget Sound. Being late November, it was mostly empty. Usually, it was packed with summertime tourists or busloads of kids on field trips. But today was quiet and they pretty much had the place to themselves.

Signage indicated the Aquarium would be closing soon for a long-anticipated expansion. Shortly after meeting Ryan and Blake at the U-Dub, they had visited the Aquarium weekly. Audrey and Blake felt lucky to see it as they remembered it, one last time.

Walking through the front doors was like time-traveling back to that short window of time when Audrey had finally grasped the reins of her future, and before the harsh realities of her father's past became her own.

They wandered rows of tanks on the first level, marveling at all the weird and wonderful creatures that came from the sea; aliens from an underwater world that covered most of the planet. Blake slipped into teaching mode, explaining a few fast facts to an Asian couple who lingered by a tank with Dungeness crabs.

His eyes became animated as he explained, "They molt periodically, a process called ecdysis... and their claws tear their food apart and pass it to the smaller appendages to stick it into its mouth. See?"

Audrey tugged on his sleeve and he followed her to the open tank to observe Mishca and Sekui—resident sea otters—floating on their backs, chomping on prickly urchins. A mom with two young children laughed when the otters tossed aside the spines and spun in the water. Audrey squatted, leveling her gaze with the two girls. "That's how they clean up after eating. They use water like a napkin."

Blake motioned her toward the stairway that dropped a couple of stories below sea level to the underwater dome; a four-hundred-thousand-gallon salt-water enclosed habitat, fenced off from the Sound.

The stairway was dark except for individual lights marking each stair, giving their eyes time to adjust to the underwater environment into which they were descending. A spry older woman coming up smiled at them, "Lucky you! You kids got the place to yourselves," she said as she slipped past.

They rounded the corner at the bottom of the stairs. The dome was roughly fifty feet across and curved high above their heads. In the center was a bench. They walked over and sat, and as the older woman said, they had the space to themselves. It was the inverse of the dome that once enclosed Tallamure, where the vitality of life was contained *inside* and the solitude and darkness of the deep sea was *outside*. And like Sinto's once vital city, she was mesmerized by the soothing gurgle of water and layers of fish and sea life that defied gravity. Some gently swayed in the current, others flitted about. In the shadows along the bottom, still others hovered or scurried.

The sea was a serene world where prey and predator coexisted in a harmonious environment.

Blake squeezed her hand. "I'll never tire of it."

"It *is* miraculous."

He let go of her hand and his gaze fell to the floor. That's when she knew. This was it, the conversation she'd been holding off for as long as possible. The easy banter over sandwiches and modern appliances and sea otter antics was merely an icebreaker for what needed to come next. She had to tell him about Sinto. The key sticking point as to why she'd been avoiding him.

She drew in a deep breath, but before she could say anything Blake said, "I know about Sinto."

She instinctively cradled her arm with the Mark buried inside. "Who told you?"

"Does it matter?"

"Not really, but..."

"You want to know how much I know."

She nodded.

"I know enough to guess that you cared a great deal for him." He paused. "I've had some time to do a little soul-searching myself.

Being involved but not remembering anything messes with your head."

She tittered. "Being involved and remembering *everything* did more than mess with my head."

That made him smile. "I can imagine." He paused, held a breath. "I can imagine it might make you rethink many aspects of your life. Like me."

Audrey's heart pounded. How to say it without hurting him. Her last conversation with Ryan revealed gaping blind spots in her life view. Especially when it came to her most cherished relationships. Dr. Wickman repeatedly pointed out that she had an unusual upbringing: no mother at a critical point of development and an overly protective father on top of that. He told her she might have to try harder to establish and maintain relationships. Oh boy, was he right.

"I'm no good at this," she said, "and if I offend you, please say something. Um, here goes—I don't think I can keep my promise. It's not because of you. It's because of me. I'm screwed up—struggling to accept—"

She couldn't bring herself to say it, but Blake did. "That Sinto's dead."

Hearing the words made her shudder. "Yes."

"I know what you're feeling."

"You do?"

He drew a deep breath, held it, let it go. His lips quivered when he said, "I lost my first love, when I was seventeen. It was not just a crush, but someone I cared deeply for."

Blake's gaze drifted to the belly of a skate passing overhead. On the far side of the aquarium a diver rolled into the water in a swirl of bubbles. Schools of fish scattered. Blake's gaze was unfazed by the sudden disruption. His thoughts were somewhere else, reliving a story from his past.

"What happened to her was so unexpected." His breath came faster. "It came from nowhere. It was a—a bolt of lightning that struck us both. I was dazed but conscious and when I looked over, she was staring back at me. I was so relieved that I drew her into my arms, ecstatic at how lucky we were, but she was limp and unresponsive. Her eyes, they weren't looking at me, but stuck open, lifeless and unseeing." He closed his eyes, opened them, blinking. "That's when I realized she was dead."

Audrey reached out and put her hand over his, fisted in his lap. He wrapped his other hand around hers, squeezing so tight she wondered if he ever planned to let go.

"I felt helpless. I replayed over and over what I could have possibly done to save her. But." He shook his head. "It took a long time to realize the only thing that would have saved her was if we had never met." The rest of his story came slowly and painfully. "And if I hadn't met her, then we never would have been exposed to—to that particular circumstance, that moment of unexpected danger." His eyes locked on a small shark and followed its trajectory across the ceiling. "I'm sorry if that's a little vague, but I found that erasing the details of that day was the only way I could live with myself."

Audrey said nothing, giving Blake space to compose himself. The diver was busy scrubbing the glass on the other side of the windows. A woman with a pair of hot-pink goggles and expressive eyes. She waved at Audrey. Audrey waved back with her free hand.

He let go of her other hand. It was moist where he had held it. "They say time heals. I don't believe that. It feels as raw today as it did in that exact moment I realized she was dead. I've only learned how to live with it. The pain and bitterness will always be a part of me and will follow me to the grave."

Audrey flashed to Sinto's dead stare and the bloom of his blood, and reflected on how cold and hollow she felt after and every day since. Would she feel this way forever, too?

They sat in silence and watched the diver merrily scrub the aquarium. Fish and crabs slithered and creepy-crawled out of her way.

"You were the only one," Blake said in a voice so quiet she could barely hear him over the sound of gurgling of water. "You made my heart dance and feel alive. You're the only one I felt like letting in. I dated, but that's all they were, dates." He sighed. "I tried but ended up breaking a lot of hearts. I just couldn't open mine for fear that if I did, I would forget her, forever."

He lifted her chin so he could look her in the eyes. "I respect your need for space. I've been waiting for someone like you for a very long time, to come into my life and show me there's still a piece of my heart left, unclaimed. Maybe it's you, maybe it's not. But I'm willing to give it time to find out. Maybe someday you will discover that too."

He stood and held out his hand. "All I ask is to be a part of your life, Audrey. If that's merely as a friend like before, then so be it. Is that the reset you were hoping for?"

She took his hand. "Thank you for understanding."

"That's what friends are for." He pulled her to her feet. "Let's get out of here. I heard something about an urgent mission." He laughed. "And here we are lolly-gagging over fish we could cite by scientific name, genus, and trophic level in the food chain."

11

Cat And Mouse

Sinto burst through the portal from Merluma to Earth and into a murky sea. His protective cocoon of lorica disintegrated, his reserves severely weakened from escaping the Terrakai Scouts through the portal. He burst to the surface gasping for air.

Rain fell from the sky in torrential sheets, tainted with the bitter taste of acid scrubbed from the sky. Dark, swollen clouds blocked the last rays of a setting sun across an endless ocean. A pier stretched from a long sandy beach to the east, ablaze with light where a giant multi-colored lit-up wheel spun lazily. Beyond the beach, the lights and sounds of Sapien civilization.

He heaved from exertion and the stench of city toxins washed from its streets by the torrential flush of rain. He rolled to his back, sucking air. Once he caught his breath he camouflaged and swam along the surface toward the pier, casting aside occasional bits of garbage. He slipped into the dark shadow of the pier, winding through concrete pilings and transparent strings with barbed hooks from fisherman's poles.

His feet found sand, then his knees. He crawled out of the water and retched a stomach full of salt water. He rolled to his back, limbs splayed and heavy, gasping. An obnoxious jumble of music from competing sources floated down from the pier. Not far from him, a couple of young males were huddled to escape the torrential rain. He was camouflaged, but if not for the noise coming from above, surely they would have heard him.

Smoke swirled around their heads as they passed a smoldering cigarette between them, sucking deep of its smoke. The smoke smelled sweet and distinct; marijuana, not tobacco. He knew not from experience but from a memory a Scout once shared with him: how it smelled, the way Sapiens rolled it up, and how it made the Scout who tried it feel. One of the Sapiens started coughing and the other stifled a laugh, trying to hold the smoke in his lungs for as long as possible.

The boys were between Sinto and the top of the beach where it met pavement. He stole a quick glance back at the sea and saw a head bobbing off shore, a glint of bronze-colored hair and amber eyes aglow. The male Scout who thought Sinto was a newborn had followed him here.

Sinto had to keep moving or he would quickly be discovered. While the boys may not see him, the Scout surely would with his heightened senses. With Sinto in his weakened state, the Scout could easily catch him.

Regardless, Sinto had no choice but to run if the Scout spotted him. He tucked his tail against his spine and flattened the fluke across his shoulders. His markings were mostly covered, except those splayed across his buttocks, around his hips and groin. If he had a pair of shorts he could easily slip into a crowd and disappear. But he didn't have shorts. So he secured his camouflage and crawled, low and slow across the sand like a chameleon, past the Sapien boys, his skin reflecting a dappled pattern of light and shadows dancing across beach grit.

"Hey, what's that? Did you see it?"

Sinto pressed his belly to the sand and froze.

"What?"

"The sand, it frickin' *moved*." The boy looked at the smoldering joint in his hand. "This shit's fire!"

The other boy laughed. "Dude, told ya."

Sinto lay frozen on the sand until they ventured into the rain, heads covered by hoods, hands thrust deep into pockets. They hopped over meandering rivers running from city streets, kicking away garbage, littering the beach. One of them said. "Look at this shit. Frickin' rain sucks." Then the other. "Only in Santa Monica!" Before fading into the darkness.

Sinto pondered this new fact of where he had washed up on Earth: Santa Monica in southern California. Thousands of miles south of the Salish Sea near the Canadian border, and even farther from his goal of Lake Superior and the City of Green located in its depths. He had never ventured beyond the protective shores of the Salish Sea and certainly nowhere this heavily populated. Scouts were the only Merahvu brave enough to travel to the more populated places, after much study of the Earth world. He had only read books from and about the Sapien world. But that was vastly different from living in it. He may as well have landed on the moon.

Sinto glanced back. The Scout had emerged from the sea. He was bent at the waist, hands to knees, catching his breath. Sinto took solace in the fact that the chase exhausted the Scout, too, though he would recover much faster than Sinto. He feared the chase was far from over.

The Scout was scanning up and down the shoreline. Sinto slowly worked his way toward the streets where voices floated down from passersby and cars whizzed by, casting sheets of spray. Darkness descended quickly and the rain eased. Bodies emerged from cars and doorways. The streets filled with Sapiens, roaming everywhere. This was good; crowds would help him easily blend in, except for one critical exception.

He was naked.

But being naked had other advantages: he could camouflage, crawl up into the space where the pier met the sand, meld into the background and rest until dawn, and upon waking, ponder his next move.

Except for the fact the Scout was now glaring in his direction.

Sinto bolted from under the pier to a parking lot of hard pavement. It took a moment for his mind to register his surroundings, another for his skin and hair to react. Camouflage worked best when he was still or moving slowly. Unlike now. His skin was a moving billboard of shifting patterns, colors, and images in the shape of a desperate man, sprinting for his life.

Sinto ran south, next to a busy street, darting between Sapiens who startled and gasped when he passed by. The Scout was not far behind, stirring up the crowd, ramming into Sapiens in his hidden form. Yelps and cries of "What was that?" erupted in his wake.

The street jaunted east, then south to an open grassy park, sparsely treed.

Nowhere to hide. Sinto kept running.

The ground was unforgiving, leg bones reverberating with each footfall, the rough cement sanding down the callused pads of his feet. His heart labored, lungs wheezed, but he didn't stop.

He saw an opening between rushing cars and darted across the street, spotted a tree-lined street heading east, followed it. He dodged between tree trunks, looking for cover. Yet still, the Scout pursued, a body of wavering air, creating a ruckus.

Sinto cut across a parking lot, staying low as he weaved between parked cars, stopping briefly to catch his breath. The Scout stopped on the street beside the lot, visible only by the wavering movement of his head, scanning in all directions.

Sinto moved slowly, trying not to make a sound or startle an unsuspecting Sapien. He timed his next move: a quick dart between cars to a sidewalk with more trees. He slipped past a restaurant, a coffee shop, and a small market, to another parking lot that spanned a city block to a street on the other side. He eased his way around the end of a building, stole a peek back. The Scout was nowhere to be seen—or maybe he was hiding, like Sinto, waiting for his next move.

Camouflage firmly in place Sinto scurried along the side of the building to the street on the other side of the parking lot. He ducked down between two parked cars.

He weighed his options. Head back to the sea, which could be heavily guarded by Scouts at this point, or assimilate into the Sapien world until they gave up. He slowly raised his head and surveyed the parking lot.

Across the street was a clothing store, advertising new and recycled clothing. On display in the store-front window was a mannequin wearing a large black leather jacket and a pair of jeans. Set beside the mannequin was a large pair of black boots. Lights blazed, offering a peek of more options inside.

A Sapien woman with dark hair and elaborate arm tattoos approached the door from inside, talking animatedly into a phone pressed to her ear. She attached a note of some kind to the front window and fiddled with the door. From this distance, Sinto heard the slide of metal against metal and a solid click. She pulled a chain hanging from an illuminated OPEN sign. The light clicked off. Several minutes later the store went dark. Running alongside the clothing store was a narrow alleyway. A door in the alleyway opened and the woman stepped out, shutting the door and giving the handle a good push and a twist to make sure it was locked and secure. She hurriedly walked away in the opposite direction, phone still pressed to ear, and slipped around the corner.

The sign said, "Sorry for the inconvenience! Today Only. Closing Early."

Surely *not* an inconvenience.

He waited a while longer, tucked between the cars, until he was absolutely sure the Scout was not lying in wait for Sinto to make a sudden and careless move.

Sinto crept around the car and swiftly moved with his back to a wall. He stopped when he reached the corner, where the sidewalk met the street. He looked back. All clear. He waited for an opening between Sapiens walking along the sidewalk and for a break in the traffic. It came, finally.

He moved slowly and smoothly across the street, camouflage in sync with every step and bend of arm. He entered the dark alleyway, eased his way to the door. He stilled, back pressed against the side of the building, next to the door the woman exited. He readied his merlux to fire, anticipating a sudden confrontation with the Scout.

None came.

Sinto relaxed a little, calculating the possibility the Scout would find him in the grid-shaped labyrinth of city streets. The likelihood a lone Scout could cover every possible street and alleyway from the time Sinto lost him was slim. He hoped the Scout considered the possibility Sinto may have returned to the shore. The odds in Sinto's favor were adding up. He held no sympathy for the Scout.

He gazed down at the keypad mounted on the door, its numbered buttons softly glowing.

While he had bought some time, he faced another more immediate challenge. Unlocking the door.

12

New And Recycled

ELECTRONIC LOCKS. SINTO HAD learned from Scouts who assimilated into the Sapien world about such things; how prevalent electronics were and how they could be easily manipulated, with a little practice. Scouts had shared how easy it was to obtain whatever one needed, whether that be money or transportation or, in Sinto's case, clothing. All that was required was patience and a little creativity.

He stood before the solid metal door where the woman had exited the clothing store—where Sinto's salvation hung in the front window in the form of a black leather coat, jeans, and a pair of extra-large boots, waiting for him to slip into and begin a new life as someone else in the Sapien world.

His journey had taken an unexpected turn. Finding the portal during the mad chase was the first step in his wild adventure. While Sinto didn't profess to know of each and every portal between Merluma and Earth, he was certain he had never heard of one off the shore of Santa Monica. San Francisco certainly, but not here. But that didn't mean it was impossible. The Merahvu believed that whenever Earth rumbled the potential of a new crack, thus a portal, could open between Merluma and Earth.

His little stunt in Merluma was sure to stir up trouble. After it was revealed he was part Seakai, surely the Terrakai rebels would be patrolling all known saltwater portals for their recent intruder, both on Merluma and Earth. Luckily, they had not discovered his true identity. Sinto imagined they would think he was a Scout sent by his mother or the Circle to sniff around Terrakai territories on Merluma looking for rebels and assessing the level of their threat. And what he found was severe.

He hadn't considered starting his search for his father on land in the Sapien world. But he knew there were rivers and bodies of fresh water dotting North America, places where he could find refuge and restorative benefits. So he could hide out in the open while he worked his way across America. It would take longer, but in the end, having eluded capture, interest in finding him here would fade. Endless were the possibilities. If they believed he was a spy for his mother, wouldn't they conclude he had beat tail to share all the atrocities he had witnessed? The chance of them continuing the chase inland grew less with every passing minute.

And yet, he debated. Should he seek his mother and warn her about the breeding caves on Merluma?

But Wantemo had been quite clear: under no circumstances was he to return until he learned what happened to this father, what his role may or may not be in the rebellion, or if he was indeed dead. Sinto's mother was desperate to learn the truth and that was Sinto's singular purpose.

Wantemo assured him, *You are not the only one seeking answers.*

Regardless, Sinto was greatly disturbed by what he had witnessed.

I must stay focused and stop wasting time. Find my answer and return promptly.

But before he embarked on this new and unpredictable journey he desperately needed clothes and a place to rest. Painted on the store's side door were the store's hours: "Open Daily 11am to 7pm." He assumed that the woman wouldn't be back until tomorrow. After stealing some clothes, he'd have plenty of time to rest and replenish his reserves.

The glowing numbers of the electronic lock beckoned. As he recalled, this particular electronic gadget required a specific series of numbers followed by a symbol to be entered. A code with too many combinations would be impossible to guess, but as the Scout told him, he wouldn't need to: *Give it a slight jolt to confuse the chip, listen for the beep. Once you see a green light, then you're in.*

Sinto fired his merlux. It purred with purpose, punctured by the knife wielded by Audrey and her father but perfectly healed by Wantemo.

Electrified flueox flowed in his bloodstream, seeping into minuscule connectors running throughout the surface of his skin, crackling like a live wire. He placed his finger on the star-shaped key. Above the keypad was a dot-sized red light indicating it was locked.

He let his mind flow on a river of electrical current, through his bloodstream, to the buzzing connectors at the tip of his finger, through the plastic key, along the wires linking to its electronic brain. He balanced the flow of electricity, summoning just the right voltage, melding with it as it looped through the micro-chip coded with a series of zeros and ones. Buried somewhere in the zeros and ones was the code.

He gave it a slight jolt, heard a beep. The red light switched to green. He turned the handle. The door popped open. He slipped inside.

Sinto paused to listen. The Scouts had warned him about something else in this world. Sapiens were distrusting of others. Locks were not always enough to keep the things important to them safe. He braced for the beep and howl of an alarm but heard nothing except the thundering of his heart. Regardless, he searched for a second keypad, near the door, behind a high counter nearby. He found none.

But still he braced for action. The Scouts also warned that sometimes alarms were silent, sent to secretly summon the authorities. He quickly set his priorities if he suddenly needed to flee: clothes, water, maybe something to eat.

Sinto wasted no time. He darted to the front window, slipped the jacket and jeans from the mannequin, grabbed the boots, and returned to the side door. Hastily, he slipped on the jeans, then the leather jacket, thankfully large enough to accommodate his broad shoulders.

The boots were another story.

While he could manage to squeeze his over-sized feet into them, they were tight and his toes quickly grew numb. He took them off. Set them by the door. They would work in a pinch, literally. Scouts always complained about shoes. Finding the right size was a problem. A big one.

Shoe problem aside, Sinto began to relax. No authorities.

He rummaged through a back room and found a trove of things to eat and drink. The food tasted strange but satisfied his hunger; something called a "power bar," a bag of salty nuts, bottled "iced" tea that was quite warm, a partially eaten bag of popcorn, two mushy apples, and an overripe banana. He ate his fill and decided to save some for later.

He searched for a good place to rest. Somewhere not obvious and where he couldn't be seen from the front window. The back room was too confining and he would be trapped if the woman came back before the morning.

There were several circular racks of clothing. He crawled beneath one where dresses brushed the floor. Beneath was a thick layer of dust, kicked up from his shuffling. He sneezed several times before settling in a tucked position, lying on his side. He supported his head on stacked arms and melted into the floor like a recently fallen leaf.

He zoned out the sound of traffic and the occasional noisy passerby on the street. He set his internal clock, closed his eyes, and fell into deep slumber.

13

Boxing Audrey

SINTO WOKE TWO HOURS later, a little groggy, but rested enough to continue his journey. He emerged with a yawn from beneath the circular rack of clothes. The glow of a street light bled through the clothing store's front windows. The store's name stretched across the carpeted floor at his feet; its shadow, printed in reverse.

It took a moment for his eyes to adjust to the faint light, pupils dilating. He stretched and surveyed the store interior. Empty and still, like the street.

He pondered his next move. How he presented himself would be crucial. He padded barefooted to a mirror against the wall, checked out his image. The leather jacket and jeans helped to conceal his true identity and to fit into this world, but...

Something's missing, he thought.

The shop was an eclectic mix of old and new, retro and nostalgic. Framed pictures lined the upper walls of Sapiens in various states of dress and posing in various states of activities. His gaze stopped at one in particular: A young man on a motorcycle wearing a black leather jacket, jeans, and thick-soled black boots like those Sinto set by the back door. The man's dark hair was slicked back and eyes were concealed by a pair of sunglasses.

His shirt was unbuttoned halfway down his chest, revealing an elaborate tattoo. Between his lips hung a cigarette.

Sinto looked at his hair in the mirror. A dead giveaway to anyone looking for him: glinting gold waves with copper streaks. His eyes cut to the man on the motorcycle. Sinto smiled, and instantly his hair darkened. He bled lorica in his palms and fingered his hair back from his forehead and along the sides. He tucked the waves behind his ears and tamed the strands in the back with his fingers. It looked wet and a little greasy just like the man in the picture.

Goldilocks no more.

Sinto plucked a pair of sunglasses like the man in the picture wore from a nearby rack. *Aviators*, the tag said. He slipped them on.

All that was missing was a tattoo.

Though he had vowed not to think of Audrey, the raw and painful memory popped into his mind: how Audrey fought her father to save Sinto; how her father tricked her into grabbing for the knife; how he had wrapped his hand around Audrey's and forced her to participate in his murder; how together they had driven the knife into Sinto's chest.

He opened the jacket, baring his hairless chest and nipple-less pecs. First, he painted a pair of nipple images, then textured and raised the skin to trick the eye into believing they were real, an absolute necessity in this world. Then he got to work on the tattoo.

He inked the image of a heart above his real heart. Then he drew the tip of a jagged-edge knife partially buried between the folds of his puckered scar where the real knife had entered. He added blood along the exposed jagged edge and a trio of tear-shape drops dripping from the puckered wound. He wrote *Audrey* on the knife's blade in a bloody, elaborate script.

Seeing Audrey's name inked across his skin caused a wave of heat to explode in his chest and ignite the Mark buried in his lower arm. He gasped from the sudden violence of it, and sucking air, he willed his mind to rid memories of her: the crush of her brow while deep in concentration, her desire to learn everything about the natural world, the satiny smoothness of her bronzed skin beneath his fingers, her lips pressed against his—

He channeled his mind to focus. *I am dead to her. Find Father, learn the truth.* He repeated these words like a mantra until his heart calmed and the Mark settled.

And after I learn the truth, I will seek out Mother and Naiada, to ensure they are safe. For surely they have foreseen the army the Terrakai are breeding...

And after, and only after, would he consider seeking out Audrey to—to *what*? Tell her his death was a lie? That he let her grieve and suffer, believing she had killed him? To endanger her life by dragging her into the middle of a new tribal war?

That last thought shook him to the core.

I must remain dead to her, now and forever, to keep her safe and far from the disruption in my world.

No matter how many times he said it or thought it, he would struggle to forget her. Audrey was a major distraction. One he couldn't afford right now. He warred with the Mark, and forced his feelings and desire into a box. He locked it and tossed away the key. He did this because he loved her more than himself. Himself, he could sacrifice. Her, he could never.

But the Mark was stubborn and quietly smoldered in his arm. The Mark and what it represented he couldn't bury. That was going to be a problem. One from which he needed constant distraction, an ever-present ghost buried in his arm and wired to his very essence.

He gazed at his image in the mirror. But what better place to find such distractions then in the Sapien world. A world where he must constantly be alert and aware and not let his disguise slip. A crash course in becoming a full-fledged Scout. A *spy*.

Sinto's mind drifted back to what a Scout once shared with him. What secretly moving about in the Sapien world entailed, the importance of being anonymous.

Take it in, swallow it whole, and live it fully. You may need to do things you find morally revolting or personally disgraceful. Scouts play an important role, many times one that is different from one's true self. A Scout must never, ever, let their guard down else risk exposure and capture, possibly their life.

He gazed up at the picture of the man on the motorcycle.

Go, be that man.

On the back wall of the store was a map of North America covered with many colorful push pins. It seemed out of place at first until he read the note beside it: "We love tourists! Mark where you're from!" On a table below it was a cup full of push pins.

Sinto studied the map, tapped his finger on Lake Superior, then traced his finger from a place called Duluth to Los Angeles, then to Santa Monica along the shore. In between were mountains, plains, lakes, and rivers. He was accustomed to traveling in a straight light through a tunneling vortex cut in the sea. He knew a direct path across these land obstacles was not possible. Sapiens constructed highways and roads that veered in many different directions. In the case of the mountains, of which there were many between Santa Monica and Lake Superior, those highways veered wildly off course.

Next, he focused on lakes and rivers. He would need to rest and replenish along the way. Finding adequate sources of water would be a requirement. He reversed his path to Lake Superior, starting from where he was. His finger stopped at a large lake in Nevada, in the middle of the desert. Lake Mead. He guessed it to be far, but a doable destination if only he could find the right type of transportation.

His gaze wandered back to the picture of the man on the motorcycle.

Be that man.

Sinto had always been intrigued by motorcycles. They were fast and nimble and, he was certain, easy to steal for someone like him.

He took a snapshot memory of the map. After, his eyes settled back on the note. "We welcome tourists!" He smiled, picked up a push pin and stuck it in the deep waters of the North Pacific, south of Kodiak, Alaska.

Then he grabbed the boots by the back door, slipped out, and mindfully reset the lock.

14

Two-Wheeled Dream

Sinto wandered the streets barefoot with boots in hand, searching for a means of transportation. The rain had stopped hours ago and the streets were free of grime and scrubbed clean, as was the air. A break in the clouds glittered with starlight and revealed a near-full moon.

While the street with the clothing store was quiet and vacant of Sapien activity, business on a street a block over was alive and bustling.

Neon lights and loud music slipped through the cracks of a night club door. A couple of women lingered outside, smoking cigarettes.

Sinto heard it coming before it rounded the corner. Dual bug-like headlights came into view. The driver whizzed past, stealing a peek at the women, then pulled a sharp U-turn. He parked his motorcycle next to the curb outside the front door, shut it down, pulled off his helmet, and hopped off.

He strapped his helmet to his bike, flashing the women a smile. "Sorry I'm late." The women dropped their cigarettes and ground them out with their high-heeled boots. The man looped his arms around their waists and led them inside the front door.

Sinto shoved his feet into the too-small boots. He imagined himself as the man in the picture, crossed the street as casually as possible with cramping toes.

His heart beat with anticipation. He had studied everything about these two-wheeled motorized vehicles from the vast library of books and magazines Scouts stole for him from the Sapien world. A form of transportation for traveling over the surface of the earth at a high rate of speed, free to experience the nuances of one's surroundings—the smells, sounds, and subtle changes in climate as the topography gave way under its rubber treads.

The matte-black and gold motorcycle beckoned; crouched and ready to pounce like some kind of wild animal. He pulled off his sunglasses and squatted on the street side of the bike to marvel at the Sapien-made machine.

Sinto couldn't believe his luck. A *Ducati Multistrada 1260 Enduro*. The latest in Italian technology with a long-range cruising capability. The perfect form of transportation for the purpose he had in mind.

He gazed across the leather seat and scanned for the owner through the night club windows. He was perched on a stool at the bar with his back to the street, nuzzling the neck of one of the women while swirling his cocktail with a finger.

Sinto rummaged through his memories, recalling the basics: electronic ignition, clutch, brake, throttle....

A surge of adrenaline pushed him to act quickly. The owner parked this wonder of technology where he could see it for a reason. Sinto fired his merlux and placed his finger on the electronic ignition. A simple spark and the motorcycle roared to life. He tossed the helmet aside, swung his leg over, and settled into the firm leather seat. He released the kick stand, tested the weight of the rumbling machine between his legs. He found the shifter with his foot, pulled in the clutch, and engaged the bike into first gear.

The owner burst from the night club, a phone glued to his ear.

"Hey, that's my bike, asshole!"

Sinto dropped the clutch and jolted forward with a slight wobble, then the bike took off like a jet down the street. He bent over and married his body to the chassis; felt the vibration and the power, fell into the rhythm of it. He marveled at how the bike moved in response to the slightest shift of his weight as he weaved around corners and the rare Sapien venturing out into the street.

He recalled the map he memorized, knew he needed to head east. Finding the right highway might be a challenge so he kept a sharp lookout for signs or other clues.

Move in harmony with force of life, flow as water, like stream around rock. Audrey's mantra. Sinto embodied it, and flowed through the streets. He was quickly rewarded. A sign pointing to the Mojave Desert and Las Vegas. And not far beyond Las Vegas was Lake Mead, his intended destination.

He veered onto I-10, then I-15. Traffic was light and he was able to easily weave through traffic.

Once he entered the desert, the lights from the city faded and the clouds cleared, revealing a blanket of stars. He shifted into sixth gear and pushed the throttle wide open, running swift as the wind.

He tricked the bike's computer to switch off the headlights. His pupils expanded, adjusting to the darkness, and he opened the secondary cavities in his ears and tuned out the whine of the engine. The light cast by the moon lit up the winding highway and desert landscape. Nocturnal wildlife scurried across the desert sands.

Sinto felt a twinge of guilt. The bike burned oil processed into gasoline, black death drawn from the bowels of Earth that expelled deadly exhaust into the atmosphere. Now, flying across the desert, he began to understand the lure of a highly tuned technology propelling his body across land at unimaginable speed.

This must be what it's like to fly.

And fly he did, into the wild unknown, deep into the Sapien world.

15

Itchy Burny Dead

AUDREY WAS RESTLESS. SHE would settle into a comfortable position, start to sink into blissful sleep, then—*bam*—her brain would click on. She fevered and sweated and the Mark would start itching. She would roll over, kick off the covers, scratch her arm raw, settle, start to sink, and—*bam*—it would start all over again.

Not only was her arm itching madly, but her mind was abuzz with the upcoming mission. The thrill of a new project and the dread of going back out to sea. The last time ended in tragedy: Tallamure obliterated, a busted-up ship, and the death of her true love.

Since then she had embraced being a Larkian. Most odd was the way she found herself warming up to Alvarez. He was a total asshole, but incredibly smart and a damn fine strategist. Any corporation would trip over themselves to learn how he was able to recruit top talent, keep them motivated, and loyal. The crew he had assembled had been granted full citizenry as Larkians. None whom she had met ever complained or grumbled about conditions.

Before she retired for the evening, Alvarez had pulled her aside for a private conversation. He reminded her that she was an official Larkian, and she would be expected to act as one. When she asked how she was expected act, he simply replied, *Like a pirate*. She had no concept how pirates were supposed to act, so Alvarez explained it to her.

The Larkians were governed by a Code of Conduct enforced by the Larkian Council. The Council was composed of her father, Alvarez, Dr. Wickman, Leonard, and the two others she had yet to meet from the original *Sea Lark* crew. The Code of Conduct had endured for hundreds of years and had originally been democratically settled by the crew at that time—as was true of most pirate crews. Over the years it had been amended as deemed necessary by the Council, and in many cases, voted on by the entirety of the Larkian citizenry. Disputes were settled democratically. If the crew or the Council could not agree, the "captain" would cast the tie-breaker vote. Her father held that role then, as he did now, regardless of his current incapacity. Alvarez also informed her that Larkian law ruled not only at sea, but on land, and since she was officially a Larkian, that meant now and from this point forward. Every action on her part would be viewed through the Code of Conduct lens.

Audrey had found this newly learned fact amusing. Turned out that her father didn't always get his way. Go figure. He'd lived most of his life under a near-complete democratic governing system, even now, as he had originally during his pirating days. But that wasn't how he ran his land-based family household. Audrey never got a vote or even a say. It was strictly authoritarian rule with Daddy deemed *King*. Oh, the hypocrisy! He conveniently disregarded the "on land" part of Larkian law when it came to her.

But at sea, her father and his crew had proved long-term success when everyone on the ship was respected and treated equally. Competition was encouraged, but regulated and fair. There were rules. Rules that had been presented, refined, and voted on. Rules that once agreed upon were added to the Larkian Code of Conduct. That didn't mean that nasty things didn't happen on a pirate ship. There were plenty, Alvarez told her. But it meant those who violated the Code of Conduct would be exposed, judged, and punished—or not—as the Council, or majority in some cases, deemed fit. Alvarez made it especially clear that Audrey would not be given special treatment.

It wasn't necessarily the Code of Conduct that worried her. She had been informed by Dr. Wickman that her father would be coming along. He was at a crucial point in his recovery and being on the ship with his crew and daughter was absolutely necessary. Audrey wasn't fond of the idea, but realized he might regress and they would have to start all over again, so she agreed. While she had yet to forgive him, she knew it was important he continue to heal and she continue her journey toward forgiveness.

But. What worried her was being drawn into a vicious cycle of therapy sessions instead of working on solving the mystery of Orange and its relationship to the orange slime mentioned in the missing ships' report. She had a distinct feeling they were one and the same.

The other thing making her toss and turn was Blake. Their agreed reset would be put to the test. After hearing his sad story and the depths of his feelings toward her she was stunned. When he had asked her to be his girlfriend months ago, she was quick to say yes, believing the physical impulses she felt around him equated to true love. While she liked Blake a lot, she realized there was a big difference between liking someone and truly loving them. Sinto had cracked open her heart and shown her the difference.

A tear slipped.

Oh, Sinto...

Just thinking of him made her heart ache and arm itch. She reached for the Mark buried in her flesh. It was hot and—*undulating*.

She sat up.

What the hell?

The Mark was on fire, setting her heart pitter-pattering faster than the rain striking the roof.

She suddenly thought of something. She switched on the light beside the bed and ran over to her dresser. She pulled open the bottom drawer. Hidden beneath old t-shirts was a very old, intricately carved, wooden box. She had found the box sitting on the shelf in the den downstairs. The carvings were like those from the Far East. It had some old coins in it. She left the coins and took the box.

Audrey pulled the box from the drawer and took it back to her bed.

She hadn't opened the box since she arrived back in Seattle after Sinto died. She had wrapped the necklace Sinto made for her on Merluma in a soft cloth and tucked it inside. The necklace was electrified and linked to him, a special token to call him from the sea. After he died, she found no use for it; the memory that clung to it too painful. But he had made it especially for her and it was exquisitely beautiful. She couldn't bring herself to get rid of it, so she had hidden it and tried to forget about it.

She opened the lid, pulled the soft cloth aside. The tiger's claw gleamed as if electrified by a tiny LED light within. A pair of pounded silver swirls gleamed. A random mix of pearls and uncut stones dangled from links of silver.

Cautiously, she touched the claw, bracing for a shock. No shock, but it was hot. Heat rippled up her arm to the Mark and set off an undulating loop of fire, circulating and feeding off each other.

She held the claw from the bluestripe tiger that nearly killed her, remembering... Sinto had saved her from a life-threatening infection. After, he told her what he was and about the conjoined relationship between Merluma and Earth. He helped her overcome her fear of water. They surfed with dolphins inside giant waves. He showed her his underwater city. She learned what it meant to be Merahvu, the good and the bad. He showed her Orange, spreading across the bottom of the Pacific.

She would never forget Club Ballo. Where the Merahvu dressed like Sapiens in wild fashions from different eras and swirled in a synchronized dance they called the Ballorue; like a ball of wild herring sharing a hive-mind connection. That was the night they first kissed, and before their lips met, Audrey had a premonition: she and Sinto were meant to be bound, heart and soul, through joy and tragedy, flowing as water through life. And when their lips touched, the Mark presented itself and they accepted, fully and wholly. After, the Mark was forever buried in the flesh in their right forearms, connecting them together until one of them... died.

Audrey gasped. The memory slipped from her mind as if suddenly waking from a dream. The undulating loop of heat between the necklace and Mark halted. The claw lay cold and lifeless in her hand, as did the Mark in her arm.

She traced the lines of the Mark and felt nothing in return. She wrapped her fingers around the claw and the chain around her hand. The necklace was cold. The heat from her hand unable to warm its sudden chill. She shivered in the cool air that filled her room and cursed herself for hoping for what would never be.

Sinto was dead.

She sighed. *All I have left are tattered memories. I must stop dreaming for that which will never be.*

She felt exhausted and empty. She switched off the lamp, crawled under the covers. Tears rained as she pressed the cold, still claw to her hollowed-out heart, and drifted into a dark empty sleep.

16

Overload

LESS THAN FIVE HOURS after leaving Santa Monica, the eastern sky brightened. Sinto clocked the hour to be just past midnight, so he was certain it wasn't from a rising sun.

He crested a hill, slowed the motorcycle, and adjusted his night vision to the sudden assault of light in the middle of nowhere. The glow of a city, drowning out the moon and the stars.

He stopped on the side of the highway and gazed in wonder at the artificial light filling the desolate desert. From his viewpoint he could see the flashing lights of Las Vegas, including a giant sphere in a motion of color and images that reminded him of Club Ballo in Tallamure. He was surprised at how fast he got here. Lake Mead was not much farther, where a much-needed fresh-water dip awaited.

But that might have to wait. The Ducati's fuel tank hovered on empty, as did his. His mouth was parched and stomach rumbled. A meal of cold, raw fish from the lake didn't sound too appetizing at the moment.

Sinto knew he should keep going, but reality dictated otherwise. Out of gas, both him and the motorcycle. Besides, he was a little curious and felt a slight detour would offer a bit of distraction from the current reality of his lonely life. Few cars passed, but those coming up from behind him flowed like a river into the city. He slipped the motorcycle into gear and fell in behind a car that veered off the highway and directly onto a multi-lane street ablaze with light and packed with a mish-mash of tall buildings.

On his right was an early century castle, on his left the Statue of Liberty and the New York City skyline. That was when he realized he was in the heart of Las Vegas, known as the Strip. The Scouts frequently shared their memories from this place, presenting them as entertainment at Club Ballo. Traveling the Strip was like traveling the world. Popular tourist destinations and cities replicated within a one-mile stretch of road. Blink and you might miss it.

The Scouts told him time meant nothing in Las Vegas, a city that never slept. Even at this late hour Sapiens strolled along the sidewalks as if it was the middle of the day, pointing at the sights, laughing, standing in circles watching magicians trick them out of their money.

He rode past the Monte Carlo and the MGM Grand. Then something caught his eye. Water, a large lake of it. Seeing it made him more aware of how dangerously parched he was from riding across the moisture-wicking desert. He stopped in the middle of the street and gaped, longingly.

A horn honked and someone yelled, "Move it asshole!" Made a rude hand gesture and buzzed by.

A car without a top stopped next to him; inside were two men. The driver was old enough to be Sinto's father, while the one beside him was Sinto's age. The younger one leaned over and touched Sinto's cheek, "Hey pretty boy, wanna come play with us?"

Play? Then it registered what they were asking. Tangling with two men wasn't the type of distraction he sought. Feeling a bit cocky from the lively vibe radiating from the city, he decided to play along. He channeled his motorcycle-man persona, cocked a smile, and said, "Maybe, if you can catch me."

He revved the engine, dropped into gear, and zipped across traffic, weaving between cars. He zipped past Planet Hollywood and the Eiffel Tower. The men followed at a fast clip, but Sinto was much more nimble on the motorcycle. He ran a red light and darted across oncoming traffic, narrowly missing a car. Horns honked angrily. Heart pounding from adrenaline, he glanced back, laughing. Stuck at the light, the two men threw their hands up in defeat.

The rush of adrenaline—now that's the distraction I need.

The motorcycle began to sputter. Sinto pulled into the nearest parking lot and cruised to a stop against a curb. The motorcycle gasped its last breath. He set the kick stand and hopped off. He took one last loving look at the two-wheeled dream. Other than adding a few miles to the odometer and a thick patina of dust, it was exactly the same as when he stole it. And because he had stolen it, he thought it best to disassociate from it. End of the road. Short and sweet. He stepped away.

A circular fountain in the center of a large sweeping driveway reminded him of his persistent thirst. Music blared from a night club to the right of the fountain. From the club's rooftop patio light pulsed to the thumping bass and screaming treble of rhythmic music. Shadows of humanity writhed to the beat. On the side of the street, a giant rotating billboard of multi-ethnic faces faded one into the another, selling something.

The lake that caught his attention earlier came alive with exploding geysers and flashing lights. Sapiens gathered and watched, *oohing* and *ahing*. His heart pounded at the absurdity of it all and the strange chill of excitement it stirred within. Adrenaline was pumping freely just from being among the noise, the light, and the chaos. Las Vegas was filled with plenty of distractions to numb him from the periodic surges of fire looping through the coils of the Mark.

Sinto considered his options. A white statue of a man draped in fabric around his waist and across his shoulder, like the skareefs

Arctakai frequently wore, stood in the center of the circular fountain. A crown of leaves topped his head. The statue reminded Sinto of Wantemo, minus the multiple loops of braided silver hair wrapped around his neck like a Sapien rapper's bling. Beyond the statue was a massive casino and hotel, channeling the decadence of old Rome. A brightly lit sign announced this place was called "Caesars Palace."

He suspected there would be food and water inside. He followed a couple through an entry with soaring white arches and automatic sliding doors. When he stepped inside it felt like he had slipped though a portal to yet another planet, just like he had in Santa Monica.

He strolled through the brightly lit lobby with more Roman-era sculptures, golden columns, highly decorated domed ceilings, and inlaid marble floors. The farther he ventured inside, he realized something odd: the feeling of being watched. He stopped and looked around, trying to determine its source.

The Scouts warned of being caught on Sapien cameras, with the phones nearly every Sapien carried in their pocket the most obvious. But they had warned of others; sometimes mounted in plain sight, sometimes not. *Assume they are everywhere in public places. Never let down your guard, best to avoid if possible.* He looked, didn't see any, but decided to act as if they were there.

He flashed back to the image of the man on the motorcycle and tucked his hair behind his ears, adjusted his sunglasses, and channeled a relaxed swagger he hoped matched his attire.

The casino was chaotic and unsettling. There was nothing natural or symbiotic about the activity surrounding him. Sapiens sat at tables, flipping cards, spinning wheels, or rolling dice. Others sat at rows upon rows of machines, mindlessly pushing buttons. Harried-looking servers carried overloaded trays of colorful beverages.

Noise warred. An eruption of frantic dinging. Outbursts of loud voices. The rhythmic and thumping clash of music. Lights flashed, an artificial and ever-changing rainbow of color and intensity. A cacophony of noise and light. A full-on assault to his keen senses.

The air grew thick and he found it difficult to breathe. A heavy dose of artificially scented chemicals swirled, as did the smell of stale smoke and sour mold blowing from vents in the ceiling.

His feet were numb from the too-small boots. Walking became difficult. He tripped and fell against a machine. He lost sense of where he was, which direction he came from. The tables and the rows of machines looked the same no matter which direction he looked. His head spun. Up was down. The ground wavered. Clinging to a machine, he spun on his heels, searching for something to give his senses grounding.

Then he saw it, on the other side of the casino, away from the heart of the chaos. A giant tank of water with silver fish, idly swimming inside. He focused on putting one foot in front of the other, ignoring his numb toes.

Be the man, be the man, he silently chanted and focused on portraying an air of relaxed confidence that he did not feel.

He did his best to maintain his footing, knowing that somewhere someone may be watching through an electronic eye.

The tank stood at the entrance to a bar outside the main casino. A statue of a mermaid hovered above the bar, her face expressionless. To Sinto she looked sad. Being stuck here as she was, Sinto could relate. He palmed the tank. The glass was cool and soothing. He reached out to the water within, grounding his senses to that which he knew. He was whisked from the chaos and the crowds, communing with the simple minds of fish gathering at his fingertips. How long he lingered in that mediative state he was unsure. But when he looked up he was surrounded by a crowd.

"Nice trick," a man said.

A woman waved a Sapien five-dollar bill. "Do another," she said.

He snapped out of his stupor. He was attracting unwanted attention. He reluctantly released his palm and slipped away, to shouts of, "Hey, come back!"

He slipped back into the casino, down a line of machines along a far wall. He passed a woman with bright-red hair teased sky high perched on a stool, pressing buttons, a cigarette pinched between fingers with excessively long and glittery fingernails. Smoke leaked from her mouth as if she was a chimney. Sinto got a nose full along with a whiff of her cloying perfume.

It happened again. Sensory overload. The Scouts mentioned it but Sinto should have known it could happen without being warned. He needed to get a grip and quick.

He ducked into a dimly lit hallway to catch his breath and claim control of his sensory receptors. His feet were completely numb and causing a great distraction, and not the good kind. He pressed his back to the wall and slid to the floor.

It was a struggle to pull off the boots. He sucked a breath of relief once his feet were free. The dense skin covering his feet was creased to match every seam and stitch from the boots. He cast them aside, vowing never to put them on again, savoring the tingling feeling of blood returning to his toes.

Las Vegas is hell for someone like me. I've got to get out of here.

He stood up a little too fast. The world spun and he forgot where he was for a moment.

Breathe, swallow. Breathe, swallow.

Stopping here was a mistake. It was too much, too soon. Scouts had grumbled about the energy required to maintain their camouflage disguise and control innate impulses when venturing deep into the Sapien world, especially heavily populated cities. Sinto was feeling a bit grumbly himself about now. But...

I'm not turning back.

He pressed his back against the wall, digging his fingers into his thighs, mustering the courage to find his way out.

"Sir, can I help you?" a man dressed in a dark crisp suit asked. Middle-aged for a Sapien, with short hair and stiff demeanor. The man didn't look as friendly as his voice portrayed.

Sinto was momentarily confused. The man seemed to come from nowhere. Sinto's tongue felt like a brick. He wasn't sure he could answer if he tried, and if he did, he was unsure how the man could help him.

The man eyed him suspiciously. "Sir, I asked if I could *help* you."

Sinto opened his mouth but nothing came out.

"Sir, please remove your sunglasses."

Sinto's hand shook when he propped them atop his head.

The man gazed suspiciously into Sinto's eyes, firmly cloaked a dark brown.

"I might have to ask you to leave."

"I—" Sinto managed to gasp. "I think I ate something that didn't agree with me." Sinto realized his hands were fisted. He uncurled his fingers, stood a little straighter, and forced a smile. "I'm feeling a little better, now."

The man's gaze cut to the tattoo on Sinto's bare chest, then to his bare feet and the boots lying on the floor beside him. He pointed to a doorway further down the hall. "The restroom's there. I suggest you tidy up. Find a shirt and put your boots back on if you intend to gamble." He pointed behind him and then to the left. "The Forum's that way, past the fish tank. Lots of stores. You'll find what you need there."

Sinto took the man's advice, grabbed his boots, and slipped through the door marked "Men."

He beelined for the sink, embedded in a solid piece of pale marble. He splashed water on his face and took several gulps from cupped hands, wincing from the strange taste of chemicals Sapiens used to keep it sterile and safe to drink. The air in the restroom was fresh and well-ventilated and soon his head cleared. The water helped, as did the reprieve from the stuffy chaos. He gulped down more water until his belly was full.

He suppressed his periphery senses. Something he should have done the moment he exited the highway. Mind sharpened and senses dulled, he grabbed his boots and stepped out the door. The man was gone, but not the tiny electronic eyes that Sinto was sure had alerted the man to his presence.

17

Rachel

MONEY DROVE THE SAPIEN world. If Sinto needed or wanted anything he needed money to get it. Like a decent meal or gasoline to fill the tank of a motorcycle.

Sinto gathered that casinos were full of it. All he had to do was look at what motivated the Sapiens around him. Based on the way the man had confronted him in the hallway, he would need to be discrete in taking it. Especially from a casino with cameras hidden everywhere.

He stepped from the sanctity of the hallway. The man told him he needed shoes and a shirt while in the casino. The problem was he had no money to purchase such things and he didn't want to risk stealing again and the possibility of getting caught. He imagined he might need quite a lot of money to complete his journey across America. The noisy machines might be his best chance to get all he would need. Many advertised the possibility of big winnings; the more you bet the better the chance to win.

He zipped up his coat and held his boots in hand ready to force his feet into them if necessary. He slowly strolled down an aisle of flashing machines far from the action, observing how they worked by watching others, hoping no one would pay him much attention.

Some of the machines were complicated, offering multiple buttons to push and electronic displays of wild and varying symbols depending on the theme of the machine. Some were simple. Push a button. Wheels spin. If they displayed a winning combination of symbols, you win. How much depended on which symbols spun up. Every push of the button cost "credits," which went up or down, depending on how much you won—if anything. Credits were registered by the machine after slipping a special piece of paper into a slot. Credits could just as easily be cashed out. All you had to do was tell the machine and it would spit out a special piece of paper.

How the special piece of paper with credits translated into money wasn't clear. That he could deal with later. What was clear was he needed a special piece of paper with enough credits to play the machines.

He stopped in front of a machine advertising a jackpot payout of five thousand dollars. Sinto wasn't sure if that was enough, but it sounded like a lot. One dollar got you one play. It was one of the simpler machines. Push a button. Wheels spin. Get three sevens and you win five thousand dollars. He looked down. A paper ticket protruded from the slot in the machine. He looked around; someone must have forgotten to take it. He pulled it out and smiled.

Twenty credits. What luck!

He set down his boots and stuck the ticket back into the slot. The machine sucked it inside. Just like that, twenty credits flashed on the display. Now to trick the machine.

Three sevens, how hard could that be.

He had twenty tries to find out.

He fired his merlux. Once it was purring smoothly and electrified flueox flowed through his veins he hovered his finger above the button. He guided the flow of electricity through the tip of his finger to the glass face of the button and on to the wiring connected to the machine's electronic brain.

He sent a jolt of electricity through his finger. The three digital wheels spun, landing one seven, one cherry, one lemon. His credits ticked down to nineteen. He tried again. Eighteen. And again. Seventeen. Sixteen. Fifteen. He tried just pressing the button hoping he might get lucky. Fourteen.

Flustered, he stepped back. *What am I missing?*

The machine was much more complicated than the lock he easy manipulated at the clothing store. The lock had preset numbers; this was a completely different mechanism. He tried again, whizzing past the first layer of zeros and ones seeking the part of the electronic brain that generated the spin. He imagined what he wanted, gave it a jolt.

The wheel spun. A seven. Another seven. And a... lemon. Twelve more tries left. He tried again, channeled his mind. The wheel spun and—up rolled three sevens.

He jumped when the machine rang out, BING! BING! BING! A domed light popped up from the top, spinning and flashing—red, white, and blue. For someone trying not to draw attention he had done just that.

Sapiens came from everywhere, drawn to the commotion. Someone slapped him on the shoulder and said, "Nice going!" Others looked dismayed and a bit jealous. Eventually, they retreated. Sinto was left standing, alone and a little baffled, at how easily he had tricked the machine, and the fact he was unsure what to do next.

A young woman in a low-cut, short red dress that hugged every curve of her body approached him and draped a hand across his arm.

"Lucky night, huh?" she said, over the noise. Her voice had a sweet, syrupy twang that sounded pleasant and friendly.

The top of her head barely reached his chest, and she was wearing high heels, *really* high heels. When she smiled, dimples dotted her cheeks. Her teeth were small and pearly white. Were it not for her heavily made-up eyes, he might have mistaken her for a teen-aged youngling on the cusp of adulthood.

She pointed to the display of credits totaling five thousand and twelve dollars. "Looks like you won a lot of money here!"

At the moment Sinto was more curious by the sound of her accent than what he had won.

Her blue eyes sparkled and she had long, wavy, dark hair draped across her shoulders, framing a remarkable display of cleavage from her well-endowed breasts.

"Cat got your tongue?"

Sinto shifted his gaze from her chest to her eyes. *What cat?* He flashed back to that same question the Scout on Merluma asked him. *What is it about cats stealing tongues in the Sapien world?*

"Do you speak English? Or are ya one of them European fellas? Français?"

"I speak English." Sinto looked at the numbers on the machine, the words Jackpot flashing on the screen. "Is this a lot of money?"

By the way she tilted her head and gazed into his eyes, he must have said something right. "Honey, that's a *lot of money*. Enough money for you to have a *very* good time." She wagged her brows. "That is, if that's what you're askin'. I suggest you cash in your credits while you're ahead and stop messin' with these machines."

Sinto looked at the machine, then back at her bright blue eyes. "How do I cash in my credits?"

"First time to Vegas, huh?" she laughed, sweet and musical. She pressed a button, snatched the special piece of paper as soon as the machine spit it out. "Come see." She grabbed his hand. He grabbed his boots. They wound through the casino to a row of windows marked "Cashier."

She looked terribly out of balance, teetering on her high heels. Her hips were narrow and waist tiny. Coupled with her ample breasts and riot of long, wavy hair, it seemed as if she would topple at any moment.

"Rachel, who have you got here?" an older woman behind the window asked.

She poked Sinto in the chest with an unusually long, bright-red fingernail. "This here is my new friend. He just won the jackpot!" She slipped the special piece of paper from the machine through a hole cut in the window. "He wants hundreds."

The woman slid a sheet of paper and a pen toward Sinto.

Rachel grabbed it and winked at the cashier. "I got this."

Sinto watched as she scribbled a random name and address of unknown origin somewhere in a state called Ohio, a series of nine numbers under "social security," then she checked a few boxes. Her tiny fingers with bright-red claws awkwardly curled around the pen.

"Just a few technicalities required by good 'ol Uncle Sam," she murmured, then handed Sinto the pen, pointed to an X with a straight line printed along the bottom. "Signature."

Sinto took the pen, having never used one, and unsure exactly what his signature would possibly look like, in a name that Rachel had written and he had never heard of.

She rolled her eyes. "Anything will do," and wrapped her tiny hand around his and drew a long and dramatic squiggle. Slid the paper and pen back to the cashier.

As the cashier counted out fifty one-hundred-dollar bills, Sinto studied this new dimpled-cheeked friend with caution. He had heard the stories from Scouts and read enough Sapien books to know not all Sapiens can be trusted, no matter what the package. Especially when money was involved.

Rachel slipped one of the bills to the cashier, picked up the stack, and held it out to Sinto.

He stared at the money in her hand. She shook her head and laughed, then pulled open his jacket and stuffed the wad into an inside pocket.

"Better keep this in a safe place," she said, patting the outside of his jacket. "Not very many people you can trust around here." She hooked a finger and said, "I gotta secret to tell ya."

He leaned over so she could whisper in his ear.

She kissed him on the cheek. "Have a nice night."

Sinto watched, confounded, when she turned and left. Thick dark waves bounced above her small taut buttocks. He knew he should let her go, having been warned about trusting some Sapiens. Especially ones in appealing packages. But her aura emitted sincerity and a heavily guarded vulnerably.

"Wait!" he yelled.

She stopped and glanced back, a smile curling at the corner of her lips.

It only took a few quick steps for him to catch up. She turned to face him. She stunned him with her sharp blue gaze and thick feathered lashes. Rachel had quite the package. She was pretty and smelled sweet and had curves in all the right places, and when she talked he found himself lingering on the way the words came out. Dangerous for someone like him, looking for a distraction from the fire burning in his arm.

He blinked, suddenly not sure why he had stopped her. "Rachel?"

"Yeah?"

He held up his too-small boots. "I need shoes." He pointed at his extra-large, bare feet. "Shoes that fit."

18

Sugar And Money

"OH MY, THEM'S BIG." Rachel looked up from his feet. "Is it true what they say?"

"Say about what?" Sinto replied.

She giggled, all dimples and blue-eyed twinkles. "Nevermind. Let's get ya some new shoes. *That fit.*"

Sinto followed Rachel through the casino, past the fish tank, and into a large open space with cathedral ceilings and storefronts as far as he could see on both sides.

Rachel stopped in front of a large back-lit map. "Anything you need, you'll find it here." She ran a tapered nail down the list, stopped on one, found it on the map. "This way."

Sinto tagged along beside her, taking it all in; the type of shops, the differing strong, perfumed smells they emitted, how most catered to women. His gaze swept across the soaring arched ceiling, how voices echoed, how he was unable to trace their source.

Rachel took his hand and pulled him inside a store with hundreds of shoes lining the walls. She sat him down in a chair and waved over a bored-looking salesman.

The man appeared no older than Sinto, or probably Rachel for that matter. He greeted them with a well-practiced, toothy smile that stopped short of his eyes. Sinto saw it for what it was, forced and focused on one outcome: To earn a buck, nothing more.

Sinto stole a glance at Rachel. Was she being genuine by helping him, or was she looking to earn a buck, too. Or maybe five thousand? He felt the weight of the one-hundred-dollar bills stuffed in his coat pocket.

Money motivates in the Sapien world.

But Rachel was the one who walked away, and he was the one who ran after her. Maybe it was a trick, and she was more practiced at relieving the unsuspecting of their money than the salesman.

Take it in, swallow it whole, and live it fully.

He decided to play along, stay alert, and gain whatever knowledge he needed to move on. After all, Rachel was helping him to find a pair of shoes that fit, and shoes were a requirement in this world.

"Biggest size you got," she told the salesman.

The man returned with a large box. Inside was a pair of bright white shoes made of something unnatural. He held one between his knees, winding laces through a series of holes. He set it down and gestured for Sinto to slip his foot inside. Not as tight as the boots, but not especially welcoming.

Rachel astutely picked up his discomfort. "Not gonna work. Got anything else?"

The man twisted his lips, obviously thinking. "Uh, I really can't..."

She reached into Sinto's coat pocket, pulled out a hundred-dollar bill. "Does this help?"

The man's gaze froze on Rachel's cleavage, then cut to the bill in her hand.

He smiled. "Maybe... I'll be right back."

He returned with another box. This one was black and much bigger than the last one. He set it down, pulled out a pair of giant black shoes with white soles and white laces, ankle high and made of soft leather. "Special ordered for an ex-basketball player who was supposed to pick them up yesterday." His gaze fell to the money in Rachel's hand. "I suppose for the right price they could accidentally be lost."

She grabbed a few more bills from Sinto's pocket, leaned forward, and gave the salesman an eyeful of her generous breasts spilling from the front of her dress. The man stopped breathing for a second.

She elbowed Sinto in the ribs, "Why dontcha try 'em on."

The man found his breath and his fingers, and splayed the black beauties open for Sinto to step into. The shoes felt like a thick layer of the lorica he wrapped around his body when diving deep into the ocean; there to offer protection, but hardly noticeable and heavenly soft.

He adjusted the laces, stood and paced back and forth a couple times. "Perfect."

Rachel glanced at the brand name printed on the side of the box, raised a brow. "Oh, my. Those are veeery nice tennys."

The salesman, nodded. "Yes, very nice, for a very nice price too."

She snagged a lot more bills from Sinto's coat pocket. Added them to those in her hand. She made a show of counting them out: ten one-hundred-dollar bills, in addition to the ones she already gave him. "Will this do?"

The salesman smiled and pocketed the money. "Definitely lost."

She gave the salesman a wave and an air kiss as they left. She turned to Sinto. "Live and learn, lucky man. Sugar and money will get you anything in this world. Now, how about gettin' somethin' to eat?"

19

Pure Distraction

SINTO FELT COMPLETE WITH a full belly and happy feet. He was ready to storm Las Vegas. Ready to find another motorcycle to take him to Lake Mead.

But Rachel had another idea.

"You like music?"

She led him back to the casino where he had hit the jackpot. She paused outside a night club called Pure, tapped a tapered nail against her lip. "Whatcha think?"

A long line of people snaked through the lobby, held back by a couple of large men in dark business-type suits and a roped barrier.

She acted before Sinto could say anything. She dragged him along with a grip that defied her size, past the line of people waiting to get inside. She asked Sinto to wait at the front of the line, behind the rope. He obeyed, not sure why; this was not what he had planned, but then again...

He watched in wonder as Rachel sashayed to a muscular bald man standing behind a counter next to the club's entrance. She began flirting with him, giving him that dimpled smile and eyeful of cleavage. The bald man's gaze swung in Sinto's direction. He scrutinized Sinto with a head-to-toe scan. Sinto acted his part and portrayed indifference from behind his aviator glasses. The bald man whispered something in Rachel's ear; she kissed him on the cheek, then waved Sinto over.

Sinto was stunned at the ease in which she moved in her world, finding solutions and working around obstacles no matter what problem was presented. Rachel was a walking, talking, winking, grinning study in persuasion.

She reached inside Sinto's pocket for a couple of bills and discretely slipped them into the bald man's hand.

The bald man smiled. "Right this way," and opened a door to the club. His mitt of a hand landed on Sinto's chest. He pointed at Sinto's sunglasses. "Lose those. Wearing sunglasses not allowed inside."

Sinto tucked his sunglasses in the pocket next to the bundle of money, which was growing thinner as the night progressed. At the rate Rachel was handing out bills he began to wonder if he underestimated how much Sapien money he needed for his journey.

The door swung shut behind him, cutting off a sudden burst of complaints from the waiting crowd.

The thought of money evaporated. Chest-thumping bass rattled every bone in his body as they passed through a white hallway with a high ceiling and neatly tied gauzy-white drapes back-lit by rose-colored light. His new shoes squeaked on shiny white marble.

Rachel grabbed his arm and pulled him into the crush of bodies beyond the hall.

Sinto was stunned by jarring music and flashing lights. Instinctively, he reached for his mind to adjust the volume and intensity of light, as he would have were he at Club Ballo in Tallamure experiencing visual images and a mash-up of Sapien music and sounds of the sea. Memories shared telepathically, and presented in an artistic way, by Scouts who frequented this world. An experience he could adjust to suit his level of participation, merely by thinking it. That loss of control made him feel vulnerable and dizzy.

A crush of bodies slithered around them. Some were lost in the motion, others watched everyone else. The ceiling soared. A network of wires held canned lights that rotated and pulsed to the beat. Mechanically controlled by a computer, not the presenter's mind. The bar was a crush of bodies, shouting for drinks. Tenders pulled bottles from shelves, ice from bins, and danced about, shaking sleek silver cups before pouring drinks into stemmed wide-mouthed glasses.

He scanned the club, seeking the source of the music and flashing lights. Opposite from the bar was an elevated stage. A woman with blue spiky hair swayed to the beat, one hand cupping a headphone to her ear, the other pressing buttons on a large flat machine. He figured she was the one in control; the DJ, he recalled from previous Scout stories. A small crowd of scantily dressed women writhed behind her, sipping pale liquid from fluted glasses.

He felt a tug on his hand. Rachel pulled him from the crowd on the dance floor and past the mass of bodies clambering at the bar.

A woman slithered up behind him and grabbed him by the buttocks. Rachel gave the woman a dirty look. Her intention clear: *Hands off, he's mine.* While he might argue he was not, at the moment he was content to act like he was. He felt like a cub in a cage filled with hyenas.

Rachel stopped at a roped barrier guarded by another man. She snagged a couple of bills from Sinto's pocket. The rope was dropped and Rachel dragged him to a more sane place where people gathered on sofas and soft chairs, some openly displaying their affections.

A man groped a woman's exposed breast, his arousal clearly pressed against his trousers. A pair of women were enthralled in a kiss, hands buried beyond the hem of their short skirts. A trio of men waved for Rachel to join them. Their eyes pawed every inch of her body-hugging red dress like slavering bluestripe tigers. A man sitting alone at a table snagged Sinto's free hand. When Sinto turned to look at him, he blew Sinto a kiss and wagged a finger for him to join him. Sinto merely smiled and respectfully extracted his hand from his grip.

These things didn't shock him; he knew of similar interactions in Tallamure. But while Merahvu wore few to no coverings, they tended to keep their more intimate interactions private.

Rachel was disappointed there was no open table for them so they left the roped-off area. For someone so little, Rachel had managed to barge her way through the crowd like a megalodon, shedding hundred-dollar bills.

"Thought I might lose ya back there." She rolled her eyes. "Honey, those people are like wild animals!"

Sinto had to agree.

She stopped outside a closed metal door and pressed a round button. The metal door slid open and she pulled him inside a small box-shaped room. The doors slid shut, trapping them inside.

Primal instinct kicked in. His merlux fired. His heart hammered and flueox flooded his bloodstream. He pressed his back against the back wall, trying to appear calm, breathing hard through his nose.

Rachel noticed his duress. "I hate these things too. They ain't natural. Where I'm from we don't have elevators. I like living on the ground." She reached out to touch him. He jumped back for fear of electrocuting her.

"You okay?"

He looked at her.

She stepped back and gasped. "Wow, how do you get your eyes to look like that? They're *glowing*. Are those special contacts or somethin'? But how? When did you—uh..."

"Contacts?" Sinto realized the camouflage shielding his natural eyes had slipped.

"You know those plastic lens thingys that make your eyes look spooky. I haven't seen green ones like that before. Lots of red and yellow ones, all these people pretendin' to be vampires or werewolves." She shivered. "Weird if you ask me."

"Sure—I mean—yes. Contacts."

The doors opened. Sinto burst onto a patio blanketed by the night sky. Fresh air filled his lungs. Car horns rose from the street below, swirling with exhilarated voices and booming music. The patio was much more tolerable with the open sky. The noise free to float away. He gazed up at the stars, took a settling breath.

Another man, another roped section. Rachel grabbed a couple bills from his pocket. Fed another hand. She dragged him past the man and the rope to a vacant sofa tucked against the far wall. To his relief, there were hardly any people sitting in this section.

Sinto felt too worked up to sit. He really should go. He glanced over the rail to the casino's entrance with the circular fountain and across to the lot where he abandoned the motorcycle. It was gone.

Rachel settled on the sofa.

"You don't like crowds."

He nodded, eyeing the knee-high, candle-lit table wedged between them.

"Me neither."

She patted the space next to her.

He gazed at her tiny hand with its long red claws, wondering how such a tiny, non-threatening person could cast such a heavy spell. He still had money in his pocket and shoes that fit on his feet. He should bolt, find another motorcycle, ride to Lake Mead.

He rounded the low table and sat beside her, caught in the web of her spell. It felt good to put his back to a wall. He relaxed for the first time since setting foot in the casino, not feeling the need to constantly look over his shoulder. He rested his head on the back of the sofa, gazing up at the sky. He breathed deep the crisp fresh air, settling into the groove of the music.

"Are you thirsty?" Rachel asked.

He licked his parched lips. He had never been so thirsty in all his life. Like a fish out of water. Literally. "Yes, water."

"I meant something stronger. You know, a drink? Liquor? Alcohol? Ever heard of that?"

She asked not in a mocking way but as if she was genuinely curious as to the extent of his knowledge and experience. He usually drank sucuvita, the elixir of life the Merahvu depended upon to keep them young and healthy. An elixir that expanded the mind and launched the body into a state of euphoria. Certainly, he would find none of that here. Only one type of liquor from the Sapien world came to mind. A drink favored by pirates.

"Rum," he said.

"Neat or on the rocks?"

He looked at her confused, thinking her question strange. "In a glass."

She laughed and out popped those incredible dimples.

"You're a funny one. I'll be right back."

He watched Rachel stroll over to the bar, wondering what he was doing. Surely, there was a nearby motorcycle he could steal to get him to Lake Mead. Yet... here he sat, butt firmly planted in a soft comfy cushion, breathing fresh air, with his feet merrily tapping to the rhythmic vibe swirling around him like an ocean breeze, watching Sapiens mingle, nuzzle, and dance.

Take it in, swallow it whole, and live it fully.

Rachel glanced back from the bar and smiled. She was a conundrum. What was she doing with him? Was it the money? Did she feel sorry for him? Was her interest for some deeper reason? Her aura was bright and had a pleasant rosy color. He sensed goodness buried within her essence along with frustration and a lingering disappointment with her life.

She was nice and had been helpful. There were many things about this world Sinto didn't understand. Maybe he needed her. Could he trust her? *Could I trust myself?* He rubbed the Mark's gristle forged in the flesh of his forearm. It lay cold and mute. If he sought distraction from it, Rachel could be it.

Take it in, swallow it whole, and live it fully.

Rachel returned and sat next to him. "Drinks are on the way. Ya feelin' better? For a while there I was wondering when you'd get your color back. It can get overwhelmin' downstairs."

She gave him a funny look, cocked a brow. "Hey! Your eyes... they look normal again." She laughed nervously. "There's some weirdness in the air tonight!" Then she rolled her eyes. "Goodness! How rude of me. I forgot to get your name."

"Sinto."

"Just Sinto? Like Shakira? Or Adele? Are you a celebrity I don't know about? Name like that, you could be one. Rock star? Pro surfer, maybe?"

He had learned about Sapiens' obsession with certain humans, labeling them as a celebrity, treating them like they were special merely because they entertained. The only celebrity he knew of in his world was his mother and that was because she was their queen, and everyone knew who she was.

"Surfer, sure." At least he wasn't lying. He intentionally left off the pro part and didn't think it necessary to explain that he didn't ride atop the wave on a pointed board but preferred riding a wave from within, like a dolphin with the flip of his tail and the arch of his body.

"Well, I'm Rachel." She held out her hand. He took it and she shook it.

He laughed. "I got that, back in the casino. So *just* Rachel?" He knew Sapiens usually had two or more names, a first and a surname, sometimes a middle one, sometimes many middle ones, depending on where they were from.

"I thought we just agreed that first names were enough."

She giggled, all dimples and perfect pearly teeth. "Works for me. Easy to remember."

He sucked a breath. *And dangerously distracting.*

"So, where you from, *Sinto*?"

Sinto hadn't thought of what to say should anyone ask. Telling the truth was out of the question.

Her eyes swept across his leather coat, the tattoo on his chest. "L.A.?"

Sinto had no idea where L.A. was.

She cocked an eyebrow. "You know, as in *Los Angeles*?"

"Yes, Los Angeles. I came from the coast, from the Pacific."

She tapped his knee with a pointed claw. "Soooo Sinto, whatcha doin' in the City of Lights?"

He watched her clawed finger circle his kneecap. "Trying to forget."

"I hear that one a lot. What's her name?"

He flinched. A sudden burst of fire rippled from the Mark and stabbed him in the heart. Rachel hooked her finger on the edge of his leather coat and pulled it aside, revealing the knife-stabbing tattoo he had painted on his chest.

"And what did *Audrey* do to you?"

"Isn't that obvious?" He frowned, sucked a deep breath. "It wasn't her fault. It's complicated. She thinks I'm dead. I am actually, to everyone I know. It wasn't supposed to work out that way, but maybe someday we will—" He shook his head. "Don't let me bore you."

She tapped the tip of the knife. "Honey, I'd never do that to you."

His mind drifted to the slow simmer in his arm. "I won't give you the chance."

"What does that mean? Don'tcha like me? You're dead, right? How would she know? Can't we just have a teeny weeny bit of fun together?"

Sinto gazed into her eyes, fierce yet innocent, searching for the true meaning of her intent.

"Maybe I could help you forget," she said softly.

His gaze fell to the smooth round mounds spilling from the front of her dress, pressed against his ribcage.

She added, "I don't kiss and tell."

Whether or not she told anyone, he would know. The Mark would know. *Take it in, swallow it whole, and live it fully.* They warred, he won. He was lonely, she could help. He needed a big dose of love about now. The Mark finally settled, sensing his need. It even expressed a surge of compassion.

He laid his arm across her shoulder and pulled her close. She smiled and he poked the dimple in her cheek. "Perhaps you can, but just a teeny weeny bit."

He leaned down and kissed her.

20

Near Miss

Sinto's head pounded.

I'm dying, for real.

It was pitch black and he had no idea where he was, only that he was dying of thirst and the drum in his head was growing louder. He rolled from his stomach to his back. Whatever was beneath him no longer was and he fell onto a lightly cushioned surface. A sliver of light bled from somewhere behind him. He rolled to his knees, opened his eyes, pupils adjusting for the darkness. The sliver of light came from a crack at the bottom of a door. It swung open, spilling bright light.

He gasped, pinching his eyes shut. Fire shot down his optic nerves straight to the back of his skull.

"Turn it off," he croaked. His tongue felt like the bottom of a dried-up lake.

"Was wonderin' when you were gonna wake up."

Sinto cracked an eye at the small silhouetted figure standing in a frame of bright light.

"Rachel?" Then it came back to him. Rum, gambling, dancing, then—

Oh, no, what have I done?

She moved from the doorway and switched on the light next to the bed. The thing he rolled off of.

He was in a hotel room kneeling on a thickly piled carpeted floor in a tangle of sheets. Rachel's bare feet brushed the side of his knee when she sat down. Her toenails were painted the same bright red as her clawed fingernails. Her hair was piled on top her head with a clip, damp and steaming as if she had just taken a hot shower. She wore an oversized robe and from the way it gaped he could tell it was all she wore.

"Howya feelin'?" she reached out and touched his cheek. "We sure had fun last night."

"More than a teeny weeny bit?" His voice actually squeaked.

She giggled. "Oh, yeah, much more than a teeny weeny bit."

A wave of panic swept over him. He looked around the room. A trail of clothing lay between the door and the bed; black high-heeled shoes, red dress, skimpy black lacy things, leather coat, and extra-large black tennys with white soles. At least his pants were still on. He looked down; the ridge of swirls around the curve of his hips peeked from underneath. He hitched them up, hoping she hadn't noticed his raised markings.

Sometime during the night he had let his coloring slip, as well as the faux-painted-on nipples and the knife-stabbing tattoo. When he looked up, she stared back, patiently waiting for him to say something.

"Water." He stood up but the room tilted under his feet. She grabbed him by the arm and pulled him down on the bed beside her.

"Sit. I'll get it." She hopped up and disappeared through the opened door. The bathroom, he guessed. He heard the soothing sound of running water.

She said loudly so he could hear. "You wore me out. I had to beg you to stop." She stuck her head out the door. "Never had that happen before." Her head popped back in. "And I'm in pretty good shape, you know." She stepped into the doorway, a glass of water in hand. "Honey, no wonder you're dehydrated."

The look on his face must have been one of utter shock. She cocked her head, lips curling into a sideways grin. "You don't remember, do ya?"

He looked away. His eyes stopped at a painting on the wall, something abstract and garish, with too many bright colors and angular shapes, a harsh contrast to the muted colors everywhere else in the room. He remembered drinking rum, lots of it. And walking the Strip, going into a blur of too many casinos, him tricking machines, Rachel cashing in the credits and carrying stacks of one-hundred-dollar bills in her hands. He remembered kissing her but not much else.

He remembered tightening down his sensory receptors to block out the confusing sights and sounds. He must have shut down the rational part of his brain—*or maybe that was the rum*—that part that remembered things and made good judgments.

"You were amazin'." Her voice broke him away from his thoughts. "I mean you can *move*."

His head swiveled in her direction, a little too quickly.

Pound. Pound.

"Move?"

"And with such grace and strength." Her eyes glazed over, remembering something he could not.

He frowned. He had to ask, had to know; his mouth worked but nothing came out. It was bone dry, like his tongue and his cracked lips. He looked back at the trail of her clothes leading to his feet. He absolutely did not remember anything about walking through that door or what happened afterward. He couldn't look at her, or those perfect pearly teeth, and certainly not at the those damn fine dimples.

The Mark felt numb in his arm. How could he have deceived Audrey, regardless of whether or not she thought him dead?

"Rachel, please tell me we didn't—did we?"

She laughed. Dimples flashed. "After cleaning up at the casinos, we danced, Sinto, *danced*. You don't remember? Like, wow, you were on fire. Had to beat the women off with a stick and some guys too. A guy from one of those male strip shows tried to recruit you on the spot. Good thing you were with me. This town eats people like you alive."

He looked over, eyes sweeping her robed figure. A knot formed in his stomach. "Then what happened?"

"We came here. You went straight for the bed and fell asleep. Passed out more like it." She handed him the glass of water.

"So we had just a teeny weeny bit of fun?"

She laughed. "Well, we did kiss, maybe once or twice if that's what you're talkin' about. I guess we tried to kiss a little more, but frankly, we both felt it was a little weird, and couldn't stop laughing when we figured it out! I think I like you better as a friend or maybe—" She snapped her fingers. "Like a brother! I never had a brother, or sister for that matter."

Sinto nearly cried with relief. *Oh, sweet Rachel. Friend, or a sister, indeed!*

"And if you call the rest of the night as having a teeny weeny bit of fun, I can't imagine what a big amount of fun with you would be like! That might be the end of me! Now, drink up. You look withered."

Sinto took a gulp, gagged, and spit it out. "Ack! Where did you get this?"

"Oh, what was I thinkin'! Old habit, I usually drink from the tap, sorry. Here," she walked over to a small refrigerator and pulled out a bottle of water, "try this." She tossed it to him.

He caught it, twisted the top open, and took a big gulp. The bottled water tasted worse, but he choked it down. "Natural spring water?" he said, reading the label. "There's nothing *natural* about it. Tastes like plastic."

"Sorry, it's all we've got." Her smile faded and brow quirked. "Hey, what happened to your hair?" She tugged on a golden lock. "And your eyes, th—they're *white*..."

He knew what that meant. Running on empty. "I need to go." He stood up slowly, fighting the wave of dizziness. He needed to recharge in a body of water, any water, and soon.

"Hey, you're not gonna leave me, just like that... are ya?"

She jumped up and started gathering her things from the floor. She opened the closet, dragged out a large bag, pulled out some clothes, stuffed her things from last night inside. "Wait! Take me with you."

She was so tiny she looked like a child in the oversized robe, holding onto a bag she could comfortably slip inside. "I don't think you'll like where I'm headed." He found his new shoes, sat on the bed and put them on.

"Please, don't leave me," she begged.

He looked up. Tears welled in her eyes. Eyes filled with desperation and a deep sadness. Her face was scrubbed clean and she looked so much younger than the woman he met last night. He stood up, grabbed his leather jacket and slipped it on.

"Here," he said, pulling a stack of hundreds from the inside pocket of his coat. "You can keep this. Not much use where I'm going and I can always get more."

She leaned over the side of the bed. Pulled three small black bags off the floor, plopped them down beside her, pulled one to her lap, yanked open the zipper. Stacks of neatly bound one-hundred-dollar bills spilled to the floor.

"It's not about the money. Besides, after this haul, my boss will be lookin' for me and he ain't very friendly. The casinos talk and we set them abuzz last night. I gotta get out of here before this place consumes me completely." She dropped the bag at her feet. "Please, I don't care where you're goin' and I don't want to die here. Maybe I can help you. You seem a little lost."

She was right. He was a fool to think he could venture into her world and assume he understood their customs and ways from reading Sapien books and after one night in Las Vegas.

"Can you take me to Lake Mead?"

"Sure, I've got a car, and with this," she picked up the bag of money, "we could go anywhere in the world."

Not quite, he thought. But he certainly needed help navigating through hers.

"Alright. Get dressed, and hurry."

21

Echo

RYAN ARRIVED THE NEXT morning shortly after Audrey woke up. Blake had picked him up from the ferry landing in Anacortes and the two of them were caffeine-juiced, bantering and bounding with energy as they climbed the stairs to the covered deck and the front door.

Audrey greeted them at the door. She was still in her pajamas with a fuzzy bathrobe thrown over. Ryan lurched and wrapped her in a bear hug, lifted her from her feet and spun her around. He kissed her on the cheek once he put her down, tears welling in his eyes.

"Missed you, kid."

Ryan said nothing about what happened. True to his word, he had wiped the slate clean and chucked it to the bottom of the Salish Sea. She mentally pinched herself, realizing how lucky she was to have a friend like him. She silently vowed never to do anything that would hurt or humiliate him again.

She led them to the kitchen. Blake and Ryan didn't skip a beat, clucking on about this and that like a couple of hens. She tried to recall if she had ever witnessed Blake this animated. She couldn't.

Audrey listened to their easy back-and-forth, missing the days when life was simple and topics didn't center around things like irrevocable connections or a life-threatening fungus.

She yawned, wondering if it was possible to plug herself into all their bounding energy. She reached for the pot of coffee instead.

She sipped, bleary-eyed from her fitful night of sleep, listening to Ryan regale them about his most-favorite classes, gossiping about so-and-so professor, and how he managed to get excused from classes for the next ten days.

She stewed quietly, jealous over having to quit the program at the Labs due to her TMFS. Blake, due to his disappearance early into the program, also had to drop out, but he didn't seem as upset about it. The orca communication research project the three of them were working on was put on hold, indefinitely.

Ryan and Blake were so busy catching up, they didn't notice Audrey pour a third cup. Her brain was finally waking up. While they jabbered she wandered back to what happened in the middle of the night, the Mark awakening and the strange loop of undulating energy swirling between it and the token necklace Sinto gave her.

She kneaded that bumpy spot on her right forearm, undeniably there and rock hard through the thick sleeve of her bathrobe. Lifeless and cold like those terrifying moments after she flushed the last of the air into the ballast tanks and the submarine bobbed weightlessly buoyant before it began a slow ascent to the surface. The reality of Sinto's death was as fresh and real at this moment as it was that frightful day.

She wondered if what she experienced was an echo. Dr. Wickman said it was possible to hallucinate as part of her PTSD. What he didn't say was how incredibly real it would feel.

She jolted to the present. The kitchen had fallen silent. Blake and Ryan were staring at her, puzzlement and concern etched on their faces.

"Sorry!" She lifted her cup. "Just slow to catch up! Did you ask me something?"

Ryan leaned back against the counter, crossed his arms and ankles. "What's the plan?"

She set down her coffee cup. "Dr. Wickman is on the ship, setting up the lab. He said he might need our help with inventory. Don't bother unpacking. Alvarez texted this morning. We're ahead of schedule. The ship's fueled and stocked. Once we board, there should be no reason to disembark. We cast off once everyone's accounted for. Most of the crew are back, only a few stragglers left to round up, including us, but that should only take a few more hours."

Blake nodded his approval of her take-charge attitude and returned an endearing, lopsided grin.

She said, with Larkian authority, "Departure in one hour."

"Yes ma'am!" Blake said with a twinkle in his eye.

Then she ran upstairs to get dressed. Her bags were already packed and ready to go by her door. She paused, wondering if what they had planned was wise. The last time she ventured into the Pacific they lost two of the crew and the ship.

22

Pirate Ship

PIER 46 WAS SOUTH of downtown along Elliott Bay and a stone's throw to Seattle's football and baseball stadiums. Audrey, Blake, and Ryan gazed up at the ship, their bags at their feet.

Ryan whistled. "So this is a pirate ship."

"Larkian research ship," Audrey corrected him.

The *Requiem Sea II* looked nothing like a research ship. It was a high-tech wonder. The sleek black hull was designed for speed and endurance, under power or sail. The decks were cleared of all clutter and the windows encircling each level were minimal in size, oval-shaped and made of reinforced glass for handling rough water. Once the ship hit the seas, a trio of carbon-steel telescoping "wings" would rise from its decks, and the counterbalancing keel would drop from the hull, converting the ship from powered vessel to sailing ship within the span of a minute.

The wonder didn't stop there. The captain tuned the sails and navigated the ship with a touchscreen and the tip of his finger. There was an extensive science laboratory for at-sea research, medical facilities for emergencies, and a cargo chamber filled with "toys" that would make most billionaires jealous with envy: dual forty-foot tenders, a deep-ocean four-seat submarine, jet skis, and six remote submersibles for deep-water surveying. On the aft deck was a heli-pad and enclosed garage for storing the ship's helicopter.

The ship was four hundred feet of proprietary technology that could accommodate a crew of up to sixty but required less than a dozen to run it comfortably. A gym with gimbaled floor and a media center kept the crew in top physical condition and entertained while at sea. Crew cabins were modest but well-appointed, and the galley churned out meals you would expect from a three-starred Michelin restaurant, from complex to practical, and all nutritionally balanced; you would never find a weevil in one of Leonard's biscuits.

"What happened to the first one?"

"Damaged beyond repair," Blake said. "I was there. It was quite the ride."

Audrey said, "The original ship was sucked down into a football-stadium-sized hole from a sudden surge of air bubbles after Tallamure imploded. The hull cracked, engines were torn from their mounts, props were wadded up like paper. The internal shafts housing the wings buckled, crumpling them inside. The stabilizing bulb snapped off, laying the ship on its side. Anything glass shattered. Anything electronic fried. Everything else was coated in diesel and oil. A total loss. Luckily, it didn't catch fire and it was a miracle no one was killed during that most unfortunate accident."

She didn't mention the fact two crewmen were electrocuted by Merahvu rebels before the ship was struck from the disturbance from below. She thought it would be a bad omen to it bring up.

She added, "Alvarez said this one's identical to the original, with a few upgrades and enhancements."

Ryan pointed to the three-hundred-sixty-degree bridge, bristling with antennas and multiple domes for communication, radar, GPS, and other proprietary technology. "Looks equipped to run a small country."

Audrey laughed. In addition to the electronics, the galley housed massive freezers and food storage, augmented by live sea specimens they kept in the lab's many tanks. Enough to last a year at sea, maybe longer.

"That's exactly what it is. A floating country complete with a Code of Conduct and its own justice system. I was warned by Alvarez to be on my best behavior. Best not to find out what that might entail."

Ryan winced. "I'll keep that in mind." He pointed to a white symbol painted on the side of the hull near the transom, a vertical oval stacked atop a sideways X. "Is that what I think it is?"

Audrey said, "Yup, remove the eye sockets and bone joints, and you've got a modern-day Jolly Roger. It's embroidered on the crew uniform too. The Larkians' logo."

"Do I get one?" Ryan asked.

"Maybe. But, you might have to earn it." Audrey remembered her initiation on the *Requiem Sea*. A game of hot potato where she was the potato. The crew had shoved her back and forth across the cafeteria while crossing a roiling sea, hands landing wherever. She survived the humiliation and gained a ton of respect from the crew. She didn't know it at the time, but that was the day she was accepted as a full-fledged Larkian. That, and the fact she was the daughter of the Larkians' original captain.

She looked at Ryan. "You're sure you want to do this? There's no turning back once you step foot on that ship."

"There's no way you're talking me out of this."

Blake grinned. "Me either."

They fist bumped, grabbed their duffel bags, and headed for the gangplank.

A ginger-haired, middle-aged man greeted them. "Well, well. Welcome Culliford! Coming with us for another adventure?"

Audrey was taken aback. She still wasn't accustomed to being called by her father's original surname. She was born Audrey Grey. Grey was her father's pseudo-surname; the one he used when he met Audrey's mother. But everyone in the crew called him Culliford and since she was his daughter, they called her that too. In the span of a month she went from Grey to Culliford.

"Wouldn't miss it." She stepped aside. "Meet Ryan, a good friend, and a marine biologist. I think you know Blake already."

"Ah, the *boyfriend*." He gave Blake a wink.

Audrey and Blake shared an awkward look.

Ryan shook the crewman's hand. "Not quite a full-fledged marine biologist. I'm still working on my masters."

Blake stuck out his hand. "Blake, Audrey's *friend*, not boyfriend. Nice to meet you."

Ryan looked amused by the whole exchange. "Hmm. Just a friend? *Really*? This should be interesting."

The man said, "Call me Copper, electrical engineer. I'm the one who keeps the lights on and water hot."

They all did a double-take at his copper-colored hair.

He shook his head. "Ah, I know what you're thinking, I've heard 'em all. Copper Top being my least favorite. It's Copper, just *Copper*. Don't forget that." He gave them a look that confirmed he meant it and slipping up would be big mistake.

"Thanks for the memo," Audrey said.

He began searching a list on a tablet he held in his hand. "Hmm, I don't see a Ryan here." He tapped the screen several times. "No Ryan."

Ryan looked like he was going to cry.

"Try Wood." Audrey said. "And Goodfellow."

"Ah, there you both are… Wood and Goodfellow. Got ya." He tapped three times, checking a box beside each of their names. "Congratulations—you've all been upgraded to level two, cabins six, seven, and eight. Aft, and next to the laboratory. Names are posted beside the door." He smiled and waved them on. "Buckle up! Only two more crew to check in before we cast off."

"Hell yeah!" Ryan said, leading them both up the gangplank.

Audrey smirked, "Just you wait! It's all fun and games until the vomiting starts."

She got a first-hand experience regurgitating her guts last time she went to sea and had no desire to repeat that again.

The gangplank dropped them in the corridor on level one, just above the waterline, mid-ship next to the main stairway. Voices drifted and light bled down the corridor from opened doorways where the crew were getting settled in their cabins. The three of them would be staying well above the waterline and aft, where lively seas would be accentuated.

Upgraded my ass, Audrey thought.

They wound their way up the main stairway that curved around the central cylinder housing the drop-down keel. They stopped and peeked inside viewing portholes cut into the cylinder, revealing the raised, oval-shaped, metal keel secured within.

The ship smelled of new paint and fresh oil but otherwise felt eerily the same as the original *Requiem Sea*, right down to the wood-paneled corridors with brass sconces and railings, polished to a bright sheen. The Larkians didn't cut any corners on interior accommodations. Not gaudy or impractical, but classically nautical with lots of wood, brass, and leather.

A schematic of the level-two layout was mounted to the wall at the top of the landing. They located the lab and their cabins. As Copper promised, they were located aft, where the ship bucked in wild seas, and across from the lab.

"Here we are," Audrey said.

The laboratory occupied the back half of level two except for a half-dozen ocean-facing cabins along the starboard side. Their last names were engraved on brass plaques mounted by each cabin door. Audrey's cabin was between Ryan's and Blake's. The doors were open and ready for occupancy. Audrey dumped her bag in the hall and followed Ryan into his room. Blake ventured into his own.

Ryan tossed his duffel bag on the single-sized bunk that ran parallel to the ship's hull. He stretched across to peek outside one of the two porthole windows. He ran a finger around the tight circumference. "Not much of a view. Kinda small don't you think?"

"For good reason."

He quirked a brow. Then he crossed the cabin, opening dresser drawers and the self-locking doors of a small closet, complete with a personal safe. He pointed at a closed door.

"The head," Audrey said.

"Right." He opened the door, stepped inside, noted the door on the other side, opened it. Another cabin, opposite layout but exactly like his and unoccupied at the moment. He shut the door.

Audrey said, "Adjoining cabins share a head." She pointed out the small green light above the knob. "Automatically detects when someone's inside. Red indicates occupied, green it's not. Try to be mindful and not walk in on your head-mate." She grinned. "Depending on who it is, you might regret it."

Within the head, a pair of cabinets and drawers framed a counter with a sink. A second, much smaller plaque, stamped with his name, was mounted to the cabinet closest to his cabin. The plaque on the opposite cabinet was blank.

"Lucky you. Seems you've got the head to yourself. No head-mate."

He turned around. Opposite the sink was a toilet.

"Don't flush your dental floss or you'll regret that too. Ship's plumber might hang you from one of those antennas for a spell. Nothing but toilet paper and, well, you know."

"Piss and shit."

She nodded.

"Good to know."

Ryan had grown strangely quiet. Audrey cocked her head. "Have you ever been on a ship before?"

"Only an old docked Navy ship, as a kid, a tourist thing. Nothing like this."

Ryan kept looking around the head, pressing against the bulkheads, peeking back inside his cabin.

"What?" Audrey asked.

Ryan went back into the head and was gazing at the sink. "How am I supposed to shower?"

"Ah, the showers are communal. Keeps things simple, less maintenance."

Ryan raised an eyebrow. "You shower with the boys?"

"Ship's rule—they respect my privacy, and I theirs," she said. "Trust me, I didn't shower with the boys."

Someone snuck up behind her and laid their chin on her shoulder, making her jump. "She's lying."

Audrey swung around. "Dyer!" She gave him a firm hug.

He winced. "Ow. Injury, remember?"

Audrey pulled back. "Oh, sorry!"

"Oh, no, don't pull back, that was nice." He pointed to his ear. "Just not here." His ear had nearly been torn off when the original ship tumbled. It was still red and puffy from Dr. Wickman sewing it back on. He wagged his fingers begging for another hug. "Come on, I'm feeling denied."

She crossed her arms.

He tsked then swung his attention to Ryan. "Oh, I see, you've got a new boyfriend. Gee, and to think I had a shot. Blow. To. Ego." Dyer mocked stabbing himself in the heart.

Audrey chuckled. Dyer had knocked her on her ass and made fun of her ill-fitting uniform the first morning she spent on the first *Requiem Sea*. He also gave her support and encouragement during their descent to the bottom of the Pacific for their ill-fated confrontation in Tallamure. His voice was the only thing that kept her from a full-blown panic attack. Dyer was a master of practical jokes but had a heart of gold.

"This is Ryan, my best friend." She turned to Ryan. "Ry, Dyer."

"Hey man, good to meet you." Ryan shook his hand.

Dyer turned to Audrey. "So I still have a chance?"

Audrey squeezed his cheeks and gave him a toying pout. "Not till hell freezes over."

"Huh." Dyer turned to Ryan, placed a hand on his hip. "How about you, big fella? You available? My first name is Jason, by the way." He wagged his brows. "But you can call me whatever you like."

Ryan's eyes bugged.

Audrey play-punched Dyer in the shoulder. "Beat it! We've got work to do."

"If you insist." He sashayed to the door, turned, batted his lashes. "Later, Wood—and oh, how I like *wood*."

Audrey closed the door once Dyer left.

"Is he really, uh—"

"I don't know. Don't take some of these guys too seriously. They like to have fun. Sometimes it's hard to tell when they're being serious or not."

Ryan shrugged. "I can deal with that."

Audrey grinned. "We'll see."

She slipped from Ryan's cabin to her own, dragging her duffel bag from the hall.

She found Blake sitting on her bunk. He pointed toward the head door. It was open, and so was the one on the other side where Blake's duffel lay on the floor. "Looks like we're in adjoining cabins. Head-mates."

"Awkward."

He cracked a nervous smile. "Yeah, awkward."

23

Nugget Of Gold

SINTO LOOKED OVER AT Rachel, sitting in the driver's seat of her white sports car. Her seat was set far forward and she sat on an extra pad to elevate her gaze above the steering wheel.

He learned she practically lived at the hotel, and when he said to hurry, she already had her things packed and ready to go. It didn't take her long to pull on a pair of jeans and a sweater two sizes too big for her petite frame, and to pile the mass of her hair atop her head with what she called a "scrunchie."

Before dragging her bag to the garage where her car was parked, she stopped briefly to talk to a man she called her boss. Rachel asked Sinto to wait outside the door. There was a lot of yelling and screaming. Her boss finally shut up and wished her well when she dumped two of the bags full of money that Sinto had won from competing casinos onto his desk. The third bag they kept. Sinto had questioned Rachel if it would be enough after witnessing how freely she spent his jackpot of five thousand dollars buying him new shoes and a VIP night on the town.

She said, "Lesson number one, Sinto: Avoid places like Las Vegas. This place will suck you dry of every penny you own and when that's gone, they'll suck the life out of ya." Then she assured him they had more than enough to provide for a year, wherever he needed to go, as long as they avoided the big cities.

She pulled the car out of the underground parking lot, into the bright sunshine, and headed for the highway. "Buckle up."

"So you worked for the hotel?" Sinto asked, clipping the belt into the clasp.

"Yep, my job was to keep the big winners—men mainly—at the hotel. I was supposed to keep 'em spending their winnin's so the owners could get all their money back, and more—at the night club, by staying in the most expensive rooms, encouragin' more gamblin', giving them a reason to come back and spend more, over and over. I was expected to do, you know, whatever it took."

"Whatever it took?"

She looked away and sighed. "I'm not proud of that."

"I don't understand."

"Are you from another planet?" She stuck out her chest. "Why do you think I got these things." Then she splayed her fingers across the steering wheel like a cat stretching its paws. Her bright red nails stretched an inch beyond the tips of her fingers. "And these stupid useless things." She banged her head against the window. "And a tangled mess of fake hair."

Sinto gazed at her overly endowed breasts, the claw-like nails, the pile of hair stacked on her head. "What is it that you do?"

"Honey, you're kiddin', right?" She looked flabbergasted and ashamed. "I guess I'll have to spell it out for ya. I please them, make them feel special, provide companionship. I'm their special escort, in the bar, the casino, their hotel room... Is any of this gettin' through?"

No, it wasn't "gettin' through." His brain had shriveled up from drinking nothing but rum in the middle of a desert.

Sinto realized how little he understood about Rachel's world. He sifted through things he had read in his vast collection of Sapien books or learned from the Scouts who shared their experiences in the Sapien world. Everything he thought he understood seemed jumbled up and incomplete. It didn't help that his brain was running at half-speed. Then it hit him like a rock slide. Something he should have known, half-witted or not. He naively came close to experiencing it firsthand less than eight hours ago.

"You're a prostitute?"

Her cheeks flamed. "A high-class escort!"

He wanted to ask why, but stopped, noting the sudden stream of tears moistening her cheeks.

"Yes, I'm a—" She sobbed. "I *was* a prostitute."

"I'm sorry I asked."

"That's okay." She wiped her tears away with the sleeve of her sweater. They sat in silence as the desert slipped by, speckled with groups of houses exposed to the intense sunshine; between each group of houses a barren and endless landscape dotted by dried-out bushes.

"It was my choice." She grabbed his hand, gave it a squeeze. "Like I chose to leave, to help you." She slipped him a sideways glance. "It's funny how easy it is, talkin' and bein' with ya. Feels natural. I don't know why. Just is. Folks say when you meet someone like that, you stick with 'em. Like finding a nugget of gold. You hold onto it, for luck."

He gave her a smile and squeezed back. "I don't care what you've done in your past. You're my gold nugget, Rachel."

She sniffed and whispered, "Thank you."

They sat in silence, the hum of tires spinning on pavement droned.

It saddened Sinto learning the things Rachel did to earn money, how she changed her body to make her more desirable to people who used her for a night. To him she looked terribly out of balance.

I bet she was perfect before.

He had read about the operations Sapiens underwent to change their bodies. Why mess with nature's gift? He had to know.

"Why did you change your body?"

"Because they made me. All part of the job description, convinced me it was a 'benefit.' They paid for the fake boobs right off, a quick in-and-out procedure, but it hurt like the dickens." A sardonic laugh slipped from between her small perfect teeth. "I don't know why you're givin' me a bad time about mutilatin' myself. I had a good chance to look ya over after you passed out last night."

Sinto stared out the window and braced himself. Perhaps she had seen his markings.

"Where are your nipples? Haven't seen that one before. If I hadn't talked to you first and figured you as a nice guy, I would've run for the hills. Come on! Your nipples? Sinto, that's kinda weird. Now the hairless thing I get. Plenty of guys are doing it now, usually those guys who work for the strip clubs. They laser off every hair below the neck."

Sinto closed his eyes. Perhaps he should tell her the truth. He didn't laser anything or cut off his nipples. He was born that way.

"Do you enjoy your job?" he asked.

"What do you think?" She laughed. "I can't believe I just quit and ran away. What am I gonna do now?" She looked at him as if he had the answer. "Where are you goin' anyway?"

"Lake Mead, remember?"

"Whatcha gonna do once you get there?"

"Dive in."

She shivered. "It's winter. I don't know what you read, but the lake is freezing this time of year."

"I like it cold."

She shrugged. "Suit yourself."

She turned right at the end of the highway, toward a town call Boulder City. Sinto could see why. This part of the desert was all boulders and desert scruff. In the distance, the lake came into view, shriveled from what he could tell by the mineral ring high up along the shore. But it was wet, dark blue and beckoning. Sinto sat up.

"Where's the dam?"

"Further south, but it's got cliffs. You want to swim, right?"

He nodded.

She rolled her eyes. "Whatever."

Rachel turned off the highway onto a desolate road. The landscape was flatter here, sloping gently toward the lake. There were no buildings or homes, just dry dirt with little vegetation. She turned onto another road, past docks lying on the beach, high and dry.

"Used to be a marina here, before the lake began to dry up. Been gettin' real bad lately. They say it might dry up completely if we don't get more rain."

She stopped the car.

"Try not to get too excited, this used to be a great place to hang out and swim." She gazed out the window. "Not anymore. Especially since they been finding dead bodies, dumped years ago."

Sinto opened his door, gazed down at his clothes and the wide-open space between him and the lake. Cars whizzed by on the highway further up the hill. There was nowhere to hide or secretly slip into the lake without someone possibly seeing.

"So, now what? You're just gonna dive in?" she said, a quizzical look on her face.

"Yes."

She turned up the heat and wrapped her arms across her chest. "Go on, I'll wait for ya here, where it's warm."

He shook his head. "No, pick me up in the morning."

Rachel's face bunched up. "The morning?"

"Met me at dawn, here." He shed his leather coat, pulled out the last of the one-hundred-dollar bills she had stuffed inside his pocket last night. "Take this, and take care of the rest."

Rachel took the money and frowned. Her dimples even popped when she was sad. "You're not gonna ditch me, are you?"

"I'll be here, I promise." He reached over and gave her chin a squeeze. "Please come back, at first light." He pulled off his new shoes, handed them to her. He left his jeans on.

She nodded and smiled.

Sinto smiled back, then got out of the car.

Rachel shook her head as she peeked at him through the door. "I hope you're not making a mistake."

"I hope not too."

24

Ghostly Presence

SINTO SHUT THE CAR door and watched Rachel drive away. She retraced the route back along the desolate road, onto the highway, back toward Boulder City. Once the gleam of her white car faded into the distance, he walked to the edge of the water.

Lake Mead was not what he was expecting. The beach, if you could even call it one, was desolate and uninviting. He was the only living thing around. No trees, no soft vegetation to sit on, not even a bush to stash his jeans behind. Just dirt and gravel, and a tired-looking picnic table.

He quickly pulled off his jeans, camouflaged his skin to match the coarse rock and sand at his feet, and left his jeans, rolled in a tight ball, behind the biggest rock he could find—which wasn't much bigger than his fist. He waded into the lake, skin shifting to match the reflective surface of the water.

He didn't bother with his gelatinous protective lorica, preferring to feel the slip of cool water across his skin and through the gills along his neck, siphoning oxygen from the water and directly into his bloodstream. Unfurling his tail felt like molting a layer of old skin. It felt good; water sliding freely along his spine. The life force in the water was weaker than he expected, but would be enough to help rejuvenate him.

He adjusted the lens shape of his eyes so he could see clearly underwater and lazily swam beneath the surface toward Hoover Dam to the southeast.

He surfaced once he rounded the point and entered a channel where the dam stopped water from freely flowing. He had read about the dam's history and found it massive compared to what he imagined. He gazed upon the man-made wonder with bitter feelings.

The Sapiens needed to generate energy, and harnessing water was clean and efficient, which was good. But before the dam, the Colorado River flowed from the Rocky Mountains to the sea and had once been a heavily traveled route for the Terrakai when they migrated to Earth hundreds of years ago. Scouts rarely visited these waters and warned of pollutants and the risk of detection by the growing Sapien population to the west. Lake Mead was one of the places Scouts had claimed to search while looking for Sinto's father. They reported finding nothing but a tired body of withered water. Sadly, he agreed with their assessment. The mineral ring on the rock surrounding the lake was growing higher than the lake was deep in some places.

As he made his way around the lake he pondered how much to tell Rachel when she returned to pick him up; what he was, where he came from, how dangerous his journey may be. The longer she stuck with him, the more difficult it would be to hide the truth. He pushed that thought from his mind to focus on himself. He would worry about Rachel tomorrow.

He swam toward the deepest part of the lake. The fresh water felt strange passing through his gills after swimming the salty sea most of his life, but he pleasured in the fact he could drink it. He fired his merlux and drew upon what little electricity he could generate to set his eyes aglow. Dual beams of green light cast an eerie landscape across the marshy bottom. Thirst satiated, he grew hungry. The hunt was on.

To his surprise he discovered schools of large fish grazing along the marshy bottom. A healthy population considering everything he had learned about the lake. Camouflaged, it was easy to sneak up on them, and with a small electrical shock, to paralyze them, so they would feel no pain or fear when he ate them alive.

He bit into the raw tender flesh of a male bass. It tasted sweet and juicy, but felt foreign in his mouth. It had been a while since he had eaten this way. It felt primal and real, and he had forgotten how much he missed it. Like the last time he had hunted live fish with his father on Merluma. It wasn't long after that his father went missing.

Thinking back, he remembered it as a particularly strange reunion. His father had asked Sinto what he believed was the best path forward for the Merahvu; if their future was best served on Merluma or Earth. Sinto thought it an odd question, citing what was obvious to him at the time: both, Merluma *and* Earth. And that there would be a time when the Merahvu would need to confront the untenable situation, probably soon; that the Merahvu would need to make official contact with Sapiens, make their presence known, formally claim Merluma as theirs, and negotiate a stake in Earth's oceans. Then he questioned his father why it mattered. His father shrugged off Sinto's question and changed the subject, saying he was curious what Sinto thought and that he was just trying to make conversation.

Now he pondered the question his father had asked. Where *did* the future of the Merahvu lie? While Merluma was certainly the birthplace of the three tribes of the Merahvu, their populations had outgrown what Merluma could reasonably sustain. The same could be said of Earth and its ever-growing Sapien populations. The ratio of humans to other species had grown radically skewed over the course of the past hundred years. One could say the Merahvu migrating to Earth was part of the problem and should rethink their long-term presence here. Maybe that was the answer his father sought.

He regretted not experiencing the ways of his ancestors more often: how they hunted and ate—and even slept—in shallower waters without protection of a lorica, siphoning oxygen from the water through their gills. He had become complacent with breathing oxywater produced from his lorica. The same oxywater the Merahvu had manufactured to fill the domed city of Tallamure. An underwater city that had mimicked life on the land combined with the beauty and bounty of the sea. A bustling city with parks and markets and vast gardens, places to gather and celebrate and flow in the dance of the Ballorue, populated with a hundred thousand Merahvu from all tribes living peacefully together. Tallamure had been a grand and successful experiment, one that also incorporated elements of Sapien life. A city nestled at the bottom of the North Pacific where the Merahvu had lived, respectfully, on Earth for nearly three hundred years.

Was Tallamure and what it represented the way forward for the Merahvu, or had it been a mistake?

Of one thing Sinto was certain: he no longer had a place he could call home, as was true for the thousands of others who survived the Sapien bombing; those who once called Tallamure home. Where had they gone?

Not only did Sinto have no place to call home, he also had no family. Dead to everyone—like his father, who may be dead or alive. This was Sinto's new existence, a *nomad*. A wanderer, to be called by whatever name he wished, with a mission to do whatever he deemed important. No one tells the wanderer what to do. The wanderer is the master of his own universe. Was that the path his father had chosen? Maybe his father didn't want to be found.

Sinto devoured the entire bass, spitting out bone and other bitter parts, and it was only after his ravenous hunger was appeased that he sensed a presence. He settled in the mud among rock along the shore and hunkered down, camouflaged, stretching his mind to see what his other senses could not.

He sensed nothing, not even a tingle. He was overreacting, maybe from an overload of sensation from the night before. He told himself it was nothing.

Perhaps it is the ghost of Father, watching over me from his ashy grave.

And with this curious and mournful thought, he slipped into a dreamless stupor.

25

Wickman's Lab

Shortly after boarding, the deck below Audrey's feet vibrated when the engines came to life. Audrey rounded up Blake and Ryan from their cabins.

"Grab your coats. Top deck, now!" she exclaimed.

They stepped out of an oval airtight door a few doors down from their cabins. They took a moment to gaze off the stern of the ship where the ship's name, in pressed gold-leaf, glinted across the expanse of the sloped, shiny black transom: *Requiem Sea II*.

Goosebumps rippled up her arms and set her heart a flutter. Ryan was grinning like a kid on Christmas morning. Blake gazed across the surface of the water, lost in thought.

The ship's thrusters engaged, fore and aft, and the ship drifted sideways away from the dock. A deep rumble and a rush of backwash burst from beneath the transom. Then the ship lurched forward followed by a single long blast from the horn. They were off.

The sky was a volatile mix of clouds, with rays of sunlight darting between spits of rain. They raced up a metal stairway to the next level, cutting across the helipad, past the garage doors where the ship's helicopter was secured inside. They continued up to the top deck which stretched the entire length of the ship. Three large hatches were marked with yellow hash-marks and warnings to stay clear. Below sat the ship's massive telescoping wings, safely tucked inside their protective cylinders, ready to deploy.

Seattle's skyline came into view as they swiftly left the channel where commercial ships docked. They leaned on the railing watching the city sweep by: The Smith Tower, the ferry terminal, the Space Needle, and many newly-built skyscrapers that had sprung up over the last decade. The ship rounded the point, leaving Elliot Bay in its wake. They passed the cliffs at the base of Magnolia Hill, past Shilshole Bay Marina and the locks to Lake Washington. Just north of that was the patch of land where her father's house, built in the eighteen-nineties, was tucked up on the hill, the metal gabled roof shimmering in a beam of sunlight, slipping through the clouds. Along the water below the bluff a train raced the ship, heading north along the tracks.

The ship quickly picked up speed. Wind tugged on their coat sleeves and pant legs. Tears were drawn from their eyes. Shivering from the cold blast of a late fall wind, they descended the stairs and headed back inside.

Stokes stepped out of the Lab, talking into a headset cupped around his ear. He disconnected once he saw them coming down the corridor. He held a hand out to Ryan.

"Welcome! You must be Ryan." He gave Ryan's hand a firm shake, let go. "I trust you all found your cabins to your satisfaction?"

They nodded, and he continued. "I want to warn you, we're in for some rough weather for the next thirty-six hours, then we expect calm seas. The good news is, we should get an extra boost in speed. The wind direction should provide for a robust sail."

He handed them each a small black pouch, drawn shut with a string, and sporting the Larkians' signature logo.

"These are for you: seasickness bands and medical patches. Patches go here," he pointed at his neck below his ear, "bands around your wrists, instructions tell you more. Should help you feel nothing."

Audrey wasted no time slipping on the wrist bands then sticking a patch behind her ear, as did Ryan. After last time, she didn't want to depend on the bands alone. Blake pocketed his pouch without putting either on.

Stokes invited the three of them into the lab. "I'll give you a tour. I've got some time before we hit the straits."

"Wow, I never had the chance to see the lab on *Requiem Sea*." Audrey said, shooting Stokes a dirty look. "I was either too sick or preparing for a deadly mission. This is amazing."

The lab was broken into three main sections. The first, the dry lab, was used for research. A bank of computers hummed quietly behind a wall of glass. Tubes of chilled electric-blue liquid and multiple fans cooled their inner state-of-the-art components. A pair of small cabins off to the side were for private office use or equipment storage. There was a wall with an oval watertight door and a row of dark windows where monitors and keyboards were set up at three workstations to observe whatever might be happening on the other side. Bookshelves lined another wall, containing journals and reference manuals. They appeared old and were well-worn. Audrey guessed them to be from Dr. Wickman's private collection.

He pointed to the wall of electronics. "This is one of three technology centers on the ship. Any one of them could be deployed as a backup should another fail. "And this," Stokes spun the wheel of the water-tight door and stepped over the threshold, "is the wet lab."

The overhead lights automatically came on when he stepped inside. They followed. The wet lab was filled with the soft sound of gurgling water and smelled strongly of fresh paint.

Stokes continued his tour. "The laboratory is identical to the one on *Requiem Sea*, as is everything else. Alvarez and the Larkian engineers stressed the importance of maintaining interchangeability and redundancy, as well as efficiency. Every ship built in the *Requiem Sea* line is identical, from the engines, to computer hardware and software, to the nuts and bolts holding everything together."

Ryan's eyes were the size of saucers as he surveyed the wet lab. A row of aquariums in varying sizes ran through the center of the large room. Tubes ran along the ceiling and dropped into each tank; one for circulating fresh salt water, the other for oxygenating. Most of the tanks were dry and empty, except for three of the larger ones. They were filled with an ample supply of prawns, lobsters, and Dungeness crabs.

Stokes gestured toward the full tanks. "By Leonard's request. We eat well."

Audrey grinned and elbowed Ryan in the ribs. "Told you."

They surveyed a bank of cabinets containing beakers, test tubes, water sample kits, sediment corers, microscopes, plankton sample splitters, neatly folded lab coats, eye protection, and more. Several plankton-gathering nets hung on hooks along one wall. A wet workspace with multiple sinks ran across the opposite wall. On the far wall was another water-tight door. Everything was spotlessly clean.

"What's in there?" Ryan asked, pointing to the door on the far side.

"Ah, we have the capability for studying larger samples of sea life." Stokes opened the door. It made a loud whisking sound as it swung in.

This part of the lab was half the size of the wet one but with a ceiling twice as high. It was dimly lit. A single spotlight lighted a circular acrylic tank big enough to comfortably contain a large sea lion. *Or a Merahvu*, Audrey thought with a shiver. At the moment it was dry and empty.

A stainless-steel gurney and other expensive-looking medical equipment were secured against the walls. A mesh and metal basket like those used in sea rescues hung above. A winch and the necessary cabling were bolted to the ceiling next to a large hatch for raising or lowering large things to or from the deck above.

Silhouetted by the glow of a laptop screen and a bow-armed lamp was Dr. Wickman, sitting at a workstation opposite the aquarium, strategically placed for observation. He was intensely focused on a stack of printed lists and his laptop screen. He sat on a stool with one foot propped on the bottom rung and the other tapping in rhythm to whatever music was pumping through a set of ear buds tucked into his ears. He startled upon seeing them.

He popped out an ear bud and smiled. "I see Stokes has given you the tour. I apologize for not seeing to it myself but I needed to reconcile our inventory."

"I thought you wanted us to help?"

"Not necessary. Alvarez wanted to leave early so I took care of it last night. I'm almost finished."

Audrey said, "This is Ryan, one of the most thorough research students at the Friday Harbor Labs." Ryan blushed. "You already know Blake."

"I look forward to working with both of you," Dr. Wickman shook Ryan's hand and nodded to Blake. "I hope the lab meets your requirements."

"Beyond, actually." Ryan pointed to the tank. "Plan on studying some extra-large plankton?"

"I like to be prepared for anything we may encounter at sea, though I've had no need for it so far. For the most part, this room has functioned as my private office."

Stokes piped up, "We should keep moving; there's more to see before we enter the Pacific."

Dr. Wickman said, "Audrey, could I talk to you for a moment?"

"Sure, you guys go ahead. I'll catch up with you later."

Stokes added, "See you at dinner. Eighteen-hundred hours. Don't be late, Chef's rules."

26

Long Over Due

DR. WICKMAN TOLD AUDREY it was urgent that she talk to her father. He had made a breakthrough, overcoming a mental block before boarding the ship. Her father had finally accepted the truth of her mother's death. Admitted the tragic role he played in Sinto's death and acknowledged the grief and guilt he had forced upon Audrey.

Afterward, Audrey meandered through the ship mustering courage, and finally wound her way up the mid-ship stairway to level four. She passed the library and ran her fingers along the corridor's long expanse of wood paneling to the aft door. Wind whipped loose strands of hair from her braid when she stepped outside and climbed the metal stairway to the upper deck.

They had just entered the Pacific, exiting the Straits of Juan de Fuca where the sea roiled and the decks wallowed. Stokes had yet to deploy the wings and set the ship to sail. He was waiting for her father to take a celestial reading.

The two of them had a gentlemen's running wager. If her father accurately predicted when they would arrive at a particular destination by using his sextant, the stars, and a chart, he would win. The prize was a bottle of rum that they ended up sharing, regardless of who won. It kept her father's navigational skills honed and Stokes on his toes.

Her father stood on the far side of the open deck, sighting the horizon, then the north star of Polaris, with the original brass sextant from his pirating past. It was one of the irreplaceable items Alvarez thought to retrieve from the ill-fated *Requiem Sea*.

The sea was lively, making it a challenge for him to get a clean sighting. He didn't notice her watching from afar as he struggled. She clung to the railing as the ship galloped along white-crested swells, the deck shuddering on the occasional rogue wave. The wind tugged at her clothes and numbed her face. Not the best conditions for a serious conversation. But Dr. Wickman said it would be a good opportunity to seek him out, while her father was in his element, breathing the brine of the sea.

It felt like déjà vu. Same ocean. Same ship. Same sextant. Same uncertainty roiling in her gut about the direction this inevitable moment would take them. It felt as if she had gone back a month in time when he taught her how to take a proper reading and she confronted him about the truth of his past. It had surprised her when he freely admitted it was true. Shortly after, he discovered the Mark in her arm and promised to fix it. At the time she didn't know he meant to "fix it" by killing Sinto. She often dwelled on the fact that if she had known, things may have played out differently.

A *wishful waste of time*, she bitterly told herself. Sinto was dead. The cold and dead gristle of flesh buried in her arm a harsh reminder.

She watched as her father pulled a small pad of paper from his coat pocket and stuck the tiny flashlight between his teeth so he could see the marks on the side of the sextant set by his reading. He used a small pencil to jot them down. The wind ruffled the paper and he fought to keep it still. Once the readings were recorded, he shoved those things inside his pocket and looked up. Their eyes met.

His face softened. Moisture rimmed his eyes, from the wind or from seeing her, she was wasn't quite sure. He froze for a beat, then he was in motion, coming to her with outstretched arms. But he stopped suddenly a few feet away. Dropped his arms, blinking. Confusion furrowed his brow. He cast his gaze to his feet, drew a shuddering breath, looked up.

"Audrey?" he said.

"Yes, it's me, Dad—your daughter, Audrey. You named me after your mother."

His gaze grew distant for a beat. "Audrey... yes. I remember my mother meant everything to me before she died." Then he gave her a sad smile. "What have I done?"

"You blew up their world—Sinto's world. You blew up my world too."

He nodded, hitched his shoulders toward his ears. "I feel so cold."

"Me too." She reached out her hand. "Come, let's go inside." He stared at it as if she was a stranger he was unsure he could trust. His gaze switched between her hand and her face, another momentary flash of confusion. Then he took it.

She led him down the stairs and through the aft door on level four. The blast of heat reddened his cheeks and made her fingers tingle.

It was nearly six o' clock. The crew would be gathering in the cafeteria one level below for the first dinner to be served on this new ship. They passed through the empty corridor in silence. Her father nodded toward the mahogany doors of the library.

They had the library to themselves. She took off her hoodie as he busied himself, polishing the sextant's mottled bronze surface before laying it in its original, red-velvet-lined case.

Déjà vu.

Audrey wondered if his heart was pounding as hard as hers. Dr. Wickman had failed to give Audrey a script for this awkward and momentous reunion. She realized that was on purpose. She would have to navigate these uncharted waters on her own.

She sat and watched as he stowed the sextant in the same place where he stored it on the previous ship. He slipped off his wool peacoat and hung it on a hook in the same location by the door, where he had on the previous ship. A creature of habit. How many habits had been etched into his brain over the past three-hundred-plus years of his existence? It boggled to imagine.

He sat in a large leather chair opposite of her and crossed his long lanky legs, like those she had inherited from him. He placed his hands in his lap and captured her eyes with an icy blue gaze.

A stare-down.

Déjà vu.

Audrey sucked on her bottom lip. "I miss her as much as you do," she said.

His face folded with fresh and raw sorrow. As if he just learned that she was gone and had yet to process the full impact of that knowledge. From what Dr. Wickman told her, that was true. The key to his therapy was reliving his past all over again, no matter how painful.

"You look just like her, tall like me, but your face..." He looked away. "I—I—can't believe she's..."

"We still have each other."

A high-pitched whine followed by a rumble reverberated throughout the ship. Her father uncrossed his legs and sat forward, eyes widened in alarm. Both swayed to a slight slowing of the ship.

"Stokes is engaging the drop-down keel. Next he'll raise the telescoping wings."

The whine of hydraulics and sound of telescoping wings clunking into place as they stretched to the sky confirmed her statement. The ship heeled several degrees. Her father jolted. There was a second of confusion, then acknowledgment, then he sat back and relaxed.

"Yes. I remember. Stokes, he took me for a tour at the shipyard and showed me the ship. Where it was built, the schematics, every detail. A competent and fine captain." He seemed to be saying it more for himself than for her. Reciting the words as if taking a test.

She was pleased with his progress but curious by his demeanor. Was this the same man she fought for the knife and who used her fatal mistake as an opportunity to make her an accomplice to Sinto's murder?

"What do you remember from the last time we were together?"

His brow furrowed and cheek twitched as if it took great exertion to recall anything from his past. "You were screaming."

"Where were we?"

"In his city."

"Whose city?"

"That—that—" His mouth twisted up like he was going to say 'boy' but instead he said his name. "Sinto's."

Hearing Sinto's name roll off her father's tongue struck a raw nerve and let loose a fresh wave of anger she thought she had buried. She swallowed it down and focused on staying calm. She asked, shakily, "Why do you think I was screaming?"

His fingers dug into the soft leather arms of his chair and he started breathing heavily. She wondered if she was making a mistake. If he might suddenly turn violent. After a moment, his fingers relaxed and he said, "Because I killed him."

Her heart pounded. "And?"

"You were trying to stop me."

"And?"

"I used you to kill him."

Audrey gasped. He admitted it. He had been using her ever since her mother died; as a thing to mold into a weapon for a personal act of vengeance, which he had successfully wielded against Sinto.

A rock lodged in her throat. He was watching her with those glacial eyes that reflected a thousand shades of blue. Eyes her mother fell in love with along with the man behind them. Was this that man before he became a monster riddled with hate?

He said, "I'm sorry." The rock in her throat grew bigger. "I'm sorry I used you. I'm sorry I blew up your world."

27

Korvasi

SINTO STIRRED WITH A strange feeling. The one he felt before, that of a presence. The water was pitch black and, based on his internal clock, sunrise was hours away. He looked up.

A pair of golden eyes cut through the darkness, close enough that Sinto could see dark pupils pulsing wildly in their centers.

He decided not to panic. While whoever it was gave him a jolt of surprise, he had the feeling they posed no threat.

Sinto snapped his fingers. A ball of electrical fire burst from the palm of his hand and set the water aglow.

"Bright light! Too bright! Too bright!" The words reverberated telepathically in Sinto's mind.

Sinto was taken aback by what he saw. A hunched and shrunken old creature with claw-like hands—gnarled knuckles and unkempt nails—shielding its eyes. Blood vessels were clearly visible through the paper-thin skin, void of its fatty layer. Sinto could hear the thrum of the stranger's heart, an odd inconsistent beat that rolled and swayed like water breaking on a sandy shore; *thumpa-thump-a-thump.*

Sinto dimmed the ball of light he held in his hand.

Wild waves of gray-green hair sprouted in every direction from the stranger's head. Based on the lack of breast mounds on the stranger's bony chest, the stranger was a male, and a Terrakai based on the intricately lacy tail gently swaying behind his hunched back.

"Boo!" The stranger yanked his gruesome hands from his face and chuckled. Thick spittle leaked from his mouth, slowly dissolving and clouding the water with a foul yellow tint. His teeth appeared too large for his mouth and were coated in green slime. His jowls had surrendered to gravity long ago.

Sinto recoiled when the smell hit him. The putrid sweetness of death, almondy and sour and something else, something unnatural, something he tasted when he drank deep of the water from the lake. The taint of Sapien-made chemicals that leached from distant lands and nearby shores.

The stranger's chuckle grew into a cackle, slipping through the folds of Sinto's mind, filling the vacant spaces in his ears and sinuses, swirling like a whirlpool, louder and louder until it burst from his nose. Seeing Sinto's reaction merely raised a thin, stranded brow. The stranger opened his mouth and Sinto's head filled with a deafening cackle, then—

Silence, except for the flutter of Sinto's working gills and the *thumpa-thump-a-thump* of the stranger's heart.

The Terrakai stranger slapped his hands across his mouth, then flipped his wrists and his hands opened palm-side out like a bird taking flight. "Oh!!" A perfectly round O formed with his mouth. "*Excuse my exuberance!*" The stranger pressed his face closer. "*What is it you seek from my fine lake?*"

Sinto drew back from the repelling smell swirling between them. "Food. *Refreshment.*"

The stranger's eyes narrowed and what little working muscle that remained in his saggy face came alive, and Sinto could imagine the face of the Terrakai this stranger once was; powerful, feared, and respected.

"*Here? In this rancid cesspool? Try again, young one.*"

Sinto hesitated.

The stranger narrowed his eyes. *"Have you come here to spy on me?"*

"No! I am not a spy. I am looking for Ramasis."

"And who are you? Why do you care about Ramasis?"

"I am a Scout sent by the future queen, Naiada. She is worried about her father. He has been missing for nearly an Earth year."

His eyes brightened. *"The future queen! Already? Have the years passed that quickly? Oh. Oh my. Does that mean—What has become of Queen Ianthe?"*

The way he inquired about Sinto's queen mother inferred sinister curiosity. As if he relished an answer that affected her continued existence. The Terrakai stranger gazed back, his eyes fierce and powerful like that of a wild animal, belying his crusty exterior. Sinto needed to tread carefully.

The Terrakai stranger poked a jagged fingernail into his chest. *"Did she meet an unfortunate fate?"* He swam in a slow circle, scrutinizing. Sinto's heart danced.

The Terrakai stranger stopped and studied Sinto's face, clawed at his hair. He opened his mouth and drew in a mouthful of water. He swished it around his mouth, then spit it out.

"You're of Terrakai blood but you taste too clean to be from the City of Green." The Terrakai cocked his head, his eyes fixated on Sinto's tail and its broad dorsal fin. *"Dual-tribe. Pacific born?"*

Then he cracked a smile, displaying a mouthful of his slimy teeth. *"What is a half-breed doing in my cesspool?"*

"I told you, I am a Scout looking for Ramasis."

"What about Korvasi?"

"Who?"

"Why are you not looking for him?"

"Who is Korvasi?"

The old Terrakai rolled his eyes and fluttered his lips.

Sinto asked, *"Are you Korvasi?"*

"*Korvasi, KORVASI! Oh, my, I haven't heard that name in such a long time. Oh, how it tickles my mind! KORVASI!*" He threw his head back and cackled like an old woman. "*My, oh, my, how good that feels.*"

Sinto mused. The Terrakai stranger was seemingly harmless, but crazy. He asked again, "Are you Korvasi?"

"*Of course! Who else might I be? Who was once the alpha of the all waters in this fine basin, from the Rocky Mountains to the sea? I AM KORVASI.*" He cackled again. "*Am I Korvasi? Korvasi am I. Am I Kor-va-seee? Korvasi, KORVASI! Oh, my, I haven't heard that name in such a long time. Oh, how it tickles my mind! KORVASI!*" He threw his head back to cackle again, but stopped. "*Oh, my. Did I already say that?*"

Sinto nodded.

"*Oh, well then, scratch that. I digress. Just you wait, young one—the years steal the mind.*"

Korvasi composed himself with an attempt to smooth his wild hair that merely sprang back exactly as it was before, utterly crazy, like this conversation. Like the man himself. He puffed up his chest, then looked at Sinto, confused. "*Where were we?*"

"*You are Korvasi and I am looking for Ramasis.*"

"*Oh, yes. I see. I see. Ramasis. Hmm, what a fine man. Ramasis... And why is it you seek Ramasis?*"

"*He has gone missing.*"

"*Missing. Yes. Oh, my. Missing. That is bad, no?*"

"*Yes, potentially, but—*" Sinto grew dizzy from the swirling direction of the conversation. At this rate it would take a month to get a straight answer and Rachel would be long gone. Time was ticking. "Are you alone?"

"*Alone? Well, well, aren't you an observant one? For an eternity!*"

"*Do you have a home? A place where we could talk? Briefly?*"

"*Oh, I suppose. It's been a long time since I had a—a guest,*" Korvasi smacked his lips and eyed Sinto as if he would be a tasty snack. Then he cackled again.

Sinto wondered if he was underestimating Korvasi, that he might be dangerous and it would be best to flee. Physically, Sinto could easily overtake him, but what about his mind? Questionable reliability, but—it could be an act, or not, or maybe a trick.

Sinto debated. *Bowing to fear will not render the truth.*

Korvasi leaned forward until his nose touched Sinto's. "*Having doubts, young one?*" The sour taste swirled strong. "*I promise I won't eat you. I've already eaten my fill. For the day.*"

28

Delicate Negotiation

KORVASI SWAM NORTH AND into the shallow waters of a narrow channel where stone ruins spread in a circle across the bottom. An old village abandoned when the waters trapped by Hoover Dam rose and buried it long ago. Above the surface of the lake the sky was still dark and a smattering of brilliant stars twinkled.

Korvasi stopped beside a square pile of stones with silt piled up around the sides. Walls built to prop up a roof that rotted away long ago. He dove down where the roof had once been. Sinto followed, descending deeper than he expected and well below the lake's original bottom. Korvasi veered, disappearing through a curtain of thick vegetation. Sinto carefully parted the slick greenery and followed him inside.

Utter darkness descended when the grass curtain swung shut. Korvasi cast balls of amber light as they ventured deeper inside the meandering tunnel, descending ever deeper into the ground beneath the lake. Sinto was surprised how well Korvasi moved with grace and speed for one appearing so old and decrepit.

The tunnel came to an end at a modestly sized cave Korvasi must have carved beneath the lake bed. The Terrakai preferred to dwell out of sight whether on land or in the water. A type of shelter that made it possible to roam and settle temporarily among Sapiens on the Earth without discovery.

Rocks of varying sizes were set throughout the underwater cave. Vines with wilted greenery clung to the ceiling like cobwebs, and the putrid smell that swirled around Korvasi was stifling in the confined space. Everything was coated in a thick layer of green slime, like his teeth.

Sinto settled gently on his feet. He decided to keep his tail at the ready in case he found it necessary to flee. Korvasi gracefully darted about the room, flicking balls of light here and there, the sound of his raspy voice humming softly in Sinto's head. The wispy fins sprouting from his back swaying side-to-side like a goldfish, unlike Sinto's single fluked tail which moved up and down like a whale's.

Korvasi busied himself, wiping away a layer of algae from a flat knee-high rock. It clouded the water and coated his gnarled fingers, which he starting licking. He turned to Sinto and smiled. Green slime dripped from his teeth.

"A *tasty snack*," he said, and gestured for Sinto to sit, which Sinto did.

Then Korvasi pointed a crooked finger coated in the stuff toward Sinto's mouth. "*Would you like some?*"

"*No, but thank you. I've already eaten my fill. For the day.*"

Korvasi's smile fell. "*Huh, aren't you the funny one.*" He muttered, "*I caught that, stealing my words.*"

Sinto shrugged. "*Merely borrowed. They were good words.*"

Korvasi busied himself trying to select the best rock to sit on, finally settling on one directly across from Sinto. He straightened his spine as best as possible and laid his gnarled hands in his lap.

"*At least you admitted it, and you thanked me. Not like them. Sapiens! No respect. And the noise... noise, noise, noise. Water toys and airplanes! My sonar receptors stopped working years ago. It's why I dug this cave, to escape the noise.*" Sinto imagined the wiring in his brain got crossed sometime years ago too.

"*Why do you stay?*"

"*Got trapped by that dam in nineteen-thirty-five. I just never left, though I suppose I could have.*" His gaze wandered. "*I can't recall why I didn't.*" He scratched his head. The surrounding water clouded with bits of soggy dandruff. "*That's it! This is my home, that's why I stay, before that I bounced around the Colorado River. I was the alpha!*" Korvasi's eyes glowed brighter. "*Those were the days. Free to travel from the mountains to the sea! Water, sweet and pure!*" He cracked a grin. "*Had my pick of many females. Merahvu and the other kind too. I used to be handsome, like you.*" He cast his eyes to his withered lap. "*Now look at me.*"

"*Nineteen-thirty-five? That would have been a mere blip in your lifetime. What happened? Why are you so—*"

Korvasi made a face. "*Old?*" His eyes bulged and gaze clouded over. "*It all started once the lights came from the west. Sucuvita was scarce and more bad than good water flowed into the lake. I didn't pay much notice until it was too late. The other water creatures are changing too. You've probably noticed the life force in the lake is weak.*"

"*And tainted with pollutants. I can taste it in the water and in a bass I ate earlier.*"

"*Humph. I can't taste anything like before.*" He reached up and pulled a leaf from the ceiling, put it in his mouth and began to chew. "*Everything tastes bitter. Blah.*" He spit it out; half chewed greens floated between them. He waved them aside. "*So tell me, is Ianthe still the queen?*"

"*Yes.*"

"*Too bad she never visits us fresh-water folk.*"

"*Ramasis, her mate, should have come to see you last year, during his annual visits. That is if he knew you were here.*"

His brows shot up and eyes bugged. "*Oh, he knows, and he did.*" Korvasi leaned closer. "*I learned something about Ramasis, and very recently.*"

The foul taste of Korvasi's too-close presence made Sinto's stomach lurch. "*What did you learn?*"

Korvasi narrowed his eyes. "*So is that the only reason you're here?*"

"*Perhaps.*"

"*There were others looking for Ramasis.*"

"*Scouts?*"

"*They weren't polite like you. I sent them away. Are you really a Scout?*"

"*I—I—*"

"*I might know where you can find him.*"

Sinto grew impatient. "*Where? You must tell me!*"

Korvasi scowled and wrapped his arms across his chest. "*Humph! Just like the others. Demanding information without offering anything in return. Why should I help you?*"

"*I don't understand. Why wouldn't you?*"

He threw his head back and cackled, startling Sinto. "*Oh, young one, so pure and innocent and ignorant of the new ways.*"

"*What do you mean, new ways? We've always helped one another, unfailingly.*"

His lips parted in a snarl. "*Nothing comes for free.*"

Sinto realized he had been foolish to think he could venture into this world and expect whoever he met to be friendly and helpful. From what he witnessed in the cave on Merluma, and Korvasi's refusal to help on principle, he was naive and out of touch with reality by living deep in the Pacific and never wandering far from the protection of Inception on Merluma. The Scouts had warned Sinto not to trust Sapiens. He hadn't considered he might not be able to trust his own kind.

Korvasi leered at Sinto, his yellow eyes glowing brighter. Sinto could sense anger and frustration building inside the old Terrakai.

Sinto shifted on the rock, preparing to bolt if necessary. "*What do you want in return?*"

"What do I *want*?" Bewilderment filled Korvasi's eyes before rolling around in their sockets like a pair of rolling rocks. "What do I *want*? What do I want!"

Sinto sensed something unpleasant about the way Korvasi wrestled with the question. He believed Korvasi was not as dangerous as he was disgusting, and feared what he may want in return. Regardless of his unease, he remained planted on that rock, waiting for Korvasi to answer his question. Sinto wondered if he was as strong as Rachel. If he could do whatever it took to find his answer.

"Ah!" Korvasi's voice jolted Sinto from his troubled musing. "*What I want is to be free—to roam the rivers, swim the oceans, to go wherever I please... And I want a mate.*" He looked down at his gnarled fingers. He tried to straighten them, but they snapped back into useless lumps. "*What I want is to be like I was before; strong, handsome—a real man.*" He gazed at Sinto with sorrow in his golden eyes. "*That's another change that has happened to me, to the fish too. We've been robbed of our manhood. Whatever the Sapiens are dumping into this lake has changed our—We're all becoming females! Even if I found a mate, I wouldn't be able to—to—*" His face bunched up like a prune. "*Now look at me, crying like an old woman.*"

Sinto averted his eyes as Korvasi sobbed for several moments.

"*Do you have a mate?*" Korvasi asked after composing himself.

"No." Sinto lied, sort of. His chosen mate was a Sapien, who believed he was dead, and was now most likely in the arms of another.

"*A young man as perfect as you without a mate?*" He rolled his eyes. "*What is the world coming to?*"

"*Let's get back to Ramasis. What did you hear?*" Sinto was eager to get an answer and leave. Sunrise was fast approaching and Rachel would be waiting.

"*Well, well, you're not so polite after all. So pushy!*" Korvasi sat up taller. His face showed no sign of his earlier sorrow.

"*Please, I must go soon. I would be grateful if you would help me find Ramasis.*"

"Not without a price." Korvasi snapped. "*I told you what I want.*"

"*How can I grant your request? I can't change you back to what you once were.*"

"No, *but there is something you could offer.*"

Sinto's stomach twisted into a knot. "What would that be?"

"*I want to feel the essence of your youth, your innocence, your virtue...*"

To give Korvasi what he asked meant he would have to touch him.

"*And share with me your memories.*" His eyes filled with yearning. "*I want to remember what it was like to be young again.*"

Sinto shivered at the thought of Korvasi entering his mind. *If I did as he asked, would his foul stench be forever etched in my mind?* Sinto scowled at his selfishness. *I made a promise. I must do whatever it takes.*

What Korvasi requested was not unusual. Sharing memories and experiences was common practice among the Merahvu, especially in situations such as this, where it was agreed that a transfer of knowledge would benefit both parties. Mind-sharing was one of the ways the Merahvu commonly communicated and shared information, such as the type Korvasi requested.

But there were rules, and Sinto didn't know if the wily old Terrakai would follow them. A risk he would have to take.

"*Well? Do we have a deal?*" Korvasi asked.

"You know the rules?" Sinto said.

"*Of course.*" He nodded greedily.

"I choose the memories."

"*Of course, of course, you choose the memories.*" Korvasi impatiently reached out. "*Let's get started.*"

Sinto knelt before him. Korvasi reached out and placed his curled fingers on Sinto's shoulders and breathed a heavy sigh. He swept his fingers across Sinto's arms, rested them on his chest, one above his heart. Korvasi's aura pulsed yellow with anticipation.

"*So much pain you harbor and for someone so young...*"

"*The rules.*" Sinto reminded him.

"Yes, *rules, rules, rules.*" Korvasi must have cackled to himself, but some of it leaked out and echoed in Sinto's mind like an approaching nightmare.

Korvasi brushed his knuckles across Sinto's temples, uncurled his claw-like fingers and clamped down like a vice around his head. Fire ripped through Sinto's ears when Korvasi slipped his telepathic tentacles down the pathway of his ears and into his mind.

29

Spilled Secrets

SINTO PRESENTED HIS OFFERINGS to Korvasi like a market of vendors hocking psychological wares along a dark and winding boulevard. Mirrored doorways played brief snippets of memories from Sinto's past. A cacophony—of laughter, human voices, gurgling water, music, rustling leaves, crashing waves, and dolphins shrilling—blared from their doorways. Accompanying images flashed across their reflective surfaces, teasing and beckoning Korvasi to step inside.

Sinto displayed an endless choice of adventures in the sea: Playing with dolphins; migrating creatures that had slipped through the portals from Merluma to Earth back to Merluma where they belonged; the false sun and rainfall in Tallamure; riding a horned stallion across grassy plains; a night of exhilarating Ballorue; and other choice memories from his youthful past. None recent, none of Audrey, or of the presentation of the Mark binding them together. None that would reveal his true identity, or the fact he was Ramasis' son. Those he buried, locked in the recesses of his mind.

Korvasi stopped in front of one of Sinto's most cherished activities as a child and smiled. Ah yes, this was an experience the old Terrakai would never forget. Sinto opened the door and Korvasi stepped inside. The noisy boulevard of memories faded away and Sinto, with Korvasi as his passenger, tumbled into a turquoise sea...

~ ~ ~

A rush of adrenaline courses through his veins as he darts past one, then two dolphins, toward the one in the front, carrying the prize—a blade of sea grass. Determined, he gains on the lead dolphin. Sinto is faster, eyes focused on the prize, trailing from his opponent's mouth. Swimming side-by-side, the dolphin veers back and forth. Sinto anticipates every move, tails whipping in tandem at ferocious speed. Sinto slithers closer and presses his body against his foe. The tail end of the blade whips in front of his mouth. He bites. Peels away with the prize.

The dolphin squeals in defeat and the others take chase. His heart hammers from exertion and the thrill of outwitting the champion.

Sinto swims faster, tail pressed against his legs, pumping in tandem. His heart is ready to explode, but he doesn't stop. He accelerates to the surface, the pressure in his ears lessens, he's almost there...

Sinto bursts from the surface as the winner. Bright sunshine fills his eyes. He is a rocket aiming for the faint outline of the moon. At the top of his ascent he curls into a ball, flips and dives into the sea, the prized blade of grass tightly clamped between his teeth.

Dolphins nip at Sinto's toes. He darts and veers, up, down, back and forth, filling their minds with laughter. Faster they follow, bursting from the sea and diving back under, over and over, until the sea boils into a frothing stew of pink and orange bleeding from the setting sky...

~ ~ ~

Sinto closed the door, casting Korvasi into the dark void of his mind space.

Korvasi smiled with glee and gasped for air. "So *playful, and such beautiful creatures!*"

"*More memories like that?*"

Korvasi's smile faded and eyes burned hot. "Not *like that. Something more... revealing.*"

And that was when Sinto lost control.

Korvasi blasted past the marketplace facade Sinto had presented and delved deeper, slipping through gray matter to neuro-connections, criss-crossing his mind. He veered along the pathways, poking around Sinto's unfiltered thoughts—what he yearned for, what he hid in shame or embarrassment, his fears, his weaknesses.

Korvasi's claws dug deeper into Sinto's skull, rendering him physically and mentally helpless.

Sinto watched in horror as Korvasi peeled away the layers of camouflage and diversion to reveal his deepest secrets. But he didn't linger on any of the embarrassing ones or those where shame or guilt warped Sinto's sense of self. The raw and the intimate Korvasi had no interest in. He was looking for something much more specific: the thing Sinto desperately hid.

But Sinto failed and his mind cracked open, spilling secrets. The wily Terrakai was a master, capable of sussing out whatever it was he sought. Holographic images bobbled in a dizzying array in the weightless space of his mind's universe. Korvasi batted aside those of no interest until he found something that drew a curious smile. The face of Sinto's younger sister.

Korvasi chuckled. "*This one.*"

~ ~ ~

Sinto is in the throes of puberty, a day many years ago. Sinto's sister giggles. Her eyes spark. Violet-colored bolts of lightning strike Sinto in the chest. He flinches when pain bursts through his ribcage and his heart pauses for a beat.

"I said stop! Lesson's over! I told you before, you need to control your voltage." Sinto plops down in a chair in their shared living space, exhausted by her antics. He grabs a book from a shelf behind his head and pretends to read. "Enough for today. Go away. I want to be alone."

"Make me." She sticks out her tongue and shocks him again.

The book falls from his splayed fingers. His heart stops. His lungs fail to draw a breath. Unimaginable time passes, paralyzed. Then he gasps. His heart sputters, resumes a steady beat, then races. Hormones surge and anger ignites suddenly. He glares, hands fisted, and struggles to contain his urge to strike something.

"Naiada, are you trying to kill me? This is not a game! Do it again and I'm going to tell Father our secret."

Ramasis fills the doorway. "What secret?"

"Daddy!" Naiada swishes across the room and leaps into his arms. "Where have you been?"

"Show him your secret, Naiada."

Naiada fires a bolt of electricity from her eyes toward a pile of Sinto's collection of motorcycle magazines. They briefly catch fire before fizzling into a burst of smoke in the moist air filling Tallamure.

"That!" she exclaims.

"My child, when did you learn to do that?"

"Just now. Sinto taught me. It's so fun. Watch Sinto jump!" She fires bolts from both eyes, searing Sinto's toes, making him jump from his chair.

A wave of testosterone surges through his bloodstream. He yells, "Father, make her stop. She needs to practice more—on a non-living subject!" He unclenches his fists before reaching down and sorting through his favorite motorcycle magazine. It crumbles in his hands. Naiada and his father stare back surprised by his sudden display of anger. He blows out an exasperated breath. "Will you both, please, just leave me alone?"

"Yes, son," Ramasis gives Sinto a knowing smile, proud of his son, cresting puberty. "Come Naiada, let's get out for a breath of fresh water."

~ ~ ~

Korvasi jerked back, severing the connection to Sinto's mind. Sinto gasped. Pain ripped through his head from the sudden withdrawal of Korvasi's telepathic claws.

"You are Sinto! Ramasis is your father." Korvasi's eyes widened understanding. "Queen Ianthe's son!"

Sinto bowed in shame. Not because of who he was, but that his secret had been revealed. That he was alive.

"I see now why you are so desperate—not so dead are you, Sinto?" He lifted Sinto's face and gazed into his eyes. Korvasi no longer appeared as a helpless old man. While his physical appearance was deceiving, his mind was sharp and he was much more powerful than Sinto imagined. His eyes were fierce and wise and filled with the desire for more.

"I will help you, young Sinto, son of Queen Ianthe and Ramasis. What you want requires more. Another truth you so desperately hide, and I so desperately need to know why."

Korvasi's eyes lit up until the yellow turned blinding white.

Sinto screamed, "No!"

Korvasi leapt into Sinto's mind without warning, Korvasi's mind-claws slipped through his nostrils like razor blades. Unprepared for the sudden intrusion, Sinto's most damning memories littered his mind space, like swirling leaves ripped from a tree by a fierce wind. He grappled for the most damning, but Korvasi was quicker, blocking his path. Korvasi's physical limitations meant nothing; his skill to ferret out a secret rivaled that of even his mother's.

Sinto snagged his darkest secret and ran. Korvasi scurried after him, along with the sound of his cackle, the sting of his mind probe, and the smell of his rotting body. When he thought Korvasi wasn't looking he disguised it and hid it in a dark corner.

But Sinto's nightmare had just begun. When he turned, dread gripped his heart. Korvasi held his secret in his hand. It writhed like a small animal trapped in a burlap bag.

Sinto pushed a thought toward Korvasi: *"The day I stole my first book. Boring."*

Korvasi shook his head. *"I think not."*

"I've got something better..." Sinto reached out to grab it.

Korvasi hugged the memory to his chest. *"Don't lie. It's about* HER.*"* His eyes dropped to Sinto's right forearm. *"The one who has Marked you."* A smile curled on his lips and a raspy chuckle slipped through his stained teeth. *"For some reason you have not completed the Joining. I want to know why."*

Then they were both tumbling...

~ ~ ~

His stomach trembles from the warmth of her lips, kneading against his. He opens his eyes to see her face, unable to believe what has happened. She opens her eyes, melted pools of chocolate behind a curtain of dark lashes. He savors the feel of her in his arms, her bare breasts pressed against his chest, the freshly forged Mark burning in his arm. Desire races through his veins, his merlux fires, and a gentle wave of electricity ripples across his skin, not enough to shock but enough to make her tingle all over. She gasps, stopping the kiss. He does it again. She giggles and asks for more. He obliges, nuzzling her neck, planting kisses across the smooth skin below her ear...

~ ~ ~

Korvasi paused on the image of her throat where she had no gills—because she was a Sapien.

Crippling pain exploded in Sinto's head as Korvasi split his mind open. Every memory, every secret he held of her laid bare for Korvasi to rummage. Sinto felt ragged nails sifting through each one, stopping on one so painful, even Sinto tried to hide it from himself...

~ ~ ~

Coddled with the same Sapien woman in the cocoon of his lorica in the depths of the Salish Sea. Nearby her boat settles on the rocky bottom, its hull ripped open. Sinto's consciousness winks. He loses his grip and she breaks free, stretching the walls of his lorica dangerously thin.

"No!" He reaches for her.

"Don't touch me."

His chest throbs and guilt suffocates him. He can't breathe, can't move. The drug circulating in his bloodstream weakens his lorica. He clings to the hope the woman who Marked him will forgive him before it fails. He tried to explain, but she refuses to forgive him for kidnapping her friend.

Her words cut like a knife. "I don't trust you anymore..."

~ ~ ~

Korvasi pinned Sinto to the wall of his mind with his gnarled hands. *"What is so special about this Sapien woman?"*

"I don't know."

"Who is she? Tell me!"

Korvasi buried his claws deeper. Sinto's vision went blank.

"Culliford's daughter!"

"Ianthe's nemesis? The pirate Robert Culliford? And she Marked you?"

"Yes."

Korvasi eased back his grip. His gaze grew distant and he muttered, "What DOES this mean? What does THIS mean? What does this MEAN?"

Korvasi's face grew slack and he foraged deeper to a brief interaction between Sinto and his sister:

~ ~ ~

"The Mark chose you both for a reason. It's unwise not to accept it. You must see this through, Sinto. Find her, seize the Mark, seal the bond. Only then will your true purpose be revealed. A mutual purpose you both must fulfill, together. Otherwise..."

"Otherwise what?"

She didn't reply. By the way she looked at him, she shouldn't need to. The answer was of unfavorable consequence.

"But Mother decreed that it's forbidden... with a Sapien."

"What we were told is a lie. There is no reason for it to be forbidden. It happened before but was interrupted. There are some paths that never fork and must be followed as presented. Sometimes I wonder what other lies we have been told, and why."

~ ~ ~

Korvasi rattled about in the confines of Sinto's mind, pondering these new found truths.

"What lies, Ianthe, what lies do you harbor?" he muttered.

Korvasi dug not for a memory but something else. Sinto fought him; electricity coursed recklessly through his body, burning up his reserves. Korvasi seized the advantage and reversed the charge, turning Sinto into a battery, charging his own weakened body. Making him stronger and Sinto weaker.

He tore beyond the depths of Sinto's mind, to the inner thoughts and emotions that motivate one to act on good or evil. The thing that makes one who they are—essence.

Anger, grief, and a raging desire for Audrey wrapped around Sinto's heart like an invasive weed. Twisted within and burning just as fierce was Sinto's loyalty to his sister and his mother. Hope for Earth, Merluma, and all living things in both worlds. Contempt for Ramasis, who he so desperately sought to find. An internal war raging. A bomb prepared to explode.

When Korvasi withdrew from his mind, Sinto slithered to the floor having learned things about himself he wished he had not.

"What other lies did your mother tell you, Sinto? What other secrets does your sister harbor?"

"I can't."

"Tell me, or I will dig them out myself, and it won't be pleasant!"

Anger slithered and loyalty bit back but Sinto was too weak to fight Korvasi. He knew he had no choice but to tell Korvasi the truth, or else he might kill Sinto trying to dig it out.

"Long ago, my other sister, Leela, Joined with a Sapien. A crewman from Robert Culliford's ship. Ianthe panicked and severed their bond, killing Leela. Naiada told me she believes their Joining was meant to be. A symbolic sign of the future. Like a joining of Earth to Merluma, Sapien to Merahvu. To strike balance between our conjoined worlds.

"Ianthe acted for selfish reasons, not bothering to pause and question why. She did it to hide her affair with Robert Culliford. Ianthe believed if the truth came out she would be cast out, her bloodline destroyed, and the tentative state of peace her mother negotiated between the tribes would collapse.

"She lied to Ramasis. Told him Culliford's crew killed Leela. Ramasis lashed out and killed many of them. Then many years later Ramasis learned of Ianthe's affair and killed Culliford's wife for revenge. Culliford blames Ianthe for all of their deaths.

"Her lies fueled Culliford's rage and the Terrakai rebellion, and have poisoned my father's essence. Rebels attacked Culliford's ship. Culliford destroyed Tallamure. So many innocents killed and scattered over a never-ending circle of lies.

"Ianthe could have stopped all of it long ago. If only she had told the truth. She lied to all of us."

Korvasi reach down and brushed the hair from Sinto's eyes. "These secrets you hide, young one, have the potential to change everything set in motion."

"What has been set in motion?"

"That I cannot say. The future has not yet been written. Especially for you and your Sapien lover. This Mark, your Joining—the truth of it. It is not a myth. And I believe your shared purpose could have profound impact for all."

"Pity me," he mockingly spat.

"Oh, I do pity you, Sinto, son of Queen Ianthe and Ramasis, I truly do."

Korvasi helped Sinto up, perched him on the rock and tenderly cradled his hands. "I will now tell you what I know of Ramasis."

30

Me Alien

After Korvasi told Sinto about his father, he bolted from his lair like a bluefin tuna with a great white nipping at its tail. It was foolish to burn what little energy reserves he had left after Korvasi's thorough and humiliating interrogation. But it was all Sinto could do to escape the stench; not of Korvasi's own stink, but of the deception clinging to Sinto's essence.

Korvasi stole more than secrets. He stole pieces of his life and dignity. A steep price to pay for information regarding his father.

I hope it was worth it.

Sinto broke the surface, waded up to the shoreline, flushed lake water from his gills, and sucked a deep breath of air into his lungs. His foot fins slurped like long wet tongues and disappeared into the end of his toes. His tail was last to be tucked with a well-deserved slap to the back that knocked him to his knees. What he needed was a swift smack to the head for being so naive, so stupid. He was a fool to trust the old one, to trust himself.

Unworthy, weak, failure.

He collapsed to the ground, facing a pink, velvety sky, naked to the world, mind in tatters and guts ripped out. He closed his eyes and ground his teeth, continuing to berate himself.

A loud gasp brought him back to the present.

Rachel's shadow landed across his naked body. Her hands flew to her mouth. "Oh, my."

He clasped his hands over the fleshy sack protecting his manhood, but it was too late. She saw everything on full display: raised markings and his genital pouch.

Rachel crouched beside him. Uncertainty and curiosity crisscrossed her face. She reached out to brush his cheek. A spark leapt from his skin, shocking her.

"Ow!" She fell back, stunned to silence. It seemed forever before she rolled to her knees. She stared at him unblinking, the color drained from her face. She reached out again, this time, cautiously. "Sinto?"

He batted her hand away and rolled to his side, with his back facing her. "Leave me."

She brushed a lock of hair from his eyes. "What happened? Why are you—"

He snapped, "I said, leave me."

"No way! You dragged me into whatever it is you're up to and I'm not going away until ya tell me some things, like how ya shocked me and why there's a weird flap of skin hanging off your shoulder. And—and what's up with your—your thingy?" Her voice shook.

"I'm a freak."

"To be honest, I am beginning to agree. But you're a nice freak, so get up and talk to me." She pushed him gently in the shoulder. "Get up."

He rolled his head around and looked at her. She gave him a brave a smile. He gave one back, sat up, and scanned the desolate landscape of dirt, sand, and gravel that she called a "park." Thankfully it was still early, with no one else around. "Are you sure you want to know?"

She nodded. "But go real slow, I'm a little freaked out right now. Uh, maybe you should get some clothes on, case someone else sees you, and all."

He noticed his jacket and shoes and a paper bag sitting on the ground beside her.

"My jeans, over there." He pointed.

She fetched his jeans, came back, tossed him the paper bag. "Got you a t-shirt."

He pulled a T-shirt with something written on it out of the bag. It read: "Mom and Dad went to Las Vegas and lost my college savings. I got this lousy t-shirt instead of a degree."

She chuckled. "Had lots in your size. Must not be a popular one."

He tucked the loose tip of his fluke against his shoulder, put on the shirt, and stood up.

Rachel nodded toward his crotch. "I wasn't gonna say anything, but, damn! You're like a Ken doll, a bump—except a good-sized man-type bump—and those wild patterns, there and all across your ass, those are kinda cool."

He slipped on his jeans, zipped them up, and pulled on his black extra-large tennys.

Her face brightened and she snapped her fingers. "I got it! You're an alien from another planet!"

Sinto sighed. Not far from the truth. At least she wasn't running away.

"I knew it! The way ya acted the other night, and your eyes, they ain't normal."

He picked up his leather jacket, slung it across his arm.

"Ya know, I believe those stories where people are kidnapped and taken to a spaceship for experiments." Her eyes grew wide. "You aren't gonna do that to me are ya?"

Sinto shook his head, amused by her imagination. "I promise, no spaceship or experiments."

"You're not? Huh." Her shoulders drooped.

"*You* asked to come along, remember?"

"So which planet you from?"

"Yours," Sinto said. "I'm not an alien, I'm human like you."

"Then how do you explain—ya know." Her face bunched up when her eyes shot to his crotch again.

"Stop with the crotch thing! I'm human! I'm male! It's there, it's just tucked away in a fleshy sack. Where I live, it's like being from a different planet. Some things about me are physically different, that's all."

"Somebody's a little grumpy this morning."

"I had a bad night."

She opened her mouth.

He raised his hand. "Do not ask why."

"Okaaay. Should we set some rules then?"

Rules? He had had enough with rules. Rules meant nothing in this world.

"Ya know, what I can ask and what I can't."

Not again.

"You can ask me about anything but what happened last night." His head suddenly felt like it was floating in outer space and he was spinning. He reached out and grabbed hold of her shoulder. "Whoa, and not till I get something to eat."

She held him until the world stopped spinning. "Better?" She was smiling, a lot of sweet with dimples on the side. "I figured you'd be hungry, so I brought breakfast." She pointed to the picnic table with a couple of white cups and a brown paper bag sitting on top. "Come see."

She wrapped her arm around his waist, helped him over to the table and sat him down.

She shoved a tall cup toward him and pulled off the lid. Steam curled up to his nose. It smelled of burnt cucuo nuts. He must have made a peculiar face because she laughed.

"Never had coffee before, am I right?" He nodded. "Coffee's an acquired taste. Best to try it with generous amounts of cream and sugar the first time." She tore open two packets of sugar, poured them in. Added three tiny containers of cream she pulled from the bag. Gave it a generous stir with a thin wooden stick.

He took a sip. It was bitter and sweet at the same time. He took another sip and savored the warmth filling his stomach. Rachel shoved a gooey roll in front of him. It was rolled up like a nautilus shell, golden brown, and smelled of cinnamon and sugar.

"That's a cinnamon roll. Try it with the coffee."

He took a bite and a sip. Then another, and before he could lick his fingers it was gone. Rachel handed him another one. They ate and sipped in silence. Sinto felt human again.

"Where on earth don't they serve coffee?"

"The sea." He gulped down the rest of his coffee, sucking the syrupy remains of sugar that had sunk to the bottom.

She gasped. "You live in the sea? Well, no wonder you've never had coffee. You'd have a heck of a time keeping the salt water out. Wait a minute, are you trying to tell me you're some kind of a sea creature—like a *mermaid*, er, mer*man*?"

"So I have been called, but no. I am a human, not a fish."

"I'm not sure that explains everything, but—*wooow*." She said it slow, her mouth forming a big round "O".

"Are you going to finish that?" He pointed to her coffee.

"Uh—you can have the rest." She pushed the cup in his direction.

"Speaking of being different..." He reached out and touched a lock of hair flipping up from the nape of her neck. "What did you do to your hair?"

"Just noticed, huh?" She flashed her dimples. "I took out those phony hair extensions and got it cut. I used to wear it short all the time." She raised her hands. "Lost the gaudy nails too." She shook her head and wriggled her fingers. "I like the way it feels, light and free. Next to go are these." She stuck out her chest.

"So you are not going back."

"Honey, you're stuck with me."

"Don't you have a place you call home, family, friends?"

"Once, before Hurricane Katrina. Dad lost his job and we moved to Texas and after that all Mom and Dad did was fight. Mom got cancer and Dad married someone else and moved to Alaska. Mom died broken and alone. I'm an only child, no sibs, no reason to stay. After, I ran away, never got further than Las Vegas. I met some other girls like me who introduced me to my boss. He set me up with a place to stay and a job and treated me nice enough. Made good money. Figured I wouldn't be any better off anywhere else. Then I met you and when you said Vegas made people go crazy I realized you were right. I was crazy to think I was happy, so here I am."

He felt dizzy trying to keep up with what her life had been like, up till now, so succinctly recited in less than sixty seconds.

He sighed. "Meeting me might be the biggest mistake of your life."

"Sinto, you just *saved* me from the biggest mistake in my life." She shoved the empty cups and dirty napkins into the brown paper bag. "So now that we got that business out of the way, where are we goin'?"

"North, to the City of Green."

"Never heard of it. Where's that?"

"Lake Superior."

31

Old Wives Tale

PITCH-ROLL-SHUDDER WENT THE NIGHT. Audrey wondered if she was reliving a nightmare. Same ship, same restless night, same wicked sea. The nausea was back and her neck was slick with sweat. She reached up. The seasickness patch she had stuck behind her ear was gone and the seasickness bands she wore did nothing to help. For someone who loved the sea, she wasn't cut out to be a sailor.

She was hit with a fresh wave of nausea. Sweaty and hot, she kicked off her covers. The cabin was cool and she shivered. It felt like fighting a fever. Hot. Cold. Hot. Cold, and—her mouth filled with saliva.

I'm going to throw up!

She blindly reached under her bunk in the dark for a trash can. The ship did another roll-dip-buck. The trash can *clanged* against the dresser on the other side of the cabin.

I can make it, she thought, hopping to her feet.

It was pitch black and she felt a sudden memory lapse.

Was the head to the left or the right? Then she remembered. *Opposite from last time.*

She patted the ceiling for the handrail, found it, and pulled herself along hand over hand to the left. Her foot struck something hard and metallic. It smashed into the far bulkhead with a loud *clang*. The trash can, hopelessly out of reach.

The ship rolled and she grasped the handrail with both hands, whipping to and fro until it settled. She hurriedly picked up the pace the rest of the way to the head door. She slapped around in the dark until she found the knob. Swallowing down what desperately fought to come up.

She slipped inside. A soft light lit the floor from beneath the cabinet. She braced a knee against the bulkhead and hurled into the toilet until nothing came up but air. She shut the lid and sat. She looked at herself in the mirror. A frightful sight; puffy eyes and lips glistening with vomit. She stood and wedged herself against the counter. She clipped her braid atop her head, splashed cold water on her face and neck, and flushed her mouth with lots of water and a glob of toothpaste.

A splash of water helped, but her stomach still roiled like an out-of-balance washing machine.

She turned to flush the toilet. The ship pitched; she lost her balance and slammed into the adjoining cabin door. It flew open and she fell to her knees. Light spilled to the bunk where Blake lay.

He stirred. "Audrey?"

Audrey crawled across the floor, spun, and sat with her back wedged against the side of his bunk, afraid if she stood the vomiting would start up again. A sudden flurry of waves tossed the ship. She gripped the edge of Blake's bunk to stay upright. "I'm seasick," she rasped.

Blake turned on the bedside light, then reached out and brushed a sweat-soaked strand of hair away from her neck. "Where's your patch?"

"Lost it, lucky me."

He reached down, placed his hand on her stomach, and began rubbing it in gentle circles. She sat like that, him rubbing, her trying to regulate her breath.

She felt her body relax and stomach settle. "That's nice."

Five minutes passed and she began to feel human again.

"I saw my dad tonight."

Blake's hand slowed, then resumed.

"It was weird. I mean, it's like he's not the same, but he is. I mean—he's like he was before Mom died."

"That's good."

"But what if he reverts? What if something triggers him? What if that something is *me*?"

"You don't know that."

"I don't know anything at this point except I'm not sure I can forgive him."

"Maybe you don't have to. Maybe the sands of time will erase the reason you feel you must."

She swiveled around to see his face. His hand stopped rubbing her stomach. "That sounds like something Dr. Wickman would say."

He chuckled. "Then I think he would agree. Time is weird. Sometimes it feels like it gets stuck, but only for you. The world marches on and leaves you behind to wrestle with your demons. I hope that won't be what happens to you."

"Deep. You come up with that?"

"Just a thought."

She found his still hand. "Please don't stop, the rubbing helps."

He started rubbing her belly again. His hand was warm in the cool cabin air. All she wore was a tank top and a pair of boxers. She shivered. He stopped rubbing.

"You're freezing."

"It's okay. I'd rather feel cold then nauseated."

He pulled back his covers; he was wearing nothing but a pair of black fitted boxers. Her eyes cut to his bare chest, then to the door leading back to her own bunk. A month ago she would not have hesitated.

"Um, I should go back." She started to stand, but he held her back.

"I have an idea." He jumped up, passed through the head to her cabin, came back with the comforter from her bunk. She was amazed at how gracefully he adjusted his movements to absorb every jolt of the ship.

He crawled under his covers, then laid her comforter on top. He pulled up one side.

"But what if I—"

"Got a bucket right here," he said, pulling a bucket out from under the bunk.

Audrey shivered. "It is a little cold."

"I'll keep my hands to myself otherwise," he said, sensing her apprehension.

"Okay." She laid down next to him. He swaddled her, then pulled her back against his chest. He slipped his hand under her covers and began to rub her belly in slow even circles.

"Where did you learn to do this?"

"Old wives' tale."

"Hmm. Old wives, good advice." They lay like that for a while until her eyes fluttered shut and glorious sleep consumed her.

When Audrey opened her eyes, gray light bled through the porthole. She was in the exact same position with her back wedged up against Blake. But sometime during the night he had rolled over, pressing his back to hers. She guessed Blake was still asleep from the sound of his breathing.

The ship was heeled hard to starboard, pitching and bucking over consistent mountainous swells. Still lively, but less chaotic than the night before. She felt better than she did during the night. At least her stomach was able to keep up, and she had managed to sleep with Blake's help, soothing her stomach with his gentle circular rubbing.

He rolled over with a loud sigh. His arm snaked inside her covers, wound around her waist, and cupped her breast. His hand kneaded a couple times and settled with her breast cradled in his hand, still asleep.

She slowly pulled his hand from her breast, but like a slap-stick comedy it sprung right back as if attached by a stretchy spring. Then it slipped from her breast and threaded its way to the top of her boxers. She heard his breathing quicken, and his fingers slipped under the band. She froze. He was still clearly asleep and unaware of what his fingers were reaching for.

"Blake," she whispered. "Wake up, wake up!"

He snorted and his hand slipped lower.

Audrey reached back, shook him. "Blake, wake up!"

"Huh?" His eyes opened to narrow slits, half asleep yet alive with an internal flame coming to life. Recognition sparked. "Audrey," he said with a sloppy grin. "I was just dreaming about you."

Audrey's eyes darted to where his hand protruded from her boxers.

"Oh," he said, pulling his hand back. "Sorry, I—" He gave her a lazy grin. "Uh, I guess that's not something friends do."

His eyes brightened, then he suddenly sat up with the comforter balled in his lap. "I think it best if you go back to your cabin."

Audrey gave him a knowing smile, fully aware of what he was hiding under the covers. She hopped up. "All good. Nothing happened that either of us would regret. Thanks for helping me last night."

Then she leaned over and kissed him on the forehead. "Catch you at breakfast, *friend.*"

32

Twice-Shattered Vow

RACHEL PUNCHED DULUTH, MINNESOTA, into her phone's mapping GPS. Being late November she fretted about the drive, especially through the mountains in Colorado and the colder states up north. She said her sporty Nissan 370Z could chew up the miles on the open freeway, but if they hit ice or snow, well, they would be grounded till the spring melt. "Two-wheel rear-drive is a bitch in the snow," she said. "And I haven't figured out how to work the clutch in slippery conditions, so all bets are off."

Sinto secretly hoped they would see snow. He had seen it only twice. Recently, when he ascended the ridge to Deep Lake and discovered the breeding cave, and a few years back when he had accompanied his father on a visit to the City of Green. It had been winter, and the lake was frozen. Sinto tagged along with his distant cousin, Arkis, and Arkis' friends for a late-night escapade on the surface. They had cut through the thick ice from underneath and leapt to the surface with a flick of their tails. Under the full moon they ran and slid on their bellies, skated on their feet, and pummeled each other with snowballs until the sun rose. Sinto had laughed so hard his stomach hurt for a week.

Rachel's GPS map estimated it was just over twenty-seven hours to drive to Duluth. A couple of long days including a short stop overnight, or longer if they hit snow. Rachel pressed down on the gas pedal when they entered the wide-open terrain of the San Rafael Desert.

"Keep your eyes peeled for cops."

Not familiar with the term "cop," Sinto wasn't sure what it was his eyes were supposed to peel for.

"Law enforcement," she clarified, "they don't like it when you go faster than the speed limit." A sign whipped by indicating the speed limit was seventy-five. He peeked at the speedometer; it said ninety-five. Rachel laughed. "Don't worry, one of my boyfriends taught me how to drive the right way after he gave me this car."

"Nice gift."

"I was good at what I did." Rachel frowned. "And they weren't really boyfriends."

Sinto could tell she was ashamed of her past occupation by the bluish tint of her aura. They rode in silence. Sinto watched desert scruff whip by.

"What's so important about this City of Green we're goin' to?"

"I'm going to the City of Green, not you."

"Why not?" she asked.

"It could be dangerous for someone like you."

"What, they don't like girls with shady pasts?"

"It has nothing to do with the fact you were a—a—"

"A whore?"

"It's because you're Sapien."

She grew strangely quiet. "Maybe this would be a good time to tell me what the heck you are and where you came from."

Sinto contemplated. She asked for something he was forbidden to reveal, but he had already inadvertently revealed enough to justify her question. He decided to give her just enough to placate her curiosity, at least that was his hope. "As I told you before, I'm human like you, with a few differences."

She glanced at his crotch, then shifted her gaze to his glowing eyes. "Go on."

"As I said, I'm human, but we call ourselves Merahvu. We've roamed your world for centuries, fiercely guarding the secret of who we are, how we came to be different from you—from Sapiens. A vow each and every one of us made, for the protection of our people. There's not much more I can tell you."

She huffed and rolled her eyes. "You think you're the only ones to have secrets? Don't the Mer-ah—whatever—understand the concept of trust?"

"Of course we do."

She held up her hand, hooked her little finger. "Give me your pinky."

Sinto was confused, but held up his small finger. She hooked it with hers and squeezed tight.

"I swear on my life I will not repeat what you're about to tell me, so help me God."

Sinto stared at their twined fingers.

"So, there you go, I gave you the pinky swear. You've got my word, Sinto, y'all can trust me with your secret. Besides, I'm going all kinds of crazy over here, dreamin' up some pretty wild reasons you are the way you are."

Rachel was asking Sinto to break a vow. One that had become so ingrained from birth that he didn't ever imagine breaking it. But he had once already, with Audrey, and that was with permission from his mother. *And that time on the beach in Oahu...*

Sinto knew Rachel well enough now that she wouldn't relent until he told her everything. *Pinky swear*, he thought chuckling to himself, a way to bond trust and not much different than the dares he and his sister, Naiada, would share whenever they divulged secrets with each other. She too was relentless when it came to ferreting out Sinto's secrets.

Sinto was dead to everyone, except Rachel—wouldn't that include his vow too? So Sinto shattered his vow, for the second time. The words spilled out like one of the many Sapiens' history books he had read, sticking to facts articulated in the simplest of language. He described how Earth splintered forty-two thousand years ago, resulting in the birth of Merluma; of early Homo-Sapiens slipping through cracks between the sister worlds; of the geographic upheaval on Merluma that covered the entire surface with water, except for a tiny island of land; of the death and suffering that followed; of how time on Merluma spins dramatically faster than on Earth, and because of that, how the few surviving Homo-Sapiens adapted so quickly to their changed environment; of how they diverged into three distinct tribes, constantly at war over limited resources.

He described how he can communicate with other Merahvu and creatures of the land or sea, telepathically, by a means called mind-speak, or *sharing*; that he can breathe underwater and cut pathways through the sea for high-speed travel; that his feet were big to accommodate his retractable fins; that he can hide his tail against his back and his fluke across his shoulders; that he was born without body hair or nipples. And because of her curious interest about his genital pouch, he explained that both males and females had protective flaps of skin covering their genitals, to protect against the cold as well as curious underwater creatures that tend to latch onto sensitive places, but other than that, the Merahvu reproduced the same as Sapiens. And finally he revealed his deepest secret: his ability to shock, like an electric eel. It was what lit his eyes and, when carefully controlled, he could use it to trick Sapien machines, like those in the casinos, and if pressed, he could easily shock another human or animal to stun. Or kill.

He stopped to take a breath, hoping she wouldn't halt the car and kick him out in the middle of nowhere after revealing that last secret. But she didn't. She wanted more. "Tell me about the tribes."

He described each, how they differ; that he was of dual-tribe, which was not unthinkable, but uncommon. He told of the Forever War that lasted thousands of years on Merluma, until their numbers dropped to near extinction. At which point the war ended and the three tribes were united as one people, the Merahvu, governed by a Circle of tribal representatives and a soothsaying queen.

"A soothsaying queen?" Rachel exclaimed. "You mean... she can predict the future?"

"Not exactly, but she can make fairly accurate guesses."

"Huh. Have you ever met her?"

Sinto gazed out the window at the wind-swept clouds. "The queen is my mother."

Rachel shot him a high-browed look. "Huh. Does that mean *you* can predict the future?"

"No!"

"But you're a prince?"

He laughed. "It means I'm busy. She always has some important task I must complete. We have no concept of royalty, so me being a *prince* is meaningless, but my sister..." He gazed down at his fingers. "Well, she's slated to be the next queen—that is, if there's still a united Merahvu to govern.

Then he turned to the dark part of his story and the tangled history between Audrey's father, Robert Culliford, and his mother, and of his father learning of their affair. Sinto's innocent role in the death of Audrey's mother and the guilt that still plagued him today; that he confessed to her murder to protect his mother from disgrace. He described the trial before the Circle, their verdict that handed Sinto over to Culliford; how Culliford intended to kill him, and how Audrey tried to stop him. And during the scuffle, how Culliford tricked her, making her an accomplice in his murder, against her will. Sinto would have died if his mentor hadn't healed him in secrecy. And how afterward his mentor suggested Sinto remain dead, to change his identity, and not trust anyone: a necessity for Sinto to learn the truth about his father's disappearance.

He wanted to leave his story at that, but Rachel still wasn't satisfied.

"You still haven't told me much about this Audrey."

Sinto closed his eyes. The Mark had taken notice when Rachel mentioned Audrey's name. He took a moment to quell the fire sparking in his arm, then started at the beginning. "We met when were young: nine, ten years old. I didn't know at the time what my father was up to, how he used me to distract the girl on the beach so he could plot how to kill her mother. Over the course of a month we became friends. Then one day, I saw her—Audrey's mother—tangled in a fishnet snagged on the reef. I—I tried to save her, but was too late. My father pulled me away. He was angry at me, but I didn't know why. It wasn't until much later that I realized he had set up her death to look like an accident. I messed it up and we had to flee. That's a secret I kept buried for years.

"I never saw Audrey again until recently, when my mother sent me on a mission, to find Audrey with the intent to settle the differences between her and Culliford. Being with Audrey again... it was as if time hadn't passed."

Then he told her about his mishaps after bringing her to Merluma; his fear she wouldn't remember him; how determined she was to escape, which she did, and the chase that ensued and ended after Audrey was attacked by a bluestripe tiger; of saving her life and the terror that filled him that he might lose her; how he realized he loved her from the day they first met as children. He described his shock when Audrey Marked him, and the joy and terror that followed.

"I can't explain how or why she was able to Mark me but I've come to believe the seed was planted long ago when we first met." He held out his arm and pressed Rachel's fingers on the hardened flesh buried in his forearm. "It lives here, as it does within her. The Mark represents an irrevocable bond of body and spirit, of our shared purpose yet to be revealed—the swirl, my world; the circle, hers. The line connects them."

The sun dipped on the horizon behind them. Hours had passed and Sinto's head thrummed. From spilling his guts to a woman he barely knew. From reliving his most recent past. From sitting in one position for so long.

Once he finished Rachel said nothing, staring at the dashed lines whipping by in the center of the road with glazed eyes. He squirmed in the tight confines of his seat, shifting his weight from one numb butt cheek to the other. His eyes burned from the dryness of the Earth world whipping by, from forgetting to blink. He wondered if he had made a mistake telling Rachel everything: of the dangers he faced, inching closer with each mile zipping by.

He secretly vowed not to get Rachel tangled up in his upside-down world. "I met someone in the lake last night and I learned of some bad things. Once we get to Lake Superior—I just need you to drop me off and—"

"And what?" She turned and glared, then set her gaze back on the road.

They sat in silence for a long time. Rachel tried to hide a tear that slid down her cheek. Sinto massaged his temples.

She turned off at an exit advertising a rest stop. "My eyeballs are floatin'." She whipped around a curve, pulled into a marked spot, and stopped rather abruptly.

She shut down the engine, glared out the front window. "You do have to pee like the rest of us, right?" Her voice was tight and sharp. She hopped out of the car and slammed the door before he could answer, stymied by the sudden chill cast between them.

33

Heart-Shaped Token

SINTO LEANED AGAINST THE driver's side door waiting for Rachel. When she saw him, she pulled her sunglasses over her eyes and reached for the door handle. He blocked her way. "What did I say?"

"It's not you."

Sinto pulled the glasses away from her eyes. They were red from crying. "You're upset."

"It's just…" She sniffed, wiped her nose with the back of her hand. "I thought we agreed to trust each other. Please, don't be like the others. Don't give me the boot!"

He looked down at his feet. "What boot?"

She rolled her eyes. "Not the ones you wear on your feet. I mean, don't you give me 'the boot,' as in dump, ditch, strand, you know, *abandon* me."

Sinto gave her a sad smile, recalling the time Audrey accused him of ditching her on the beach on Merluma. It was after he directed the orcas to attack her boat and he took her to Merluma. Sinto had sent Moonstone to watch over her while he fetched his leather coverings. But she woke in a panic, and his bird companion scared her, and the snowball of Sinto's mishaps began, ending with

Audrey nearly losing her life. An eternity ago. Sinto could relate. Being abandoned made his guts knot.

"I didn't say I was abandoning you. I'm merely worried about your safety. Where I'm going—it might be dangerous."

She frowned. "I was hoping for an adventure."

Sinto reached out and touched her cheek. "After all of this, I promise I will take you on an adventure. I can show you places that will blow your mind. Just not there."

"Tell me I'm not makin' a mistake, takin' this trip with you."

"I can't promise you that. I might be making a mistake."

She huffed and stared back.

"I would understand if *you* gave me the boot, but I need your help. Get me to Lake Superior. After that..." he shrugged.

"Then what?" she said.

"The answer to your question is complicated." He ran his fingers through his hair. "I won't let you get involved."

"Afraid I'm already involved with everthin' you told me. Pinky swear, remember?" She wagged her little finger. "Look, all I want is to be your friend. Been a long time since I had a friend like you."

"Me too."

She cracked a one-dimple smile. "We make quite the team don't we, the merman and the whore."

"I am not a merman and you are not a whore. We're friends watching out for each other. If I tell you it's dangerous then I expect you to give me your trust and do as I say. I would only do so to protect you. Do you understand?"

She studied his face, then nodded.

It was getting dark fast. An overhead light flickered then engaged, lighting the parking lot. A beam of light glinted off a heart-shaped locket hanging around Rachel's neck. He hadn't noticed it before. She wasn't wearing it the night they met and must have slipped it on after they left Las Vegas.

"Can I see that?" he asked.

"Sure," Rachel released the gold clasp and handed it over. "It was Momma's. Dad gave it to her when they got married. She said it would probably mean more to me than it did to her, gave it to me right before she died."

Sinto rolled the necklace over in his hand; it was a simple gold chain with a heart-shaped locket. He popped it open. Inside was a picture of a man and woman. Rachel inherited her dimples from her mom. "They seem happy."

"Once. Damn hurricane ruined everthin'."

Sinto yanked some hair from his head, glanced behind his shoulder to make sure no one was watching, and snapped his fingers. A ball the size of a marble filled with green threads of electricity hovered above his fingertip. He fed his hair into the ball; it sucked it inside, twisting the strands into a tight dark knot. He tapped the ball several times until it was the size of a small seed. He tucked it behind the picture then snapped the locket shut.

"I'm not even gonna ask what you just did, probably wouldn't understand anyway. I never was any good at science."

He smiled. "Then think of it as magic." He placed the locket around her neck and secured the clasp.

"It feels hot, no cold, no—both," she exclaimed. "Magic!"

"Now you have a part of me with you, a token of myself. I will be able to find you as long as you are wearing it. If you need me, think of me, call to me. Say the words in your mind."

A tear leaked from the corner of her eye. "Like a silent prayer?"

"Something like that."

She grinned. "Thank you, friend."

"Anytime Rachel."

"Okay, that bein' settled and all," she tossed him the keys, "I'm tired of drivin'. Lesson time. Know anything about a clutch?"

PART TWO

34

Flow, Swift, Fierce

DAY TWO ON THE high seas. The ship was still lively but Audrey was feeling much better. Stokes told her sometimes nothing works to quell the seasickness bug except time; once the inner ears catch up to the motion, you can take anything the sea will throw at you and feel fine. She vaguely remembered this from before but kept her seasickness bands on just in case.

The thing about being at sea is time. Lots of it. Traveling the sea from point A to point B was slow. Even in a fast-sailing ship with wings, flying along at what felt like mach speed for ocean travel. Given other circumstances she would embrace it. But with lives potentially at stake and a mysterious orange fungus to investigate, she, along with everyone on the ship, was a little on edge and anxious.

Audrey, Blake, and Ryan reviewed all the systems and equipment in the lab with Dr. Wickman. Drag nets and containers for capturing bits of plastic and other sea life were ready to deploy once they reached the gyre where the missing ships were last reported. A specific plan of how to handle a potentially destructive organism had been defined and distributed to the crew.

That left eating, sleeping, reading, games, movies, doing one's daily chores, annoying those doing their own chores, or getting a sweat on in the gym as remaining options to fill the time.

Audrey easily finished her chores after breakfast, which included keeping her workspace tidy and keeping Leonard's sea-life fed and the tanks clean. Tasks that occupied a small part of the day which meant she was antsy and restless and plenty bored.

Time to sweat.

She pulled on leggings and a tank top and padded barefoot to the gym. Along the way she ran into Ryan and Blake. They had been hanging with Tucker, the ship's tech guru, in his bat cave tucked beneath the bridge.

Audrey had worked with Tucker to find Sinto's underwater city the last time they went to sea. The bat cave doubled as Tucker's cabin and workspace. His bunk was wedged between racks of computers and other strange bits of technology. To say he lived and breathed his job was an understatement. He had modified sonobuoy technology used by the Navy for decades: shrunk it down, lightened it up for drone deployment, expanded its range, and adapted it to listen for Merahvu tunneling through the sea. He was the reason her father was able to track Sinto back to Tallamure at the bottom of the North Pacific. She wouldn't be surprised if Tucker had been responsible for designing the bombs that were used to blow it up. She was certain he was the one to guide the submersibles on their kamikaze mission, and may have been the one to push the buttons that detonated the bombs. She tried not to think about that. He was doing what he was asked. Destroy the enemy. What was done was done.

Because of her father and his original crew's past experiences with the Merahvu, Tucker along with every other Larkian believed they were an evil enemy and extremely dangerous. It was true the Merahvu could be extremely dangerous, but Audrey didn't share the assessment that they were all enemies. She believed the Merahvu could prove to be valuable allies in the fight to restore

Earth's oceans and much more, something she'd hoped to dedicate her life to one day.

Audrey couldn't blame Tucker for what happened, nor anyone else in the crew. They had been misinformed and misguided. She hoped to change that, and soon.

Tucker wasn't your typical tech geek. He was a total badass and had the scars and the hat to prove it. A prized black hat that spelled it out in bold white letters: BADASS. Anyone could challenge the current owner for it, who of course was Tucker. No one had successfully won it back from him, though many had tried. The challenge was civilized and straightforward; three rounds on the mat, supervised, which was usually done by the ship's captain. Stokes, in this case. But everyone knew that to challenge Tucker meant trying to live long enough to reach the third round. Like everything on the ship, the crew voted on who they felt performed best. That was *if* you made it to the end of the third round.

Audrey teetered on sea legs, counteracting the motion of the ship. Damn, she wanted that hat, more than she wanted to set her feet on quiet ground.

"He show you all the cameras?" she asked Ryan.

"What cameras?"

She laughed. "My point exactly. Watch out for that one—he's sneaky and seems to know everything." She tugged on Ryan's shirt. "Heading to the gym. Change and join me."

Ryan looked at Blake. Blake shrugged. "Why not?"

Ryan looked worried. "As long as you promise not to hurt me."

"Naw, come on, it'll be fun. Got to burn off all those calories. Leonard's cooking sneaks up on your waistline." She patted her belly. "Got some to burn off myself."

Ryan looked unsure. Blake looked like he had enjoyed checking out that extra padding the night before.

Audrey entered the gym, a large open space with a gimbaled floor covered with mats. The mats were firm enough for balancing but cushioned enough to lessen the impact of a smack down. The gimbaled part was necessary. A sailing ship was usually heeled either to port or starboard, depending on the direction of the wind. And because the crew were required to stay in top condition and battle-ready form, a space where they could safely train was required. The gym floor was the only space on the ship that was gimbaled. A floating floor that equalized and remained level no matter the heel of the ship. There was still some movement, but it was muted by where the gym was located, mid-ship. In times of extreme seas, the floor was locked in place and the gym closed. Today wasn't one of those days.

Audrey stepped onto the gimbaled floor. There were no weight machines or stationary bikes or treadmills. Her father didn't believe in them, said they were a crutch. The real work lies in one's own body. Throw in some tools to heft and swing, or ropes to climb, and you'll find muscles you never knew existed. His crew trained like true warriors of the past.

She recognized the various tools from the training center her father built in Seattle. Secured in custom slots along the walls were practice staffs, clubbells, steel maces, and kettlebells. Pull-up bars were mounted to the wall. Rings were bolted to the ceiling, pulled aside with line and cleated to the wall. A couple of punching bags swung with the ship's motion. An angled rock-climbing wall was molded into the far corner.

She wasn't the only one who felt like sweating. A couple of guys were practicing take-downs and other defensive moves, while another swung a twenty-pound mace with the ease and grace of a Viking warrior.

Audrey selected a patch of mat in the far corner where she wouldn't get in anyone's way. She worked every joint from head to toe and ripped out a few yoga salutations to warm up. It felt good to move after being hunched over with a tender belly.

She hadn't pre-planned her workout and just started to flow, linking body-weight and animal-flow movements together. She dropped down on tucked toes, arms stretched forward, and surged forward on hands and toes, with her knees hovering a couple of inches above the floor. She bounced back and forth like that a couple of times, like a cat ready to pounce.

She surged forward, kicking one foot forward and punching her opposite elbow—*bam*. She hopped back and repeated it on the other side, imagining fending off an attack forward and back—*bam-bam!* Then she kicked to the side, low to the ground, ankle height of an imaginary opponent—*bam!* She curled her other leg under her hips and kicked the opposite direction, as if punching a hole in an imaginary wall with the heel of her flexed foot—*strike!* She planted her hands over her outstretched leg, rose up, head down, hands to floor, and kicked one leg up and over, pointing her toe as if a scorpion readying its stinger. She held the pose for a beat before rolling over and landing lightly on her stinger foot—*sting!* She whipped her opposite leg up and over—*sting!* She linked these movements together, flowing without hesitation.

Bam! Strike! Sting!

Sweat poured from her temples and she switched it up. Loaded on hands and toes she threaded a leg under and flipped over, belly up, propped on feet and hands. She flowed these moves together into a fast series of linked switches—belly up, belly down—in a blur of switching hands and feet, rolling her way across the mat one direction, then reversing her way back. When she got dizzy she crept along the floor like a crab, belly up, raising opposite foot and hand, stopping every third step to arch back into a full bridge, belly to the sky. Then she'd move in the opposite direction.

Roll, creep, arch up...

Tiring of crabbing about, she squatted low and mimicked an ape shuffling sideways, keeping her body low to the ground, landing softly and gracefully on her hands and feet. She planted her hands between bent knees and hopped forward, and once she reached the edge of the mat, she rolled backwards over her shoulder, switching sides with each roll until she had traversed the entire length of mat. Back and forth she hopped and rolled until her heart pounded and she needed to catch her breath.

She was just warming up and dropped to the floor for more. She combined these moves and others that felt prime at that particular moment: Kick, roll, arch, hop—performed with the grace of a ballerina—on and on she went, flowing from one movement to another. She tuned out everything—the others in the gym, worrying thoughts about the mission, the rumble of the ship—and flowed. A meditation of movement and breath and surging blood. It was a challenge, timing each move with the gentle motion of the gimbaled floor, but that too became part of her mind and body connection, adjusting each move to the sway; hanging in air, landing swiftly on her feet, then striking with precise force.

Flow as water, swift as wind, fierce as fire...

She repeated this mantra and didn't stop until her shoulders fatigued, wrists screamed, and legs ached. She rolled to her feet and stood, chugging breath, heart pounding and sweat dripping. She reeled her mind back to the gym and the present moment.

She had drawn a crowd. The clock on the wall said more than twenty minutes had passed. But to her it felt like time had stopped.

Blake whistled. "Nice!"

The guys she saw earlier had gathered to watch and were clapping their approval along with some others who must have come in while she was locked in her flow state of mind.

"No way am I doing that," Ryan said. "What are you, made of rubber?"

Audrey smiled. She had avoided doing anything like this when she was around her friends. Mainly because it had been forced upon her by her father as part of her training. Moving to Friday Harbor and doing nothing of this sort was one way to rebel against her father.

"Just warming up," she lied, as every muscle in her body quivered. It had been too long since she practiced those moves and knew she would pay the price in the morning.

Ryan rolled his eyes and looked around. "Isn't there a weight bench or stationary bike somewhere?"

"Unnecessary. Your body is all you need. Moving it right will get your heart pumping aplenty."

She came up with a simple list of movements that would work him over and have him screaming at her in the morning. She was glad she brought her phone and pulled up a timer app. "We'll start you off with an easy Tabata. Five movements, six rounds each for thirty seconds with a fifteen-second rest in between."

Ryan laughed nervously. "I can do anything for thirty seconds."

Blake said, "Sure, me too."

"We start with practice rounds." She clapped her hands. "Boys, show me your squat."

35

Orientation

Day three on the high seas. Audrey rolled out of bed with a groan. Every muscle screamed as she padded to the head. She splashed cold water on her face and attempted to brush her hair—a challenging process, untangling knots that tied themselves while she slept.

Her hair was in desperate need of a trim; dried jagged ends reached below her ribcage. She rolled her eyes and began braiding it. When would she ever have time for a haircut? Maybe she should shave her head and fully embrace being one of the guys.

That thought quickly evaporated when she heard a gentle knock on the other head door. She swung it open. Blake gazed back wearing tight-fitting black boxers and a tank top. Typical crew sleeping attire. Normally he wore something with color: his sweater, a shirt, or chinos. But he looked good in black, mysterious. Almost like a different person.

"Morning," he said with a yawn.

She smiled back and grabbed her toothbrush. "Almost done."

"No rush." He swayed to the pitching motion of the ship, hands braced against the door frame, watching her brush her teeth while chasing the sleep from his eyes.

He reached up, grabbed the top of the door frame and stretched. Exposing his flat stomach and line of short dark hair rising from his boxers to his belly button. "Man, I feel good, thanks for the workout."

She spit, rinsed her mouth and toothbrush. "Not so sure Ryan will feel the same. I thought he was going to lie on the mat the rest of the day afterwards. Had some choice words and I don't recall any of them including 'thanks.'"

He chuckled. "He needed it. I've been trying to get him out for a while. Glad I'm not you this morning."

"All yours. Don't be late." She slipped out and shut the door behind her so both could have privacy. She slipped on a pair of black pants and opened the middle drawer of her dresser. Neatly folded was an official uniform: long-sleeved fitted shirt made from anti-sweat, breathable fabric. A white Larkian logo was embroidered where it would lay across her left pec. She pulled it on, sat on her bunk, and put on a pair of socks and black leather tennis shoes.

She stood, ready to go.

Her heart began to pound. Stokes and Alvarez had asked her to present to the entire crew everything she knew about the orange substance she had witnessed. They also wanted her to relay all she had learned about the Merahvu from Sinto and from what she observed while in Tallamure during her initial visit. She had no experience talking in front of people, but Stokes assured her she had nothing to worry about. She wasn't so sure after their impromptu game of hot potato the first time she was the center of their focus.

She stepped into the hall, tapped on Ryan's door. "Hey, you awake?"

No response.

His door was unlocked. She opened it. His bunk was made and head door open. No Ryan.

She checked her watch. Five minutes till breakfast. Maybe he found a closet to crawl into and die. She had to go. Ryan was on his own. She shoved off from his door frame, closed the door.

She scurried down the corridor and raced up the mid-ship stairway to level three, her thighs screaming in revolt. She cursed herself for overdoing it in the gym the day before.

Alvarez had already claimed a table near the windows on the far side of the cafeteria. The ship was heeled to starboard as it had been most of the trip. Keeping things put was a matter of safety. The tables and chairs were bolted to the floor. Between the tables were floor-to-ceiling bronze poles for navigating across the open space in rough seas. She pulled her way over to Alvarez's table, the muscles in her shoulders tender.

She sat across from Alvarez. His laptop sat on the table in front of him, lid closed. His round glasses were smudged with fingerprints. He sat with his arms crossed, regarding her, then slipped her a rare smile.

His teeth were yellowed like aged ivory and ground short by years of use. Obviously original. Not bad for a very old guy. He must have flossed or used a pick to clean them everyday. She recently learned her father had titanium implants, not just caps as she thought. He lost his teeth to rot long ago. Now they were perfectly straight and white thanks to twenty-first century technology. Sucuvita may extend the life of cells, but teeth were something entirely different.

"Taking a break?" she asked.

"I do once and awhile. Leonard's put out the morning's spread. You might want to grab a bite before the others arrive."

She wasn't hungry but knew she needed to feed her aching muscles. She wandered over to a long serving counter that opened into the galley. Leonard was busy loading up warming trays with steaming piles of scrambled eggs with creamy herbed cheese folded in, plus a pan of fried ham.

"Aren't ya a sight for sore eyes! Ready for yer big speech?"

She drew a jittery breath. "Not really."

"Just imagine they're naked and you'll do fine."

She winced. "That might be a little too distracting."

"Imagine them all dressed as clowns then."

She laughed. "Now that's a little closer to the truth."

He scooped some eggs and dropped a slab of ham onto a plate and handed it to her. "You've nothin' to fear. Fill yer gut. That'll give ya something to help calm yer nerves." He winked at her, spun on his heel, and barked an order to his sous chef, busily cutting up melons.

She wandered back to Alvarez's table. Stokes had slipped in while she was talking to Leonard and was sitting next to Alvarez. She set down her plate and carefully sat on her sore glutes.

She picked up a fork. "So is there anything I *shouldn't* say?" She lowered her voice, looked at Alvarez. "Like how old you'll be on your next birthday?"

Alvarez fixed her with a beady-eyed gaze and leaned forward. "Do *you* know how old I'll be on my next birthday?"

"No..."

"Then there will be no reason to say anything."

She looked at Stokes. "Do they know—you know?"

"Know what?" Alvarez said.

She scoffed. "What is this game we're playing?"

"No game. We tell them what they need to know. So far there has been no need for them to know how old I really am, nor your father, or anyone else from the original crew. When it becomes necessary, then we'll tell them. That's what we call 'need to know'. It's a strategy, not a game." He sat back.

She took a bite of creamy eggs. "I'll try not to let it slip out." As if she didn't have enough to be nervous about, now she had to guard every word.

The cafeteria filled up quickly, black-clad Larkians lining up for their morning grub. Ryan was one of the last to wander in, Blake by his side. His hair was wet and he was moving slow, like every movement took a great deal of effort. But his eyes were bright and he was quick to strike up conversation with the guys in line—even Dyer who playfully flirted with him that first day. That made her smile.

When her father entered with Dr. Wickman there was a noticeable shift in the crew's demeanor. One of great reverence for the man they still considered their captain, even though he was too infirm to command the bridge. He stopped and chatted with a couple of guys. Simple interactions including a hand shake, good-to-see-you's, and looking-forward-to-working-with-you-on-the-bridge type of encouragements.

Her father and Dr. Wickman filled the remaining two seats at Audrey's table.

Her father greeted her with a nod and a smile. While he was making progress with regaining his past memories, physically he had aged noticeably. His hair was shot with more silver radiating from his temples. The wrinkles around his eyes were more deeply etched and his cheeks sagged more than usual. He also wasn't very talkative. Dr. Wickman said that was to be expected. Lots of processing going on in his head.

She smiled back and gave his hand a squeeze. "Morning, Dad."

"I heard rumors you put on quite a show in the gym," he said.

She rolled her eyes. "Ah, just keeping everything limber."

He smiled. It took him a moment to find his words. "More than that from what I heard. I'm proud to have you as my daughter."

Forward progress. Daughter not wife. His memories were finally sticking.

Audrey ate, listening to the idle chatter exploding around her and the rattle of dishes from the ship's motion, trying to keep her mind off the fact that soon it would be quiet and she would be the one commanding the entire crew's attention.

Dishes were cleared and mugs refreshed.

The time had come. First up, Stokes.

He stood and wedged himself against a pole. "Hope everyone is feeling well and ready for our next mission."

There was a rousing reply of ayes and finger salutes between the clanking of dishes coming from the galley.

"Two vessels are presumed missing in the North Pacific Gyre. Ships working in tandem to sweep up plastic on the surface. They first reported there was very little to collect, which is unusual for that location. Their last report mentioned an orange slime coating what little bits of plastic they were able to sift from the water. We believe it might be a type of water-borne fungus. They also reported that crew members who came into contact with it developed a rash and began acting agitated and restless. They wisely isolated the crew. Neither ship has been heard from since.

"We intercepted and buried their transmissions. We are the only ship going to investigate. Alvarez has ensured no other search and rescue has been launched. For good reason. It's possible this orange fungus is rising up from the ocean floor. The reason we know about it is because of the Merahvu."

A sudden shift of bodies and quiet whispers rippled throughout the cafeteria.

"This may be a simple in-and-out rescue mission, which we've done many times before. Or," he paused for deep breath, "we may discover a new and incredibly harmful substance that is quickly spreading through the North Pacific.

"Regardless, we'll proceed with caution under the assumption that what we may find is dangerous and the reason we've lost contact with these ships. Procedures have been put in place to ensure full containment should anyone or any part of the ship come in contact with this substance. They've been sent to each of your phones. I expect you to confirm you've read them shortly after this meeting.

"I've asked Culliford." He looked to Audrey. "*Audrey* Culliford..." Every eye swung in her direction. "To share with us everything she knows. I don't think I need to rattle off her credentials on why she is our resident expert on the Merahvu, but I expect you to give her your full attention and respect." He turned to her. "Audrey?"

She stood up. The ship lurched; so did the eggs in her belly. She grabbed the nearest pole with a sweaty palm, pulled her body against it. She felt heat rise in her cheeks and was thankful for her dark coloring, hoping no one would notice. She looked up at a sea of curious faces. Faces she recalled from their last mission, young and old, dark and light, intense and seemingly calm. Faces of men who were recruited from all walks of life—mostly from the dark side—and from many different countries. All spoke English and would understand every word she had to say, if only she could find them.

Her mind went momentarily blank and she wondered if she could go through with it. The room filled with silence and pulsed with every pound of her wildly beating heart. Even the ship seemed to still, waiting for her to say something.

She opened her mouth. "Hi, um, can you hear me okay?" She was pretty sure she squeaked out the words, but to her, her voice sounded like a lion roaring in her head.

"Speak louder," someone shouted from the back of the room.

She cleared the frog from her throat, tried again. "How about now?"

Nods all around.

"Er, I'm not used to—to talking in front of a crowd this big so I apologize in advance. If I stumble a bit, um, I'm sure many of you would be happy enough to toss me around the room like a hot potato till I get my wits adjusted and my station among you properly equalized."

Smiles and chuckles rippled throughout.

"You were one hot potato," someone shouted.

"*Our* hot potato," another shouted.

The ice was broken. She smiled, surprised at how easily they responded, and for the unexpected way she wrangled their respect. She drew a satisfying breath and stood a bit taller. She finally found the words she wanted to say.

"I want you to abandon every belief you may have about the Merahvu. They are not fish, nor are they innately evil. The Merahvu are descendants from early versions of Homo-Sapien, like you and I, but they come from a world spawned from ours, tens of thousands of years ago. A world much more hostile and water-based than ours.

"Because of this, their bodies and methods of communication have evolved in ways different than our own. It's how they're able to live underwater as well as on land. Many have lived peacefully in our oceans and even roamed our cities without the general populous being aware. They're human just like us. And like us, most are good, but some are evil and find no guilt in harming others, for sport or for power."

She looked directly at her father, whose face was as emotionless as a stone. "I am aware of past conflicts. They were horrible and regrettable. We have all been victims. My mother was murdered, and this crew are two fewer because of them. But the Merahvu were attacked and scattered when their city was destroyed. By us."

She locked eyes with Tucker. He was wearing his badass hat, staring her down with a white-hot gaze.

"Nobody should blame anyone for what has happened. I blame no one for what happened. I understand how some of you might be feeling right now and consider the Merahvu as our enemy. I was manipulated and used by one I befriended, and trusted."

She pointed at Blake. "My friend Blake was kidnapped and imprisoned for weeks. They're capable and guilty of the same sins as anyone, because they're human. It's ingrained into our nature. And because they're like us, they can be our enemy, or they can become a resourceful and powerful ally."

She paused to let the words sink in before getting to the real reason she was standing before them. "My—" Her throat caught. "My friend, Sinto, who is now deceased, showed me an orange fungus growing at the bottom of the Pacific. It stretched as far as I could see, latching onto and consuming pieces of plastic that sank to the bottom under the weight of organic matter growing on their surfaces. It stripped away all but the plastic and consumed it, quickly and purposefully. During the short time I witnessed this strange phenomenon, the fungus spread, noticeably. Sinto called it 'Orange'

"Orange is heating the ocean and smothering whatever organic matter gets in its way, including innocent sea life. The size of the reef, it was... stunning, and its impact severe. The Merahvu discovered it less than a year ago."

She paused, not sure if there was much else she wanted to add. She looked over at the table where her father sat with his original crew and Captain Stokes. At least she didn't bring up their tumultuous past with Ianthe. "I think I pretty much covered everything you need to know."

Dyer's hand shot up. "How do they differ from us?" He wagged his brows. "I hear you got real up close and personal with your friend."

There were plenty of murmurs and Audrey wondered how many of them were privy to the recordings Tucker's little cameras had captured of Audrey and Sinto on the beach on Andrews Island when she tried to seduce him into coming to her boat so she could drug and kidnap him. A time that felt like eons ago.

She channeled that possibility proudly and meandered through the tables, gripping the poles. "I can tell you they are deadly. They can shock you like an electric eel, to stun or kill." She tapped Dyer on the forehead. "They can permeate your mind and uncover whatever secrets you wish to hide. Plant an idea you might think your own. Suppress a memory and make you forget something important. I know, because it happened to me."

She paused and let that sink in.

"They possess vast knowledge of the natural world. They can reanimate damaged flesh. They communicate with, and master, creatures in the sea and on the land." She wove her way to Tucker's table. She tipped back the brim of his badass hat, and gazed into his pale blue eyes. "They can burrow tunnels—vortexes—in the sea and fly at unfathomable speeds within them, quiet as a mouse, guided by geomagnetic and sonar receptors as well as their vast knowledge of what lies beneath the surface. I know, because I experienced it, first hand."

She meandered around the tables, locking eyes with everyone she passed. "They can seamlessly blend into the environment by camouflaging their skin, their hair, their eyes. A dynamic trick of color and texturing. A thick layer of insulation lies beneath their skin, providing built-in thermal protection against hot or cold environments. They have no need for clothing and feel at ease in their naked form. When naked they can be invisible. I know, because I've seen this."

She closed her eyes, remembering the day Sinto took her to the House of Healing, where the sick and weak fought for their lives and Healers were unable to save them. Remembered watching a young boy die. "When they die their body rapidly disintegrates until all that is left is ash." She raised her hand, opened her fingers. "Poof—then they're gone. That's why we've never discovered any trace of their existence. I know, because I've seen them die, smelled the vestiges of their death—musty and metallic."

She ended her meandering through the cafeteria at Dyer. She leaned over and gazed into his eyes. "So, yes, Dyer, I got real 'up close and personal' with my friend, and everything he showed me."

The cafeteria grew eerily quiet. She turned toward her father. His eyes were particularly glacial. Maybe she imagined it but he appeared to be breathing a little harder than normal. She probably should have bit her tongue but the words slipped out before she could stop them.

"And I am very sad that he is dead."

36

Unicorn Devil

SINTO AND RACHEL ARRIVED in Duluth mid-day, after deciding to drive through the night. Rachel suggested getting a hotel room along the Lakewalk near the Duluth North Pier Lighthouse. She planned to wait while Sinto dove to the bottom of Lake Superior to find out if the price he paid for Korvasi's information about his father was worth it.

As Rachel called it, "weather weirdness" had hit the region early, with a stubborn deep freeze that refused to budge and a recent storm that had buried the city with a foot of snow. There was a flurry of activity as snowplows scraped the streets, and Sapiens shoveled sidewalks and braved the cold to hunt down provisions before the next round of heavy snow, expected the next day.

Rachel took over the driving once the first flakes started to fall. While Sinto managed to get used to the clutch—which perplexed him at first, being the opposite of a motorcycle when it came to what you did with your hand versus your foot—she was not at all confident of his driving ability in the snow. She had expressed her reservations about driving in the snow earlier but persevered, knowing Sinto's sense of urgency to reach Lake Superior. She managed better than she predicted about driving a clutch in the snow. Though she said it might be a good idea if Sinto didn't watch. He took it as a sign to get some rest while she slid her way into Duluth. She blew a sigh of relief once they were safely parked in a hotel parking lot.

The lake had frozen hard over a week ago. While that would not be a problem for Sinto, it meant he may attract attention blasting his way through the ice before diving in. They decided he should wait until dark before descending the depths to the City of Green.

But before he dove to the bottom of Lake Superior, he needed a favor.

Rachel held a section of Sinto's hair pinched between her fingers, a pair of sharp pointy scissors in hand. "Momma taught me how to cut hair. When she got sick, she wanted it short before it all fell out." She sighed. "Honey, you sure about this?"

Rachel stood behind Sinto. He sat in a chair she had dragged from the desk in their hotel room into the stark-white bathroom. A white bath towel lay across his bare shoulders. He gazed at their reflection in a mirror as wide as the bathroom was deep, then shifted to a picture on her phone that she had found on the Internet; a famous movie star Sinto had never heard of. His golden streaked bangs were swept back and the rest of his hair was short and clear of his ears.

"It's all the rage," Rachel said.

He wasn't sure what raging had to do with it, but agreed it would work for his intended purpose: to change his look and sport a hairstyle more attuned to a Scout who frequently roamed the Sapien world.

He looked at her reflection in the mirror. "Do it."

Snip.

A wavy lock of Sinto's golden hair, laced with dark copper streaks, floated to the tile floor.

Snip. Snip. Snip.

It did not take long for the pile to grow. After cutting most of his hair off, and styling the top, she grabbed a mechanical device she called a buzzer. She attacked the side of his head with speed and confidence, pulling his ears back from the sharp vibrating blades. She tipped his head forward and cut crisp sharp lines along the sides of his neck into a pointed V at the top of his spine.

When she finished, Sinto ran his hands through the longer layer on top, and felt the bristly ends along the side. His hair looked much darker than before, glistening with more copper than gold, which would help his disguise. His head tingled from the sudden access to air.

Rachel dug in her bag and pulled out a small spray bottle filled with clear liquid. She sprayed some of it into her hand. It smelled like flowers mixed with sticky chemicals.

"The great thing about this haircut is the different ways you can style it." She rubbed her hands together and combed his bangs back like the movie star in the picture. "Or you can do this…" She picked and fluffed and fussed, drawing the layered strands up and forward and into a messy point sticking out from his forehead.

"Put on your sunglasses."

He did.

"You don't look like you anymore; still handsome, but different."

"Good."

"Do that trick."

"What trick?"

"Where you color it."

He colored what hair remained on his head pitch black with the pointy part in the front red.

She laughed. "You look like a unicorn devil!"

He laughed. "They're real, what you call unicorns, on Merluma."

"No kidding!"

The lighthearted mood grew somber. Cut short, the color of Sinto's hair was darker. A reverse from before and a trend that began once he reached adulthood, with more and more dark coppery-bronze strands emerging amongst the gold. He was becoming more Terrakai as the years passed by. He completed the effect, darkening his skin to a warm bronze glow. While the green color of his eyes were inherited from his father, they were rare for a Terrakai so he switched his eyes to a deep amber to deepen his disguise. He stood, shaking off bits of hair clinging to his neck. He felt like a different man.

Rachel stepped back. "You definitely don't look like you anymore."

She was right; he looked like a full-blooded Terrakai. The almond-shaped, upward-slanting eyes and angular facial structure were like his father's. What he couldn't change was his tail, but that was easily solvable. The Scouts he had known kept their tails tucked—an enduring habit—pretty much most of the time.

He had practiced locking his camouflaged disguise into place and controlling it while they traveled in the car. It felt automatic now, requiring little concentration, like walking and breathing. He was confident it wouldn't slip even in the most dire circumstances. Though he hoped he wouldn't need to put that confidence to the test.

And with his new hairstyle, he was as ready as he could possibly be.

The sun had set. He stole a peek from behind the light-blocking curtain covering the window with a view of the lake. The North Pier was vacant of human life.

Sinto said, "Time to go."

37

Cold Farewell

A FRIGID WIND BLEW from the north. Sinto and Rachel stood in the dark of early evening at the end of the Duluth North Pier huddled around a glowing ball of electrical fire lying at their feet. The lighthouse towered above them. The lake spread out below from the edge of the pier, frozen and windswept and disappearing into the darkness.

Sinto took off his shirt and shoes. Even with the high-density layer of insulation beneath his skin, he felt the brutal cold.

"Don't worry about me." Rachel's teeth chattered in fits and starts. "I'll go sh—shopping or somethin', read Reese's current pick, check out the spa at the hotel, practice drivin' in the snow." Snuggled into his oversized leather jacket, she looked like a child afraid to be left alone for the first time. A trickle of snot ran from her nose. He wiped it away with his finger.

"I might be gone several days, maybe longer," he said.

"I'll wait. I have nowhere else to go. Besides, it's a nice hotel and I got lots of money. Thanks to you." She forced a smile and pulled his leather coat tighter around her shoulders. "Now skedaddle, you got stuff to do and I'm fr—freezing."

He slipped off his jeans.

"Make la—la—lots of new friends."

He cradled her hands, gave them a squeeze. "Remember the locket. You get in trouble, call for me. I will return..." *If I can*, he almost added, but thought best not to say it.

He handed her his things. She hugged the wad of clothes and his giant shoes to her chest. She sniffed. "I hate goodbyes."

"I'm beginning to hate them too."

He picked up the ball of light and placed it in the palm of Rachel's free hand. "To help light your way. It should last long enough for you to get back." He leaned over and kissed her on the top of the head. "Take care and don't wander off too far."

Her mouth wadded up when she nodded.

He stepped to the edge of the pier, facing the lake naked. Rachel gasped when his tail peeled away from his back and the fluke flopped on the icy dock. He had told her about it, but seeing it; that was a different thing and garnered the same reaction of shock and awe as he got when he showed Sapiens on Oahu what he was.

He flicked his wrist and a thread-thin bolt of lightning shot from his fingertips. It exploded on the frozen surface of the lake. A low rumbling sound came from below and the ice suddenly cracked with a resounding *pop*. A web of cracks radiated from where the bolt had struck. He fired a second, more powerful bolt. A geyser of steam erupted and rained down. The steam cleared and revealed a hole big enough for Sinto to dive into.

"Good lu—" Rachel's voice was abruptly cut off when his head hit the water.

A thick gelatinous layer of lorica bled from pores in his skin until he was completely encased by its protective cocoon. Oxygen siphoned from the water filled his protective shell and he sucked a deep breath of dense, moist oxywater. It felt strange after spending so much time on land, breathing light dry air.

Life force from the water permeated the protective layer and gave his reserves a jolt. He swam beyond the shoreline and into the deeper waters and sank to the bottom to recharge. He needed to top off his reserves before approaching the city. Especially after pondering the tenor in Korvasi's voice when he asked, *When was the last time you visited the City of Green?* That was right before Sinto bolted from his lair.

Sinto never answered his question and regretted not staying long enough to inquire why Korvasi would ask him that, especially in the way he had.

Sinto decided to keep watch while he rested. He closed one eye and left the other open, along with the small part of his brain that sensed movement, sound, and heat. While he was familiar with these waters, he knew there were potential dangers. Lampreys occupied the lake and were merciless creatures and dangerous in large numbers.

Soon, the sound of his heartbeat surrounded by dead silence lulled him into a deep restorative slumber.

38

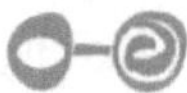

Challenge

DAY FOUR ON THE high seas. Early in the morning Audrey sneaked into the gym before breakfast. She needed a good stretch and a light workout to flush the ache from her muscles.

She was hanging a ten-pound mace on the wall when Tucker sneaked up behind her like a ninja. She startled, believing she had the gym to herself. He must have slipped in while she was distracted. He was wearing his badass hat and gym shorts, and nothing else except a towel slung around his neck.

When she turned to face him, he poked her hard in the chest with the tip of his index finger. "I 'ear a Sheila wants my hat and being that you're the only Sheila on the ship that must mean you."

"I was thinking about it." Though she didn't recall saying it to anyone. "Who told you?"

He ignored her question. "No Sheila ever gets to wear my hat."

"What a shame."

"All the Sheila's I know are smart enough to know better."

Her face burned. "Oh yeah? One never challenged you for it?"

He yanked the ends of the towel hanging around his neck. "What was that business yesterday about regretin' blowing up fish city? You're the one who found it." When he didn't like something she noticed he poured his Australian accent on real thick. It suddenly became thick as Vegemite.

"That's true, I did help find it. But I meant what I said. Being the genius you are, I would think you of all people would be able to put the past behind. Intrigued by what you could learn from the Merahvu, if given the chance. That is, if you can accept that they're intelligent human beings, like you and me."

"Hmm."

She poked him in the chest with her index finger. "You trying to change the subject?"

"Right, the hat." He studied her for a beat. Ran a finger down the scar running along the side of his face. Ear to mouth. "Could be fun takin' a tumble with you on the mat." The scar distorted his upper lip when he smiled.

She smiled back. "Could be." Her heart pounded. What was she thinking? This guy was confident and was the best fighter on the ship. But, damn, she wanted that hat. It was times like these that being determined and stubborn equated to being stupid.

"Who trained you?" he asked.

"My dad."

"Hmm." He scrunched up his mouth, ran his tongue across his teeth. Made a loud sucking sound when he pulled it away. "Suppose we do it."

"Yeah?"

"Weapons?"

"Hand to hand."

His eyes narrowed. "Hmm."

"Three rounds, three minutes each. Supervised. That's how it's done, right?"

"And 'ow do we know who wins?"

"Crew votes, right? Usual training etiquette applies. Someone taps out, you stop, start going again." She smiled. "Remember we're on the same team. Injure your opponent, you lose. Injuring them will you get penalized. What that penalty might be, the Council determines."

"Who supervises?"

"Captain decides who and when."

"Hmm."

"Well?"

"You've done yer homework."

"I know how to sniff around."

He studied her. It was impossible to get a read from his eyes, pale and always calculating. Then he nodded, held out a fist.

She punched it. "Game on."

"I'll talk to Stokes. Set it up."

39

Braided Advice

LATER THAT DAY, THINGS started coming together. Stokes estimated they would be arriving at the last known location of the missing ships within twenty-four hours.

Every crew member had been required to review the operating procedures Dr. Wickman outlined for handling samples they hoped to collect. Stokes worked with the ship's engineers and mechanics to identify the ship's vulnerabilities. Procedures for how to protect and isolate the crew and ship systems should an outbreak occur were defined and distributed. Afterward, everyone was tested, and everyone passed. No one was taking any chances. Sailors were superstitious, the crew on this ship no exception. No one wanted to end up in the fabled Davy Jones Locker.

Audrey was impressed by the professionalism and thoroughness of the crew. From Stokes down to the guy who kept the cargo bay spotless and equipment tuned and ready to go. The last time she was on the ship she was distracted by the revelation of the Mark, fear for Blake's safety, mental preparation for a deadly dive, and the imminent standoff between her father and Ianthe. She didn't have the bandwidth to observe the detailed workings of the ship.

Being a part of the crew meant she shared in the responsibility to act for the protection of the crew and the ship by whatever means necessary. There were forty-four souls aboard, including the senior crew and her friends, Blake and Ryan. The total number of crew were broken down into four teams in case of emergency situations. Working within organized and cohesive units was what saved most of the crew when the *Requiem Sea* was attacked by Terrakai rebels and destroyed when Tallamure imploded.

Basic procedures were reviewed by each team; distribution of weapons and protective gear, communications, who did what, who backed up whom, the process for abandoning ship, and basic first aid. Most importantly, they reviewed what to do if the command structure and everything else fell apart—the dreaded fucked-up-beyond-all-recognition FUBAR situation—where the best strategy was to rely on independent problem solving; do all you could to protect your team and live to greet another day.

Audrey, Blake, and Ryan were each assigned to a different team. Stokes, Alvarez, and Dr. Wickman were team leaders. Because her father was still recovering, Leonard took over the fourth team. Audrey was with Alvarez, Ryan with Stokes, Blake with Leonard, and her father with Dr. Wickman. The three of them were outfitted with spare rubber suits and dive equipment in case entering the water was necessary. Who got what weapon was a bit of a stumbling block since no one wanted to end up a victim of friendly fire, but in the end Ryan and Blake proved they were quite proficient at escaping and hiding with nothing but their wits and fists. Audrey knew that on the very slight chance they were attacked by Merahvu, their rubber suits might be their best defense against electric shock.

She tried not to think about that possibility and certainly didn't raise the issue with Ryan or Blake except to tell them to save themselves and hide *if* it came to that. She reminded them their greatest concern was a plastic-consuming fungus running amok on the ship and fouling the electronics.

Ryan and Audrey were stowing their dragging gear in the cargo bay when Stokes came looking for her.

"Are you sure you want to challenge Tucker?"

She made a face. "I might have been feeling a little more confident this morning."

"You don't have to do this."

She nibbled a lip, pondering.

"Yeah, she does." Ryan said. "Once she gets an idea in her head, nothing will stop her. A character asset and a curse. She's got it in spades."

"I estimate we'll be arriving late tomorrow afternoon. If this is going to happen, it's got to be before dinner, today. You up for that?"

Blake walked up with the last of the gear from the lab. "Up for what?"

"The big face-off. Culliford vs. Tucker." Ryan said.

"Hmm."

Audrey's face felt hot. "That's what Tucker said, a lot of 'hmms' and quote, 'No Sheila ever gets to wear my hat,' end quote."

"Oh, boy, here we go." Ryan said. "Gasoline on fire. I'm off to place bets."

She turned to Stokes. "I'll be there. Tell me when."

"Gym, sixteen-thirty hours."

Blake waited with Audrey as Ryan and Stokes left.

"My bet's on you. But."

"But what?"

"You've got to tame this." He lifted the braid lying across her shoulder. "I bet he'll go for this right off. Spin you around like a ball on a chain."

"I suppose I could bun it on top." She rolled it up and knotted it on top her head.

He flipped the over-sized bun back and forth. "Too floppy."

She sighed.

"Or," he smiled, "braid it tight to your head."

"Right," she rolled her eyes, "I only know how to do the one I've got."

"I'll do it for you. Not much different than origami."

"Can you make it look badass?"

"I'll try. Come on."

They wound their way back to Audrey's cabin and she dug out every hair band she brought. Six total. Blake ran across to the lab and came back with a dozen Sharpee pens.

"What are those for?"

"The master never gives away his secrets."

She sat sideways on her bunk, with Blake sitting behind her. He undid her single braid and brushed her hair. He raised up on his knees to get above her and separated her hair into two sections with a rat-tail comb. Each section started at the side of her forehead and spanned across the top of her head to the opposite side, ending at the top of her neck. He secured each with a hair band. Then he pulled the rest of her hair into four sections. One started from the origin at her forehead along the same side, straight back, over her ear. He secured it. He repeated that for three more sections, paralleling the previous section. He secured those.

He started braiding the first section crossing over from the front of her head. His fingers deftly picked up small but equal sections of new hair with each wrap. Audrey felt her scalp tighten as he worked his way across her skull, a wrap followed by a firm tug. Every few inches he inserted a Sharpee pen and looped the braid around it.

"Interested in some advice?" he asked.

She clasped her hands in her lap. They'd been shaking ever since making the challenge. She would take any advice at this point. "Sure."

"From watching him spar with some of the other guys, I bet he's going to come at you rigid and aggressive. Guys fight like that, all testosterone. He'll expect you to do the same. Remember he's been training with *guys* on this ship. Plus, I noticed he tends to use the same moves; good ones, but he's consistent."

"Consistent at winning too."

"Guys like that tend to fall apart when you don't play by their rules. Be random. Don't give him what he expects. Do the opposite. If he needs you rigid to complete his next move, go limp. Surrender at times, then strike when he eases up. Keep him off balance. Do something to distract him. I don't know, just some thoughts. I just don't want you to get hurt."

"My dad slammed me pretty hard a few times. I'm still walking. That doesn't mean I liked it."

"Tucker's smart. Use it against him." He stopped and craned his face around to look at her. "Is it true he called you a *Sheila*?"

She nodded.

"How did that make you feel?

"Royally pissed off."

"Good, use that against him."

They sat in silence. Blake worked through the sections with surprising skill and speed. She used the moment of quiet to get inside her head and prepare for the standoff with Tucker. Blake's wise advice simmered in her thoughts.

When he finished the last of the six braids he blew out a deep breath.

She was quite the sight with a dozen pens sticking out in random directions from her head.

"Now for the fun part. I hope this works. I'm kinda making it up as I go."

He looped the long end of each of the six braids through the spaces left in the tight wraps when he withdrew the pens. Weaving the braids back inside themselves. He followed a circular pattern with each remaining braided end, securing them at the crown of her head in a five-inch-long tight ponytail.

He led her to the mirror in the head.

Audrey gasped in disbelief at the creation Blake made with her hair. Braids encircled her scalp. A short ponytail stuck up from the top of her head, like a spouting fountain. She looked like a true warrior with a braided helmet and majestic tassel.

Blake had always been mysterious and quiet. With his origami creations and well-thought-out messages and advice, she realized she'd never really appreciated the extent of his creative mind until now.

She whipped around. "I love it!" Then she kissed him, short and sweet, but enough to set a tiny piece of her heart aflutter. By the way he reacted, she'd also lit a flame she hadn't intended.

40

Badass Sheila

A COUPLE HOURS LATER Ryan and Blake came to get Audrey from her cabin. She sat on the cabin floor in a state of meditation, playing through various possible attacks.

Neck lock. Leg lock. Elbow to neck. Leg around neck. Arms pinned behind her back...

She remembered being chased by bluestripe tigers, running for her life, scurrying up a tree on Merluma. The way the adrenaline flowed through her body. The terror of facing true death. The blind focus to live.

To win.

She gazed up, rose to her feet from a cross-legged position without use of her hands. Rolled her neck, her shoulders, circled her hips. She tucked her body-hugging sleeveless top into her full-length leggings. The fit was snug and fabric slick. She patted her freshly braided hair, finger-combed the high pony. Everything clicked into place.

"I'm ready, let's go."

She led, and Ryan and Blake followed her down the corridor to the main stairway. She cast her gaze forward but at nothing in particular; a killer's stare. She sensed Ryan giving Blake a fist bump for the creation he created with her hair. She bolted up the stairs to the gym level. She didn't hesitate at the gym door. She hopped onto the gimbaled floor and picked a spot just outside a large circle printed in the center of the mat.

She ripped off a couple yoga salutations, flowing smooth and sure. She dropped to her hands and feet, pumped forward and back into a low plank, juicing up her shoulders. She rolled to a side plank, free hand and leg pointing to the sky, flipped back, rose up, belly to sky, walked forward and back before rolling back to where she started on her hands and feet.

She laid down some forward and backward rolls to get a feel for the mat. She rolled atop her hands and drew her knees to her elbows, holding a crow pose, testing her balance. She rolled up her hips, then straightened her legs into a handstand, held it, gauging the extent of motion from the ship and how that might impact her balance. She rolled out of it, super slow, and landed with a whisper on her bare feet.

The ship wasn't still but it wasn't galloping like it sometimes did. She felt good, balanced and limber, no sticky spots.

The crew filed into the gym, lining up around the gimbaled floor. She pretended to look over the crowd but blurred her gaze to minimize distraction. All she saw was a sea of black blobs, no faces.

Tucker entered with a tight and light swagger, wearing the badass hat. He circled like a tiger stalking his prey. He found his spot on the other side of the circle. She stood at five-feet, ten-inches tall; he was the same. Both lithe and lean. It was his custom-fitted rubber suit she had borrowed when they dove to Tallamure the month before. Equally matched physically, but him fueled with testosterone, her with determination. She kept her eyes low, avoiding direct eye contact. Adrenaline flowed and words of advice from her father's training looped through her mind.

Never look your enemy in the eye. It humanizes them. Tickles your compassion. Compassion is a distraction in battle. It will get you killed—Be spontaneous. Focus on opportunity. You won't know what it is until they act—Use their weakness against them—Keep your enemy guessing—Fury is fuel, draw on it to—

"Audrey?"

She startled. Stoke addressing her.

"You ready?" he asked.

She nodded.

Stokes was the referee. A whistle hung from a string around his neck. He raised a hand, silencing the gym, commanding everyone's attention.

"Audrey has challenged Tucker."

A round of whistles and woohoos erupted from the mass of blurred bodies ringed around the gym.

Stokes waited until the crowd quieted. "May I remind everyone, this is a challenge of *skill*, not a fight." He shifted his attention to the two of them. "The same rules of training engagement apply. Tap out if you feel your opponent is pushing too far, then resume. You injure your opponent, you lose. Council will determine the penalty, which will be determined by the intention and severity of the injury. With me so far?"

Stokes looked at Tucker. He nodded. Then at Audrey. She nodded.

"Three, three-minute rounds. Crew decides the winner. Extra points for style and creativity."

Audrey smiled to herself.

Stokes held his hand out to Tucker. He took off the hat and handed it over, not looking too happy about it.

Stokes lifted the whistle to his mouth, hesitated when her father entered the gym with Dr. Wickman. They took a front-row spot among the crowd.

Her heart thundered. She looked up. Stopped her gaze on Tucker's nose. No eye contact. This was it. Was she ready?

Tucker flared his nostrils. Big mistake. Memories exploded inside her. She never realized it to be a trigger. *Flared nostrils.* Just like her father, preparing for the attack. He did it too, every time before teaching her a brutal lesson of hand-to-hand combat. Ten years of humiliation and bruises came back to her; the anger, the pain, the hatred she felt after, toward her father but also herself.

Fury is fuel.

She felt it in spades, lit the match, and focused on a single purpose.

Win the hat.

The whistle blared.

Tucker shoved her. She stepped back and to the side, didn't react. He did it again, testing. Then, a third time. She sensed his frustration. She was waiting for a sloppy move. The fourth time was sloppy with low intent. She slipped sideways, squatted, ducked, and surged forward, driving her elbow to his sternum. It tapped hard, barely within the rules but enough to catch him off guard. She took advantage of his backwards momentum, followed it with a swift hook of her lower leg around his ankle. He fell to the ground.

The crowd reacted with a loud round of *ohs*.

He was up. A bull raging. Breathing hard, not from physical excursion but humiliation. She knew exactly how it felt.

Hate to be you.

Her breath was even. In control.

Keep it together.

He came at her, fists guarding his face, readying a punch, but where? His lower body was exposed. She hopped to the side of him, dropped and rolled into the side of his legs. He crumpled, recovered, landing on top of her.

He smiled.

Not where I want to be!

He was fast, winding his legs around hers, locking them at the ankles. Within the same swift move, he rolled her to her side, pinning one of her arms. He slid an arm around her neck, the other around her free arm. Her neck was locked in the crook of his elbow. He began to squeeze. She engaged her neck muscles to protect her windpipe from collapsing. She grunted, twisted, and bucked, making him believe he had her fully locked and she was suffering from lack of air. Then she stilled but didn't tap out. His grip loosened, ever so slightly as if she might. The fault she was hoping for. She liquefied her muscles. Controlling something firm was much easier than something squishy and slick. She slithered around in his arms to face him.

Noses pressing, she said, "Having fun yet?" Then slipped an arm free, drew back and raised her hand with fingers pointed, as if she meant to poke his eyes out. It worked. Tucker was momentarily distracted, and she slithered down and out from his embrace, folded her body around their locked legs and dug her fingers into the arches of his bare feet.

Instinct was a bitch.

He recoiled as she expected. His legs released their lock and she slithered free. She rolled backwards and hopped to her feet. Crouched and ready for his next advance.

Stokes blew the whistle. End of round one and she still had all her teeth.

This next round scared her. Tucker was smart and would be ready for her tricks. This next round would be a true test of her skill.

Tucker paced like a tiger. "Nice baby boop," he sneered.

Good, she thought, *he's mimicking my tricks of distraction.*

Time for something different.

The whistle blew.

She dropped to the mat and laid on her back, arms splayed, knees bent up. He made a what-the-hell face, then pounced, straddling her hips and pinning her wrists to the mat. Smart move. Wrists are vulnerable. But he did exactly what she hoped. Tucker was solid as stone and very heavy for his size and she suddenly feared she had made a mistake. She tugged to break free.

He leaned over and shoved his face into hers. "Be a good 'ol girl and roll over for me."

Damn, he's heavy!

She focused every ounce of will to her hips, visualized what she wanted. A hip snap up, back arching, right hip hiking up a little higher. A sudden upward thrust was the trick to this move, especially against weight like Tuckers. Get it moving and roll with the momentum, up and over...

It worked! He popped off and rolled to his back, his grip fast on her wrists, taking her with him.

Big mistake, Aussie man!

She drove her knee between his legs, brushing up against his tender bits, enough for him to squirm and gasp, but not to trigger a penalty. She was on top, knee married to his groin. Noses touching, real up close and personal. Her wrists felt like they might snap from his ironclad grip. She had to break it.

"Roll over like this?" She ground her knee higher, felt bone. It had to smart.

He let go of her wrists. She rolled off and onto her feet before he could say "ow".

They circled each other. Tucker was pissed. He came at her in a blur, from behind. They crashed to the mat, her splayed face down beneath him. He looped his arms around her elbows, yanked back, and clasped his hands behind her neck. She hated this move. Being the weaker one made it nearly impossible to escape from. She was rendered armless, neck vulnerable to snapping, shoulders stretching back to their limit. On the pain scale, this one teetered near the top.

Tucker's breath rained hot and moist against her cheek. "This was what I meant."

He wormed her legs apart with his. Those tender bits she crushed seconds before ground into her butt cheeks. This is one of the most vulnerable positions to be held hostage for obvious reasons, for a male or a female.

Her primal instincts kicked in. Reptilian brain awakening. Compassion and rules and whistles meant nothing. As someone who has trained, you learn to control that fine line of knowing when to stop. This is that move and Tucker knew it. He was waiting for her to tap out. Big score for Tucker!

But she couldn't do it; she freed her mind to embrace it. With the hold he had on her neck, whatever she did would be dangerous. Not to him. But to her.

She coiled, hollowing out her core, shoving her butt up with a wiggle, giving Tucker's bits a ride.

Damn, he's heavy!

She didn't stop; somehow her muscles defied Tucker's weight and gravity. He rose from her effort, grip locked, wrenching her neck. His legs bent unwillingly, giving her the break she needed to draw her legs together, for her knees to bend. He still had her arms yanked back, with his hands pressed to her neck. What she planned to do next was risky, with the hope that he'd ease up before her neck snapped.

In one swift and explosive movement she tucked her knees and chin to chest, and rolled. Tethered to her arms, Tucker rolled beneath her and suddenly she was top, her bound elbows grinding into his chest. She planted her feet in a wide stance, knees bent, creating a wedge. She silently thanked her father for giving her strong, long legs.

Tucker still had her elbows locked with his hands clasped behind her neck. He would have to struggle mightily to break the wedge she'd created with her legs. They crabbed-walked around in circles, spinning on his sweat-slicked back. They were stuck, both too stubborn to give in. He grunted in frustration, she grunted from the strain.

The whistle blew.

Tucker released her. She rolled to her hands and knees, did a quick check of her neck, rolled her shoulders. Both were still intact but they were going to hurt like hell in the morning. She stood. Drawing deep breaths and chugging to calm her thundering heart.

She felt like she might throw up at any second. That lull before you get your second wind. The final sprint in a marathon, where the body's pushed to the extreme. Where your body screams to quit. That last round scared her. One more to go. At this point she wanted it to end with her body intact. And her dignity.

Stokes glared at both of them. "Last round. *Rules*. Keep it clean." He blew the whistle.

Audrey launched at Tucker in a daze of subconscious thought. Imagining the fight in her mind, guiding the movement of her body. A strike to his hip flexor, him bending over, him spinning and landing a couple of firm hits to her kidneys. Her blocking another strike, ducking, giving him a round-house kick to the ass. Him slamming her to the mat, a roll, slithering out from another of his ironclad holds, her hopping to her feet. Another take-down, another knot on the mat. She could tell he was feeling it too, but then he would pour on the juice, going hard and rigid, and she would loosen every muscle and wriggle free just as Blake suggested.

Damn, he's heavy and he's fast!

They were both sweating and breathing hard. He had her face down again, trying to pin her arms like before. She tucked them beneath her body, straightened her legs, zipped them together; rigid and unbendable like a staff, her face pressed into a puddle of their combined sweat. He tried to loop an arm around her neck; she coiled beneath him, rolling into a tight ball, setting him off balance. She rolled out from underneath, spun around facing his feet, and straddled his chest with her hips. He grabbed her legs as she hoped, then she pressed back, shoving her crotch in his face. She threaded his knees with her arms, locked her hands behind her neck, engaged her shoulders, her lats, her core—then thrust her chest forward and rose up. His ass lifted off the mat with his shoulders and head pinned by her hips. He bucked and squirmed beneath her, his breath hot and face smothered by a part of her she tried not to think about.

The whistle blew.

She released Tucker and hopped to her feet. Tucker hopped up after her, gasping.

Blood surged in her ears. She looked at Stokes. The whistle was no longer clamped between his teeth but swinging loosely around his neck.

Was that really three rounds?

She felt arms around her, pats to her back. Ryan and Blake by her side. Shit-eating grins on their faces.

Tucker was pacing, breath steaming from his nostrils.

Stokes prompted the bystanders for votes. They punched their votes into their phones. Stokes reviewed the results, called for silence. He moved to the center of the circle, gestured for Tucker and Audrey to come forward.

Stokes glanced at his phone, swept his gaze across the bystanders, then back to Tucker and Audrey.

He nodded at them both. "A little dirty, but a fair fight."

Sweat trickled down Audrey's neck. Tucker's lip twitched. Stoked looked one last time at his phone, arched a brow. He opened his mouth. Audrey held her breath.

Stokes grabbed her hand, raised it. "Audrey wins by two-thirds vote, with bonus points for creativity."

Her heart stopped a beat, then it raced. Stokes perched the badass hat atop her head, squishing her baby-boop of a ponytail. It felt safe to smile. It was over. She won. She won! Tears mixed with sweat poured down her face.

Tucker looked like he wanted to punch something. He grabbed her hand and pulled her to his bare chest, glistening with sweat. He was still breathing hard, like her. Hot breath swirled between them. They lingered like that for a beat, gazing into each other's eyes, not in anger or hatred, but respect.

Finally, he said, "You're *scary*. Wily as a witch and slippery as a fish... and that move you did—whatcha call it—the sixty-nine? *That* was certainly unexpected."

She laughed. "I don't call it anything, it just... came to me, felt like the right thing to do at the time."

He smiled that twisted-lip smile and poked her in the chest. "I want you on my team, any day, any time."

She smiled back in disbelief. The ultimate compliment, and coming from Tucker, one that meant as much as winning the hat.

41

City Of Slime

IN THE DEPTHS OF Lake Superior, Sinto slept, waking after a full night's rest. He stretched and pressed on. No breakfast. He missed the ritual he had shared every morning with Rachel. A steaming cup of sweet and creamy coffee and a cinnamon roll served up with a smile and a pair of dimples.

Sinto recalled the last time he had traveled to the City of Green with his father, Ramasis. They had passed through the portal at the bottom of Deep Lake on Merluma directly to the City of Green on Earth. The same portal he discovered was now heavily guarded by Terrakai Scouts.

He cranked up his sonar receptors, listened for the hum and pulse of the city's electrified organic dome, and swam in that direction.

Sinto was troubled. The City of Green was the first place the Scouts searched for Ramasis. They were told Ramasis was not there and would send a messenger if he returned. That was the last time his mother had heard from the City of Green, many months ago. He wondered if the Scouts who guarded the portal were the same Scouts who sent that message and if they had been sincere.

Korvasi told Sinto that Ramasis had been in the City of Green ever since he and Naiada were poisoned by Culliford while trying to deliver a message for his mother. He was well hidden, and only a select few knew he was there. When Sinto inquired how Korvasi knew, he refused to answer and merely chuckled, *You are so close to the answer, it might bite you on the nose, young one.*

Korvasi told Sinto that Ramasis had nearly died from the poisoning and his recovery was slow and painful, but he eventually recovered. Though he would have died if he had not had help, like Sinto had helped Naiada with blood infusions. The question that Sinto could not answer, nor extract from Korvasi, was who had helped Ramasis. Sinto was able to help his sister because she was of shared blood. Who in the City of Green could have helped Ramasis? He had no other family Sinto was aware of. And what answer did Korvasi believe Sinto knew? Sinto had rummaged through the possibilities during the long drive from Lake Mead to Duluth. He came up with nothing. How could Korvasi possibly know what had happened to Ramasis? He was a lonely old man living alone in a stagnant lake he refused to leave.

If Ramasis was alive Sinto was puzzled as to why he had not returned to Tallamure. Naiada was ill. He must have known. She had been exposed to the same toxin. It was Ramasis who rushed her back to Tallamure before disappearing. What was more important than coming home to his family? Ramasis and Naiada were very close, closer than Sinto had ever been to his father. They shared a special bond neither Sinto nor his mother understood. Why had he not at least sent a message?

Why would the Terrakai Scouts lie to his mother about his father's whereabouts, and did that lie have something to do with what he witnessed in the caves on Merluma?

Distracted by thoughts, Sinto collided with a very large fish. Its tail lashed out and struck him in the chest before disappearing into the murky depths. Sinto stopped and tuned his receptors. He sensed several large creatures circling in the waters above him and just out of sight. Large like a shark or a young whale. Unusual for the lake, here or in the others connected to it.

One of the creatures dove down and swam around Sinto in a wide circle, its eyes scanning him like an early morning meal.

Sinto got a good look. A lamprey. A long thin fish that looked and swam like an eel, but that was where their similarities ended. The lamprey had a circular mouth with multiple rows of sharp teeth that clamped onto the body of an unsuspecting fish and bored holes in the flesh, consuming it alive. The lamprey was a deadly predator that inflicted a slow and painful death and typically grew no longer than the length of Sinto's arm. This one was at least six feet long. He sensed the others, swimming just out of his sight, were even larger.

The lampreys followed Sinto at a discrete distance. Every so often one would emerge and brush against him, testing. Sinto fired his merlux, sent a burst of electricity through the water. A warning to stay back. He picked up his pace when he saw the green glow of the city in the distance. As he neared the city, more lampreys joined the pack. Sinto released another burst of electricity.

A thick layer of algae coated the city's dome, which cast an eerie olive-green glow. The presence of algae was new, like the circling swarm of giant lampreys.

Something felt off.

He landed on the marshy bottom and wiped a layer of algae from the side of the dome. It did little to help. Star-like blooms of mold covered the inner surface of the dome, hindering his view of what lay inside. What he could see was dead and rotting. Once-healthy trees were bare of greenery and stood as giant gnarled snags. It was as if the photosynthetic-generating light had been sucked from the city.

The city was once brightly lit and bursting with organic life, colored in a thousand shades of green, thus giving the city its name. But now the city inside the dome was gray and oppressive. He hesitated. So far all the signs screamed for him to flee. But where would he go? He had a plan and it led him here. He had survived many trials and made it this far.

I must be brave and act. I am nothing, my life meaningless, without the truth I seek.

Sinto glanced over his shoulder. The lampreys circled, waiting for his next move, unafraid of his earlier warnings. No turning back. Enter the city or face their wrath. With his disguise firmly in place, merlux charged, and body energized, he pressed his hand to the dome. Duty overpowered his fear. He took a deep breath and stepped inside. His lorica rolled off his skin and was absorbed by the dome, a living organism that slurped it away as he passed through.

A cold chill swept through his veins. As he had observed, the once-flowering plants, fruit trees, and ground covers that grew inside the dome sagged under a layer of smothering algae. The distinct floral scent he remembered was replaced with the sickening smell of rotting vegetation. Trees as far as he could see were barren of greenery. Dead vines hung like loose wires and gray-green moss clung to their gnarled branches like wiry coiled hair. The mock sun cast dreary light that sucked the color out of everything. The oxywater was thick with carbon dioxide and low in oxygen, an imbalance that can occur when too many Merahvu are confined in a domed space without the proper vegetation to replenish it with oxygen.

It took him a moment to figure out where he was. It was as if this was a different city. The city he remembered was bustling with diversity and life. This one was eerily quiet and vacant.

Two figures were headed in his direction, swimming fast. He pressed his back to a tree, camouflaged, and since he was hiding from his fellow kind, cranked down the vents of his aura.

A pair of Terrakai males landed next to the dome where the lampreys still circled. The shorter of the two said, "Are you sure you saw something?"

The other replied, "Certain. Why would the lampreys still linger? Someone entered, and very recently."

They spread out and searched, poking dead bushes, kicking up silt. "Come out, come out wherever you are... No use hiding, stranger, we'll find you eventually."

Sinto edged his way around the trunk of the tree as they came closer, absorbing the reality of what he was witnessing. Two guards dressed in matching black leather uniforms; knee-length wraps and vests adorned with several rows of shiny silver buttons. Stamped across the chest in the vest's thick leather were three rings in the shape of a triangle. Sinto recognized the significance immediately. It was the same pattern of dots that made up his father's markings. The same pattern found in the Mark symbolizing his parents' irrevocably fused bond.

The shorter of the two guards passed in front of Sinto. His eyes were bright orange and aglow. He intently scanned the dead snags above Sinto's head, then the ground at his feet.

"Suevo, come look."

Suevo, the taller guard, flicked his multi-finned tail, protruding from a slit in the back of his leather vest, and disappeared around the other side of the tree trunk.

"Fresh footprints."

Sinto heard a deep draw of breath though nostrils. "I can smell him, Taylee. Definitely male, and mature. Either he was just here or—shh, be still."

The guards Suevo and Taylee were just on the other side of the tree trunk from Sinto. He could hear the oxywater flushing in and out of their nostrils. Sinto held his breath knowing they could hear the same. But it was his heart, pounding like thunder, he could not still.

The silence was suddenly broken by a loud and distant horn, blaring inside his head.

Dah-woo. It repeated three more times.

"Damn, the timing!" the one called Suevo said. "Summoned."

"You're one lucky son of a bitch, for now, but we'll sniff you out eventually," Taylee said before they departed.

Sinto watched them swim away toward the center of the city and the sound of the summoning horn. He released his pent-up breath.

He stepped from the side of the tree and readjusted his camouflage back to Terrakai coloring.

A band of crackling energy descended from above. It dropped over his head and tightened around his chest, binding his arms to his sides.

A deep voice said. "Boy, are you thick. That old trick works. Every time."

42

Acting Leader

THE GUARD WHO CAPTURED Sinto spun him around. Sinto recognized him immediately. Not a guard, a Scout. His hair was cut short on the sides with windswept bangs, like Sinto's recent haircut. The Scout was naked and must have been camouflaged, lying in wait after the guards failed to find him.

"Nice haircut, *Goldilocks*." Sinto stared into the golden eyes of the Scout who had captured him on Merluma and wrongly believed he was a newborn who had escaped from the breeding caves. The same Scout who chased him though the portal to Earth and onto the streets of Santa Monica, California.

The band wrapped around Sinto's chest crackled and buzzed. He suddenly felt weaker.

The Scout flicked the band with a finger. "Like it? It's a parasitic draw. Sucks the energy from your merlux, like a reverse battery. The harder you fight, the more it sucks."

"You followed me?"

The Scout scowled. "Tracked you to Lake Mead, then lost you. But lucky me. I guessed you'd come here, eventually. Figured you were trying to pass through the portal at Deep Lake when we first found you. I should have figured it out when we caught that bird around the same time. Your Scout. I won't make that mistake again."

Sinto thought the same to himself, quickly formulating what he hoped was a believable story. "I'm just trying to survive. I was there when Tallamure was attacked. Everyone I knew perished. I barely escaped myself. I have nowhere else to go, don't know who to trust. It would have been careless not to use caution, so I used a bird Scout. I heard about a rebellion—is it true?"

"Why did you attack my partner back there in the caves?"

"Act of self-preservation. If you'd witnessed what I had at Tallamure, you would be leery of a trap too." Sinto stood firm, trying to ignore the band sucking down his reserves. "So, what of this rebellion?"

The Scout gazed back for a beat, then he grabbed Sinto's chin between his fingers, turned his head, left then right, studying every detail. He cocked his head and gazed into the distance; a vacant look filled his golden eyes. Sinto was certain he was communicating with someone through a telepathic link. His gaze shifted back to Sinto.

He raised a brow. "You don't say..." he muttered to himself. Then he smiled. "I think you can drop that ridiculous disguise. Show your true coloring, *Sinto*, son of Queen Ianthe and Circle representative Ramasis. Not so dead after all, hmm?"

Sinto's skin paled and his eyes blazed true green. "Who were you talking to?" he demanded.

The Scout laughed. "You shall know soon enough." He wagged his brows. "You've been summoned."

Sinto had mentally prepared for this moment. The only way to understand the enemy was to become one. "My desire has not changed. My sacrifice was for nothing. My mother used me to placate Culliford, and yet the city and many lives were destroyed. And for what? I have seen the error of her ways, too trusting of the Larkians. She deceived me. That is why I hide. So I can cause her more grief than she ever imagined, because I am *dead*."

The Scout flipped his bangs from his intensely glowing eyes. "We'll see."

The Scout grabbed some clothes he had hidden beneath a rotting bush. He pulled on a pair of gray jeans and a black T-shirt with a skull and "Metallica" written on it.

He bent, bound Sinto's ankles with a leather strap. He shoved Sinto down, grabbed him by the strap, and took off with a flick of his tail, stirring up a cloud of silt in his wake. Sinto was dragged upside down across the city landscape, his chest bound by the life-sucking band.

Sinto had the distinct feeling he wouldn't be welcome to freely roam the city no matter what he said, at least not yet. Dread nestled in his belly at what he might be asked to do to prove his worthiness to the rebel's cause. He hadn't planned much beyond weaving a story. He wasn't sure what actions he was mentally prepared to take should he be forced to prove his story's integrity.

Onward the Scout swam, over a barren forest of trees whose trunks had been fully hollowed for additional dwellings. A once-living forest decimated for what? Housing for a population they were breeding on Merluma? The movement of shadows within indicated the city was indeed not vacant. Sinto calculated the population of the city must have quadrupled since he was last here, perhaps to the size of Tallamure before it was destroyed, over one hundred thousand. Numbers much too great for an underwater city of this size to sustain. The poor quality of the oxywater and abundance of algae were solid proof.

Sinto considered fleeing but was already feeling the effects of the band drawing down his reserves. He guessed it had dropped by an eighth in the short time it had been wrapped around his chest. While his fluked fin gave him a speed advantage over the multi-finned tail of the Terrakai, he was uncertain if he could out-run the over-sized lampreys guarding the city before he could cut a vortex tunnel and escape.

He cursed smelly old Korvasi. Had the Scout found him once Sinto left Lake Mead? Had Korvasi told him what his romp through Sinto's mind revealed? Had Korvasi knowingly led Sinto into a trap? While the Scout had acted surprised by who he was, was that supposed interaction with someone else just an act? Scouts were master-class actors, and as Sinto was quickly learning, can't be trusted.

The Scout swam past the once-vital mother tree of the city, which spawned the forest and sheltered surrounding greenery. Dead. She was planted at the center of the City of Green at its inception, a symbol representing eternity and life.

The diameter of the mother tree's massive trunk spanned the length of a Sapien city block, and what was left of her upper branches brushed the top of the dome. Windows were cut into her gutted trunk and along massive branches where there was once vibrant wood. Her heart had been ripped out and her fibrous skin was reduced to multi-family dwellings. Seeing what had become of the city disgusted and angered him.

The dead forest blurred and gave way to a low-sprawling dwelling. Half of the trees in the forest had been cut down and stumps cleared. This new dwelling was uniform and unnatural. Forged not by the whims of nature but by an unimaginative mind.

The dwelling was quite large, black, and formed from an unidentifiable substance Sinto doubted came organically from nature. It was composed of three flat-topped circles laid out in a triangle like the symbol pressed into the guards' vests. Fingers radiated outward from the three circles like spokes from a hub at the center of a wheel. They stretched into the dead forest and butted up against the edge of the dome like venom radiating from the poisonous bite of a deadly snake.

One of the spokes intercepted a massive outwardly curved wall pressed up against the dome with an unencumbered view of the lake beyond. An auditorium, facing the lake, massive enough to seat thousands. That too was new.

Sinto was stunned by the magnitude of changes that had occurred in the city since he last visited. He wondered how his mother and the Circle had been so complacent and unaware. He recalled the first time he had been invited to occupy his father's seat as a member of the Circle and the acceptance of his presence, especially by Jabal, the other representative of the Terrakai. Did Jabal know what was happening in his home city? Sinto's mother had warned him of spies in Tallamure when they spoke afterwards. Was Jabal, an active member of the Circle, one of these spies? How deep did the rot go?

The Scout descended toward one of the circular structures. Sinto pulled himself into a ball to avoid landing on his head. He landed hard on his back. The surface of the structure was rough and unforgiving, like pavement in Sapien cities. The Scout released his bound ankles and Sinto rolled to his feet.

What struck Sinto most was the uniformity, like Taylee's and Suevo's uniforms: the silver buttons, the triangle of three circles, and throughout the city, the lack of color, rigid and uniform dwellings, and complete disregard to nature. This was nothing like the city Sinto experienced previously, where a large population of Terrakai lived; raising families, nurturing the natural environment, teaching and sharing and creating, helping neighbors and friends, and reaping the rewards of creative spirit that flourishes within a healthy and free society. Sinto saw not one trace of that here.

The Scout grabbed Sinto by the shoulder and together they dropped down through a mirrored doorway cut into the roof. They landed on a plush rug in a darkly lit living area.

A sofa and chairs upholstered in dark velvety fabric encircled a gnarled root ball from an old tree, honed flat. A sheer curtain hung across the far side of the room, blocking the full view of what appeared to be a bedroom. The sound of running water drifted from an arched doorway opposite the bedroom. Paintings of Terrakai females striking shockingly intimate poses decorated the walls. Glowing orbs of golden light floated above Sinto's head like a gaudy chandelier with invisible arms. More balls of light hovered along the edge of the room. There were no windows. Except for the golden light, the space was dark and muted, like the city outside. The oxywater still and thick. Even though Sinto's internal clock registered daytime, it could be day or night. There would be no way to tell.

"Sinto," a soft and familiar voice. A man stepped from behind the sheer curtain, his face cast in shadow. He balanced a ball of amber fire on the tip of his finger. He cast it aside and loosely tied a silken wrap around his waist. "How long has it been?"

Sinto's voice caught. "Arkis?"

Arkis stepped from behind the curtain and gave Sinto a broad smile. He looked different from what Sinto remembered. It had been at least a year since he last saw him, but he seemed much older, a bit tired and used up for someone in his early twenties. His hair was long, colored black, cut unevenly, and messy. His once bright golden eyes were barely open and ringed with kohl. Behind the slits the irises burned a dark sienna. Creases from lying in one position on wadded-up bed coverings for too long were stamped on his chest. He looked as if he was recovering from a hard night of partying and nursing a hangover; fuzzy-headed and disheveled.

"Why so chary?" His smile faded when he saw the parasitic band buzzing around Sinto's chest. "Oh, I see."

He turned to the Scout. "I think you can release him now. Sinto and I go way back, don't we Sinto?"

The Scout unwound the band, coiled it up, and secured it to his jeans with a chain and a clip.

Arkis embraced Sinto. "How have you been, good friend?" Sinto caught a whiff of alcohol on his breath.

Sinto had known Arkis since they were younglings. They had been born in the same year, Arkis a few months older. Sinto's father had introduced Sinto to Arkis and told him they were distant cousins. Since the Merahvu lived such long lives, one may have many relatives from multiple generations, and being a distant cousin of someone was quite common. Sinto and Arkis shared many common interests and had bonded quickly as if they had been siblings. They competed in almost everything and had their disagreements as Terrakai and Seakai usually did. But in the end, Arkis and Sinto respected each other's differences, physically and in opinion. Arkis was dark while Sinto was light. And when they did something wrong, Sinto got caught while Arkis did not. As they got older, Sinto noticed Arkis was prone to more indulgent behaviors. There was always a dark glint in his eye and he always got his way, regardless of who may or may not be harmed in the process. Yet, Arkis had remained a friend, and Sinto always reached out to him whenever he visited the City of Green.

Sinto glanced at the Scout observing. "I see a lot has changed since we last met—what, a year, two years ago?"

"Two, I believe." Arkis waved for the Scout to depart. The Scout launched upward and out the mirrored opening in the ceiling. It sealed with a soft pop. Sinto's only means for escape from what he could tell.

"Come sit, would you like refreshment?" Arkis gestured for Sinto to sit on the sofa.

"Water would be good. Thank you."

"Sinto, you're too polite!" Arkis sat beside Sinto and slapped him on the knee. "Still reading all those books written by Sapiens?"

That was one interest they did not have in common. Arkis thought Sinto was wasting his time reading their stories, or learning of their technology, or marveling at their discoveries of the universe. Arkis considered Sapiens an enemy as did many Terrakai.

Sinto ignored his jab. "That was an interesting reception. Between the lampreys and those mutts who greeted me. And what of that Scout with his band of life-sucking evil? I was beginning to wonder if I was welcome here."

"You can never be too careful these days." Arkis turned his head toward the curtained space behind him and ordered, "Zayra, bring drinks."

"Zayra? Have you found your mate?" Sinto asked, sitting forward.

"A mate, you ask?" Arkis laughed and gave Sinto a sinful smile. "Look at the walls." He gestured to the nude paintings covering his walls. "*Mates*, my friend—all of them. Aren't they a precious sight? Much has changed since you were last here."

Sinto studied Arkis' face, unsure if he was telling the truth or joking. You could never know for sure with Arkis. He loved to taunt his friends. Sinto decided he was being serious, and to play along.

"That must be interesting," Sinto replied.

Arkis rolled his eyes and slumped back on the sofa. "More like exhausting, not that I'm complaining." He sat up and barked, "Zayra! Drinks! Now!"

"Not to sound rude, but you look so much older than the last time I saw you."

He grinned. "It's the lifestyle." He patted his rounded belly and yawned. "And worth it."

A beautiful young female quietly slipped from behind the curtain, carrying a tray with two cut-crystal glasses half-filled with brown liquid. She was void of any covering. Her long bronze-colored hair hung limply over engorged breasts covered by protective skin adorned with her markings. Her belly was swollen with child, nearing full gestation. She set down the tray on the table and settled ungracefully beside Arkis. Her gaze fell on Sinto. Her fiery-orange eyes sparked with a hint of danger.

Arkis regarded her with a curt nod and a gesture that meant she wasn't welcome to stay. The expression on her face made it clear he told her the same, in so many words, via mind-speak, that he wanted her to leave. She struggled to stand up as if the mere act of bending forward to put the weight on her feet would burst her water. She left without Arkis making an introduction.

Sinto watched, appalled. While she had struggled to extract her overwhelming bulk from the sofa, Arkis merely studied his fingernails. Yet she left, submitting without complaint.

Sinto found the entire interaction demeaning, but he was not entirely surprised. Based on the paintings on Arkis' walls and what Sinto had observed of Arkis in the past, he knew Arkis had a mean streak and a disturbing disrespect for women.

Sinto prodded, "So, you're going to be a father. You must be thrilled!"

He sighed. "I suppose I am—again. But it's not my first child. Nor is Zayra my only mate." Sinto cast his gaze to the lurid paintings on the walls. Twelve total, with plenty of room to hang more.

"Mm, what are you implying?"

"No doubt you noticed the city has grown substantially."

"I was going to ask about that."

Arkis sat forward. "Don't you want to know why?"

"Of course, but why ask. I can see you're dying to tell me. You weren't one for keeping secrets for very long."

Arkis exploded into a high-pitched laugh. "You certainly know me well!" He gave Sinto a sinister grin. "We've been ordered to populate as fast as possible and I'm in charge of making it happen." He paused for that last part to sink in. It did, like a bomb dropping. "But I must admit, with all the..." He waved his hands as if Sinto knew exactly what he meant by "all the" of whatever was going on. "It can be so *exhausting*. Some nights I just want to sleep!"

Sinto ignored his last flippant comment. His gut churned for another reason. "Ordered?"

Arkis raised a brow. "That's right, Sinto, and the order didn't come from your mother. It came from our new leader."

Sinto stared at Arkis, not quite sure whether to believe him or not. Arkis' face didn't reveal the usual mocking grin nor did he burst into his maniacal laughter as he usually did while stringing Sinto along with another of his wild and unbelievable fictional stories. Arkis was a jokester and Sinto had fallen for too many of his outlandish ideas or suggestions.

Sinto hid his alarm behind a stone mask and put on another, one with sinister curiosity. "Who's this new leader?"

A long silence passed while Arkis' measured the sincerity of Sinto's question. Sinto felt the familiar prick in his ear as Arkis attempted to slip a probe into Sinto's thoughts. If anything was gained from his short time with Korvasi it was to trust no one and triple lock the gates to his mind. In reality, alarms were going off inside his head. The lampreys, the number of those who had strange orange eyes, the desecration of the city, the population explosion, Arkis' callous treatment of Zayra, his many mates immortalized in demeaning poses on his walls, the order to procreate at an unfathomable rate. Sinto's mother had not shared whether or not she had seen these things in her visions. Only Naiada had an inkling that something was happening. But she couldn't quite decipher the details. Only that it was unsettling.

And unsettled he was.

Arkis grinned ear-to-ear. "That, my dear friend, would be me. *Technically*," he bobbled his head, rolled his eyes. "For now, I'm only the *acting* leader. That is, until we get our new queen and she chooses me to be her mate, which I have utmost confidence she will. Only it will be her chosen mate calling all the shots, not her, in this new world. Ha! Can you believe it! Me in charge of all this!"

"You? You're the one who has transformed the city?"

"Of course!"

Sinto had listened to Arkis with troubled heart, absorbing these new facts. Arkis as acting leader of the City of Green and what had become of it. Arkis in charge of a critical portal between the City of Green and Merluma. Arkis as keeper of the lands where the breeding caves lay. Arkis who lied and cheated whenever he couldn't get his way.

Who in their right mind would put Arkis in charge?

Sinto swallowed down the bile burning in his stomach at what he must do. He nodded, then smiled as if giving Arkis his full approval. "So tell me, what can I do to help with your little rebellion?"

43

Rock Stars

ARKIS REPLIED, "HELP? WHY, Sinto, I need for you to deliver me a queen."

The Merahvu had had one queen since the end of the Forever War over three hundred years ago. Sinto's mother. Part of the peace agreement was the establishment of the Circle, a new and consolidated governing entity consisting of two members from each of the three tribes—Arctakai, Seakai, and Terrakai. Each tribe equally represented. All peoples of all three tribes unified as one under a common name: Merahvu. Tallamure was built shortly after to represent the union of the tribes and was declared the primary seat of Circle affairs, with his mother as their guiding queen.

But not all had agreed with the arrangement, arguing the imbalance. Sinto's grandmother—the former queen—was a Seakai and many felt her participation in setting up the new governing system gave the Seakai an unfair advantage should disagreements arise. That was when she decreed that her daughter, Ianthe—who was entering adulthood and was the soon-to-be queen—would take a Terrakai as her mate. Ianthe chose Ramasis, son of the Terrakai leader at the time. And as expected, the Terrakai elected Ramasis to be one of the two representatives for the Terrakai tribe to join the Circle, a seat Sinto's father was grooming Sinto to fill one day, with hopes the Terrakai would choose his son to be one of their representatives.

Wantemo informed Sinto before he left on his mission to find Ramasis that Ianthe was actively training Naiada to take over her responsibilities as soon as possible. The Merahvu people had lost confidence in Ianthe and she was desperate to maintain peace in these troubled times. Naiada was the key to holding onto what little support the Circle had, especially of the Terrakai. She would be the first-ever dual-tribe queen, and one with Terrakai blood running through her veins.

Was Naiada the queen Arkis hoped Sinto would deliver? She was far too young and untrained. Or was his idea of "queen" radically different from what his mother represented? At this point, Sinto decided not to assume anything until he learned more.

How Arkis fit into all this was a mystery, and Sinto had a difficult time imagining him in any position of authority, now or ever. Korvasi was quite certain Ramasis had been in the City of Green since he went missing a year ago. If true, what did he think of what Arkis had done to his cherished city? Or was he part of the rebellion? If so, did he intend to draw Sinto's sister, Naiada, into it as a key accomplice?

Or did his father disagree with what Arkis was doing and was being held captive, not willing to hand over Sinto's sister? Korvasi didn't offer any clues to that question, only speculation. *Ramasis is a complicated man,* he told Sinto, *one who can be easily bent by the wind once you discover his greatest weakness.* Sinto had asked what that weakness may be, but Korvasi merely shrugged. *Don't ask me, ask the one who discovers it.* Needless to say, Korvasi hadn't been much help in this regard. The words he offered could be true of anyone.

Sinto treaded carefully. "And who may that be, this queen you wish me to deliver?"

"Now, now, Sinto. You know I can't tell you. Not yet."

Nausea swirled in his stomach. Why did he refuse to say his sister's name? She was the most obvious choice. Unless Arkis had another option, one that Sinto was unaware of, which troubled Sinto deeply. Almost as deeply as it troubled Sinto that Arkis wasn't willing to reveal this new and troubling fact, *yet*. Though it made sense. Ianthe was Sinto's mother. In Arkis' eyes Sinto was her dedicated servant, of dual-tribe and potentially sympathetic to the Seakai. So was Naiada. Both a wild card to his power play. Arkis may be a partying troublemaker but he wasn't stupid. Sinto sensed a test of some sort in his immediate future.

"Open your eyes, Sinto. There's a new world order coming. We've been standing by far too long while the Sapiens run rampant, over-breeding and consuming every resource they can get their greedy little hands on. It's only a matter of time before they discover a new resource on Earth we've been very busy nurturing and harvesting. One that is key to our success. We must confront them, and the time to act is now, before Earth fevers completely and takes Merluma with it."

"Ianthe knows of these challenges. Starting a war won't solve our problems."

"Ha! Like the one Culliford started? Is it true Ianthe invited him to Tallamure? Asked you to help? You of all people should be furious! She used you, sacrificed you to that madman. So you tell me, Sinto, who was it that suggested you fake your death? Was that her plan all along? So her personal spy could sneak around inside *my* city?"

Arkis would hound him for the truth no matter how much Sinto tried to stall. He quickly wove the threads of a story, stitched up from a patchwork of memories—carefully edited with a few embellishments added—to buy time and lead Arkis into thinking Sinto was on his side.

"Arkis... always spinning your crazy theories." Sinto sat forward. "Want to see for yourself? What really happened?" Sinto pushed his fabricated story into Arkis' mind before he could respond; a collection of the important bits, played out in fast forward...

~ ~ ~

Sinto kidnapping and seducing Culliford's daughter, a girl named Audrey, a mere pawn to bend Culliford to Ianthe's will. Sinto convincing her to lead Culliford to Tallamure...

The confrontation in Tallamure as it happened in front of the witnesses—twisted with a few added false interactions privately exchanged between Sinto and Ianthe to back up their planned ruse to trick Culliford...

Culliford and Audrey fighting for the knife—twisted to seem that Audrey, as well as her father, wanted to kill Sinto after Sinto confessed to killing Culliford's wife...

Sinto leaning to the left as Naiada had warned him to do—but to Arkis he presented it as Ianthe's idea...

The blade buried in his chest. Sinto collapsing, the touching effect of blood and flueox blooming above his broken body—Ianthe giving a heartfelt performance of grief over Sinto's body while he pretended to die. Culliford satisfied, the Circle buying the ruse, like sheep drawn into a wolf's lair with promise of protection. Fools as they were...

~ ~ ~

Sinto stopped his game of show and tell, and jolted Arkis from his mind.

"But then," Sinto said, "Rebels attacked Culliford's ship at that most inopportune moment and prompted him to blow up Tallamure." Sinto paused, and still performing, gave Arkis a sly smile. "Or perhaps you planned it that way?"

Arkis was strangely quiet, so Sinto finished his embellished story. "So after I was whisked to Merluma to be healed and heard what happened, I decided to fake my death. After the Healer patched me up, he sent a message to my mother, saying I was dead. Naturally, I dispatched that Healer so there would be no witness to the truth." Sinto gazed deeply into Arkis' kohl-smudged eyes.

"So you see, I was freed, finally. Dead to everyone, especially my mother. She has no hold on me any longer."

Arkis said, "That is quite a story."

He eyed Sinto as he sucked down the drink Zayra had brought him. He stood and paced. He stopped and cast his gaze back to Sinto. He paced some more, scrubbing his fingers through his messy hair. This went on for several agonizing minutes, during which Sinto sat calmly, regulating his heartbeat and his breath. It was the first time he had lied so blatantly and worried Arkis would see right through it. All he could hope was that his story melded with whatever story Arkis had heard from his Scouts, many of whom he seemed to control completely and who seemed to be everywhere.

Arkis finally sat. He gave Sinto his signature madman grin.

"My, oh my, I never thought you had it in you Sinto. And killing a Healer? Unbelievable! I always thought you were so pure and innocent, the *good* one." He picked up the other drink, handed it to Sinto. Sinto took it, but didn't drink. Arkis' maniacal smile faded and he pinned Sinto with a fiery gaze. "Just answer me one question."

Sinto's heart skipped a beat and he fought to still his fingers holding the glass of brown liquid.

"What do you think we ought to do about our little *problem,* on the surface?"

Sinto put down his drink. "Ah, you mean, what do we do about the Sapiens." Sinto fixed Arkis with an equally fiery gaze. He chose his words carefully, speaking to that thing he was certain Arkis wanted to hear. "After studying those Sapien books you so fondly mocked me about, I have come to a conclusion. While you can lop off the head of the snake, more will arise in its place. There is only one way to topple those who cannot be made to see the error of their ways. Kill them all, like an invasive species." Arkis may believe Sinto was referring to the Sapiens, but in reality Sinto was vague enough that he could have been referring to Arkis and his rebellion.

Arkis patted Sinto on the thigh. "Well done, Sinto. Welcome to the team! Everyone in this city believes in The Eradication, and those who don't, well... let's just say, we escort them outside."

A chill ran down Sinto's spine.

Is that what happened to Ramasis? Or would happen to me if Arkis learned of my lies? Join or die. Not many options.

Arkis laughed hysterically. "Sinto, you look like you've seen a ghost! Have a drink, *relax.*" He shoved the full glass toward Sinto. Then refreshed his own from a bottle he found on the floor beside the sofa. He leaned forward. Sinto could smell his last drink on his breath mingling with whatever was left over from the night before.

"I'm going to show you my kingdom. Tonight we party like rock stars!"

Sinto raised his drink. "To rock stars." He tipped back the fiery drink and closed his eyes as the thick liquid swirled around his tongue and down his throat.

I must find Ramasis and get the hell out of here before Arkis learns the truth.

44

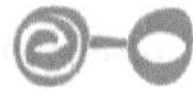

Symbolism

ARKIS' PRIVATE RESIDENCE WAS only one of many spaces in the sprawling compound. When Sinto asked what the other spaces were for, he went on about the yet-to-be-set-in-place governing members, and the soon-to-be-instated queen. When Sinto pointed out that the spaces seemed excessive, he muttered something about recruits and needing housing for all of them.

Arkis was quite proud of his accomplishments, including the destruction of the forest to make way for his "personally designed" compound that, he claimed, *set the whole city abuzz* during its construction.

Sinto had no doubt about the buzz. He was buzzing about it and not in a good way.

And when Sinto slipped in a subtle reference as to who his chosen queen might be, Arkis demurred with a bat of his kohl-ringed eyes and thick lashes, followed by howling laughter. Sinto began to wonder if he had gone mad from breathing all of the rotting vegetation that was a result of his proud accomplishments.

After their disturbing conversation, Arkis led Sinto to a spare room within his residence. "I suggest you rest up for this evening's festivities." When Sinto asked what that may be, he became strangely giddy. "It's a surprise! No time to waste! Only a few hours to *prepare*." Then he left Sinto alone in a room sparsely furnished with a bed and a side table with a tall glass of water. There were no windows, no art on the walls, no reading material. Floor, ceiling, walls painted a dreary shade of green. On the bed was a simple bed sheet and a pillow, and lying on top was a black leather wrap like those Arkis' guards wore.

Sinto was unsure what Arkis meant by "prepare," other than to put on the wrap left for him. His internal clock guessed it to be mid-day. He eyed the glass, gave it a sniff. He detected pure water, nothing else. So he drank half of it.

He surveyed the room, looking for anything out of the ordinary. While the Merahvu didn't use technology such as cameras to spy, he wouldn't put it past Arkis to wield a similar technique. He found nothing suspicious and relaxed a little. Maybe he had sufficiently convinced Arkis that the story he spun and the change in his beliefs were genuine.

Play along, see where the river flows.

He wrapped the knee-length leather covering around his waist and looped the leather strings through holes bound with metal rings along his left thigh. He left his tail tucked and gazed at his reflection in the mirrored doorway. He no longer needed to hide behind a disguise. He was certain that word he was alive and in Arkis' complex would spread through the city like an oxywater-borne virus. Though he hardly recognized himself with the oppressively colored wrap and his darker-than-usual short hair.

Curious how far Arkis trusted him, he reached out to see if it the reflective door was locked. His hand was suddenly sucked to the surface, like a magnet. He felt that same life-sucking draw.

A parasitic draw like the band the Scout wrapped me in. Great.

Sinto yanked his hand back, breaking the connection with a loud zap and a bone-numbing shock to his fingers. He hadn't noticed it before, but now he did: subtle as it was, the life-sucking draw was meant to weaken him, but why? He moved to the farthest corner of the windowless room, pressed his back to the wall and slid to the floor, drawing his knees to his chest. He could still sense the parasitic draw, a bit weaker because of the distance from the door, but it was still there, doing its damage. If Sinto spent more than a few hours under its influence, it would deplete his reserves and render him helpless should he need to fire up his merlux and defend himself. Was that Arkis' idea of "prepare"?

He hoped Arkis was sincere when he said, *Only a few hours...*

At this point, Sinto had no choice but to go along with Arkis' plan, prove to Arkis the sincerity of his lie, and hope an opportunity to escape would arise. He had no doubt Arkis had ordered his guards to keep an eye on him and employ their parasitic leashes if he misbehaved. His first priority was to survive the night and whatever Arkis had planned.

But at the moment Sinto was stuck in this room that was sucking the life from him with only his thoughts to distract him; thoughts that kept coming back to the mystery of his missing father and how wide and deep the roots of the rebellion against his mother and the Circle had spread.

Korvasi told Sinto his father returned to the City of Green after falling ill. If true, who helped him heal? Naiada required Sinto's blood to save her from the effects of the toxin Culliford infected her with. Perhaps she was more vulnerable because of her young age; perhaps the older Ramasis was able to fight off the effects on his own.

Or perhaps the toxin finally took him.

Naiada shared a secret with Sinto shortly before Tallamure's fall. She had begun having visions, even though she shouldn't have been able. Being on the cusp of puberty, her powers were a mere bud yet to bloom. Or had they already? She claimed her power of foresight had manifested much earlier than was to be expected. She told Sinto she could no longer sense their father and worried something had happened to him, and recently. Was it just a fluke?

She did confess her newly discovered visions were sporadic and sometimes unreliable and might mean nothing.

But still... Naiada could be right. Ramasis may have been discovered. And, as Arkis suggested, escorted outside.

Outside where the lampreys lie in wait.

As awful as that seemed, Sinto wrestled with another more troubling, and realistic, probability: his father was part of the rebellion and Naiada's unreliable vision was indeed wrong.

Sinto knew his parents had a tumultuous relationship from the start—a forced Joining arranged by Ianthe's mother to appease the Terrakai during a time of great upheaval between the tribes. Ramasis was the optimal candidate for political reasons, the popular and charismatic son of the leader of the Terrakai tribe. Their Joining marked the end of the Forever War. Peace had finally come to the three tribes and Merahvu of all tribes were ecstatic and hopeful for the future.

But history told a different story. One of mistrust and violence played out beyond the watchful gaze of the people and the Circle.

After the death of their first-born, Leela, and Ramasis' discovery of Ianthe's affair with Culliford, he left her, telling the Circle he needed to focus on understanding the concerns of the people he was elected to represent. For well over a century he resided mostly in the City of Green or on Merluma amongst the Terrakai settlements, fulfilling his duties with aplomb. As did Ianthe in Tallamure.

Then one day he returned to Tallamure and Ianthe's bed, claiming he forgave her for what happened with Leela and Culliford. Sinto and Naiada were born shortly after. A son to mold in his image and a new queen to govern the people.

But for which people?

Sinto felt uneasy as he rehashed this tumultuous history. Ramasis' essence had been poisoned long before his last encounter with Culliford, and what better way to strike down Ianthe than to destroy everything she stood for, using his own offspring to ensure his success?

And what would stop Ramasis from delivering Naiada to Arkis himself? But then why was Arkis so anxious for Sinto to join his rebellion and find him a queen?

The most damning fact supporting his father's involvement with Arkis was the triangular trio of rings stamped on the guards' uniforms and the layout of the buildings constructed for a new, yet-to-be-installed government.

Ramasis' markings were dots in varying sizes and randomly placed, but not completely. A distinct pattern of that same triangle of three dots was peppered in small groupings along his father's spine, across his buttocks, and speckled prominently over his genital pouch.

Sinto dropped his gaze to the same pattern of dots twined with swirls, curving around his hip. He had many instances of the same triangle of dots peppered throughout his unique markings. So did Naiada.

Dots were quite common among Terrakai. Yet he felt sick to his stomach. How likely was the triangular-shaped pattern a coincidence?

The more he pondered, the more confused he became as to the fate of his father.

I must assume Father is alive. Find him. Learn the truth. That is the sole purpose of why I am here.

Sinto huddled in the corner behind the bed in an effort to escape the worst of the parasitic draw that was draining critical energy he would need to find answers, then escape. He laid his head upon his knees, hugged his body into a tight protective ball, and set his mind into a restful meditative state. By the rundown look of Arkis, Sinto believed he would need every bit of strength he could muster to survive whatever Arkis had planned for him.

45

Butterfly

Day five. The Requiem *Sea II* arrived at the last known location of the missing ships in the North Pacific Gyre. The sun was setting with a glorious show that gave Audrey goosebumps.

As the sun dipped in the west the ship was alive with activity. The cargo chamber crew began deployment of a grid of sonobuoys. Because they were made of metal with internal watertight rubber seals, Tucker believed they would be safe from possible Orange intrusion. Even if some failed, there would be more than enough to transmit soundings and other vital readings from the ocean floor.

The ship tracked along preprogrammed grid-lines covering a square area measuring twenty-five nautical miles per side. Deep water "Big Boy" sonobuoys were dropped at every nautical mile of the grid—east, west, north, and south—for relaying information to a network of sonobouys deployed nearer to the surface. Surface sonobuoys were dispersed every two and a half nautical miles for relaying readings from the Big Boys to Tucker's command center.

Dyer was the cargo chamber team leader and coordinated the sonobuoy drops. His team was also readying a submersible that would drop to the bottom, scan and record whatever possible from the ocean floor, and scoop up a sample. It would be untethered from the ship, since the communication cables were coated in a petroleum-based plastic Orange would consume. So Tucker programmed it to navigate along the bottom, guided by wireless signals sent through the grid of sonobuoys. It was programmed to follow the heat, scoop up the stuff creating it, then ascend to the surface. He even programmed a plan B. To simply drop, scoop, and ascend should the ship lose contact.

Because the submersible had plastic integrated throughout, they replaced whatever they could with non-petroleum-based flexible materials then coated the entire thing in a thick layer of beeswax. The heat Orange radiated was an issue to consider. Beeswax would melt at one hundred forty degrees Fahrenheit or higher. Not that it mattered, the electronics would fail shortly after reaching that temperature. Not a super high-tech solution but, possibly, enough to fool Orange.

Give six shrewd pirates from the eighteenth-century advance knowledge of the future, and an elixir that rendered them ageless, and what do you get? A grossly wealthy secret nation employing the most advanced technology on Earth, yet not ashamed to employ beeswax in a pinch. It surprised Audrey how practical the Larkians were given their technological advancements.

Audrey, Ryan, and Blake were on standby until the crew was finished deploying the sonobuoys. That meant dragging their plankton nets all night.

Ryan pointed out the advantage. "Sifting for sea life is just as important as searching for Orange. We'll be able to gauge if Orange has affected those that rise up from the bottom at night to feed on the surface." He cracked a mischievous grin. "Besides, it'll be like the old days, pulling an all-nighter, but without the beer."

They worked out a schedule—three shifts of two. Blake and Ryan taking the first one, Audrey and Blake second, then Ryan and Audrey rounding out the third.

Thankfully, they had calm seas all through the night, but, unfortunately, found nothing. With less than an hour to go before sunrise, Audrey and Ryan sat on the cargo chamber platform, open and overhanging a quiet sea, feeling melancholy. The ship cruised the grid at four knots as it had all night, gently rising and falling on slight swells. Light from the cargo chamber flooded the deck. The only light they had seen all night. The moon and stars had been blocked by cloud cover. Beyond the spread of the ship's light the sea faded to black, which was soon broken by the glow of the rising sun.

Blake dropped by for a report. Audrey merely shook her head. Blake merely nodded, as depressed as her by the lack of anything, then left to share the news with Dr. Wickman.

It was chilly and Audrey was thankful for the hugging warmth of her rubber suit with built-in booties and gloves. Dr. Wickman had insisted they wear them to protect from possible exposure to Orange that could be clinging to whatever they might sift from the sea.

Dyer had laid out rubber matting with a lipped edge along the ship's swim step where the nets would be pulled. Anything that came in the nets wouldn't touch the deck and would drain overboard. A hose was at the ready to rinse everything away between pulls.

They waited another thirty minutes. The line between the sea and sky came into focus as the day announced its imminent arrival.

"Time for another pull," Ryan said. Audrey yawned and flicked the switch to engage the winch. The winch hummed quietly as Ryan tailed the half-inch line and wound it into a coil at his feet. One hundred feet off the stern of the ship a large plankton net skimmed along the surface. This was their tenth pull.

"Why does the ocean have to wake up in the middle of the night?" Audrey asked with another yawn.

"To eat and not be eaten," Ryan said.

"I know what Diel Vertical Migration is."

"Then stop whining."

"Not whining, just making conversation. This would be much more pleasant during the day, soaking up some Vitamin D."

"Speak for yourself. I'm sweating like a pig in this suit."

The net came into view and Audrey turned off the winch. Together they wrestled the four-foot-wide, twenty-foot-long net onto the swim step. Just like all the other pulls. Nothing.

A deep-red glow filled the eastern sky as the sun crept closer to the horizon. The sound of voices drifted from the cargo chamber. The smell of freshly brewed coffee and frying bacon swirled in the gentle breeze, venting from the galley and circulating around the back of the ship.

Ryan took a deep whiff through his nostrils. "Ah, the ship awakens. Shall we call it a day?"

"You mean night? Sounds good to me."

Ryan disconnected the rope from a clip attached to the net. Together they rolled it up, heavy and unwieldy. The coiled rope and net were laid in a rubber-lined bin with a chunk of plastic. They stripped off their suits and shoved them into another rubber-lined bin with another chunk of plastic. Both bins were sealed shut and left on the swim step.

Since they didn't know what type of fungus they were dealing with Dr. Wickman concluded the best test for contamination was to isolate it with something it wants. Give it time and see if it consumes it. Not super scientific but the simplest test for what little they currently knew. A crafty solution that made her grin.

A couple of guys were milling around the cargo chamber waiting for something to happen. For all the urgency to get here there wasn't a lot going on. Everyone was on edge waiting for a discovery or for something exciting to happen. Audrey and Ryan introduced themselves.

"Burns," said a petite middle-aged man of Indian origin. He looked more like a science professor than a combat-trained Larkian.

"Tobe," said a tall Scotsman, red-bearded with an accent thick as a malted brew.

Both had been pledged as Larkian for nearly a decade, picked by Alvarez in his first round of recruits.

Burns pointed to the sky, fiery red. "Check out that sunrise."

"Red sky in morning, sailor take warning," Tobe said.

"You really believe in that crap?" Ryan asked.

They both gazed at Ryan like he just told them Santa Claus didn't exist.

Audrey piped up. "Saw it the morning we dove on Tallamure. Didn't work out so well. Let's hope Ryan's right. Just a lot of crap; just a random coincidence."

Tobe and Burns looked at each other and shrugged. "Let's hope."

Ryan and Audrey said farewell and slipped away to the cafeteria. They grabbed a quick bite then headed up to the bridge to see if Tucker had picked up any unusual readings from the network of sonobuoys.

Audrey and Ryan stopped at the top of the circular stairway that led down to Tucker's command center below the bridge. She heard him talking to someone about their recent challenge. Curious, she held Ryan back and paused to listen.

Tucker's voice floated up, "Odds were twenty to one. Can't believe she outwitted me and I lost my fucking hat. And you, you lucky son-of-a-bitch, pocketed a fortune."

She heard Blake chuckle. "Gotta know your horses. I chose wisely."

Tucker huffed. "You mean *wisely* by using insider information."

"I'm not going to respond to that," Blake said, curtly.

Audrey waited a few seconds before announcing her presence. She yelled down, "Permission to enter."

Tucker replied, "Oy."

Audrey and Ryan wound down the circular stairway. It was dark and warm and abuzz with banks of electronics. The air was stuffy and swirled with the smell of dirty socks, sweat, and hot electronics. Blake was sprawled in a chair next to Tucker fiddling with something in his hand. Tucker was sitting at his command station, shirt off, with a semi-circle of six glowing screens hovering above his keyboard. Three on top, three below. A bank of electronics filled the wall behind him. Tucked into the far end of the space was his unmade bunk and a dresser with a couple of drawers ajar. Spanning the width of the small rectangular space was a pull-up bar with a pair of pants slung over it.

He swirled to face her. "Well, well, speak of the she-devil."

"Still smartin'?"

"Careful, I might demand a rematch. Won't be so lucky next time. I'm wise to your ways, you wily witch."

She pinched his cheek. "And I yours. Hell of a tumble, wouldn't you say? How about we give it a rest, let me enjoy the glory for a few more days."

He looked at Blake. "Is it true you did that to her 'air?"

"Yep." He set something on the desk next to Tucker's mouse. A small folded creation. Tucker picked it up—an origami butterfly—and twirled it in his fingers.

Blake turned to address Tucker as if she wasn't there listening. "She's not a she-devil or a wily witch. She's a butterfly." He plucked the paper butterfly from Tucker's fingers, and folded the wings together. "The butterfly may appear weak and vulnerable, but it adapts to whatever situation it may find itself in, folding its wings to hide and blend in." Then he spread the wings open. "The butterfly spreads its wings to display a full spectrum of color and patterns. It is this beautiful display that stuns and frightens the predator but brings joy and brilliance to those who pose it no harm. We all witnessed the transformation. You helped her spread her wings, Tucker, and she proved crafty and resilient." Blake gave her a smile. "She justly earned her reward."

"Yeah, yeah. She's all those things but she whipped my ass and that *stings*. I'd add scorpion to that list of stuff she's like." Tucker pointed to the paper butterfly Blake held between his fingers. "Braids now this. Aren't you a hopeless romantic."

"Not hopeless." Blake reached over and handed his paper creation to her.

Audrey held back tears, gazing at the beautiful little butterfly lying in the palm of her hand, wings spread wide. She never thought of herself as a butterfly, a thing of mystery and beauty and crafty resilience. She sucked a sudden breath, fixing Blake with a watery gaze. "That's the kindest, sweetest thing anyone has ever said about me."

The bat cave fell silent except for the ever-present rumble of the ship and buzz of electronics.

Ryan snapped his fingers in front of Audrey's face. "Uh, guys, we've got slime to catch, lost ships to find."

Audrey blinked. "Right, sorry." Her head buzzed; from lack of sleep, from the intensity of Blake's gaze and thoughtful words, from the paper creation she held in her hand.

Then the moment was gone. Back to business. She plopped down in a chair next to Blake.

Tucker said, "So, you guys find anything?"

Audrey yawned. "Nothing, literally."

Ryan said, "Speaking of which, I'm gonna head back, stow our stuff."

Audrey waved him adieu while focusing on what was displayed on Tucker's screens.

"Water temps are higher than usual, especially on the bottom. Just like you described." Tucker was watching two screens, one showing readings coming back from the grid of sonobuoys, the other a topographical map of the ocean floor publicly available on the Internet. Not much variation, and not nearly as detailed as the one he had when they were searching for Tallamure. Those had been scanned by him and offered incredible detail. He hadn't had the opportunity to do the same in this part of the Pacific.

Audrey slouched in her chair and exhaled. Blake rubbed her neck. It was pretty stiff from one of Tucker's head locks. She sighed and melted into his fingers.

"Damn," Tucker whispered. Audrey cracked an eye. Tucker was zooming in on the grid. "Just lost a couple sonobuoys in sector five-F." He sat back with a sigh. "Probably nothing, could be weak batteries. Happens sometimes."

46

Attack

TUCKER CONTINUED TO SCAN the status of sonobuoys throughout the grid. He found no new failures. Audrey sat back, prompting Blake to keep massaging her neck. If Tucker wasn't worried about a few sonobuoys falling off line, then she wasn't going to worry either. He confirmed it happened frequently. Salt water and pressure were a bitch on electronics.

The submersible was nearly on the bottom ready to scoop up a sample and record what was down there, like possibly the hull of one of the missing ships. It was a long shot whether they would find anything at all. The proverbial needle in a haystack. Unfortunately, they wouldn't be able to see whatever was recorded until the submersible was retrieved. Only simple transmissions worked across the sonobuoy network, not a live video stream.

Tucker fingered his scar while staring at the main screen of his command center where a grid of active sonobuoys pulsed as individual points of light. Ten of them were now dark. Audrey imagined the gears spinning in his head.

"Gotta be weak batteries, that's all—" He lurched forward. "What the—" He attacked his keyboard, grabbed his mouse, scrolled around, dropped it, flipped on his comm channel to the bridge above. "Stokes, I just lost ten more sonobuoys—wait, twenty! Not a fluke! Something's happening!"

Tucker zoomed in on the grid where the sonobuoys were missing.

Tucker continued, "Stokes, the ship's positioned directly above the off-line sonobuoys."

"I'm seeing it too." His voice boomed over the comm speaker. "What's our position relative to target?"

"Directly above where those ships were last recorded."

Audrey's senses began to tingle. Something didn't feel right. Nervous energy flooded her body. Her heart raced. She looked around confused. "Where's Ryan?"

"Said he was heading to the cargo chamber to stow your stuff," Tucker said.

A strange, squirrelly feeling fluttered in her chest. That feeling you get right before impending doom. As if there's a force in the universe that emits a pulse of energy, giving a sixty-second warning before everything went to shit.

She jumped up. "I've got to warn Ryan." Then she bolted up the circular stairs to the bridge, Blake hot on her heels.

Stokes was scanning the horizon. "I don't like the look of those clouds."

The sky had darkened significantly since Audrey and Blake descended into Tucker's windowless command center. Thirty minutes had passed. Fifteen since Ryan departed for the cargo chamber.

Stokes clicked a button on his headset. "Dyer, seal the cargo chamber." Clicked it off. He turned to his second in command. "Lovric, open ship's comm." He raised a pair of binoculars to his eyes. Scanned a line of dark clouds forming all around them.

"Aye," Lovric said, "you're hot."

Stokes clicked on his headset. His voice boomed from speakers throughout the ship. "Code blue. Clear the decks, seal the cargo chamber. Possible rough weather. Possible compromise to ship. Repeat. Code blue."

Code blue also meant to prepare to muster with your teams, to stand by for further instruction.

Tucker's voice rang out through the bridge speakers. "Somethin's coming up from the bottom."

On the ship's depth and sonar display a large red blob emerged, edged with orange then yellow. The ship was lying solidly above the orange zone. "It's warm, whatever it is," Lovric said.

"Two hundred meters and rising," Tucker said. "The thermal reads thirty-two degrees Celsius and rising." He paused. "More sonobuoys down! Someone get a visual, what the hell's going on out there?"

Audrey and Blake stepped out a side door, Stokes following. Thunderheads surrounded the ship, blooming to the upper stratosphere. A water spout dropped from the center of one, drew water from the sea like a giant sucking from a straw. More water spouts dropped down. The ship was surrounded by water-borne tornadoes.

Quarter-sized drops fell from the sky, splattering Audrey's cheeks and bouncing off Stokes' bald head. Audrey licked a drop snaking down her cheek. "Salt water."

Gusts of wind swept across the water. The sea frothed. A deluge poured from a purple sky, blotting out the horizon, moving steadily toward the ship.

From below, a sudden upwelling of krill, plankton, and other unrecognizable sea creatures rose to the surface. Small fish leaped into the air, flapping frantically.

Audrey gasped. "We captured nothing during the night—why are they migrating to the surface now?"

"It's as if they're running from a predator," Blake said.

The body of a giant squid floated to the surface. Then another, and another, tentacles slapping the hull as if looking for a way to escape from the sea. Hundreds of them.

Lovric stepped to the door, yelling over the screaming wind. "Tucker's reporting thermal readings from separate entities. One thousand meters and rising. Dyer reports the cargo door's stuck. Working to clear."

Stokes ran back to the bridge, "Tell him to clear the chamber, seal the inner doors."

"Ryan's down there," Audrey yelled.

"I'm sure Dyer will keep him safe," Stokes said.

"You don't know Ryan!"

Audrey and Blake bolted across the upper deck to the aft end of the ship, racing down three flights of stairs. They leaned over the railing one level up from the cargo platform. Down below Ryan was helping Dyer wrestle with the containers and the rubber mat they had laid across the platform to protect from potential fungus spread.

Audrey screamed, "Leave them! Get out of there! Seal off the inner doors!"

Ryan look up. In the water below, a head popped to the surface; eyes glowing orange, face dark-skinned, and hair of burnt-bronze.

Terrakai!

The Terrakai grabbed Ryan by the leg and yanked him into the sea.

Audrey flew down the stairway to the platform. She hopped over the railing, sucked a lungful of air, then dove into the water. Sea life writhed around her. She tried to open her eyes, but they were walloped by krill and fuzzed with plankton, forcing her to narrow her lids to slits.

She swam to a glowing shape not far below. Krill and plankton gave it a wide berth. She pinched her nose, equalizing the pressure building in her ears, and swam deeper. The Terrakai had Ryan cocooned within his lorica, with his arm wrapped around Ryan's neck. Ryan's eyes were wild with shock and fear.

She had no weapon. She had no rubber suit for protection. Her lungs were on fire.

A silver string of air slipped past her lips. She felt the swirl of electrical current. She tried to maintain calm but reality dictated otherwise as panic filled her. She had seconds before she involuntarily sucked a lungful of water.

Spears pierced the water, then the gelatinous lorica; one found the Terrakai's neck. Blood bloomed and the arm around Ryan's neck went limp. The Terrakai's lorica swelled then disintegrated with a blinding flash of light and a jolt of electricity. Audrey's heart faltered. The last of her air slipped past her lips.

Someone grabbed her around the waist. She gasped when she broke the surface. Blake held her in his arms, aggressively swimming toward the platform. He propped her arms on a rung of the ladder, hanging in the water. Dyer popped up beside her with Ryan in his arms. He was limp and unconscious. Hands grabbed her by the wrists and pulled her up. She flopped onto the platform. Ryan's lifeless body followed.

Blake and Dyer were still in the water.

She rolled to her side, helpless, and gasping, "Get out! Get out of the water!"

Blake's head suddenly went under.

"Somebody help him!" Audrey yelled, tugging against hands that held her back.

Dyer dove down. There was a brilliant flash of light below. The surface of the water danced with tiny sharp peaks, then lay flat as a mirror. No sign of either of them.

She was suddenly airborne and bouncing across Tobe's shoulder, heading into the cargo chamber. Burns grabbed Ryan. They were dumped against the hull of a tender tucked against the hull of the ship.

Audrey sat up and felt for Ryan's pulse. Weak but beating evenly. And he was breathing.

Stokes' voice boomed from the ship's speakers. "Code Red! Code Red!"

Eight rubber-suited crewmen poured through the inner door. Cabinets lining the forward bulkhead were pulled open. Crossbows sailed through the air to waiting hands, followed by spare preloaded barrels of exploding-tip arrows. Safeties clicked off.

A couple of guys were helping Burns and Tobe drag Blake and Dyer from the water. Two others kicked the containers with the drag equipment and their suits overboard. Together they dragged the rubber mat off the platform. Someone engaged the platform hydraulics. There was a loud *clunk*. Then it rose slowly.

"Come on, come on, faster!" someone yelled. The platform slowed with a shimmy, then emitted a sick grinding sound and stopped halfway closed. A burst of ash followed. A corner of the rubber mat was stuck on one side.

Burns and Tobe dragged Blake and Dyer by their arms away from the stuck platform and dumped them beside Ryan. Both were weak and writhing.

The air rippled around the platform opening. Camouflaged bodies launched from the sea and skidded down the sloped platform. More clunking and grinding as Dyer struggled to close it. Threads of smoke and the smell of burnt plastic rose from the winch.

Audrey screamed, "They're getting inside! Camouflaged! Watch for rippled air!"

Bolts of electrical fire exploded from rippled air, striking the aft bulkhead, whizzing over their heads. Storage cabinets buckled. A jet ski exploded. The hiss of an extinguisher followed as a brave crewmen put out the fire.

Arrows fired back. Invisible bodies suddenly appeared once struck. Their orange eyes widened in shock when the multi-bladed tips detonated, shredding whatever flesh it had found. Terrakai fell to their knees, crumpled over, and exploded into ash.

A rubber-suited crewman had freed the mat that was blocking the platform door. He threw it at Audrey's feet. "Cover yourselves!"

Then he rejoined the fight. Audrey yanked the mat over the four of them, prone and vulnerable.

Five more rubber-suited crewman came from inside the ship and joined the fight. One was struck in the chest by a bolt of electrical fire. He fell to a knee for a beat, then jumped to his feet and fired his thirty-round, auto-fire crossbow in a controlled sweep across the lip of the platform.

Ping! Ping! Ping!

Poof! Poof! Poof! Terrakai burst to ash.

The ship rolled violently. Crewmen formed a wall and advanced determinedly as one unit toward the platform opening, fighting the sway of the ship, firing at every inch of air. Beyond the opening, the seas were lively; black clouds spit bolts of lightning.

Fatally wounded Terrakai crumpled. Ash was set aloft by gusts of wind that slipped past the cracked opening and filled the chamber, coating everything in a layer of gray snow. The air was thick with it and the taste of metal and must. Audrey whipped off her shirt and covered Ryan's mouth and nose with a sleeve, then her own with the other. She helped Blake and Dyer cover their faces to protect their lungs.

She could barely see across the chamber through the smoke and ash. Voices shouted. There was a loud *clunk*. The platform shuddered and whined, then slammed shut. A camouflaged body trapped between the hull and the platform burst into ash. Audrey's ears popped from the sudden change in pressure.

The crewmen formed a tight circle around the four of them lying on the cargo floor, kneeling with crossbows raised, ready to defend.

Burns yelled, "Tucker, run thermal scans!"

There was a tense pause filled with the sound of adrenaline-fueled breath and the roll and groan of the ship and things clanking around in cupboards.

Then, Tucker's voice: "All clear outside the circle!"

The crew took no chances and told Audrey and the others to stay put beneath the mat. They fanned out, searching every nook and cranny—around the submarine, the jet skis, the tenders.

The ship shuddered and rolled violently. Audible gasps as bodies swayed to stay upright.

Stokes' voice boomed over the ship speakers, "Rough seas! Hold tight. Trying to outrun it!"

The engines rumbled; the ship lurched when they accelerated and the props bit water.

Ryan stirred. "Where am I?"

Audrey grabbed his hand. "You're alive, that's all that matters."

Then he threw up a gallon of salt water.

Dyer made a face, tried to sit up. "Gross," he wheezed. "You got me, Wood. Not how I wanted, but you did." He looked pale and shaky.

"Bad time for jokes, Dyer, take it easy," Audrey pushed him down.

Blake worked his fingers. "That was terrifying, paralyzed underwater but totally aware. I thought I was going to drown."

Dyer slurred. "Yeah, that asshole shocked us good, but I got him."

Dr. Wickman came through the inner door, dropped to a knee beside Blake and scanned his eyes with a small light pen. He checked his pulse. "Your heartbeat is still accelerated. Stay put. Calming breath."

Blake nodded.

Then Dr. Wickman turned to Audrey. She waved him off. "See to Dyer and Ryan. I gulped a little sea water, that's all."

She stood up. The ship shuddered, sending her to her knees. Metal groaned in protest and spent arrows slid across the metal floor.

The motion of the ship, the urgency to escape whatever was happening outside, and the worried sound of Stokes' voice brought her back to her feet. She moved low and slightly crouched to the side of the chamber, grabbing onto to whatever she could find to keep her on her feet. She peered out a porthole.

The sea ran in confused circles. Foam swirled and twisted into mini-tornadoes. A hundred yards off from the ship a giant whirlpool bored a hole in the sea. Directly above it was the biggest, darkest, most evil cloud she'd ever seen. The thing they were running from.

A bolt of lightning sprang from the cloud's mouth like a forked tongue and lashed out at the ship. It struck the water in a blinding flash, lighting a sea coated in Orange. A deluge of Orange-tainted rain followed.

47

Elite Orankai

SINTO BROKE FROM HIS restorative meditation several hours later. The parasitic draw still did its damage. Between the last several hours and the short time wrapped in the Scout's band, his merlux was down to about a third of its peak reserves. A critical means of his defense was compromised, not by accident but by Arkis' order.

Arkis wasn't stupid; in fact he could be quite cunning and manipulative. He was systematically weakening Sinto's resolve. First the pleasantries, then the questioning of Sinto's trust, then the weakening of his body. Pushing Sinto into a state of mind that could make him vulnerable to persuasion. How else could he have taken control over the city in such a short period of time? Sinto found it hard to believe the remaining residents would readily join his "new world order" and voluntarily participate in the destruction of this once beautiful and thriving city.

Suevo stepped into the room and jolted in surprise, eyes moving to the empty bed until finally landing on Sinto huddled in the corner, chin tucked and gazing back through a fringe of lashes.

Suevo crossed the room and grabbed Sinto by the chin, forcing Sinto to look at him.

He regarded Sinto with his fiery orange eyes. "Time to go pretty boy. Wouldn't want to be late for your party, now would you?"

Sinto sensed a hint of jealously in his voice, and stood. "Where's Arkis?"

"He's meeting us there." Suevo was of equal stature and met Sinto's gaze, the warning in his eyes clear. Suevo grabbed Sinto's elbow and led him through the door. Sinto directed his gaze to the floor, thankful the life-sucking band was secured to Suevo's waist and not wrapped around his chest.

Sinto asked in as non-threatening a voice as possible. "Where's *there*?"

"The auditorium. He said not to be late."

"Then best we hurry," Sinto said.

Taylee was waiting outside the room and they marched in formation: Suevo in the lead, Sinto in the middle, Taylee in the rear. The shorter guard prodded Sinto forward with a stiff finger and jeered whenever Sinto looked back, irritated.

They passed through a locked doorway out of Arkis' private residence and into a hallway that extended as far as Sinto could see. Fiery balls of light hovered along the dreary ceiling. Mirrored doors lined both sides, their parasitic draw reaching for Sinto's dwindling energy reserve. Housing for Arkis' recruits. Of which, Sinto came to realize, he was considered one.

As they marched in silence, Sinto noted Taylee's and Suevo's routines and individual habits, calculating their advantages and disadvantages. The guards moved slower and with less grace than Sinto, but their bodies were more muscular and stronger. Sinto had the advantage of his fluked whale-like tail. He was faster and more flexible and especially good at worming his way out of most tight physical situations. But if Sinto bolted and was caught, the two of them could easily out-power him physically. Plus they had the benefit of the parasitic bands, neatly tied at their waists and ready to deploy.

The one uncertainty was their electrical strength. That depended on individual genetics, not tribal descent. The only other Merahvu who had out-shocked Sinto was his sister Naiada. Electrical superiority was a strong characteristic in his family, passed down by their father, Ramasis. No one outside Sinto's family was aware of Sinto's exceptional gift except a very few. Unfortunately, Arkis had learned of Sinto's talent when they were younglings. Arkis had challenged Sinto to an ill-fated contest of who could out-shock the other. Sinto won and had to restart Arkis' heart. By the way Arkis was treating him he had not forgotten that lesson.

Recruits from all three tribes emerged from some of the doors they passed by, bare-chested and wearing black leather wraps like Sinto's. All were males and each was led by guards in uniforms like Suevo's and Taylee's. The recruits had eyes colored by their heritage: gemstone for Seakai, golden or amber for Terrakai, and pale blue for Arctakai. The guards' eyes were all a distinct fiery orange.

Arkis' eyes had once been a simmering amber, lively and mischievous. Now they burned a dark reddish-orange, wicked and venomous like a deadly snake. Was it an act of camouflage or from something else?

They reached the end of the long hallway. Sinto was first to be led through an arched doorway to a small courtyard beside the auditorium. Its massive wall soared and intersected the city's dome wall. Beyond the dome the lake was steeped in darkness. Based on the outward curve of the auditorium wall, the view from within was clearly oriented toward the lake waters outside the dome.

Sinto drew a deep breath. The oxygen mix was no better than the mix inside Arkis' rigid and gloomy structure; heavy with carbon dioxide and light with oxygen. Every breath triggered a feeling of suffocation. Not to the point of panic, but enough to keep him off balance and distracted. Another control mechanism.

The courtyard filled quickly and the group of confused recruits was shuffled by an equal number of guards toward an unmarked door cut in the auditorium wall. Sinto counted twenty-one recruits including himself.

A horn, like the one he heard earlier, rang out three times—*dah-woo*—a pause then it repeated. No lungs pushed air through an object to make the mind-numbing sound; it was transmitted telepathically to every mind in the city, a summoning impossible to ignore.

Suevo and Taylee stood with Sinto sandwiched in between. They took turns prodding his mind, daring him to flee. He did not. Not the place or the time. He ignored their mind-meddling thoughts between summoning blasts.

Terrakai streamed in from all around the city in response to the summoning. Their coverings included a wrap and a vest similar to those that Arkis' guards wore but were colored either gray or green and made of cloth instead of animal skins. Some appeared more tattered than others. Uniforms.

They all had buttons sewn on their vests. Not silver and shiny like the guards', but carved from wood—and far fewer of them.

A chaotic buzz of activity ensued as the mass of bodies gathered. The entrances to the auditorium were guarded. Terrakai lined up, waiting to be let inside. Sinto and the other heavily guarded recruits were held aside within the private courtyard and given a respectable distance.

"What are they waiting for?" Sinto asked.

"To be sorted," Taylee said.

At first the noisy greetings and scurrying of bodies through the doorways appeared to be random, but Sinto quickly saw an order to the chaos. Each door was marked with dots, like the buttons sewn on their uniformed vests. One, three, seven, and so on, each entering a doorway marked to match the number of buttons attached to their vests.

Uniforms, buttons, assigned doorways…

Enforced sorting into societal classes.

Sinto looked down at his bare chest. The recruits had no vests.

Suevo noticed. "You'll get yours once you prove your loyalty and your worth."

Sinto also noticed the guards were handing out small cups of liquid, which were greedily gulped down before those approved for passage slipped through the doors.

"Required refreshment," Suevo said. "Don't worry, you'll get yours soon enough."

The unmarked door to the auditorium opened, revealing a small sparse room.

"Everyone inside," Taylee yelled.

Sinto held back until the others passed through and was the last to step inside.

Suevo sealed the door with a lock. He gave Sinto a wicked smile. "Please, do something stupid."

The recruits shuffled around in the small space. Some chatted excitedly, some nervously adjusted their wraps, some sized up the others in the room. All eyes suspiciously landed on Sinto at some point. He suspected they had been told who he was.

Sinto heard Arkis' hyena laughter over the banter. He stepped away from a circle of men, waved to Sinto. "Come here, Sinto." An order not a suggestion.

Arkis wore the same black leather wrap as the other recruits, along with a red silk shirt, partially buttoned and exposing his chest but not the swell of his belly.

Sinto forced a smile and greeted Arkis as if he had nothing to worry about.

Arkis gazed into Sinto's eyes over a pair of round tinted glasses perched on his broad nose. The kohl around his eyes had been refreshed and his irises blazed orange, glowing much brighter than a few hours ago.

He put his arm around Sinto's shoulders. He was clearly worked up, literally bouncing on his feet. "I'm tickled you're here, finally, where you belong. I was sad to hear of your death, but alas, I now understand the genius of your reasoning and will do everything I can to keep your secret! I have high expectations and great plans for you, good friend!"

He said it with such enthusiasm, Sinto thought he was joking. *Good friend?* Sinto couldn't imagine how one might be treated if they were not Arkis' friend or loyal dog like Suevo and Taylee. Sinto had the sneaking suspicion he was about to find out.

And Arkis keep a secret? That would be a first. By the way everyone was looking at him, the secret was out.

Arkis released him and stepped up on a circular platform placed in the middle of the sparse room. "Listen up!" He demanded.

The room quieted and all eyes turned to Sinto's troublesome cousin with a level of awe and respect Sinto did not believe he deserved.

"I want to personally welcome all of you to the Elites. Yes, you heard that right. *Elites.* Each and every one of you have been chosen for a very important and specific purpose. As the name implies you are the best of the best, possessing the highest order of excellence and *inherited* assets. You are the strongest and most powerful of mind and body."

He clasped his hands at his chest and drew a dramatic breath. "It is with great pleasure I announce the formation of a new tribe. A perfect blending of Terrakai, Seakai, and Arctakai, one never achieved before. You all are perfect specimens to create and help populate this new tribe. Say goodbye to Merahvu and hello to *Orankai!*" He opened his hands. "You have been especially chosen for this specific and honored role and will be rewarded, based on your performance during your initiation."

A combined buzz of unease, fear, and competitiveness colored the collective aura, filling the room. Sinto sensed not everyone was here by their own volition.

"I know what you might be thinking... and it is true you will not be the first to wonder why this is necessary. But please hear me out. We have been suppressed by the current rule of the Circle and Queen Ianthe, compromising our ideals and ignoring our concerns. They have lied about what is happening on Merluma. They discourage integration with the Sapien world. They want you to cower and hide in fear at the bottom of Earth's oceans, or sequester on Merluma."

He paused to let his words sink in before continuing. "But why? Why do we allow the Sapiens to rule Earth, to use its resources for themselves, to claim ownership to its lands and oceans? The Circle claims it is for the greater good. But what have we gained? We have grown weak and complacent while the Sapiens have overrun Earth, stripped its oceans, depleted and tainted its fresh waters. It is only a matter of time before they discover Merluma, stake claim to her, and strip her of her dwindling resources; to root us out and destroy us as they have done to so many in the past. This city is rotting because of them!"

He frowned. "Remember sucuvita? Our most sacred life-giving and vital elixir—now in short supply." He put his hand to his ear. "Why, you ask?" He dropped his hand and glared at Sinto accusingly. "Because our queen has horded it, doling it out only to her most loyal. She decides who lives or dies. But do not fear. This and future generations of Orankai will benefit from a new and improved elixir! We will no longer need sucuvita. We will no long have to conserve! I offer it to all of you freely! While I can't reveal the source of this amazing new discovery, you must trust me when I say its supply is *endless*."

Sinto's heart pounded. Lies! He struggled to remain calm, from hearing the twisted truths Arkis told and the feel of suffocation with each and every stifling breath.

Arkis swept his fiery gaze across each of his recruits, pausing on Sinto the longest. He swept his hand toward the dark waters beyond the dome. "We must not forget what happened to the indigenous Sapiens who once thrived on the lands surrounding these Great Waters. Long before Merahvu was established and

Tallamure was built, the Terrakai had befriended them—treaties were established and communities integrated. And when invading Sapiens came from the east the Terrakai were threatened by the queen and ordered to retreat to Merluma. Many did not and were murdered, along with their dual-blood children, by the sharp blade of her Seakai army."

Sinto fumed. More lies. That was not what happened. It was the queen who warned them to leave and they did, and after, it was the Sapiens who murdered their own kind.

Arkis continued his fantastical story. "Look where we are now! Those same capitalizing Sapiens are coming for you! Queen Ianthe and those before her failed to warn us of these threats. We can no longer trust her or the Circle to lead the next generation. We must rise up against the forces that threaten to destroy our world. Earth is as much ours as it is the Sapiens'. We must stop all who threaten our future, crush them in a way they least expect it!"

He raised his arms. "You are no longer Merahvu, Seakai, Arctakai, or Terrakai. From the failings of a unified Merahvu and the ashes of Tallamure, I give rise to the Orankai!" He paused with raised brows as those around Sinto shuffled with unease or huffed in agreement. "As Orankai elites you will be respected for the station you occupy, offered the best residences, entertainment, and—" He smirked. "Whatever else you might desire."

He pointed around the room. "You are elites of blood and station. The best of the best. Elite of the Orankai!" And with that Arkis raised his arm with his hand fisted, folded it across his chest, pressed his fist to his forehead, then punched it outward before dropping his arm to his side. Sinto recognized it as a salute eerily similar to those adopted in the past by Sapien fascist movements.

The guards prodded the recruits to return the salute, the most competitive recruits first to act, then the others joining in. Sinto included.

Someone started chanting, "Orankai, Orankai, Orankai," a chant growing louder as voices joined in. Sinto moved his lips but could not bring himself to vocalize the word.

Arkis beamed, waving his hands for it to continue.

Sinto's mind shut out the voices and reeled at the implication of what Arkis described. He preached truths and fantasies all tangled up into one scary story to make him feel important and powerful. He proposed abolishing what had naturally transpired, disregarding history that dated back to the days of the Homo-Sapien ancestors who first slipped through the cracks between Earth and Merahvu.

There was a reason the Merahvu evolved their way. Splintered groups of Homo-Sapiens evolved to survive the harsh environments they found themselves thrust into, naturally and organically.

As time passed and environmental conditions settled and the seamless migration to Earth became routine and accepted, the Merahvu evolved from barbaric tribalism into a sophisticated society that celebrated their differences. A society devoid of violence, of communities where members were free to choose how to contribute, where to live, and with whom. A society where tribal members were given equal voice.

Sapien history was filled with leaders who believed the rigidity of one rule and one lineage led to longevity and success. Logic that defies nature. One type of bee cannot be designed to suit every purpose. Diversity is nature's secret elixir to longevity. All of the stories Sinto read about these experiments ended with tragedy and death and the eventual collapse of what was once a functioning society. Arkis' proposed Orankai sounded a lot like one of these stories on a fast track to utter destruction. Like the destruction of this city in such a short period of time. All by Arkis' design.

Merahvu history was far from perfect but so too was nature. Some are born stronger, some weaker. Some die because of environmental conditions while others thrive. Some are born evil and act out in brutal ways. Others group together and fight back. Some are lucky, some are not.

Nature is brutal for a reason. Balance. Like the doe who must choose which of her two fawns will live because she only has the capacity to nurse one to full maturity. That fawn did not die because of greed or an insecure ego. It died because it was the weaker of the two and by bad luck was born in a year of drought. Sooner or later nature catches up. She always does. Arkis lacked this sensible understanding. Evidenced by what had become of his city.

Arkis and those who enabled him promised false hope. A distraction from the true threats facing the Merahvu, and the Sapiens. The Orankai tribe he was forming was the first and foremost threat of all.

Filled with these troubling thoughts, Sinto lined up with the others, wondering what awaited on the other side of the auditorium door.

48

Elite Slave

Sinto stepped through the mirrored door and into the auditorium. He became one in the shuffle of bodies being led by Arkis.

The gathering crowd exploded into cheers once they saw Arkis. He beamed and waved, a cult leader greeting his fervent followers. Rows of seats stretched high and wide to the extreme ends and top of the massive auditorium, large enough to seat many residents of the city. Everyone remained standing, the reason clear. Arkis turned to Sinto and the others, encouraged them to wave at the crowd. Sinto plastered on a smile and did as Arkis demanded, fighting brewing nausea.

Sinto mapped out his surroundings as he faced the cheering crowd. Uniformed males stood guard at every possible exit on every level. Regardless, Sinto calculated distances from the front row seats where he stood to each exit. He counted the number of guards with parasitic bands hanging from their waists. There were too many and, with all the commotion, he lost count before he reached one hundred.

The crowd present was predominantly Terrakai, like Arkis' elite guards. A small smattering were Seakai or Arctakai, sorted among the lower classes, standing at the top of the auditorium by the seats farthest away from the dome wall. Still, no one sat; all remained standing.

The recruits lined up along the seats in the front row. Arkis circled back to stand by the seat beside Sinto, front and center. The row behind them remained unclaimed and empty.

The dome wall soared before him, forming a backdrop to a small platform between the first row of seats and the waters of the lake beyond. Suevo and Taylee, along with the other guards, took places beside the platform and all along the outer walls.

In the lake, Seakai and Arctakai in gray uniforms with vests marked by a single wooden button scraped sheets of algae from the outer dome wall with their hands. They were not as well-fed as Arkis' guards or even Arkis' followers filling the auditorium. Those laboring outside the dome were gaunt and thin-limbed with lifeless orange eyes.

Slaves.

The slaves outside the dome stole nervous glances at the dark void behind them while they worked. Scores of opossum shrimp swarmed, nibbling on the bits of algae drifting down from their hands and piling up on the lake bed. Schools of small fish gobbled up the shrimp, and even bigger schools of siscowet lake trout circled, picking off the smaller fish. Large dark shadows lurked in the distance. Lamprey. The lake's food web on display. Where the slaves would fit into it was clear.

Sinto knew he had no chance of punching through the dome wall and making a mad dash for the dock in Duluth, where Rachel waited for his return. The slaves cleaning the dome wall didn't worry him, nor the distant lampreys. He calculated he had just enough reserves and time to launch a tunnel to the pier before they could organize and gather for a deadly attack.

But he was certain that the dome wall was locked, especially for him. And even more certain that Arkis controlled the lock, deciding who could come and go. By the way Suevo and Taylee shadowed him, Sinto knew he was a slave just as much as those reduced to scrubbing algae from the dome's outer surface. If the dome was locked he would bounce off, probably after receiving a punishing shock. Or perhaps he would be sucked against the surface with a reverse polar current, like the door to the prison cell Arkis had called a "nice place to prepare" for this event. In that case, the life would literally be sucked out of him in a matter of moments.

Suevo and Taylee glared at Sinto as if they knew what he was thinking. Taylee slowly shook his head. Suevo gave Sinto that wicked grin that screamed, *Go ahead, try it. Be stupid.*

A procession of guards equally as threatening as Suevo and Taylee entered the auditorium and claimed the row of empty seats behind Sinto. They too remained standing, like everyone else in the auditorium including the recruits, some of whom were looking around wondering what to do.

Arkis stopped waving to the crowd and faced the row of guards. In unison they punched their right fists forward, across their chests, then to forehead before punching the air and dropping their fists to their sides. Arkis nodded his approval at the impenetrable wall of thuggery to Sinto's back and sides.

No way of escape. Not here, not now, he decided, modifying his earlier mantra. *Take it in, swallow it whole, live to escape—and warn others.*

Silence befell the auditorium but for the squeak of slaves' hands slipping across the outer dome wall. All eyes were locked on Arkis. He stood for several beats, savoring the power, then he motioned for the recruits to sit, then the guards behind them. He paused, holding that power in his hands before motioning for everyone else to sit. Arkis was the last to claim his seat beside Sinto.

Outside the dome, a trio of females swam into view and proceeded to put on a show, grasping each other's hands and tails and spinning in a circle, then coming together and swimming apart as if a flower blooming. An unexpected display of grace and beauty in such a morbid place. These were the first females, other than

Zayra, that Sinto had seen since entering the city. He assumed they were a warm-up act for what came next.

Sinto shifted in his seat to face Arkis. "So, tell me about the buttons, this *sorting* Suevo mentioned to me earlier."

"Ah, yes, the sorting." Arkis clicked his tongue against his teeth. "With the increase in our population we found it necessary to instill some rather strict rules and methods to manage the masses."

Arkis gestured toward the crowd.

"Everyone is given a fair chance to earn merits, to improve their station among others. The more buttons you earn, the higher your station. Each and every resident of the city must display them at all times to identify their rank. Rank is based on one's demonstrated talents and accomplishments. Those with the most buttons are part of my Elite Force: Guards, Scouts, and those with other valuable and unique contributions they may have to offer..." His lips curled into a wicked grin. "Such as yourself."

He didn't give Sinto a chance to respond, and continued, "Our servants—cooks, tailors, food gatherers, and others, like those out there polishing the dome—keep our city humming along smoothly. They are the lowest ranked. Healers and the educators, who are teaching our younglings the Orankai ways, rank somewhere in between. Behind you, the keepers of the law—my elite guard—rank high. Hand-picked by yours truly for their strength and aggression and fortitude to carry out orders, no matter what that may entail." Arkis leaned closer and lowered his voice. "And my most trusted, ranked at the highest order. Let's just say, there are few, *very* few, but you, Sinto, *you* have the unique opportunity to become one of them."

He sat back and sighed. "It has been a difficult and challenging job to be the one responsible for peace and harmony amongst the growing population of this very fine city. It requires making difficult decisions, especially when dealing with those who, shall I say, *disagree* with the Orankai way."

Sounds like a cult, not a civilized tribe, Sinto thought.

"Where are the females?" Sinto pointed to the trio gracefully swimming in the waters outside. "Other than those lovelies."

Arkis elbowed Sinto in the ribs. "Oh, Sinto, I do like the way you think. Most of them are on Merluma, gestating and nurturing our next generation. But don't worry, not *all* of them are there. Oops!" His hand flew to his mouth, stifling an exaggerated giggle. "I mustn't tell you more. I'd hate to ruin the surprise."

"Surprise?" Sinto feigned enthusiasm, not the surge of dread he suddenly felt.

Before Arkis could answer, the mock sun hovering at the top of the city's dome dimmed, simulating the glow of twilight. The trio of females darted out of view. The auditorium darkened and quieted.

Balls of electrical fire burst to life from the fingertips of the remaining slaves bobbing in the waters outside the dome. Simultaneously, they launched glowing orbs of light above their heads, creating a fiery ring that illuminated a large watery stage. The trunk of a dead tree stood prominently in the center, shaved of its bark and limbs, its base buried in the mucky bottom. The slaves swam away and out of sight. Lamprey darted just outside the ring of light.

From the sidelines, Suevo launched a ball of fire above the platform wedged between the front row of seats and the dome wall, the watery stage as its backdrop. Arkis bolted from his seat with a flourish of his wispy-finned tail and landed in the circle of the fireball's light.

The crowd stood and chanted boldly, "ARKIS, ARKIS, ARKIS."

The recruits next to Sinto stood and joined them. Sinto did the same, moved his lips but said nothing. Praising his friend felt horribly wrong—as wrong as the fanatical and righteous auras swirling around him.

Arkis beamed, eating it up. Sinto watched with quiet horror, wondering how his cousin had captured the minds and essences of those who apparently worshiped him as if he was a god. It was true that Arkis could be funny and charismatic—the life of the party—and as he was growing up, Sinto as well as others had been drawn to him because of his dramatic and adventuresome flair. But there had been a darker side to him as well. One that Sinto had avoided and discouraged whenever they were together. One that Sinto now realized ran deeper than he ever imagined. That all of the tricks he pulled, especially those more harmful than funny, had been a reflection of who Arkis truly was.

A dark aura clung to Arkis. One Sinto had never noticed before. Maybe Sinto never really knew Arkis that well or maybe Arkis was a master at hiding his true essence; a mask he now cast aside, revealing his true self. Sinto reflected back to the way he had treated his mate Zayra. His lack of respect and gratitude. How he feigned joy at seeing Sinto, only to lock him up in a room designed to weaken and demoralize him. How he seemed intent to make Sinto another slave to his new tribe.

Arkis had made *everyone* in the auditorium slaves to his new tribe, and they seemed to love him for it. Sinto kept coming around to that question of how. *How* was Arkis able to garner their complete and total compliance?

Arkis waved for silence and the crowd instantly obliged. "Do I sense an unusual level of anticipation tonight?" He held his hand to his ear.

A roar erupted from the crowd.

"As you should! But before we begin, I've got a very important and exciting announcement to make. One that will blow your mind!" He used his hands in gesture. "Kaboom!"

"BOOM! BOOM! BOOM!" the crowd chanted.

"Tonight we accept a new member into our tribe. Can you guess who?" He put his hands palm sides out against ears, eyes bugged and mouth wide, prompting for their telepathic reply. "Yes! YES! I hear your telepathic voices! The rumors are true!"

He waved his hands for Sinto to stand up.

"Don't be shy, my friend, pop up, and show the people who you are!"

Put on the spot with no warning, Sinto's heart thundered, and he struggled to mute the fear bleeding through his aura. But he did as Arkis asked, as a slave would for its master. He flicked his mighty fluked tail and rose above the other recruits who were jealously watching. He swam in a slow circle, knowing this would please Arkis. His prized pet, performing on cue.

"May we all give Sinto, son of Queen Ianthe…" Arkis paused for a loud round of hissing from the crowd, "and our own beloved Ramasis an Orankai welcome!"

The crowd erupted, "SINTO, SINTO, SINTO," followed by a clamor of stomping feet.

A simple flick of Arkis' wrist silenced them.

Sinto felt hopeful at the mention of his father's name but sickened by the response it evoked. He spun one more time scanning the faces in the crowd and a small group of those perched at the very back of the auditorium masked in the shadows of a low overhang. Could one of them be his father?

It made Sinto sick to do what he knew he must. The way Arkis was staring at him, it was expected. A test of Sinto's sincerity to Arkis' cause. He spun to face Arkis, punched his fist straight out, across his chest, fist to forehead, up in the air, then down to his side. The symbolic salute to the Orankai order.

Arkis nodded his approval, beaming in front of his adoring crowd and pleased with the performance of his newest slave.

Arkis' gaze never left Sinto's eyes when he said, "Sinto has made a very wise choice to join the Orankai. I have high expectations that he will play a very, *very* important role in delivering our new queen."

Sinto dropped to his seat as the crowd went crazy, stomping their feet and roaring their approval.

Sinto's mouth went bone dry.

Not Naiada. Not while I still live.

"I also want to welcome our other new recruits! And as tradition dictates, it is now time to celebrate our continued advance toward imminent victory. What do we say?" He held his hand to his ear.

"In with the new, out with the old!" The crowd roared back.

Arkis gave the salute. The crowd stood and gave it back. And with that Arkis swam back to his seat and settled in by Sinto's side.

Sinto seethed. It took every ounce of strength for Sinto to still his hands and not wrap them around Arkis' neck.

49

Deathly Show

THE THRUM OF EXCITEMENT swirled through the auditorium and radiated from the crowd, with eyes aglow and fiery orange. They stomped their feet and clicked their teeth as if chomping on invisible meat. The lampreys beyond the ring of light became animated, flicking about like sharks catching the whiff of fresh blood.

The crowd screamed, "In with the new, out with the old!"

That pit in Sinto's stomach grew deeper.

The crowd roared when two guards swam into the ring of light outside the dome, dragging a male Seakai by his golden hair. His arms and tail were lashed to his body by three electrified bands. A body-length piece of rope was wound around his neck. The guards attached the rope to a ring at the top of the pole. The Seakai prisoner thrashed his legs to escape but bounced back when he reached the end of the rope. Live bait tethered. The movement provoked a frenzy of movement beyond the light.

The guards retreated.

The prisoner hid his face from the crowd with his splayed hair and kicked madly to keep his back toward the crowd. He had been stripped of coverings and it was difficult to distinguish who it might be based on his unique markings, obscured by distance and his bound tail.

The crowd behind Sinto booed.

"Show us your face, coward," one heckled.

Others screamed, "Sever the rope! Try to run! Give us a show!"

The lampreys swam just outside the ring of light. The prisoner twisted and yanked his shoulders, fighting to free his arms. Electricity crackled across the bands with every attempt to escape. The more he thrashed, the weaker and more defeated he became and the more frenzied the shadows swirling in the dark wings of the watery stage became. The lampreys were ready and eager to attack, but they were being held back by something. Or someone.

Sinto had witnessed sharks attacking a weakened prey, but never a Merahvu. It was futile to attack a Merahvu—all creatures instinctively knew of their physical power to shock and kill and their mental acumen to master and manipulate a lesser creature's mind. Merahvu were the masters of the natural world, especially the underwater world.

Arkis stood up, and yelled, "Let the show begin!"

The lampreys burst into view and circled their prey in a blur of rippling fins and snapping tails and yawning round mouths filled with rows upon rows of razor-sharp teeth.

A lamprey struck the prisoner on the shoulder, spinning him around to face the crowd, his long golden hair flowing behind him.

Sinto inhaled a sharp breath.

The prisoner was Beech, one of two Seakai representatives in the Circle. Beech had been a good friend of his father's and they had worked together on many projects that mutually benefited the Merahvu, including those now screaming for his blood.

Sinto's heart thundered and urgent questions filled his mind. How many members of the Circle have fallen at Arkis' command? Was Beech the first? Could his father have shared this same fate?

Beech did not deserve to die. He was a peaceful man, compassionate and generous, not like the monsters screaming for his blood. How had he fallen victim to Arkis and his Orankai? Had he come to the city freely? Or was he captured and brought here for this night's entertainment?

Sinto tried not to watch, but that insatiable need for his mind to grasp the reality of what was happening won over. His eyes failed to blink at the horrible scene unfolding.

Two lampreys broke out of the pack; one butted Beech in the back, the other struck him in the stomach. Neither latched on.

They're softening up his flesh!

They took nibbles from his shoulders and his buttocks, teasingly torturing their prey. A lamprey struck one of the parasitic bands. It cracked and fell to the lake bed. Beech struggled harder to escape.

The crowd chanted, "PLAY, PLAY, PLAY!"

The lampreys were fueled by the taunting and Beech's thrashing. One severed the rope mooring Beech to the pole. Floating free, the lampreys began tossing Beech back and forth like orcas tenderizing the flesh of a seal before gulping it down. Beech's head whipped violently with each powerful hit. Blood stained the water and bits of Beech's flesh dropped to the lake bed where daring trout darted in for a bite.

Sinto swallowed bile rising in the back of his throat. His merlux hummed and tail twitched with each blow to Beech's helpless body. It took every ounce of strength not to act.

He must have been breathing hard. Arkis elbowed him in the ribs. "Got you excited I see! Save your energy, the night's just begun."

Sinto closed his eyes and concentrated on reining in his emotions and the impulse to try and save Beech. Sinto knew any attempt would be futile, between the number of guards and the frenzied lamprey. He locked down his merlux and took Arkis' warning seriously.

There would be nothing gained and much lost if Sinto gave in to his impulse and suffered Beech's fate.

Live today, fight tomorrow.

Sinto blocked the tragedy unfolding before him from his mind. He locked unseeing eyes on the frenzied massacre; he filled his mind with the vision of his sister Naiada and his need to escape alive. The urgency to warn his mother and the remaining members of the Circle. His goal of finding his father was slipping farther down the list of what he must do.

Arkis stood and yelled, "Stop!"

The lampreys stopped playing and Beech settled to the lake bed on his knees. Torn flesh hung from his body. His head hung in defeat. Only a single band remained around his torso.

"*Fight, Beech, fight!*" Sinto pushed his plea into Beech's mind.

Beech slowly raised his head and fixed his eyes on Sinto. A wave of despair rippled through their telepathic link.

"*Too late for me. Run while you still can.*"

"*Ramasis... have you seen Ramasis?*"

Beech's gaze drifted across the crowd before shifting back to Sinto.

"*The Ramasis I knew died long ago. Run Sinto, warn Ianthe! Protect your sister!*"

Then Beech fixed his dull gaze upon the crowd in the stands and pushed his telepathic message to the crowd's collective minds. "*I am proud to be Merahvu. I am not ashamed. Are you?*"

Arkis jumped to his feet. "You are the one who chose to die, traitor, and die you will." He waved his hands, signaling to the crowd, and chanted, "EAT, EAT, EAT."

The crowd joined in, a deafening sound that rattled Sinto to his core. Their fiery orange eyes glowed with a blood-lust Sinto had never seen before in the natural world. The stink of rot and evil swirled from their collective aura.

The lampreys whipped into a feeding frenzy. One after another attacked, latching their razor-sharp teeth onto Beech's body like a ball of writhing snakes. Bursts of blood stained the water. The crowd's roar couldn't overpower Beech's screams reverberating through Sinto's mind.

Sinto could take it no longer. He shut down his sensory receptors. Not knowing what else Arkis had planned, he questioned if he was strong enough to make it through the night, free, sane, and alive.

How could Sinto have been so naive to walk into Arkis' trap? His father's well-being was no longer a priority. Survive he must. Long enough to escape, and warn his mother and his sister. Ramasis must be dead, or worse, one of them. He needed no other evidence. From what was done to Beech it was clear. Join or die.

Sinto didn't want to die. He *couldn't* die. His sister's fate was his only tether to sanity. He had no choice but to go along with Arkis' little game. To convince him Sinto was ready to fully embrace the Orankai. To become one of the very special few. And maybe, just maybe, Arkis would loosen his grip enough that Sinto could slip away before anyone would notice.

"Sinto. Sinto?" Arkis wrapped an arm around his shoulder and shook him.

Sinto focused his eyes and escaped the terror he held bottled up inside. Outside the dome, schools of fish of all kinds nibbled on the scattered remains of his father's once good friend. Eaten alive and torn to bits and left to feed the bottom of the food chain.

Sinto tore his gaze from the morbid scene, put on a stony mask, and faced Arkis.

"Sorry, Arkis. It's been a while since I last ate and watching all the feasting has made me a bit lightheaded. Did you mention something about dinner?" He laughed and added, "That was one hell of a show, made me realize I was hungry."

Arkis grinned. "That's my boy. We will feast, and more. Much more!"

50

Orange Effect

REQUIEM SEA II RAN hard to the south to escape the stormy mayhem. No one was allowed outside. Every door, porthole, and hatch was buttoned up. The generators and water-making equipment had been shut down so as not to suck up tainted seawater for cooling or desalinating. Luckily, the engines were cooled by radiator-like keel coolers built into the ship's hull and sealed from salt water intrusion. Exhaust was released through dry stacks running from the lower engine room to the top deck. Without them the ship would have been a sitting duck. Dead in the water. Like the two ships they never found.

Stokes wisely guided the ship into a deluge of rain once they cleared the thick patch of Orange. Untainted rainwater washed what they could see through the windows free of any Orange-tainted water that might have rained on the ship.

Being aware of what Orange was capable of and acting fast saved the ship and, most likely, all forty-four lives on board. A somber mood befell the crew on the realization that the missing research ships and their crew had not been so lucky.

Dr. Wickman and a small team surveyed the outside state of the ship and signaled an all-clear, but not before scraping tiny samples of the fungus puddled in dips around the rubber seals of the ship's communication domes. The samples were hermetically sealed in glass jars with rubber stoppers and placed inside a second hermetically sealed glass box, then delivered to the lab for observation. They were never able to retrieve the submersible sent to the bottom for a sample. Dr. Wickman felt lucky they got what they got. A least half their mission was accomplished.

They raced south toward the Hawaiian Islands and Isla Salvación, the island where Audrey was born, located west of Kauai. It wasn't until now that Audrey learned Isla Salvación was designated as an independent country: created, owned, and governed by none other than her father and his original crew. The Larkian Nation. Every recruit was given Larkian citizenship, including her. Her Larkian passport had been under the safe-keeping of her father all this time. He ensured she had been given dual-citizenship as an American before she was able to talk.

Audrey had not been back to Isla Salvación since her mother died. It was with mixed emotion she anticipated their arrival. Dr. Wickman said the island had changed greatly over the past decade but the house on the south end where she had lived was exactly as they left it over ten years ago. It made sense now; her father had been vague about the island, claiming it was independently owned—just not by whom. She had never felt the need to dig farther and reopen old wounds.

The island was the seat of the Larkian Nation with a harbor, staffing, and facilities able to perform whatever ship repairs may be necessary. *Requiem Sea II* was most certainly in need of it. Most of the damage was exterior. The two-part epoxy paint coating every surface of the ship was literally eaten away in strips when Orange rained down from the sky. A deluge of rain had interrupted its feast but not before it left its mark. Streaks of bare metal and etched paint marred the hull and the topsides. The ship took on a ghostly zebra-striped look and was quite a fright.

After running for twelve hours, a break in the weather brought sunshine and calm seas, and anyone who was off duty littered the helipad deck, shooting hoops, practicing golf swings, and playing pickle ball with a heavier, more-solid ball less susceptible to the wind. Others simply lounged in the sun. Audrey had learned that these modern-day pirates were dead serious about combat and protecting their own, and keeping a clean and well-functioning ship—but even more serious about playing and partying hard. Music boomed from outdoor speakers. Beer and rum drinks flowed. A much-needed break from the disaster they barely escaped.

Audrey and Blake were involved in a heated match of pickle ball with Burns and Tucker. At match point, Tucker slammed it down the line just beyond Audrey's reach.

"Yesss," he hissed, grabbing a fist full of air above his head and pulling it to his chest.

They gathered at the net to give the winners deserved congrats. Tucker tapped the rim of the badass hat sitting on Audrey's head. "One step closer..."

"And a mile behind," she finished for him. She tapped his nose; it was bright red. "You might want to cover that."

"Oy, right. Sunshine can be hell on the skin after livin' in a cave all day."

"You should get out more."

"Oh, I plan too. Find me a sweet lady-friend and get lost in paradise."

Blake and Burns bantered about catching some waves once they reached the island. Audrey wasn't sure what she planned to do and demurred from joining the conversation.

She waved goodbye. "Enough sun for me. I'm heading inside to find Ryan. He said something about helping Dyer in the cargo chamber." After their near-death experience they'd become best buddies.

Audrey wound her way down the outside stairway to level two and ducked inside. She was still sweating from the heated match with Burns and Tucker and felt a sudden chill from the cool air circulating inside the ship. It took a few seconds for her eyes to adjust to the artificial light. She paused at the lab door and peeked inside.

Dr. Wickman and her father were in the wet lab, hunched over the glass box containing samples of Orange. Sealed arm holes were cut into the side and lined with rubber gloves for manipulating the samples.

Curious, she joined them.

Her father perked up. "Audrey!"

"Hiya, thought I'd stop by, see what you've learned so far."

Her father looked at Dr. Wickman. Dr. Wickman said, "More than I think we want to know. This stuff is remarkable and terrifying. As you know, it consumes petroleum-based polymers at an extraordinary rate. I dabbled with something like this long ago as a method for breaking down recycled plastics, but we scrapped that project when other priorities arose. But this—this is like nothing I've seen in all my years."

"Nor mine," her father said.

Dr. Wickman stuck his hands inside the rubber gloves. "It's what it does to a host if ingested that is most disturbing." He opened one of the water-filled glass jars with a quarter-sized blob of Orange settled at the bottom and extracted a small sample with a glass syringe. Then he capped the top with a rubber stopper, sealed the jar, and placed the syringe on a pull-out metal tray. He removed his hands from the rubber gloves, pulled out the tray, and carefully picked up the syringe.

They followed him to a small glass tank littered with seaweed and a lone Dungeness crab. He removed the rubber cap, dipped the syringe in the water. The entire blob of Orange slipped out and settled at the bottom of the tank amongst the seaweed. Then he placed the syringe in a sterilizing unit and flipped on the infrared light.

Dr. Wickman said, "It tends to stick to itself. I've yet to witness it leaving any kind of residue. But I'm not taking any chances."

The crab circled the blob of Orange wriggling around in its new environment. At first the crab stood back, but grew curious, poking it with one of its walking appendages. Then it stuck it, picked it up, and ate it. The crab carried on, picking its way across the bottom of the tank looking for something else to eat.

After a minute or so, the crab began shaking as if having a seizure. Then it perked up, rising on its appendages, and turned to face them. Its beady eyes were no longer black. They were an orange color so brilliant that they appeared to glow. The crab reared up on its swimming appendages and threw itself against the glass, pinchers clicking. It became desperate, pounding on the glass, staring them down with its strange orange eyes.

A shiver ran down her spine. "Its eyes—like the Terrakai that attacked us."

Her father added, "Agitated and restless like the missing ships reported."

"Watch this." Dr. Wickman pulled another crab from a large tank of live crabs reserved for crew meals and dropped it in with the orange-eyed one.

The orange-eyed crab turned and circled the intruder. It reached out with its front pinchers, clamped down on the other crab's own pinchers, and snapped them off. Then it went for the innocent crab's eyes, snipping them away one by one, then it knocked the crab on his back and ripped into its underbelly. With swift precise strokes it peeled back its shell and ripped its guts out. Then the orange-eyed crab stepped defiantly away. The attack was not to feed but to kill, an attack so ruthless, targeted, and sudden that the innocent crab didn't have a chance to fight back.

"We observed that if both crabs ingest the organism, they don't attack each other. Instead they work together to attack any innocent bystander, as if they've formed an alliance."

Audrey swallowed. "That's enough to make you lose sleep at night."

He nodded. "It's hard to say what would happen if this organism infected the aquatic food web."

Audrey pointed at the orange-eyed crab. "The Terrakai that attacked us, their eyes were orange too. Every single one. Terrakai typically have gold or amber eye coloring. I never saw one with eyes like that."

Her father glanced at Dr. Wickman. "Neither have we."

"Do you think it's a virus?" Audrey asked.

"It doesn't appear to cause any breakdown of function; if anything, it enhances, like a drug. Once the effects wear off, though, this specimen will return to normal. At least as far as I've observed. I haven't had enough time to determine if there are long-term effects from ingesting it."

"Sinto showed me that reef as a warning. This is new to the Merahvu. He believed it posed a danger to all of us, Merahvu and Sapien."

Dr. Wickman said, "It does make you wonder what those Terrakai were doing there."

The orange-eyed crab had been watching their interaction, its pincher claw *tap-tap-tapping* against the side of the tank, staring back as if it knew the answer to Dr. Wickman's question.

"Let's keep this to ourselves. For now," her father said, turning to Audrey. "I don't want to spook the crew. No one must learn what we just witnessed, is that clear?"

Audrey swallowed down an objection, nodded.

He said to Dr. Wickman. "Destroy that crab and quarantine the samples on level zero."

He grasped Audrey by the arm. "No one gets access except Dr. Wickman. *Understand?*"

"Yes."

He squeezed a little tighter. "Say nothing to anybody."

"Say nothing, got it."

He shook her arm, gently. "And keep your hands off the samples."

"Absolutely, no touchy."

He released her arm, then studied her for a beat. "Good."

51

Deadly Seduction

Audrey left the lab deeply troubled. While the crew was celebrating escaping a tragic fate, her father and Dr. Wickman were discovering the depth of the catastrophe brewing in the Pacific, one with a huge impact to Earth's future.

She was forbidden to say anything to anybody, not even Ryan, which would be a challenge. Ryan was the one and only person she trusted whenever she needed help. He was the one she told about the Merahvu after she was reunited with Sinto and learned of his world. Not that Ryan believed her at first, but he was the only one with whom she shared her secret. But she also understood that what Dr. Wickman discovered had to remain a secret, or else risk panicking the crew. So she vowed to say nothing, as she promised—even to Ryan.

She forced the image of the orange-eyed crab massacre from her mind and worked her way down the mid-ship stairway and aft to the cargo chamber.

The transom door was secured shut. Beams of sunlight cut through small portholes in the side of the hull. Circles of light swept across the spotlessly clean diamond-patterned steel floor from the gentle sway of the ship. The rubber mat under which Audrey had huddled with Ryan as the crew fought attacking Terrakai had been stowed. Spent arrows had been picked up, refurbished, and loaded back into their auto-firing barrels and secured in the arsenal lockers along the back wall. There were a few remaining boxes, stacked and yet to be stored, lying between the ship's tenders near the transom.

One invisible clue remained of what had happened. That haunting smell she would never forget. The metallic musty smell of ashy remains, though not a speck of ash remained. Otherwise the chamber was spotless with the exception of scorched metal along the aft port side of the hull where one of the jet skis had taken a full hit of electrical fire and exploded.

Ryan was alone, fiddling with something at the work bench on the opposite side of the chamber next to one of the tenders.

"Where's your new best buddy?"

"Went to get something to eat."

"Whatcha working on?"

He held up a crossbow. "The barrel froze."

"When did you become an engineer?"

"I don't know. I like to tinker with stuff from time to time. More interesting than getting a sunburn. These things are fascinating. Never knew they existed."

"Probably don't except here on this ship." She laughed. "I've been around this stuff for so long, I guess I never really thought about it. Just assumed it was standard equipment my dad ordered off the Internet."

"Not this."

Ryan handed it to her; she fingered the barrel. It was indeed stuck in place. "From what I've learned over the last month I'd be willing to bet the government has an entire office dedicated to approving the patents filed by the Larkians." She handed the crossbow back to Ryan.

"Never imagined this was what I'd be doing when you asked if I wanted to come on this trip."

"Welcome to my nightmare!"

"What? This isn't a nightmare, this is the coolest gig. Ever. Sign me up for next time."

"Ha. I guess, you're right. I mean, now it seems pretty cool, but growing up around all this secrecy messed with my head."

"I can imagine."

"You saw the wall around the perimeter of the house. Like a prison. Now I understand why my dad was so paranoid." She drew a deep breath. That smell. Metal and must. Maybe it was imagined or just residual ash stuck in her sinuses.

Ryan asked, "Speaking of secrets, do you know what Dyer did before working for your father?"

"Probably something he'd like to forget. I think it best to let that secret remain just that. These guys were recruited from all over, pulled from the streets, rejected from society. Alvarez has the knack for finding the roughest of diamonds and Dr. Wickman for polishing them into something spectacular."

"Yeah. From what Dyer told me I would agree. Said the guy he once was is dead and buried."

Audrey thought she heard something. A creak like a door opening. "Did you hear that?"

Ryan shook his head, rolled the crossbow from side to side, inspecting the retractable pin that secured the barrel. He pulled open a metal drawer below the workbench and rummaged for some pliers.

Audrey left him to his project, curious about the sound. She was sure it came from the direction of the ship's tender on the other side of the chamber. She walked around it, scanning the darkly tinted side windows, rounding the bow where the plowed end of the chrome-plated anchor curled around the stubby pulpit. She continued down the other side where sunlight bled through portholes. She decided it was something that shifted from the ship's gentle motion. Or nerves. Especially after what she witnessed in the lab.

She rounded the tender's transom, was struck in the chest, and lifted clean off her feet. Her last breath was knocked from her lungs when she slammed into a metal cabinet. Her head struck with a solid crack and a sudden burst of pain reverberated through her skull. Her feet slid out from under her and she landed in a heap with her legs crumpled beneath her and her back pinned against cool metal. The room spun and dark spots danced in her eyes. It was so sudden it took her a beat to acknowledge what happened. She shook her head trying to shake the dizziness and sudden bout of nausea.

Ryan slowly turned to see what happened. The crossbow slipped from his fingers and clattered to his feet. He froze, eyes wide, his empty hands splayed from dropping the crossbow.

A female Terrakai cowered in the center of the chamber, her gaze whipping between them. She was shaking and appeared frightened. Her eyes were an orangy-amber color, weakly glowing. She was a girl probably no older than sixteen.

Audrey tried to get up but dizziness pulled her back. The girl crouched lower as if preparing to strike. Camouflage flickered across her feet, blending seamlessly with the diamond-patterned floor. Ryan hadn't moved, frozen by fear, as if stuck in a time warp. Seconds passed. Audrey worked her fingers, sucked shallow breaths, swallowed down nausea.

The girl looked all around. Left, right, up. Her eyes locked on the inner door, assessing danger or maybe looking for a means of escape.

Ryan finally snapped out of his stupor, raised his hands as if to surrender. He said, "It's okay, I won't hurt you."

The girl snapped her gaze in his direction. Cocked her head. Slowly she stood, stole a glance back at Audrey.

Audrey pretended to be unconscious, chin to chest, eyes narrowed to slits.

Still slumped, she breathed more purposefully. Her vision started to clear and the dizziness subsided. She had one chance to act and she wanted to be sure she was ready. Deep breath in, slow count out. Adrenaline sputtered through her veins.

The girl took a step toward Ryan. Then another. She was at least twenty feet away from him. Audrey heard the crackle and buzz of her merlux firing. A very subtle sound, but thanks to everything Sinto taught her, she understood exactly what it meant. Audrey was twice the distance away on the other side. She had no weapon. No rubber suit to protect her from being electrocuted. Attacking the girl unprotected was incredibly risky, suicidal even.

Her heart thundered. Ryan was in grave danger. She had to act.

If Audrey warned Ryan the girl would respond. The girl was scared and charged and possibly unpredictable. If she was a native Terrakai she may not understand English. Negotiation out of the question. Bad situation.

The girl was still facing Ryan. Ryan's gaze shifted from the girl to Audrey. Audrey held a finger to her lips. Then dropped her chin to chest anticipating the girl to look back. She did. *Good,* Audrey thought. Might buy Ryan time if she thought Audrey was no longer a danger.

Ryan started talking, in a soothing voice, "I won't hurt you... you must be hungry." He mimicked putting something in his mouth. "Hungry?"

Brilliant Ryan! Just the distraction she needed.

Audrey rose to her feet and slithered behind the tender, quiet as a snake, scanning for anything she could use as a weapon. A toolbox stood open next to the scorched spot of metal and rack of jet skis. She moved toward it quickly. Lying next to the toolbox was a large wrench. The kind used for tightening engine mounts. About eighteen inches long with a head about four inches across. Hefty, with more weight at the end, like a steel mace.

Ryan was still talking. The girl was inching closer. Curious, very curious. Distracted but getting dangerously close to Ryan.

Audrey darted from the cover of the tender's bow, to the stack of boxes, then again to the bow of the second tender, secured on rails on the other side of the chamber, closer to Ryan. She could see Ryan down the alleyway between the tender and the hull of the ship. The girl just beyond the tender's transom. Audrey ducked down; saw her feet, actively reflecting the metal flooring. The girl continued her slow march toward Ryan. Twelve feet. Ten. Nine...

Audrey's best chance was to come from behind. She retraced her steps, circling back and around the bow along the other side of the tender, stopping just short of the aft end of the chamber. She crouched, looked for the girl's feet. Eight feet from Ryan and still moving forward.

Ryan had stopped talking. Audrey peered around the end of the transom. His gaze was transfixed and odd. "You want to what?" he said. He ran his fingers through his hair, a nervous laugh, a shake of his head. "I mean, you're just a—no way! But—but how?"

The girl was six feet from him, merlux buzzing like a hive. Audrey had no doubt the surface of her skin was electrified.

Then the girl reached up and peeled back the protective flaps of skin covering her breasts. She smoothed them back around her ribs. Ryan blinked. She took another step closer. Four feet. Then she reached for the flaps of skin covering her groin.

Ryan gasped. "Ohh, no, no. I really shouldn't..." His eyes bugged and mind warred, the effects of manipulation clearly rippling across his face. Then something changed. His face relaxed, and an odd smile curled his lips. Audrey had seen that smile before. Ryan was a lady's man in a teddy bear package; he frequently used that smile when picking up a date. He looked to be genuinely flirting. But Ryan was a man of integrity. He would never take advantage of someone so young.

She's gotten into his mind! Using the universal language of seduction! No words required! Images would do just fine!

The girl reached out at the same time she dropped to a knee. Ryan was fully transfixed, breathing hard. A bead of sweat trickled down his cheek. Audrey barely recognized him, acting like a stranger. He gave the girl a nervous grin then reached out to take her hand.

The girl's chest crackled. Her brightly glowing eyes lighted Ryan's face. She was fully charged and ready to shock.

Audrey jumped from behind the tender's transom, wrench gripped in her hands like a baseball bat. Using her forward momentum, she coiled and swung.

The wrench struck the girl in the temple. She crumpled to the floor, knees bent to the side, arms splayed, lying on her back with a wide-eyed gaze, body twitching. Blood bloomed like a halo from the concaved place in her skull, a fast-growing puddle encircling Ryan's feet. She blinked once, twice. The fire in her eyes faded, light orange, then yellow, then white. She twitched a couple more times, then stilled. Audrey covered her nose and mouth and stepped back, expecting her to disintegrate into a cloud of musty ash.

The girl lay dead at their feet. Eyes dead. No movement. No ash.

Ryan stepped back and shook his head, utterly confused. "What the fuck just happened?"

Audrey dropped the wrench. It landed on the metal deck with a loud *clank*. Her fingers ached, bone-deep and throbbing. In that brief contact to the girl's electrified skin, she took a powerful jolt that zinged up her spine to the back of her skull. Like striking a live wire before it fizzled.

Ryan slid to the floor with his back against the metal drawers. At his feet lay the dead girl, his shoes stained with her spreading blood. He buried his face in his hands, chest heaving.

Audrey froze over the body, hand to mouth, unblinking. The girl looked even younger than Audrey first guessed. The girl's breasts were small, either barely developed or just that way. Her face was round and full of youthful innocence.

Barely a young woman, more like a child.

Dyer burst through the inner door and started yelling for help. Dr. Wickman knelt beside the fallen girl, hesitated at first, then pressed his fingers to her neck.

Audrey's father came to her side.

Dr. Wickman looked up and said, "She's dead."

Audrey looked at the girl, then Dr. Wickman, then to her father, disbelieving the girl was truly dead. It happened so fast, acting on trained instinct, like a soldier in battle. She was that soldier, and she *murdered a child*. She tried to say something. Nothing came out. She couldn't move or talk or think. She started shaking uncontrollably. Her father wrapped his arms around her, crushing her to his chest.

She looked up into those eyes that reflected a thousand shades of blue. There was pride and love for her in those glacial warrior eyes but she didn't feel she deserved it.

"What have I done?"

52

Mind Fuck

THE CHAMBER TURNED INTO a murder investigation scene. Dr. Wickman asked everyone to stand back. He scooped up blood samples, cut off a large lock of hair, and used a large pair of tweezers to inspect the splayed layer of protective skin lying across the dead girl's ribs. Then he respectfully laid them across her breasts. He stood up, a look of confusion and disbelief on his gentle face. His eyes scanned every inch of the dead girl as if she would disintegrate at any moment and he was determined to burn every detail into memory.

Audrey was still wrapped in her father's embrace. "Why didn't she disintegrate? Sinto said they're programmed to once they die. To leave no trace."

Dr. Wickman said, "I don't know." He looked at her father. "We've never seen one dead before."

Her father was staring at her crushed skull. "Perhaps because her brain was damaged."

A fresh wave of despair roiled through her and she started shaking, again. Brain damaged. *I did that.*

Ryan hadn't moved. He sat pale and quiet, mindlessly gazing at floor.

Blake knelt beside him. "What do you say we get out of here?"

He didn't answer, and stood. He stole one last glance back at the dead girl. Blake wrapped an arm across his shoulder and led him away.

Audrey's father released her. "Go with them."

She didn't object; she didn't steal another glance at the dead girl. She'd seen enough.

The three of them climbed the mid-ship stairway quiet as ghosts. Blake suggested they decompress somewhere quiet. Maybe find a shot of something strong to drink.

Blake led them to the library. A couple of guys were playing a game of chess, another was intently reading. Soothing music played softly. Something nostalgic from the seventies.

They settled in a far corner with seating for four around a coffee table. Ryan sat. The soft chestnut-brown leather chair engulfed him. Blake pressed Audrey down into a small sofa across from Ryan. Headed for the bar, returned with a full bottle of rum and three highball glasses.

He sat next to Audrey on the sofa. Poured them all a generous shot. Ryan grabbed his glass and threw it back. Signaled Blake to give him another. They sipped in silence. The smooth liquor slipped down her throat and warmed her belly. The effects were instantaneous. Slowly she started to relax. To *breathe*. She hadn't realized every muscle in her body was taut, ready to fight.

"I keep going over it in my mind," Ryan said. "I was feeling things, wanting to *do* things, but—" his mouth froze open.

"She was manipulating you. It wasn't you."

He looked at Audrey. "I was ready to get down on the floor and—" His eyes widened in horror. "Jesus!"

"She seduced you. She planted suggestions in your mind. Things you would not normally think or do."

"I feel gross and disgusted just thinking about it. You saw her. She was practically a kid!"

"It's not your fault."

He scrubbed his face as if trying to expel what just happened. "I just can't shake how utterly real it felt. My thoughts, my actions, my *desire*. I couldn't—I couldn't help myself. I couldn't stop."

"That's exactly right. It wasn't *you*. She planted those ideas in your mind. A total mind fuck. You should be angry she did that you—a violation, akin to rape. Keep telling yourself that. Else it will eat you alive."

Ryan sighed. "Maybe you ought to train us all what to do, you know, for if this happens again."

Audrey nodded. "Not a bad idea. The trick is to identify when it happens, then ignore it. Dr. Wickman might have some suggestions we all could use."

Blake pressed his shoulder against hers. "And what about you?"

"What about me?"

He cocked his head. "You know what. You can't kill someone and be perfectly all right after."

She looked away. Tears stung her eyes. She rolled her lips into a tight grimace. He was right. She wasn't perfectly all right. She was a disaster. Maybe she ought to ask Tucker to pummel it out of her in the gym later.

Blake put his arm around her and pulled her close. "You're just like your father. Brave and honorable and good at hiding behind a mask whenever something deeply troubles you."

She opened her mouth to refute what Blake said, but stopped. She had never thought of herself that way. Masks were a coping mechanism. Dr. Wickman often mentioned that, but she thought he was talking about her father, not her. But right now, she didn't need therapy; that was something she could deal with later. What she needed at this moment was sitting right beside her. She sank into Blake's embrace, the warmth of his body pressed against hers, the solidness of his arms cradling her. This was much-needed therapy.

Though, she was curious about what Blake just said. "How do you know that about my father?"

It took him a beat to answer. "Observation. I've known his type, and I know you."

53

Initiation

ARKIS WAS STRANGELY QUIET as he led Sinto and the other Elite recruits to a doorway cut into the floor of the room where they had gathered prior to entering the auditorium. He stood alongside Suevo and Taylee as the recruits dropped through to a room below one at a time.

Arkis stopped Sinto when it was his turn. "Be honest, Sinto, what did you think of the show?"

An atrocity directed by a madman to entertain his blind followers, was what Sinto wanted to say, but bit his tongue, smiled, and told Arkis what he wanted to hear, "Entertaining, to say the least, and I very much look forward to this 'surprise' you have planned for me."

Arkis studied Sinto carefully, then burst into laughter. "Oh, yes, the best is yet to come."

Taylee held Sinto back while Suevo dropped to the room below. Then he gave Sinto a not-so-friendly nudge to follow.

Sinto landed beside Suevo. Taylee dropped down next, sandwiching Sinto between them. No matter how hard Sinto tried to feign enthusiasm and support toward Arkis' new world order, Arkis kept Sinto on a tight leash. Sinto decided it best to ignore his guard dogs like pesky flies.

He turned his attention away from the brawn surrounding him to focus on his next challenge.

The room was smaller than he expected. It was circular and intimate, with tables set around a gently flowing fountain of orange-colored liquid, ringed by small empty pitchers. Pin-pricks of light shone down from the ceiling like twinkling stars. The walls were darkly colored and the arched ceiling gave the effect of being in a cave. A natural habitat preferred by Terrakai.

Sinto flashed back to his discovery on Merluma; of caves, orange liquid, and suffering.

But there was a profound difference. Each table was festively set with crystal glasses, cloth napkins folded to look like a blooming flowers, fine china and silver utensils. A feast awaited on shelves carved into the outer walls. The fountain emitted the soothing sound of trickling water. Had Sinto not sensed the danger he was in, he would have felt lulled into relaxation, ready to enjoy a satisfying meal with new acquaintances.

But he knew it for what it was. A trap.

Eight darkened doorways lead to dark hallways that radiated out from the banquet hall like spokes on a wheel. A similar shape to the structure that included Arkis' residence and the long hallways with rooms for new recruits. Sinto sensed each hallway led to a dead end. The opening in the ceiling appeared to be the only way in or out.

Nervous and excited voices filled the hall as the last of the recruits dropped down from above. Arkis being the last. Suevo set a seal and locked the opening, cutting off Sinto's only means of escape.

Arkis took up position next to the fountain and a respectful hush descended.

"Welcome my friends, my Elites. As many of you may have observed, we've grown our population significantly over the past year. This is only the beginning. Orankai are born every day to aid in our cause. You have been chosen to lead those young minds and bodies in the fight for what we believe is right and just. The time has come to celebrate your fine assets, the reason you were chosen. Tonight you will cast aside your origins to become Orankai! And as part of your initiation, you will be rewarded for your commitment to the new world order."

He gestured for Sinto to come forward. Sinto set an earnest face and fulfilled Arkis' request.

Murmurs quickly spread throughout the room.

"I'd like to thank my special guest for the evening. As I mentioned earlier, Sinto has come to join our ranks and help us recruit others to join the Orankai, including our new queen."

It felt like dying when Sinto said, "I'm honored Arkis chose me for this essential task, as I am sure all of you are as well."

The recruits cheered. Arkis beamed. Sinto suffered a vile burn deep in his gut.

Arkis said, "But first, let's replenish our souls and fill our bellies!" Then he clapped his hands twice.

Young Terrakai-featured females poured from the darkened doorways carrying trays of drinks. Sinto counted twenty-one total, the same number of male recruits. Each one a perfect specimen of utmost beauty. Each with blank golden eyes.

Sinto probed some of their minds. Open like a book to be read by all, only the pages were blank. Minds void of memories or opinions. It was clear by the way they strutted past the tables, passing out drinks, that they weren't here for simply serving drinks or meaningful conversation.

Arkis leaned over and whispered into Sinto's ear, "Fresh from Merluma, ripe and ready for seed."

Sinto looked up at a young female handing him a drink. Like a child, she looked scared and uncomfortable until she noticed Sinto watching her. Her demeanor shifted and she gave him a seductive smile. A newborn bred for one purpose and one purpose only.

Procreation.

Arkis had not advanced the Merahvu way of life—he had thrown it back in time where murder was deemed entertainment, the disgruntled became slaves, and females were solely for procreation and pleasuring.

Sinto felt nauseous. Did Arkis intend to reduce Naiada to a pleasuring female should she fail to provide him what he so desperately sought?

Arkis ribbed Sinto, then held out a platter of sliced meats. "Eat, Sinto, you look paler than usual."

Sinto took the platter and gazed at the parade of young females circling the fountain. "Of course, I can see I must fuel my body." He winked at Arkis. "For later."

As Sinto ate, he felt the familiar pin-prick in his ear. Arkis probing. But his attempted probes were no match for the lock on Sinto's mind.

"You sure you're not having second thoughts?" Arkis asked.

Sinto feigned surprise. "Why would I?" Sinto shot a leering gaze toward a young female who had stopped beside their table. "I am looking forward to this *initiation* you have promised."

Arkis laughed. "Sinto, you surprise me. I thought you, of all people, would put up a fight."

"Why would I want to do that? I've been held prisoner by my birthright all my life. What you offer is freedom." Sinto raised his drink. "To the Orankai."

Arkis raised his drink and shouted to all, "To the Orankai!"

The other recruits raised their drinks and joined Arkis and Sinto as they drank down their sweet liquor.

"Refills!" Arkis ordered.

The young female standing beside him poured Sinto and Arkis fresh drinks. She continued to linger, casting flirtatious glances in Sinto's direction.

"I think she likes you," Arkis whispered in his ear. "She could be yours and no one else's. The one who will bear your first offspring. Your true mate. The one you will share the initiation with, like I did with Zayra. But of course, that doesn't mean you can't... *stray*, in fact, you must! We want many little Sintos filling our ranks! But be assured, she cannot stray, nor be with another. She would be yours and only yours to do with as you please, to provide offspring, to serve you as you command, for many years to come."

Sinto swept his gaze the full length of the young female's body. "Hmm."

Arkis ribbed Sinto. "What do you think? She is a beauty, open-minded too—you can make her do whatever you want, as a true mate must."

The Mark in his forearm prickled. *Mate.* His heart throbbed at the thought of Audrey. To be far from this place and safe in another with her. The thought bloomed in his mind, threatening to unravel the charade he was growing more and more certain Arkis was buying. He tamped it down, focused on one thing: escape.

He looked up at the young female. Her vacant mind was an open book ready to be written. He sensed she was a little unsure and frightened, putting on a show with the hopes of being chosen. Sinto hated to think what might happen to her if she was rejected.

She swam around the back of the table with the grace of a ballerina and leaned over to whisper in Sinto's ear. Her long silky hair brushed his bare back.

"My name is Mianna."

Her golden eyes brightened when Sinto turned and looked up.

"Please, choose me."

Her breath was fresh and sweet, her teeth straight and white, her nose pert and perfectly proportioned to her heart-shaped face. Her upwardly slanted eyes were warm and inviting.

Sweet. Innocent. A victim.

Could he trust her if he decided to flee once they were alone? His eyes shifted to the other females parading around the room. Was there someone else he should choose?

Sinto felt a pang of fear. Not for himself, but for sweet, innocent Mianna. If he chose her and he managed to escape, would she be punished for his actions? He gazed around the room at the other males. Would another do her no harm and keep her safe? Was life, any life, sacred in Arkis' barbaric new world?

Arkis gave Sinto an encouraging smile and wag of brow.

Sinto ran his fingers through Mianna's hair and breathed it in, absorbing the sweet fragrance of innocence. Innocent like the newly born.

It made him sick. The decision he was about to make.

War punishes the innocent long before its mongers fall.

Sinto stood and held out is hand. "My name is Sinto. Please join me."

Mianna shot a nervous glance at Arkis. He nodded his approval, then she turned to Sinto and bowed, accepting his offer. She looked up, smiled, then quickly swam to the fountain. She grabbed one of the empty pitchers and filled it with the orange liquid trickling from the fountain.

Arkis smiled wickedly. "Great choice, Sinto—now go with her. I assure you, Mianna will take *excellent* care of you."

54

Mianna Of Merluma

EVERYTHING SINTO FEARED WAS suddenly happening. His eyes cut to the opening in the ceiling, locked and sealed with Suevo and Taylee below, standing guard. They eyed the young female by his side, then glared at Sinto, faces taut with jealousy.

Mianna grasped his hand and tugged him toward one of the darkened hallways. Sinto mindlessly followed, thoughts reeling as he tried to formulate a plan. Certainly, he could overpower her, but what next? Perhaps there would be another exit wherever she was taking him. He sincerely doubted that, knowing Arkis, and the fact Suevo and Taylee were guarding the banquet hall where they entered.

The hallway curved dramatically to the left, blocking the view of the banquet hall, and ended at a single doorway. Mianna didn't bother palming the reflective surface of door; she easily passed through, pulling Sinto inside.

Sinto scanned the room. No doors. No windows. A room much like the one Sinto was imprisoned in before. Bed. Side table. Nothing else.

Mianna set the pitcher down on the table. She pushed Sinto toward the bed. Began to untie her wrap.

Sinto grabbed her hands, stopping her. "No."

She blinked, utterly confused. "Am I not pretty enough? Do you want another?"

"No, I meant..." Sinto reeled. *What do I say?*

He glanced around the room, trying to find an excuse to string her along, so he could think.

He gave her a reassuring smile. "You are the most beautiful of all of them. That is why I chose you. Please, sit and let me look at you. We have all night, do we not?" He sat and pulled her down on the bed beside him.

She looked toward the door then gave Sinto a nervous smile. "They didn't say."

Sinto debated. He knew she was innocent, a victim like him, but this was *war*.

Interrogate her.

"Arkis said you came from Merluma. Did you grow up there?"

She bristled.

"Relax." Sinto put his arm around her shoulders and laughed nervously. "I'm just trying to break the ice, making small talk. I would like to get to know you first, before, you know..." He cradled her chin.

She furrowed her brow. "They told me not to talk."

"What else did they tell you?"

"Just to—" Her gaze fell to his lap. "To give you pleasure."

She reached for the side of his neck, straight for the highly sensitive skin of his gills. A particularly sensitive place where once caressed would make him physically susceptible to her sexual advances.

He pulled back.

"Mianna, stop, please." He grabbed her hands and gave them each a gentle kiss. "Tell me about Merluma."

She looked nervously about the room. "The others will be coming soon, to make sure I've not failed."

"Tell me quickly then."

"I don't remember much, except growing up really fast, and it hurt. Some whispered about experimentation, which is why some of us die. They say it's because we're growing too fast. The caves where I was born are overcrowded with so many—too many to feed. I was one of the lucky ones, I got to come here." She batted her lashes. "I was born beautiful; some aren't so lucky. With the experiments and everything—some are born with—some don't come out quite right."

"When were you born?"

"Six months ago."

Sinto stifled a gasp. He had only observed a small part of what was happening in the caves carved into the bowels of the Black Mountains on Merluma; he would never forget witnessing the agonies of infants and younglings, forced to grow unnaturally.

He gazed at the pitcher of orange liquid, sitting on the table. It looked the same as the orange liquid the guards passed to the residents to drink before granting them passage into the auditorium, and the same orange liquid intravenously fed into the bodies of newborns in the caves. He pictured the scars where every joint on a newborn had been punctured, and the suffering screams and bodily gyrations as the newborn visibly grew before his eyes. The restless, panting sleep that followed.

Sinto thought back to a time before he had reunited with Audrey and nearly died at Culliford's hand. He reflected on the unexplained changes he had noticed on Merluma over the past year. Creatures mating in off-season, the overgrowth of flora, the hyper-aggression he experienced with the bluestripe tigers that nearly claimed Audrey's life. Perhaps these experiments were the cause of these strange occurrences on Merluma.

Sinto gazed into her eyes. They were amber, not orange. "Why are your eyes not orange like the others?"

Her mouth opened but nothing came out at first. "I don't know."

He pointed to the pitcher. "Do you drink this regularly?"

She shook her head. "I've never drank of Arkis' orange nectar." She smiled. "The first time will be with you, as part of the initiation. Together, we will be reborn."

She suddenly grew nervous and stood. "Enough talking, they're coming." She removed her wrap. It floated to the floor and puddled at her feet. Her markings were strange. A mix of random slashes as if she'd been cut with a knife to make the skin pucker and mimic markings which Merahvu naturally inherited from biological parents.

He picked up her wrap, forced it into her hands. "I'm sorry. It has nothing to do with you, but I cannot do this."

"They'll kill you if you don't cooperate." She pushed him down with a strength and tone of voice that surprised him. "They'll kill me too, and I don't want to die like the others."

"What others?"

Sinto heard the soft padding of feet approaching and soft voices, rounding the sharp bend in the hallway. Footsteps too light to be from Arkis' brawny guards.

Mianna jumped on the bed, pulled Sinto on top of her and wound her legs around his ankles.

Sinto was growing desperate. He whispered, "Please, help me. I must escape, but I need your help. Help me convince them I am a believer. We can pretend. Kiss me!"

Four females entered the room. One of them was Zayra, heavy with child. He recognized the sound of her heavy pant.

She crossed the room, observed the full pitcher. "What's taking you so long, Mianna? Did you do as instructed?"

Sinto rolled off Mianna and gave Zayra a disgruntled scoff. "Excuse me? This is my party, not yours. I am a man who likes to savor his prize." He licked Mianna's cheek. "I want to experience every tiny detail of my beautiful mate." Sinto tickled Mianna's belly. She giggled, but her eyes were filled with fear.

"Maybe Arkis wasn't clear. You'll have time to *savor* later," an older female said, stepping forward. "Mianna, do as you were instructed. Now!"

Sinto could feel every fiber of Mianna's body clench. "I told you," she whispered.

A tear fell from her eye as she reached for the side of his neck and slipped her fingers across the sensitive slits on the side of his neck.

55

Blood-Bond

Mianna stroked the sensitive receptors along the gills on the side of his neck. A dangerous mix of testosterone and dopamine shot through his bloodstream. His heart hammered and he gasped, his lungs starved of oxygen in the stagnant oxywater, heavy with carbon dioxide, swirling within the small room.

The females who had entered the room grabbed him. One grabbed Sinto's arm, another grabbed his other. A third female stripped him of his wrap. They rolled him from his side to his back, and yanked his arms into a T. Sinto struggled to break free but they wielded an unnatural strength.

Arkis' mate, Zayra, stood back while one of the females prodded Mianna to act, barking out detailed instructions.

Mianna slipped on top of him. Her hands reached toward his groin, which stirred traitorously. He tried imagining he was swimming in a freezing lake, that he was running from bluestripe tigers slavering for his flesh; he thought of Arkis siccing lamprey at Beech, the blood-curdling scream as he died... but his efforts were for naught. No matter how much he tried to distract his mind, there was little he could do to stop the primal reaction to Mianna's stimulation.

He bucked, flipped her off, then twisted and kicked wildly. The females held fast to his arms, digging their fingers deeper into his flesh. Three more females entered the room. Two grabbed his legs, the third his tail. They pulled his appendages in opposite directions until he was splayed like a starfish, belly up and vulnerable. At least Mianna had stopped her advances. Pressing her back to the far wall, eyes darting and wild like a cornered animal and as much a victim as he.

Zayra came forward, swung a leg over his body, and straddled him at the chest. She cradled his head between her fingers and wrenched his head back, exposing his neck. She rolled forward, pressing the mass of her swollen belly against his larynx. It was a fight for each breath. She gleefully watched him struggle, capturing his gaze with her fiery orange eyes.

"He's strong, untamed," one of the females said.

Zayra leaned forward, her breath hot against his face. "But he can be broken." Her unborn child kicked where her belly lay on his chest as if it too was waging a war, unaware of which side it had chosen.

Zayra slipped her fingers through Sinto's hair, then dug them into the tender flesh covering his skull. A mind probe slipped effortlessly past his carefully set defenses. "Go, get Arkis," she ordered.

Sinto writhed. Trying to break free an arm or leg, anything to break Zayra's connection to his mind, but the strength and the weight bearing down from the six of them was too much of a match.

Zayra scurried across the landscape of his mind. He ran ahead, severing pathways to memories, thoughts, and feelings. But that didn't stop her. Like Korvasi, she was well-practiced at mind-mining, easily batting away the distractions Sinto haphazardly tossed her way.

Zayra smiled. "Mianna, demonstrate the tricks we taught you."

Mianna dropped to her knees beside the bed and began fondling his genital pouch. They shared a brief, frantic glance. She looked away, ashamed, moisture pooled in her eyes.

Zayra's eyes glowed brighter, deepened to a simmering red. "Succumb, Sinto. Mianna is a lovely mate you have chosen. You can trust her, she will guide you through the initiation and then you will become one of us. An Orankai of the highest order, an honor only Arkis can bestow. Join him, stand by his side, together as you are intended."

"No," he gasped.

"You're hiding something from me. A dark, private secret. It is the reason you resist so strongly. Show me your secret, Sinto, *show me*."

Zayra dug deeper. Her mind probe was no longer slippery and whisper-like, but a scalpel, slicing and peeling back layers of gray matter, and with each slice, his fortitude slipped.

Sinto begged, "Stop. Please."

Arkis slipped into the room and sidled up next to Zayra. He placed his hand on Sinto's head and melded with Zayra's telepathic probe, doubling its strength. Arkis' eyes rolled back in his head and he moaned deeply. Like lovers passionately entwined they danced and slithered over and under the noodles of his brain, wriggling deeper and deeper. The lovers conceived and birthed worms that multiplied—two became ten, then a hundred—writhing against the bounds of his skull, burning scorched trails across his mind.

Sinto's hold was tenuous, the iron bulwark around the secrets they must not find crumbling: The Mark he shared with Audrey; Naiada's new-found powers.

Arkis locked eyes with Sinto's. "Join us or die."

Zayra's belly crushed his windpipe. Mianna's fingers slipped beneath the protective skin of his genital pouch. He couldn't breathe. His vision faltered. He struggled to weigh his options.

If I succumb... Gasp. I will be a threat to Naiada.

If I reveal my secret... Gasp. I put Audrey in danger.

If I refuse... Gasp. Arkis will kill me.

If I die, there will be no one to warn them!

Must... Gasp.

Escape. Gasp.

Zayra slid off his chest. He was free from her unbearable weight but not of her violating probe. Sinto gasped, drawing deep unsatisfying breaths, but what little oxygen he could draw helped bolster the bulwark barely holding Zayra back.

If only he could concentrate enough to fire his merlux...

"Bring the nectar," Arkis said, then forced his fingers into Sinto's mouth and yanked it open.

"It's time, Mianna," Zayra said.

Mianna yanked back his genital pouch. He felt the sudden tingle of full exposure. Mianna mounted him, slipped a leg across his hips, and captured him in her hands.

Orange liquid poured into his mouth. Arkis pinched his lips and yanked his head back by his hair, forcing him to swallow.

Arkis' nectar ran swift and sure down his throat and exploded like a bolt of fire in his belly.

The multi-prong attack was more than Sinto could fend off: Mianna's sexual advances; Zayra's incessant mining; Arkis' nectar burning a hole in his belly.

A dam burst in his mind—Audrey. The Mark. Naiada's vulnerability—spilling like a raging river.

Zayra gasped from the discovery and withdrew her fingers.

Arkis' nectar flooded his bloodstream. All he saw was orange. All he felt was rage. A wellspring of dark and violent emotions bubbling up from the deep recesses of his mind. Every bad memory, every negative emotion, every wrong waged against him laid bare. Voices buzzed in his head. Strange voices. Angry voices. Hundreds of them. Their collective rage filled him.

Sinto felt a surge of power, gained unthinkable strength. It was what he needed. It fueled him. He burned with it.

He fired his merlux. Flueox crackled throughout his bloodstream and ignited the receptors on the surface of his skin. Threads of current filled the room, a tangled mass of blinding light, stunning all in its path.

A human bomb, and it went *kaboom.*

Bodies flew across the room. Zayra's water broke. Mianna struck the ceiling, fell to the floor. Arkis tumbled atop Zayra. Those who had held him cradled scorched hands.

Arkis yelled for his guards.

Sinto sprang up, distancing himself from the others.

Zayra lay on the floor, screaming and cradling her belly; a cloud of blood seeped from between her legs. Mianna cowered in the corner, sobbing.

Suevo and Taylee entered the room and launched for Sinto, crackling bands in hand.

Sinto was a dead man, of that he was certain. He had exhausted his reserves, was left weak and trembling. He didn't fight when Suevo grabbed him by the neck and Taylee wrapped a band around his torso.

Arkis bolted from Zayra's side and pressed his face into Sinto's, smashing his nose against Sinto's. His eyes burned white-hot and spittle shot from his mouth. "You son-of-a-bitch!"

He backed off, visibly shaken; ran his fingers through his singed hair. His voice quivered with rage, "I had a bright future planned for you, Sinto, but no, you had to be the hero, a loyal dog to your *mother* and her silly little Circle of tired old fools."

Arkis sucked a breath through clenched teeth. "You have made me a fool. I knew I shouldn't have trusted you, should have fed you to the lampreys the moment you entered the city, made every Scout in my employ record it, to share with all as a lesson to those who betray us."

Then he screamed and stomped about the room, deafening and unhinged, like a howler monkey suffering a defeat.

It took him a beat to settle, to find his voice, gruff and shaky. "But, I promised him! I promised him I would make you see, to *believe*." He shook his head. "I told him—I told him you were dogmatic, a fool—reading all those Sapien books—I told him you would be unwilling to do what needs to be done—sympathetic to Sapiens, to the Circle, to that whore of a mother." He spun on his heel to face Sinto. "And I was right!"

Promised who? Sinto wondered. *Who is he talking about?*

Arkis grabbed Sinto by the neck. His eyes were a manic red, and on fire.

"To tell you the truth Sinto, I never really liked you much. I pretended to care, I pretended to be your friend." He spat. "I never saw you as anything but a spoiled, entitled *prince*." He gave Sinto a wicked grin. "I shall truly enjoy watching you die."

Arkis released him and nodded to Suevo.

Suevo punched Sinto in the stomach with a force that rendered him powerless and served to help empty his stomach. Hot orange nectar exploded from his mouth and swirled at Arkis' feet. The orange glow that tainted his vision faded, as did whatever lingering strength it had given him.

Arkis turned up his nose. "So vile. That's how I will remember you after you're dead. Only this time, you will die, for real." Then he laughed his hyena laugh, the one Sinto once found amusing. Now it sounded as vile as his city of slime and Sinto's orange vomit, swirling at his feet.

Sinto glared. "I would rather die than join you."

"Oh, I have every intention of fulfilling your wish. But before that happens, I want you to spend your remaining hours pondering all the juicy secrets you've revealed, to imagine what I will do with them. I want you to die knowing I will find your precious Audrey and kill her myself in a most spectacular way. And that's not the only one I will go after."

Sinto jerked against his guards' grip. They slammed him against the wall. Pain radiated through his head.

Arkis' lips curled into a devilish grin. "That's right, Sinto—after I kill your Sapien plaything, I'm going after Naiada. Only I might not ask as nicely as you may have."

"Leave her out of this!"

His eyes glittered with malice. "Oh, but I can't. You see, she is key to my success. Your little sister will be my queen, and I her king."

Sinto choked. "No!"

Suevo's grip around his throat tightened.

"So young and impressionable. She should easily succumb under the influence of my precious nectar." Arkis stabbed his finger to Sinto's forehead. "Thanks to your weak mind we now know her secret. We won't have to wait for her transition, for she already possesses a power much greater than her mother's."

Suevo sneered in his face. His breath stank. "Cherish this thought: Arkis sharing her initiation with his most loyal, me and Taylee."

The thought of them touching his sister ignited an inferno of rage that rendered him blind.

Arkis circled. "And if your sister proves to be as resistive and foolish as you, then we have other ways of harnessing that power. All we need is an egg, or two. We'll breed another, and another, until we get it right. We always do, eventually. After all, Merluma's accelerated time has worked wonders in our favor thus far.

"Though, I must admit, it pains me to destroy such a perfect breeding specimen as you." His eyes swept to Mianna huddled in the corner, shook his head. "You two could have made strong, beautiful babies." He grabbed Sinto by the chin. "And you did look quite handsome with orange eyes, not that vile color of green."

Arkis paced and continued to berate. "You do realize that you've always been the expendable one. A lowly male in a female-dominated world, son of the queen, worthless, really. You see, it is your *sister* the people clamor for, not you." He raised his hand to his ear. "Wait, what? Did I hear that they offered you a seat on the Circle? How naive of you! There is no longer a Circle, you fool!"

Sinto squirmed under the guards' grip.

"How does it feel knowing you were worthless all along? It could have been much different for you. You could have joined me, by my side. A fate I will no longer have to suffer. Female queens once had all the power, but no longer." Arkis grinned, "And as for—for—*Ramasis*..." He tapped his chin with a finger. "I think I'll let you die wondering what happened to him, whether he is dead or alive, which side he was, or *is* on. But I will tell you this: he had secrets of his own. Care to guess what they may be?"

Arkis gazed into his eyes. "Think hard, Sinto. Why was it we were always together, you and me, whenever you visited the City of Green. Who encouraged us? And why was it that Ramasis always invited me to join the two of you when running errands on Merluma." He tapped Sinto's forehead. "Figure it out yet?"

He's toying with me, a master manipulator. Don't give in!

"He was quite lonely all those years, separated from Ianthe, citing his work as his mistress..."

Sinto felt sand building in his chest, the birth of a quivering sinkhole.

"What do you think he was doing, here in the City of Green, while your mother and the Circle toiled over the building of Tallamure? Shouldn't he have been by her side, especially since their widely celebrated union represented the creation of the Merahvu and the newfound peace established between the tribes? Was not Tallamure a symbol of that union?"

Sinto's heart slipped closer to that sinkhole.

"Who do you suppose kept his bed warm at night whilst he was away from his whoring mate?"

Sinto gasped out, "You're toying with me, like you toy with your followers. Manipulations to prop up your tenuous and fragile ego."

"Am I? Why was it that you and Ramasis were always offered a place to stay in my mother's home whenever you visited the City of Green? Our home was a small and humble residence, certainly not one fit for the queen's mate and their son. Why was it that Ramasis never rejected such an offer? And tell me, Sinto, did you ever witness your father slumbering on the sofa?"

"Purely a coincidence."

"Are you sure?" He reached for a knife tucked in a sheath strapped to his thigh. He slashed a small slit on the inside of his wrist, then another on Sinto's. He clasped Sinto's tethered arm and pressed their cuts together. The skin fused naturally, opening a pathway for their blood to intermix. Blood surged between them, his flowing into Sinto's arm, Sinto's flowing back. Twined blood, perfectly matched. Just as he once shared with his sister in order to save her life.

Sinto felt the blood drain from his face when his heart slipped into that sinkhole, occupying his chest.

"So finally, I have your attention, do I not? It is not a lie. It is the undeniable truth. You and I, Sinto, are blood-bonded brothers."

What little energy Sinto had left to argue slipped from his grasp. His mouth gaped, a gesture of weakness he was powerless to stop.

"That's right, brother, all along I've kept our blood-bond a secret, relegated to silence by our father. And when he came limping back after Culliford poisoned him, who do you think saved him? Why, of course, it was me. Can you believe it? You and me, mighty sons of Ramasis! And why was that? Why did he insist on burying this truth? Any ideas?"

Sinto's chin fell to his chest. He couldn't say it. But it was clear. The Orankai wasn't an idea conceived by Arkis in the past year. It was born a long time ago by someone else. Someone broken and deeply resentful—his father.

"Where is he?" Sinto rasped.

"Our father?" Arkis laughed. "I told you, he could be anywhere—bedding one of our newly born females, or could be fish turds, having fallen victim to the lampreys. I can promise you this, though: he has been given what he justly deserves."

Sinto looked up and shook his head.

"Too weak to accept the truth, I see." He tsked. "I suppose I should feel sorry for you, but alas, I do not. In fact, I should thank you for being so righteous, brother, for I no longer need to challenge you for the throne of our happy little tribe."

Arkis snapped his fingers at his guards.

"Lock him up and crank up the drain. I want him limp as a noodle. Tomorrow night's show should be quite entertaining. The lamprey will get an extra special feast tomorrow—royal flesh!"

56

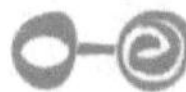

Pseudo Autopsy

AUDREY HAD TO FACE the truth. See it, touch it, smell it. After bidding Ryan and Blake farewell after dinner, she returned to her cabin to think. She laid down on top of her bunk fully dressed. The lingering stress of the day still pumped through her veins. Her resting pulse topped out in the nineties.

She got up and paced, fighting the inevitable.

She slipped out of her cabin and across to the lab. The dry lab was dark; so was the wet lab with the exception to the giant tanks, now empty. Leonard had served up the prawns and lobster the first couple of nights, and a crab lasagna for tonight's dinner. It was one of the best pasta meals she'd ever tasted. Unfortunately, she could only down a few bites. Especially after witnessing what Orange did to that crab. Her stomach was bound up in knots that would take forever to untangle. Maybe never.

She passed through the wet lab to the inner lab door. She knocked before opening. Dr. Wickman was inside, typing something into his laptop.

The stainless-steel gurney was positioned in the center of the room. The dead girl lay on top. A sheet covered her body except for her face. Her colorless eyes stared up at the basket hanging above as if patiently waiting for someone to take her home. Maybe a sibling or her mother or her father. Was someone out there worried sick about where she might be?

Audrey reached out and touched her brow. Cold and sticky. She closed her eyes and drew a deep breath.

We are of salt and earth, her and I.

When she opened her eyes they fell upon the concaved side of the girl's head where the wrench had crushed her skull. Bits of bone and brain clung to the crusted blood laced through her coppery-colored hair. A large lock of it was missing. It lay on the counter in a plastic bag along with vials of her blood.

Audrey looked down at her fisted hands, the same that had wielded the wrench that took the girl's life. She opened them, palmed her thighs. She looked back at the girl's glazed eyes.

You're dead because of me.

Audrey imagined the girl taking a sudden breath, orange fire animating her eyes; sitting up and swinging her legs over the side of the gurney and giving Audrey another stunning punch to the chest.

God knows I deserve it.

But the dead girl didn't sit up or face her murderer. She just stared. Up. At the hanging basket and the outline of the hatch. A way to escape.

Audrey stepped back and bumped into Dr. Wickman. He had slipped in behind her while she wasn't paying attention. "Couldn't you have at least closed her eyes?"

He swept his fingers across the girl's lids. Stiff from death, he only made it worse. Now the dead girl's gaze was directed toward Audrey. Narrowed and accusing.

"What are you planning to do with the body?" Saliva filled her mouth. She swallowed. She already knew the answer.

"Find out what makes her tick."

The knots in her stomach rolled tighter. "You plan to cut her up."

"That's usually the way it works."

"She's a human being, not a lab rat."

"*Was*. She *was* a human being. What lies before you is merely," he took a deep whiff, "rotting flesh, nothing else. The part that animated her is long gone. Regardless, I always use the greatest respect while studying a human body."

She shook her head. "No." She turned, putting her back to the girl, and faced Dr. Wickman. "I won't let you cut her."

"You've got no say in this matter Audrey."

"The hell I don't! I was the one who killed her!"

"Yes, it was you who killed her and we should thank you for that. From what both of you told me, she had every intention of killing Ryan. She boarded during the attack, hid and eluded all of us. And who knows what happened to the people on those missing ships. Twenty-six lives lost. When you play a dangerous game, people die."

"That doesn't justify murder."

"War is messy. They attacked us. It was self-defense, not murder."

"What if we were the intruders and they were defending themselves from a perceived threat? Like you said, self-defense. The ocean is their world. We are merely guests."

"That is irrelevant now. We have been given a gift. You want to be a scientist? This is a critical first step. I can help you become the scientist you've always dreamed of becoming."

Her eyes swept across the sheet-covered body, a body that held many secrets. Secrets she was burning to uncover. Pushing buttons. Dr. Wickman knew her well.

He stepped to the bottom of the gurney and snapped the sheet away from the body. Sudden, like ripping a band-aid off a hairy patch of skin. The sweet smell of decay assaulted her nostrils. Audrey covered her mouth and nose with one hand and grasped the edge of the gurney with the other. Tears blurred her vision. It took several moments to process the image of the girl's naked dead body.

The protective layer of skin that had covered her groin and breasts had begun to dry and curl into transparent crisps along the edges. Her markings looked as if she'd been slashed by a sharp knife in an angry pattern of crisscrossing lines and the skin had been left to scar and pucker. Not a graceful embellishment like Sinto's swirls and dots. It was as if her markings revealed a part of her past, a childhood filled with pain and abuse. If true, who would do such a thing? Who made her angry and violent? Who taught her to seduce a male the way she did Ryan? Why would one so young want to murder an innocent human being?

Dr. Wickman rolled a tray with several instruments next to the gurney. He picked up a scalpel.

Audrey grabbed his wrist. "No cutting; only fluid and hair samples, nothing else." She gazed into the dead Terrakai's accusing eyes. "And we should return her body to the sea."

"It's not up to you." The silver blade reflected in the bright overhead lights.

"Who then?"

"Alvarez."

"Fine," she said sharply. "I'll talk to Alvarez."

Dr. Wickman regarded her for a tense moment. "Fair enough." He set down the scalpel and walked over to a tall machine covered with a dust cover tucked against the bulkhead, wheeled it over. "I've got other options to keep me busy for now."

He pulled the dust cover off the machine.

"What's that?"

"Ultrasound machine. We can investigate without cutting. That is if you approve?" he said with a hint of sarcasm.

Audrey bit her tongue.

He turned to a set of cabinets, opened a drawer. "But first let's start with the basics." He pulled out two sets of blue examination gloves, tossed her a pair. They put them on. Then he pulled out an otoscope, a large tongue depressor, a pair of microscopic glasses, and several swabs and accompanying tubes for storing swabbed samples.

Audrey stood across from him as he examined her ears and nose. He took swabbed samples. Audrey labeled and capped the tubes, set them aside. He put on the microscopic glasses, which cast a narrow beam of light. He peeled back her lips, inspected and counted her teeth. He depressed her tongue and gazed deeply into her throat, took a swab sample.

"Hmm," was all he said. Then he set his tools on the tray with the scalpel, jotted down a few notes on a pad of paper next to his computer. He went over to the ultrasound machine and turned it on. The monitor flashed on. A quiet buzz filled the room.

He pointed. "See that bottle on the counter over there? Could you get it for me?"

She hesitated.

He sighed, obviously irritated. "I'm trying to do what I can without *cutting*. The least you could do is try to help."

"Sorry." Audrey retrieved the bottle and handed it to him. He squirted a cookie-sized blob of clear gel on the girl's stomach. He picked up an attached object the size of his hand. Lifted it so she could see.

"This is a transducer. It transmits sound waves that echo back and produce an image." He pressed the transducer into the blob of gel.

He started scanning the places where you'd expect to find vital organs. He ticked off each as he zeroed in on their locations in the girl's body. "Kidneys, liver, stomach... everything I'd expect in a human." He stopped just below the sternum. He took several sweeps and zeroed in on a flat baseball-sized object.

Audrey furrowed her brow. Her studies only briefly touched on the use of ultrasound technology in live marine specimen research. Having never seen one before, she was intrigued but had no idea what she was looking at. While the shapes changed slightly, everything looked the same in varying shades of gray. "That must be the merlux, the organ that generates electricity."

He took pictures and measurements, shifting the transducer around for different angles. Took more pictures and measurements.

"Maybe you could cut up a knife fish, to see how it works."

He stopped and cut her an icy gaze. He was clearly unhappy. Normally, he was the calm one, smoothing over emotional reactions with everyone around him. She didn't ever recall Dr. Wickman being so agitated.

"You know what a knife fish is, don't you?"

"An electric eel." He rolled his eyes murmuring, "Not born yesterday..."

She sighed. "Just trying to think outside the box."

"Don't get me wrong, I appreciate your input, but studying a fish is not the same." He plopped gel on the place above her pubic bone where the protective flap of skin parted. Her genitals were free of hair like the rest of her body except for the hair on her head.

Dr. Wickman picked up the transducer and resumed, fiddling with knobs and pushing different buttons that helped to clarify the image. He swept across that place where her uterus and ovaries should be, then he stopped and studied something intently on the screen. Audrey noted the slight twitch on his brow. He shifted the transducer, stopped, studied the screen a second time. His eyes registering somewhat shock.

"What is it?"

"I'm not sure, but I found something perplexing."

"What?"

"I need to perform an internal exam to be sure."

He looked genuinely curious and concerned.

She placed her hand atop his. "Is that necessary?"

"Audrey, I'm a *doctor*. You must trust me. I've delivered babies and performed many vaginal examinations. I'm very familiar with the female anatomy. I *am* treating her with utmost respect. You can leave if you don't want to watch." He glared at her. "By the way, I delivered you."

She had never thought to ask. *Of course* he would have, being her father's personal doctor. The one person her father trusted to care for his family. She felt stupid for questioning his intentions. She may have won her first objection, but she was being selfish and unreasonable. He was doing all he could, respectfully. For this she was acting ungrateful.

"I'm sorry. I'm struggling with this."

He smiled, relaxed a little. "I know you are and we should talk about it, but not now. Later."

"Okay. Tell me what to do."

He reached for the corner of the gurney. "Pull out the stirrup on that side."

They both struggled to unhook the stirrups from the underside of the gurney and lock them into place. It was obvious they had never been used. He went to the end of the gurney, slipped his arms under the girl's hips and carefully slid her down a couple of feet.

"Try to get her foot into the stirrup." It was a little bit of struggle. The leg was limp and knee stiff.

He wagged a gloved hand. "Gel." She squirted some in his palm.

He positioned himself between the girl's knees and slipped the fingers of one hand inside. The other he placed on top of her pelvis, pressing, adjusting position, pressing again.

Audrey shifted uncomfortably, thinking of the last time she'd had a pelvic exam. "Is everything down there the same as us? I mean, like me?" Audrey felt the heat rise to her cheeks. That was a question she'd been too embarrassed to ask Sinto, no matter how scientifically she had attempted to formulate it in her mind.

"From what I can tell, yes."

He stopped, focusing on one spot in particular for several seconds. Then he removed his hands. Snapped off his examination gloves, dropped them into a waste basket.

He peeled off his glasses and rubbed his eyes. "She was pregnant. Maybe sixteen weeks along."

Audrey gasped. It felt like she'd been stabbed in the heart. Her body went numb. She gripped the gurney, fearing her knees would buckle. She killed a girl *and* her unborn baby. Not one life extinguished, but two.

Dr. Wickman picked up the dead girl's arm, rolled it over and looked at the skin below her right elbow. A raised circle with a slash running through it was carved in the flesh, shaped like the universal symbol for "no". Where it was positioned and how the skin puckered looked vaguely like a Mark, but wasn't a true one from what Audrey could tell.

"Hmm. Mated?" He laid the girl's arm across her stomach, placed the other on top.

Audrey fingered the girl's arm. "It's not a real Mark but made to look like one. Maybe it's more like a brand, symbolizing she belongs to someone."

Seeing the girl's fake Mark made Audrey realize she had been ignoring the burning itch of her own, very real one, buried deep in her forearm lying just below the surface. The burning itch ebbed and flowed randomly. Sometimes she didn't feel it at all. Sometimes it was intolerable. An impossibility, she thought, with Sinto dead. She wondered if maybe the Mark was reaching for a mate that no longer existed.

Dr. Wickman looked at her hand kneading the Mark in her right arm.

"Are you alright?"

"It's nothing, really."

"Can I see?"

She held out her arm. He grasped it and gently pressed his fingers against the hardened coils of the Mark. "It's yet to fade. Interesting." He looked at her, eyes distance, calculating.

"Should it be fading?"

"I'm not sure. I would imagine with Sinto gone, the Mark would eventually fade."

She itched it. It felt as prominent as the day she brought it into being for both of them.

"Now I'm curious—did you actually see Sinto disintegrate?"

Audrey hadn't thought about that. Everything happened so fast. The urgency to escape the city with their lives.

"No... But we did have to escape rather quickly. Maybe he was still clinging to life at that point. Those last moments once the heart stops beating, but the brain is still alive."

"Hmm."

After a beat, he pushed off from the gurney. "Let's make her more comfortable, shall we?"

Her heart warmed at his concern for the dead girl's comfort.

They took her feet out of the stirrups and returned them underneath the table. Pulled her body up to where it was before. They covered the body with the sheet, including her face.

They washed their hands in silence. Dr. Wickman grabbed his laptop, switched off the lights, and escorted her out of the inner lab, gently closing the door.

"That's all I can do without cutting. I suggest you have your conversation with Alvarez soon. You've got twenty-four hours." He avoided looking her in the eyes. "Try to get some rest. We'll talk in the morning."

He turned on his heel and disappeared into the ship's main stairway.

Audrey watched him depart, scratching that burning itch in her forearm that wouldn't go away.

57

Denied

AUDREY SOUGHT OUT ALVAREZ immediately after leaving the lab. Dr. Wickman's discovery weighed heavy in her heart.

Pregnant and so young!

It was going to take a lot of discussions with Dr. Wickman to untangle the mess jerking around her emotions and setting her body on edge. Not all was right with Audrey Grey-Culliford. She needed to do something to right the wrong that didn't involve jumping off the back of the ship.

All was quiet. Most crew members were tucked away in their cabins for the night. She wandered the quiet corridors of the ship, nibbling her thumbnail, trying to calm her anxious thoughts. The mood among the crew had become somber after the near-attack on Ryan. While the Terrakai girl was considered the enemy, it had been difficult for some to accept an enemy so young, as well as female. Most believed war was for men over the age of eighteen who had been trained and understood the consequence of going into battle. Audrey begged to differ on the male part, but agreed otherwise.

What was gnawing at her gut was if the girl had merely been a victim of unfortunate circumstance. Being in the wrong place at the wrong time kind of thing.

Audrey replayed the entire scenario in her mind. She believed the girl had been trapped on the ship when the platform doors were sealed. She imagined herself in the girl's situation. How would she have acted? Basically the same. Prioritizing self-preservation, using whatever weapon she could find. She would fight to escape and upon coming face-to-face with a supposed enemy, maim or kill to save herself. The girl had used one of the Merahvu's greatest assets. Mind manipulation. And being a young female confronted by a male, she used her next best weapon. Seduction. Normally harmless tools. But put together, and anything could happen, especially with a Merahvu when all it took was a touch to shock and kill.

Audrey remembered how scared the girl looked. The way her body trembled. The way her eyes frantically sought a means of escape. If only they could have negotiated, shown her a way out. No one needed to die. It pained Audrey to imagine how many innocents had died over the past millennium during times of war merely because of a language barrier.

She looked down at her thumbnail. It was bleeding. She had chewed it to the quick. She knew why. Avoidance. She was certain what Alvarez would say and wondered why she should bother asking. She was sure he would agree with Dr. Wickman. That the girl should be cut into a hundred pieces, preserved and studied.

But she had to try.

Halfway up the mid-ship stairway her phone buzzed; a message from Alvarez: *Let's talk.*

Dr. Wickman must have alerted him!

She typed, *What's up?*

She stared at the screen, heart pounding.

Alvarez responded, *The answer is no.*

Her jaw dropped. No? To *what*?

Wickman told me about your conversation. Your request is denied.

She typed, *What about my opinion?*

It's unreasonable and unfounded.

She stifled a scream. Found herself huffing like a bull. *Calm down. Tell him what you think.*

She typed, *How would you know? You haven't given me a chance to state my case.*

Okay, then, speak.

She sat on a stair, drew a deep breath. *I should not have killed her. It was a mistake. I missed the signs. She was looking for a way off the ship. Feeling trapped she made a move for Ryan, who she saw as a threat.*

Alvarez replied, *That's not the story I heard.*

She was defending herself. How was she to know that Ryan had no intention of hurting her? If it had been me, I would have acted the same way. It's what my father trained me to do. Self-preservation at all costs. She just witnessed a massacre! We could have killed her mate or brother for all we know!

What does that have to do with your objection to an autopsy?

She pinched her eyes shut. Alvarez was dissecting her objection as certainly as Wickman wanted to dissect the girl's body.

She typed, *Have you no respect??*

She's dead, Audrey, dead. The being she once was is gone. She should have disintegrated, but didn't for some reason. We were given a gift. We will not waste it. We have never had this chance to learn more about their anatomy. EVER. If the tables were turned and it was your dead body lying on the gurney we'd do the same to you, and you would not feel it or know about it. Because you would be dead.

Audrey gasped at the cold-hearted audacity of his argument. She typed, *Please, can we talk more? Face-to-face? Where are you? I can be there in a—*

Before she could press send, he sent another text: YOU ARE OFFICIALLY ORDERED TO BACK OFF AND LEAVE WICKMAN TO DO WHAT HE NEEDS TO DO. END OF DISCUSSION.

She sent her unfinished text anyway, then sat in the stairway for ten agonizing minutes waiting for a reply. Nothing. Edict officially issued. Dr. Wickman won.

Audrey fumed. Then she got an idea. A wickedly bad idea. One she couldn't shake. Morally it was right, though Dr. Wickman and Alvarez would think otherwise.

She tapped out another message, only this one went to Ryan, *You awake?*

He sent back an emoji with one eye cracked, yawning.

I have a proposition for you.

One I might regret?

She tapped her phone against her temple. She debated. Tell him the truth or offer plausible deniability. *Hmm, don't think so. Looking for help cleaning up a mess I made.*

Will either of us get hurt cleaning up this mess of yours?

She made a face. *It's not that kind of mess.*

Maybe then.

She stood up. *You in your cabin?*

Affirmative.

She typed as she scurried up the stairway, *Be right there.*

58

Burial At Sea

A UDREY KNOCKED LIGHTLY ON Ryan's cabin door. The door swung open. Ryan yawned, "Sorry, I was half asleep when you texted me. Come on in."

She told him her plan, but nothing about Dr. Wickman's planned autopsy. She stressed she was righting a wrong.

His eyes narrowed. "Are you sure you want to do this?"

"Yep."

"I don't know..."

"I take full responsibility."

"You are a dangerous friend to have, Audrey *Culliford*."

"Remember, two AM. Set your alarm. Wear black."

"What other color is there?"

She chuckled. "Right."

She left Ryan, then raced through the ship collecting things that would be necessary for what she had planned: a twenty-five-pound mace from the gym and a coil of quarter-inch rope from the cargo chamber. She staged the mace where she needed it, looped the rope over her shoulder, and returned to her cabin.

She lay on her bunk too wound up to sleep, playing through every aspect of her plan. It was solid.

At two AM sharp she lightly tapped on Ryan's door. He opened it, pulling on a black sweatshirt. He wore a pair of Larkian-issued black chinos, the fabric straining across his ass a little more than usual. Audrey smiled to herself. Leonard's cooking had a way of making clothes shrink.

They quietly tiptoed their way down the corridor toward the lab.

The door at the end of the corridor began to open. Someone coming in from outside. They turned and bolted in the opposite direction, around the corner to the mid-ship stairway. They quietly padded up to level three. Audrey pointed to the cafeteria door. They ducked inside, closed the door, and pressed their backs against the wall. The main eating area was lit by a soft light coming from the galley.

Footsteps echoed in the corridor outside the cafeteria, then stopped.

Audrey and Ryan inched their way next to the door. If it opened they would be concealed behind it. Whoever it was opened the door and stepped inside. Stokes. He headed straight for the galley.

Audrey held her breath and wrapped her fingers around Ryan's hand. It was hot and clammy. Luckily, Stokes hadn't seen them. They watched him round the service counter and open the refrigerator. When he leaned over to rummage inside, they slipped out the door and into the hallway.

Audrey started breathing again once they reached the stairway. "That was close."

"Let's hope Dr. Wickman isn't a night owl too," Ryan added.

Luck was on their side. The lab was dark and empty.

Audrey turned the handle to the inner lab door. It swung in with a loud creak. Ryan winced.

"I swear it wasn't like that earlier!" she said, in a hissing whisper.

She carefully closed the door without a sound.

"So what's the plan?" Ryan asked.

Audrey's teeth tugged at her lip. "We take the body to the back of the ship and dump it overboard."

"You and I carry a hundred-twenty-five-pound corpse through the ship without making a sound or getting caught by the insomniac Captain Hook? That's your plan?"

"You forgot the part where we weight her down, so she sinks."

"With what?"

"A twenty-five-pound mace."

"So add twenty-five pounds. You've got to be kidding. Do you know what those beefcakes on this ship made me do all afternoon? 'You need a distraction,' they said, 'Come join us for a little exercise'. Man, my arms are shredded. I barely got my sweatshirt over my head."

"And did it work?"

"What?"

"Distract you."

"Sure, hammer your shins a couple of times swinging a steel mace and you won't be thinking of anything else."

That made her laugh.

Ryan rolled his eyes. "Not funny. Let's get this done so I can drift off to la-la land and dream of some brunette with blue eyes seducing me. A brunette without a tail and odd markings who isn't trying to electrocute me."

Her eyes zeroed in on the basket hanging above the body of the dead girl. "I've got an idea."

He looked up. "Now you're thinking."

"We take her up and out. We'll have an extra stairway to carry her down but less of a chance someone will hear us. Plus, gravity will be on our side."

Audrey found a set of switches on the wall marked with self-explanatory labels. She pressed the top one, marked HATCH. A whirling sound drifted down from the ceiling. The hatch slowly swung upward. She pressed a second one marked BASKET. The basket lowered and came to a stop next to the body on the gurney.

"Easy peasy!" Audrey said.

Cool fresh air drifted down from the open hatch. They may be heading south but it was early December and still cool on the high seas at night.

Ryan rummaged through several drawers. "We need some rope."

Audrey unzipped her sweatshirt where the coil of quarter-inch rope she stole earlier hung around her neck. "Got it."

Ryan started tucking the sheet under the body. Audrey grabbed his hand. "Wait. Do you want to… see her?"

"No." He promptly replied. "I want closure to this nightmare. Let's just get this done."

They worked in silence as they rolled the body one way, then another, tucking the sheet around it and wrapping the rope from head to toe, tying a half-hitch with each wrap. Ryan secured the ends with a square knot across the girl's chest.

"So who gets to steal the mace from the gym?"

"Already handled. Let's get her in the basket." The basket was slightly lower than the gurney and the body easily slid into the basket. It creaked from the added weight.

"That was easy," Audrey said.

Ryan gave her a dirty look. "Stop jinxing us. None of this is easy."

Audrey pressed the BASKET switch on the panel. A simple switch system: open, close, up, down, depending on the current position of the basket or the hatch.

The basket rose. When it reached the top a pair of mechanical arms unfolded, and the basket continued rising a few feet above the level of the deck. It stopped, followed by silence. It hung there silhouetted by the night sky bursting with stars.

"I'm beginning to get a bad feeling about this," Ryan said.

"Can't turn back now."

"She's not overboard yet. All you have to do is push that button. We put her back and walk away."

Audrey glared.

Ryan shrugged. "Okay, okay. But don't say I didn't warn you. Dr. Wickman's not going to be happy when he discovers the body missing."

"I'll take all the blame."

"You know I can't let you do that. I'm here, aren't I?"

They switched off the lights and used care to close the inner lab door without making a sound, then slipped down the corridor and out the aft door.

The night air was cool and humid, a bone-chilling combination. Salt crusted every surface from mist rising off the sea. They hiked up the exterior stairway to the helipad. The open hatch was near the far bulkhead, next to the heli-garage. The body gently swung in the basket from the motion of the ship.

Audrey stopped. Her throat hitched. The body looked like a swaddled baby being lulled to sleep in a cradle.

A girl and her unborn baby. Dead because of me.

Ryan took the lead. "Let's get this over with."

The wind flattened his spiked-up hair and whipped loose strands from the braids crisscrossing Audrey's head.

"You get the feet, I'll get her by the shoulders," Ryan said, slipping his arms under her chest.

Audrey grabbed the girl's feet, took a step, and slipped, nearly losing her grip. She let out a sigh of relief a little too soon. The basket swung out from under the body, swung back, and nailed her in the elbow. The numbing twang of a direct hit to her funny bone loosened her grip. The dead girl's feet slipped from her hands and fell down the hole where the gurney sat twelve feet below.

Ryan let out a yelp which was followed by a loud rip. "Little—help—please," he huffed, hugging the girl's body to his chest, her feet dangling down the hatch. Veins bulged across his brow and down his neck. She hopped over and wrapped her arms below Ryan's and together they pulled the body out of the hole. Once clear, she let go and hopped back. Ryan fell back. The body rolled and landed on top of him, face down. The sheet had loosened, revealing her pale face and gaping mouth.

"Gross, she stinks!" Ryan writhed out from under her. He hopped to his feet and bent over, hands to knees, gasping for air.

Audrey winced. "Oh geez!" Then she averted her eyes. The back of Ryan's pants gaped and Audrey witnessed more than she ever wanted to know about Ryan's male anatomy.

His face turned a bright shade of red when he reached back and felt bare skin.

"*Commando*? Really? Ryan!"

"Hey, you're the one who rousted me out of bed in the middle of the night. So help me, if you say anything to anybody about this, I'll never help you again." The wind ripped spittle from his mouth.

"Of course, cross my heart, hope to die." Audrey sucked in a breath. It hit her suddenly, the absurdity of the situation. She fought to keep from bursting out laughing. She cleared her throat and stood up, a giggle threatening to slip.

Ryan cocked his head and glared back. She forced it down.

"Alright, let's finish this." She found a panel on the nearby bulkhead, opened it. Same buttons, HATCH and BASKET. She pressed HATCH. The mechanical arms that lifted the basket above the deck folded, and the basket lowered to its upper position next to the ceiling, just below the hatch opening. The hatch swung closed with a soft *clunk*. "That was convenient."

"Maybe for you." He looked totally humiliated, standing with his backside away from her, a hand attempting to hold the seam together.

Audrey nodded toward his occupied hand. "You're going to need that," she said squatting down to lift the body's feet.

"No shit, Sherlock." He squatted down to lift the girl's shoulders. "On three. One, two, *three*."

The night air filled with gasps and grunts as they half-dragged, half-carried the body across the deck, down two stairways to level one and the partial deck beside the closed transom door.

The ship's name glowed in the pale moonlight on the raked-back transom. They wrestled the girl's body to the edge of the deck. The sea whizzed by three feet below. Audrey grabbed the twenty-five-pound steel mace she stole earlier and had left wedged against the hull.

The roar of water churned up from the props made it difficult to hear anything.

"I think we should say something." Audrey yelled.

"She tried to kill me. How about 'good riddance?'"

Ryan kept his backside to the stairway. Sweat beaded his brow and he looked ready to bolt.

"I was thinking 'forgive me'!"

Ryan rolled his eyes and yelled back, "As if anyone would care. Certainly not her!"

She looked up at the star-strewn sky, remembered the fake Mark carved in her arm. "Someone must care."

A light on the deck above clicked on. The deck where the body lay was flooded with light. They quickly rolled the body back against the hull and into a tight band of shadow. Then glued their backs to the hull. The body lay at their feet.

"Someone must have heard us," Ryan whispered. His eyes pinched shut and he mouthed several four-lettered words.

A shadow washed across the deck, someone leaning over the railing. Audrey drew back her foot, awash with light.

Pleasedon'tcomedownthestairs! Pleasedon'tcomedownthestairs!

The shadow retreated. The lights went out.

They waited just in case it was a trick. A couple of minutes passed.

Audrey slithered up the stairway, came back down. "All clear."

"Geez, how can you be so calm? I think I just had a heart attack."

Audrey slid the body back to the edge of the deck where the sea roiled below. She grabbed the steel mace. Ryan untied the knot at the dead girl's chest, and together they slipped the handle through the half-hitched loops of rope. Ryan retied the knot. The dead girl looked like a Viking warrior ready for a fiery burial.

"Before we do this there's something I need to tell you."

Ryan sat back.

"Dr. Wickman discovered she was pregnant."

Ryan looked away. "That's doubly harsh."

She nodded, fighting back tears. He leaned over and hugged her, then leaned back.

"It's time to let her go, Aud."

She nodded again. "Okay." Her hands shook when she placed them on the sheet-shrouded body.

I'm sorry I murdered your baby.

"Any time now. I am literally freezing my ass off," Ryan said, impatiently.

She swallowed down a lump of guilt. "With heavy heart I commit your body to the sea. May loving hands collect your troubled soul; may you find peace and love and reconnect with loved ones who have passed before you."

Then Audrey pushed the body off the edge into the churning wake of the ship. The girl's body floated for a split second, then slipped beneath the dark swirling surface.

59

Show Time

Sɪɴᴛᴏ ᴡᴏᴋᴇ, ʟʏɪɴɢ ᴏɴ his back with his arms and legs splayed across the cold stone floor of a windowless and empty room. After dumping him there, Suevo and Taylee released the bands that had bound him after his attempt to end his initiation with Mianna.

Before sealing the lock on the door they made sure to let him know they had amped up the parasitic draw in the door more than usual. "A parting gift, pretty boy. Sweet dreams," Suevo said, before slipping out.

Sinto had no idea how long he had been lying there or how much longer he had before they came for him. Of this he was sure: Arkis' threats were genuine. His heart ached with dread. He had failed. Audrey and Naiada would have no warning.

Tears snaked from the corners of his eyes only to die in a puddle on the floor. He whispered apologies to Audrey, Naiada, and his mother. He pushed a warning to Audrey through the Mark, and to Naiada and his mother through mind-share, hoping they would somehow hear his faint voice, or discover that he was indeed alive and held captive during their wanderings through the Timeless Dimension. Try as he might, he knew these gestures were pure folly.

And as he lay in his state of despair Sinto noticed something was different.

Something *not* happening.

He sat up. Just inside the door was a bowl and a pitcher of water. It wasn't there when he went to sleep. But that wasn't the something that aroused his senses. His heart beat with hope. He felt much better than he expected. In fact, he felt surprisingly energized.

He crawled to the door and placed his hand on its mirrored surface, pulled it back. Nothing. No magnetic pull or electrical shock. He looked at the contents of the bowl. Whatever it was had grown cold, but it was edible, packed with protein and other vital nutrients. A welcome relief to his undernourished body. He slurped down the chunky soup-like meal and gulped down the pitcher of water.

The effects were swift and encouraging. With a full belly and thirst quenched he tested the strength of his merlux, measured the level of his electrical reserves. Not a hundred percent, but enough to give him a fighting chance against the lamprey.

He pondered who might have slipped him food and water. Certainly not Mianna. He feared her fate might be tied to his. It had to be someone who would have the means to unlock the seal and disable the parasitic draw Suevo had set on his departure.

He wondered if a spy could have slipped through Arkis' defenses or had managed to slip past the initiation process. It could certainly not be anyone who completed it.

Sinto shuddered at the memory of how it felt when Arkis' orange nectar entered his bloodstream, like someone controlled by everything bad or evil that had happened to them or had thought or been exposed to. He remembered the buzz of other voices in his head, an angry and persistent chant of the Orankai world view that Arkis preached. A mind-speak of looping propaganda. The feeling of connectedness to others under its control, like being an orphan suddenly embraced and protected by a like-minded family. Like a member of a cult-like hive.

Arkis' nectar was a weapon he wielded upon the masses to bend them to his will. Without his precious nectar, would he lose the ironclad grip he had over them?

The small amount Sinto had ingested still lingered in his system. The voices threaded in and out of his consciousness, but had grown weaker. His hand shook like never before and he craved more of Arkis' orange nectar. A festering want woven around every thought. He could only imagine what it must feel like after ingesting large quantities in periodic doses, with time deepening its effect, creating a society of addiction. Sinto wondered how long he would feel its pull. Wondered what would happen should Arkis withdraw his addictive nectar from a follower for whatever reason. As punishment. As entertainment. Maybe just to watch one suffer and then use that lesson to instill fear among the others.

A strange voice whispered in his mind, "*It is true, that is what happens if you disobey the master.*"

Sinto shuddered at the message, no doubt slipped through from another imprisoned by Arkis. A message confirming that falling victim to his nectar was a fate far worse than being ripped to shreds by razor-sharp lamprey teeth.

Could Arkis' addicts escape its lure and physical effects and recover? Sinto doubted it.

He felt sick remembering what he witnessed. The newborns in the cave. The orange liquid flowing into their tiny helpless bodies. A generation of addicts born every day, every hour, every second on Merluma. Addicts bred to fight or breed more, and for nothing else. He thought of Mianna, her blank mind, her fear, the way she performed as commanded, actions forced against her will. What kind of life was Arkis creating for the future? Who would benefit?

Arkis mocked Sinto for his desire to learn from the Sapien world, its history and advances, and knew little of the consequences from the Forever War: a slaughter, spanning thousands of years, that drove the Merahvu to near extinction. Arkis was marching along that same barbaric and well-trodden path that ran through human history, Sapien and Merahvu. What was to be gained? What would be lost? Sinto knew the truth. Much was lost, little was gained, and the cycle would perpetuate into the future, toward the next conflict. Grievances were never reconciled, passing from one generation to the next, lying dormant to rear up once the blood and the ash and the trauma of watching loved ones and the innocent die were swept aside by a fresh layer of earth and a new season of vegetation—the mind's way of justifying atrocities that happened to someone else.

Was murder the solution to solving the problems facing the natural world? If this city was any indication, Arkis was blind to reality. He did not care. The natural world was his to use and cast aside when it no longer served him, like the people who objected to his new world order. Arkis was a monster that needed to be destroyed.

Sinto's reverie was interrupted when Suevo and Taylee slipped through the door with bands in hand. He was thankful they didn't notice the empty bowl and pitcher he had set aside in the corner behind them. He tamped down the glow in his eyes, colored them a pale green. He slowly rose to his knees, adding a convincing waver as if the mere act of standing was beyond his physical capacity.

They yanked him up by his armpits. Sinto turned to liquid. His knees buckled and he slithered to the floor. This made them smile. Sinto, the noodle Arkis requested.

"Won't need to power these," Taylee said, as he secured his band around Sinto's chest, binding his arms and tail. "I'll need my energy for later." He ribbed Sinto. "Arkis invited us to join the group romp tonight, thanks to you," he added with a chuckle.

Suevo wove his band around Sinto's thighs. "I'm not taking any chances. This one's unpredictable." Sinto felt its draw wind up. He was confident he could withstand it for a short time, but only a short time.

Suevo yanked Sinto's slumped head up by his hair, studied his eyes.

"Feeling a little sad, pretty boy? Your eyes aren't as bright as they use to be. Too bad for you, looks like my special lock worked. Say goodbye to your lovely accommodations."

"Not a pretty boy for long." Taylee said. They grabbed Sinto by the bands wrapped around his torso, and Sinto dragged his feet, forcing them to carry him. They dragged him through the door and along the outer auditorium wall. The sound of the gathering crowd drifted from the other side.

Suevo whispered in Sinto's ear. "How does it feel, knowing you're going to die?"

"Wonderful. I'll no longer have to breathe your retched breath."

Suevo smacked him in the head in response.

They halted at the dome wall. Slaves were scurrying away from the circle of light, lighting the dark waters where two poles stood, buried in the soft lake bottom. Lamprey darted impatiently in the shadows.

A hush filled the auditorium.

Arkis' voice cut through the silence. "It is with deep despair that I have called you all here to witness this special event. Let this serve as a lesson for those who stray from the Orankai way. I was tricked by my own flesh and blood! My half-brother, Sinto, son of Queen Ianthe and my beloved father, Ramasis."

An audible gasp from the crowd.

"Yes, I know, a shocking betrayal."

Suevo and Taylee pulled Sinto through the dome wall and into the lake waters. The shock of cold reverberated throughout his body, firing nerve endings on the surface of his skin, awakening instincts he would soon need. He sucked a watery breath through the slits in his neck, the deep chill seeping into his bloodstream where the filters pressed against his jugular. He savored it and drew more. Full of oxygen, unlike the fizzy water filling the city. His mind cleared and blood sang and he felt truly awake for the first time since he arrived.

Sinto hung his head sideways, so he could observe the crowd in the auditorium. Arkis stood facing him on the platform before the crowd, his gaze fiery red and filled with rage.

The seats were completely filled except for the upper last row where a single observer sat, hidden in shadow. The observer's eyes flickered between orange and green. It happened so fast that Sinto was unsure if it was real or a trick of light. He cast it off as a fluke.

The crowd booed and made foul gestures with their hands upon seeing him gaze in their direction.

Taylee looped a rope around Sinto's neck and attached the other end to the nearest pole. Sinto hung free but tethered. Suevo gave him a swift kick and Sinto wound around the pole until the rope had reached its end, then he slowly unwound back. Sinto acted like a limp noodle.

Arkis turned to the crowd and continued his diatribe. He shook his head. "A tragedy, really, and most unfortunate that Sinto didn't reveal his true intentions—he lied, in fact. *Lied!* To his own flesh and blood. He lied to *you!* What kind of man does that?" He held his hand to his ear.

"TRAITOR, TRAITOR, TRAITOR."

"Any ideas who may have sent him and for what?"

The crowd hissed, then started chanting. "SPY, SPY, SPY."

Sinto was disgusted at how well the crowd was trained.

"I would like to thank my beloved mate, Zayra, for revealing his deceit." Arkis paused, feigning great sadness, wiping away fake tears, mimicking a sob. "And it is with deep sadness I tell you that our precious child she was about to bear was—was—*lost.*" Then he swung his fiery gaze toward Sinto and pointed. "He killed our child deliberately. Sinto is a traitor, a spy, and a MURDERER!"

Another audible gasp and murmurings from the crowd.

Arkis held up his hands for silence. "And more troubling, he had help. Yes, one of our own. A newborn from Merluma, lovingly cared for and groomed to be his mate. The beautiful and sweet Mianna. A traitor in our midst."

A pair of guards entered from the other side of the auditorium, dragging Mianna by her hair. Her arms and legs were bound with rope instead of parasitic bands like those wrapped around Sinto. Her face was awash with fear when they tied her to the other pole.

The crowed hissed and booed.

Sinto's heart sank.

"*Yeah, your girlfriend gets it too, lover boy,*" Suevo's voice piped into his head.

"*Now you'll have her death on your conscience too,*" Taylee added.

"*Not for long.*" Suevo laughed, then shoved Sinto one last time, before swimming away.

Mianna struggled against her ropes.

"*Stay still!*" Sinto mind-spoke to her and only her. She stopped struggling, but her body quivered. Sinto could sense her fear rippling through the water, as surely as the lampreys would.

"*Stay calm. Lamprey are drawn to fear.*"

Arkis yelled, "Tell them what happens to traitors."

"They die!" The crowd yelled.

"Tell them what happens to murderers and spies!"

"They die!"

The lampreys skirted the edge of light, preparing to bolt from the darkness.

Arkis turned and regarded Sinto. "Like to change your mind, Sinto? I might have a job for you, emptying shit buckets on Merluma." He howled, and the crowd went crazy.

Sinto gazed back, head hanging on limp neck. Arkis didn't deserve the satisfaction of an answer.

Arkis continued, "As if I'd give *you* a second chance! You shall die, fool!"

The crowd cheered and chanted, "DIE, DIE, DIE."

Sinto blocked the ruckus erupting inside the auditorium and turned his gaze to Mianna.

"*Did they teach you how to tunnel the waters?*"

"*To what?*" Her eyes darted to the moving shadows.

"*Did they teach you to control the waters?*"

Her face wrenched in despair. "*Only to mate.*"

A single lamprey swam into the light and circled them.

The crowd shouted, "PLAY, PLAY, PLAY."

A second lamprey emerged and struck Sinto, spinning him around the pole. The first one struck Mianna in the back. They circled for a second strike. Sinto tucked his knees. When the lamprey drew closer, he kicked it in the eye. It screamed and writhed and swam back to the shadows.

"Ooohh. Still got fight!" Arkis yelled.

The crowd screamed their approval.

Sinto's attack and the men's taunts infuriated the lampreys. Two more emerged from the darkness and circled impatiently.

"FIGHT, FIGHT, FIGHT!"

"*Burn the ropes!*" Sinto told Mianna. "*Free yourself. Flee as fast as you can—I will distract them.*"

"*No, you run!*" She thrashed her legs, arched and twisted her body.

The lampreys swam to her.

"*Fight! Kick them—fight!*" Sinto screamed in her mind.

She stopped thrashing and looked at him with sad eyes. She shook her head. "*I am nothing. I have no future.*"

She fired her merlux and burned the ropes binding her. They fizzed into twisted shreds. She floated down and landed on her knees in the soft mud. She spread her arms, offering herself as a sacrifice. A lamprey slammed into her, latching onto the flesh of her back, clipping her wispy tail. It bore into her flesh with its circular rows of teeth. Blood swirled. A trickle leaked past her clenched teeth.

The scent of blood excited the others. Lampreys burst from shadows and frenzied around her, but they didn't attack. Held back by Arkis, no doubt, drawing out Mianna's suffering to appease his followers.

Sinto still had time to save her. He bit the rope tethering him to the pole, then fired his merlux to burn through the strands with the electricity flowing from his lips.

He opened his mouth and fell free. Arms and tail bound, he pumped his tethered legs, swimming toward Mianna.

He coiled and kicked the lamprey, latched to her back, in the head. Momentarily stunned, it broke free. Mianna's flesh filled its teeth and lacy bits of her fin floated from its mouth.

The crowd frenzied. "EAT, EAT. EAT!"

Drawn by the scent of blood and Sinto's thrashing, the lampreys closed in. More arrived, smelling easy prey. Sinto counted five with more lurking in the shadows. He yanked on his arms and twisted his torso, but the band binding his chest held strong. He dropped to the lake bed on his back, kicking to fend off an attack.

A lamprey latched onto Mianna's side. Screams of pain filled his head. She pleaded for a sudden death.

Sinto knew he couldn't kick his way out of sure death but feared if he revealed his true strength before he was ready, Arkis' guards would be on top of him before he could flee. He grew frantic. Mianna was dying. Her screams filled his head, distracting him from focusing his energy toward the bands locked around his body.

He rolled to his knees and closed his eyes. Shut out Mianna's screams, the chanting audience, Arkis' mocking laughter. He focused on the band around his legs, sucking energy from his reserves. He fired his merlux. A dance of polarized current ensued, electrified flueox tangled with the parasitic draw. If he made a wrong move it would backfire, possibly shocking himself to death. He focused on the powerless band Taylee had wrapped around his chest, pin-pointing on the weakest spot. He fired a jolt through his chest. It split and fell away.

A lamprey slammed into his side and latched on.

Razor-sharp teeth ripped through the top layer of skin and began shredding the fatty layer beneath.

Now or never. Sinto screamed and fired. Blinding threads burst from his chest. The electrified band around his legs disintegrated. The chanting stopped, and when Sinto looked up, mouths hungry for blood gaped. Arkis included.

Then Arkis' face folded with anger. He snapped his fingers, calling his guards.

"*You'll never get away!*" he screamed in Sinto's head.

Sinto swam for Mianna. She was engulfed by lamprey. Blood and flueox bloomed all around him. He kicked, punched, walloped, and elbowed his way through the writhing ball of frenzied fish boring into her youthful flesh. He sensed she was alive, but barely. Her screams had turned to weak whimpers. He fought off the last lamprey clamped to her back.

His eyes slid closed to the horror when he saw what they had done to her. Flesh hung from her body like confetti, white bone shone where muscle used to be, her tail was gone, and her arms were barely attached to her shoulders. Blood flowed freely from her weakening heart. He opened his eyes and focused on her face. It was untouched and beautiful. Her gaze was filled with regret.

Arkis taunted. "How sweet, she offered herself as a sacrifice, trying to save him!"

The crowd yelled, "MARTYR, MARTYR, MARTYR."

"*Leave me, I'm already dead.*" Mianna said.

Sinto nodded, acknowledging, and kissed her on the forehead.

"*You're the hero they could never be. Your sacrifice will never be forgotten. Go. Find peace.*"

He captured her mind and guided her to the edge of death and wrapped her in the love she had never experienced in her short sad life. She smiled back as she passed over into everlasting sleep. Her head slipped from his fingers when her broken body fell into a crumpled heap. The lampreys set up to pounce on what remained of her flesh but what was left exploded into a cloud of ash.

The audience booed.

The lampreys circled for a final attack. Sinto crouched on the lake bed, head whipping, counting how many were circling. He froze when he saw something inside the auditorium that utterly shocked him. He swung around to face the crowd.

His father stood beside Arkis and gazed back with fiery orange eyes. His face emotionless and stone cold. He had a ragged unkempt look and appeared heavily drugged, like the rest.

Alive and one of them!

A lamprey latched onto the unfinished hole in Sinto's side, razor-sharp teeth slicing into fatty flesh. He punched the fish eating him alive, but it held fast and bit deeper. He stifled a scream and ducked as a second aimed for his head. A third lamprey took aim for his back. Sinto wound up his tail and smacked the fish in the head, killing it instantly.

The simple-minded lampreys latched onto their dead brother. A brief reprieve for Sinto to deal with the one burrowing into his side. Teeth ground away at the fatty thermal layer, with sharp tips nipping at the muscle beneath. He had scant moments before teeth cleared muscle and found his liver. Blood fogged the water. He struggled to free its mouth from his side but the deadly fish was determined.

He revved up his merlux, weakened from fighting off lampreys, freeing himself from the electrified band, and the shock of seeing his father at Arkis' side.

Sinto spun to face the crowd, lamprey latched to his side. Suevo and Taylee gloated from the sidelines outside the dome. Ready to give chase if he tried to flee. The angry mob was on their feet, screaming for his blood. His father and half-brother anxious to see him die.

His merlux hummed barely at half power. Flueox flowed to the remaining fibers of muscle where the lamprey's mouth worked it raw. He channeled fury and let it fly. Threads of electricity burst from the lamprey's mouth. It gaped and fell away. Scorched bits of Sinto's flesh spilled from its smoldering mouth.

He was wounded, but not yet fatally. Weak and bitter, he summoned the last remnants of the orange nectar coursing through his body. He glared at his father and Arkis. Thought of Naiada and what they had planned for her. Pictured Audrey picking up the pieces of her life unaware of the danger coming for her. Remembered Mianna, innocent fodder for a few moments of entertainment.

Rage rose swift and sure. The angry voices returned and Sinto felt the surge of their collective rage fill him. At the pinnacle of that rage he screamed—fired his merlux—and it roared.

Ka-BOOM!

Bolts of electricity exploded from his chest. The dome wall buckled, knocking Arkis and Ramasis and rows of spectators off their feet. Dozens of lamprey stilled and drifted to the bottom, stunned or dead. Suevo and Taylee floated, unconscious.

Sinto drew what power he had left. Cut a tunnel through the water and dove inside.

60

Bloody Pursuit

SINTO ZIPPED AT TOP speed through the dark cold waters of Lake Superior, fighting to stay conscious. Dizziness threatened to disrupt his concentration and the trajectory of the vortex tunnel boring through the water. Blood streamed through his fingers grasped around the open wound in his side.

Pin-pricks of light burst into view behind him. Arkis' guards racing to catch him. Sinto tamped down the searing pain radiating through his torso and focused on his escape.

He locked onto the faint pulse coming from Rachel's locket. His mind's eye saw the locket lying against her chest, sensed her heart beating calmly and her breath shallow and even. Asleep in the hotel room where she agreed to wait for him, close to the North Pier.

Sinto called to her, pushing an urgent warning, unsure she would be able to interpret it. He regretted not teaching her how his message might manifest. If asleep, she may believe it just a dream.

The surrounding water brightened as he neared the shores skirting the city of Duluth. The tunnel spat him out. He swam haphazardly toward the ice-covered surface, favoring the wound in his side. He wasted no time firing bolts of fire, first to crack the ice, and again to blast it open. Frantically pumping his tail, he burst into the air.

Suddenly Sinto was flying. He waved his arms and wagged his tail to right himself, and landed on the icy dock. He skidded, then beat feet for the shore, running on pure adrenaline.

Sinto honed in on Rachel's locket. The signal was strong and came from the direction of the hotel. The night sky was still and dark and Sinto hoped Rachel got his message. Behind him, he heard the ice crack and two pairs of feet land on the dock. Two followed by six more. Eight against one.

He ran to a side door of the hotel. Rattled the knob. Locked. Panting, he circled to the front and burst into the lobby.

A man sitting behind the reception desk took a double take as he stumbled through the lobby, naked with a shredded hole in his side, a trail of blood in his wake. The man picked up a phone and started to dial.

Sinto limped up a stairway to the second floor and down the hall, guided by the locket around Rachel's neck, his vision winking in and out and legs growing weaker. All the doors looked alike. A high-pitched buzz filled his head. Consciousness fading, he forgot which room was Rachel's. He began knocking on doors, calling her name.

A door down the hall opened, Rachel stuck her head out.

"Sinto!" she whispered loudly.

He gasped in relief. "Must go, now."

He tried to run to her, tripped and fell to his knees.

"Car," he said, panting heavily.

"Oh my god, you're bleeding."

She was fully dressed and ready to go, wearing a winter coat, hat, gloves, and a long scarf wound around her neck. Sinto cried out in relief. She got his message.

His head fell to his chest and he blacked out momentarily. His eyes popped open. Seeing her, and realizing she had been waiting for him, gave him a boost of energy he desperately needed.

Rachel pulled the scarf from around her neck and wound it tightly around his torso, tying a secure knot. Sinto gasped from the pressure and rough fibers rubbing against raw nerve endings.

"Sorry!"

"Car—where?

"In the parking lot—wait, my stuff."

"Others—coming—forget it."

"No need," She grabbed a couple bags just inside the door of her room and slung them across her shoulder.

She slipped her arm around his waist, avoiding the side with his wound. They retraced Sinto's steps toward the stairway to the lobby, her eyes wide and alarmed by the wide swath of blood staining the carpet.

He sensed the others nearby and pulled her to a stop. He heard voices coming from the lobby and unwound her arm from his waist.

"They came to kill me—you can't know me. They will kill you too," he gasped.

He wavered on his feet.

She shook her head. "Nope, not happening." Then she gritted her teeth, grabbed him around his waist, slung his arm across her shoulders, and with a strength that defied her size, dragged him back the other way. She stopped, gazed at the trail of blood leading to the door of her room. She grabbed Sinto's bloody hand and pressed it to the door, leaving a clear print.

"That should slow them down a bit."

She resumed dragging Sinto down the hall to the end and the emergency exit. They slipped through the door into a brightly lit stairwell. Rachel quietly shut the door and helped Sinto down a flight of cement steps to the first floor and a door leading outside. She opened it, stuck her head out.

"All clear."

She dragged him out the door and slipped her arm out from under his shoulder. He slid to the ground with his back pressed against a cold hard wall.

"Shit," she said, looking up and squinting under a blinding light haloing Sinto where he sat. She dropped the duffel bag at her feet, dug for something inside her purse, and pulled out a small metal object no longer than her hand. A folded knife with a pointed metal stub on one end.

"I gotta get on your shoulders, can you hold me?"

He nodded, stiffened his spine, engaging the muscles on his good side. The other side screamed.

She climbed on top of Sinto's shoulders.

"Look away."

She rammed the stub end of the folded knife into the bulb. Glass rained. Sinto was cast into darkness.

She hopped down. "Stay." Then she ran into the dark night toward the parking lot.

Over the din roaring in his head, Sinto heard sirens in the distance.

A squeal of tires rounded the corner of the building. Rachel's car jumped the curb, headlights bouncing. She bounded across the snow-covered grass, looped in a tight circle, and slid to a stop beside him. She left the car running, hopped out, opened the passenger door, and dragged him on his butt to the door. It took all of his energy to lift himself up and roll onto the seat with her help.

She dumped her bag in the trunk, then jumped in and stomped on the gas, rear end swerving sideways in the snow-slicked grass. She flew off the curb and swerved into the parking lot, narrowly missing a parked car. Sinto ducked down as she passed by the hotel lobby.

Suevo and Taylee and two other guards burst through the doors.

Rachel flipped them a middle finger as she passed by, then fishtailed onto the road.

They pursued. Suevo and Taylee sprinted alongside the car along with two other guards. One of the guards leaped onto the roof and landed with a muffled *thud*. The hair on Rachel's head began to rise. The scent of ozone filled the air.

"Slam on the brakes!" Sinto screamed.

The car slid to a stop. The guard slid off the roof and rolled down the hood. Rachel wrestled the stick shift into reverse and stepped on the gas. Suevo and Taylee ran after them as the car careened wildly backwards. The car hit a guard running up from behind. Rachel didn't stop. The car hopped as the tires rolled up and over, crushing him. She stopped with a gasp. His body lay in the street, his dead gaze staring back. Then his body melted into itself and exploded into ash.

Rachel blinked as if what she just saw was an illusion.

"Oh, God," she whispered.

Sinto grabbed her hand frozen on the stick shift. She stared at the pile of ash. Suevo and Taylee ran toward them, gaining fast. The guard who slid off the roof was slowly getting to his feet.

"They *will* kill us, Rachel."

The words sunk in. She slammed the car into gear and stomped on the gas, heading directly for Suevo and Taylee. Suevo jumped out of the way but she managed to nick Taylee. She careened toward the guard who had rolled off the roof and was getting on his feet, her eyes ablaze in fury and teeth set in a grimace. Rachel hit him head on. He flipped up and over the car, landed on his head on the icy street.

Sinto looked back. Another poof of ash. Taylee was still on the ground. Suevo punched air in defeat. Sinto managed a weak smile. Victories, no matter how small, added up.

Rachel, sweet Rachel, what a true warrior princess!

A police car with red and blue flashing lights rounded the corner and roared past them, toward the hotel. Suevo dragged Taylee into the shadows, like cockroaches escaping daylight. The others who had chased them followed.

Sinto blinked away the darkness that threatened to overcome him. His side was on fire; Rachel's scarf was soaked through with his blood. He drew what little energy he had left and burned it away. Then he laid has hands across the hole the lamprey tore in his side. He clenched his teeth and swallowed a scream when he cauterized his own flesh.

Rachel raced through the icy city streets. Sinto was aghast at what he saw. Scouts hid in doorways and sat on benches, easily recognizable to Sinto's keen eye by the dim glow emitted by their watchful gaze. They seemed to be everywhere, watching—a Sapien city overrun and unaware.

The next light turned yellow. Rachel eased up on the gas.

"Run it—west—to the ocean—don't stop." Then Sinto passed out.

61

Pirate Law

SOMEONE RAPPED ANGRILY ON Audrey's cabin door. Six AM and still dark outside her porthole.

Audrey cringed, slipped out of her bunk and reluctantly answered it. Stokes. To say he looked pissed off was putting it mildly. He looked like he wanted to beat somebody to a bloody pulp.

A somebody like me.

His fake grin of gritted teeth was blinding. "Morning, Audrey. Would you care to join us for breakfast?"

She looked at her wrist. She had no watch, but it seemed the thing to do. "A little early for breakfast don't you think?"

He glared.

She nodded sheepishly. "Do I have time to wash my face?"

"I think not," he said icily. "Let's go, *now.*"

Stokes watched, arms crossed, filling the entire doorway while she grabbed a pair of sweatpants and pulled them over her sleeping shorts. She snagged her sweatshirt from the floor where she dropped it after the big heist a few short hours ago.

She followed Stokes in silence. Down the corridor, up the stairs. She could *feel* the steam wafting from him.

She was a child again, marching to a forthcoming punishment. This was the part she dreaded the most. Not the actual punishment but the anticipation leading up to it. The crime was obvious. Not knowing the price for it was the agonizing part, and whether or not they knew of Ryan's participation.

She quickly got her answer.

Posted on the wall next to the cafeteria door was a flyer. It said:

HAVE YOU SEEN THIS MAN?
WANTED FOR INDECENT EXPOSURE

Below the words was a photo of Audrey and Ryan struggling with the girl's body. The angle of the picture said it all. Audrey was clearly in it, in the background, slightly out of focus, but it was obvious it was her; eyes bugged, cheeks puffed, and face strained. Front and center and in perfect focus was Ryan's exposed backside, feet spread and bent at the waist to accommodate the heavy load in his hands. His bare ass and male anatomy prominently displayed through the rip in his pants. Indisputable evidence of indecent exposure. Someone had drawn a conversation bubble coming from her mouth with a Sharpie pen. Inside they had scribbled the words: "Nice balls!"

"Peachy," she whispered.

Stokes shot a glance at the poster, then her face. So much for keeping Ryan out of it. "Are you coming?"

Not hungry, how about a rain check?

Her feet refused to move. Stokes grabbed her by the wrist. His fingers were hot and sweaty. He literally dragged her through the cafeteria door.

Everyone on the ship was there, seated and waiting. Blake was tucked quietly at a table in the back sitting by himself. He gave her a reassuring smile and a quick wave. Lot of good that would do her.

Her stomach dropped. Ryan was there too. Sitting alone at a table in the front, facing the entire crew. His chin cast to chest in shame. An empty chair beside him.

Stokes dragged her across the room and sat her down in the empty chair next to Ryan.

Sitting at a table in the front row were her father, Alvarez, Leonard, and Dr. Wickman. Alvarez had his laptop open and ready to record whatever would come from this little gathering. Her father fixed her with a glacial gaze. Leonard looked uncomfortable. Dr. Wickman sat with arms crossed. He would not even look at her.

The room was still and silent. Audrey looked over at Ryan. He looked away. Her wrist ached where Stokes had grabbed her. Her heart thundered and her throat was parched. She could really use a glass of water. She tucked her hands in her lap and rubbed her wrist nervously.

Stokes stood above her. Based on the look on his face this was going to be one bloody fight.

He turned to address the whole room. "We have rules on the high seas. Rules defined and agreed upon by every Larkian member. And when the rules are broken, we must uphold them. Punish the offenders."

Alvarez handed Stokes a sheet of paper. Stokes held it pinched between his fingers. Turned to face her.

"Audrey, you are a Larkian. An integral part of this crew. Of this *family*. Before you boarded the ship Alvarez explained the rules and how they applied to you as a Larkian citizen. Is that correct?"

She recalled some document Alvarez had sent her on her cell phone. It was marked urgent and that she was to read it and agree to it. She didn't read it but had skipped to the bottom and checked the box to confirm her agreement to all the language printed before. Just like she did whenever faced with pages of legalese when she downloaded some new app on her phone. For all she knew she had signed away her first-born years ago. *Stupid. Stupid. Stupid.*

She nodded.

"Speak up so all can hear you."

"Yes." It came out a loud rasp.

He looked at Ryan. "Ryan, you understand that you are a guest on this ship. Is that correct?"

He didn't bother looking up. "Yes."

Leonard got up and retrieved a glass of water for each of them. Audrey looked up. He winced, giving her a face that said things might not end well. Then he sat down.

She took a sip, then piped up. "Ryan had nothing to do with this."

"We got the whole escapade on video," Stokes said.

She slouched in her seat. Tucker's damn cameras. She should have known better. Didn't she even mention it to Ryan? *Stupid. Stupid. Stupid.* This was not the first time Tucker's cameras caught her doing something she'd rather not become public.

She sighed. "Of course you do."

Alvarez piped up. "That includes heisting a piece of equipment from the gym and rope from the cargo chamber, breaking into the lab after working hours… We even recorded your touching little speech right before you dumped the body into the sea."

Stokes continued, "Is it true you discussed your concerns about Dr. Wickman's plan to study the body with Alvarez? And that he made it explicitly clear your request was denied?"

"Yes, and yes."

"Regardless, you defied his order. A direct order from a senior officer. Is this true?"

"Yes."

Audrey swallowed. This was definitely worse than any punishment her father had doled out. The way Dr. Wickman glared back, she wondered if it would be her who would be rolled off the back of the ship in the middle of the night. Or worse, that he would never talk to her again.

"Did you take a twenty-five-pound steel mace from the gym?"

"Yes."

"And twenty feet of quarter-inch rope from the cargo chamber?"

"I don't know how long it was exactly, but yes, I took a coil of rope from the cargo chamber."

"Did you remove the deceased body from the lab?"

She didn't answer.

"Audrey?"

She huffed. "Yes."

"And did you dispose of these items you took into the sea? Essentially ensuring the disintegration or destruction of each of these items?"

"Yes, and yes."

Stokes looked at her father. He stood up. It took him a few moments to find his words.

"I am disappointed. It is an honor to be accepted into the Larkian family. To be one of us." He paused. Dr. Wickman gave him a reassuring nod. "Larkian Law dictates anyone who is found guilty of breaking the Code of Conduct must pay the consequence. No matter who you are." He sat.

She slapped her hands on the table and stood up. "She was just a child! Dr. Wickman was going to cut her up like a frog!"

Ryan squirmed in his seat. Whispered, "Not helping."

She sat.

Her father said, "It doesn't matter what Dr. Wickman was going to do. You are a budding scientist, given the opportunity to do what you've always dreamed of. You are well aware that dissecting things is part of being a scientist, especially a biologist. Human cadavers are carved up in medical school, for God's sake." He was fuming now. "When are you going to grow up?"

That last bit stung. Deeply. She took a deep breath.

Calm down. Stop screaming. Prove you are grown up.

She took a sip of water. Leaned forward, hands clasped together on the top of the table. "Those cadavers gave their permission. Before they die, they sign the necessary paperwork to donate their bodies to science. She never gave Dr. Wickman that permission. She was human, like us. Isn't that written somewhere in your Code of Conduct?"

No one said anything. Her pits sprung a leak that trickled down her ribs and pooled in the folds of her sweatshirt.

Her father let out an exasperated breath. "I'm deeply disappointed in you. I thought I raised you better."

Her face burned; she snapped, "*You* didn't raise me."

He jolted upright. "Pardon? What did you say?"

There was a commotion of movement and quiet murmurs. Everyone in the room heard their exchange. Airing dirty laundry. It felt like the temperature suddenly rose another ten degrees. She was in hot shit up to her nostrils and sinking fast.

Ryan glared at her. The look in his eyes said everything.

SHUT. THE. FUCK. UP.

She gazed at her fingers knotted in her lap. "I'm sorry. That was grossly inappropriate to say, here, in front of everyone." She looked up at her father. "To say at all."

Stokes said, his voice softening a little. "We're all family. It happens. Apology accepted. Let's get back on point." He cleared his voice. Rattled the sheet of paper in his hands. He stepped forward and set it on the table in front of her. It read:

Audrey Culliford (Grey) is charged with the following offenses:

1. Defying a direct order by a senior officer.

2. Stealing ship property as listed: 25 lb. Mace, 20' of 1/4" rope, 1 cadaver scheduled for autopsy.

3. Destroying said property listed in #2.

4. Enlisting a guest on a Larkian ship to aid and abet in said offenses.

By signing, you plead guilty to all listed offenses.

There was a line awaiting her signature. Stokes handed her a pen.

She looked up, meeting the gaze of Dr. Wickman, Alvarez, Leonard, and finally her father sitting before her. None of them looked happy.

She signed her name, handed the sheet of paper and the pen back to Stokes.

Stokes said, "You may speak before we discuss your punishment."

Audrey sat there stunned. What could she say? She was guilty of every offense. Caught in the act; on Tucker's cameras, on that humiliating poster hanging in the hall. No matter what she said or how hard she argued as to the moral reasons for her actions she knew they would still find a damning way to punish her.

"I've nothing left to say."

"Audrey, Ryan, you are dismissed until called upon. I suggest you go back to your cabins and wait until someone retrieves you."

62

Regrets

AUDREY LEARNED THERE WAS no appeal process as part of Larkian law. Even if she hadn't admitted guilt, they would have found her guilty based on the overwhelming evidence. Book closed. Move on. No more discussion.

Ryan was reprimanded for participating in the act of retrieving the body from the lab and helping Audrey dispose of it. He should have known better, and had, but he was found guilty by association and, of course, there was the indecent exposure. Any punishment for such acts was waived but he had become the butt of all jokes amongst the crew. Pun intended.

For every poster proving their transgression that Audrey ripped down, ten more appeared. Ryan believed his dream of being offered another chance to participate in future missions on the *Requiem Sea* II, and even the possibility of being recruited as a Larkian, evaporated that night they dumped the girl's body in the sea. Humiliation atop disappointment.

Audrey recalled the conversation they had shortly before boarding the ship, how he had been willing to start over, clean slate. She had vowed to herself she would never ask him to do anything that might cause grief or harm. Yet selfishly she had, again. Audrey wouldn't be surprised if he never spoke to her again, doubted he'd be willing to start afresh. Clean slate be damned.

Since this was Audrey's first offense, the crew had been lenient and the penalty unanimous; to be deported off the ship as soon as possible, and until that time, to perform community services. Once the ship was within helicopter range of the Hawaiian Islands, she would be flown off. Until then, she was to spend every waking hour working through a laundry list of tasks defined by the crew, including scrubbing the showers with a toothbrush. Tucker even reverted to using a chamber pot and made her empty it daily.

Since Ryan was near the end of his ten-day leave from the Labs, he was to accompany Audrey on the helicopter. He spent most of his time in the lab, in his cabin, or hanging out with Blake.

While she should feel relieved that her punishment didn't jeopardize her life or infringe on her basic rights, she was deeply ashamed and humiliated. She had alienated the one person she admired the most and aspired to emulate, Dr. Wickman. Every time she passed one of the guys in the crew, the disappointment in their eyes was palpable. Even Dyer avoided her. Tucker stayed buried in his cave, tinkering with his next technological breakthrough and, of course, filling his chamber pot. She was only allowed to enter for that duty and for nothing else.

Humiliation was a powerful lesson. Especially after her father came to visit after her punishment was announced.

"You got off easy. Two hundred years ago you would have gotten a keel-hauling or twenty lashes. Most didn't survive. I suggest you tread carefully. Dr. Wickman is more upset than I've seen him, *ever*. He has waited patiently his whole life to study one of them and you took that lifelong dream away from him. And for what? Why Audrey, *why*?"

Why indeed. She asked herself that question as she lay in her bunk, the nautical miles slipping beneath the hull, edging her closer to full rejection. The entire mood of the ship had shifted. To describe it as a buzzkill was an understatement. It was as if she had been infected with a deadly virus and anyone who came near would catch it.

Blake came around periodically to check in with her, offering sympathy as she churned through her unpleasant chores, but not to help—stating justice was justice and sometimes we do things we shouldn't, and as Newton's third law says: For every action, there is an equal and opposite reaction, and that was how the world worked. And she'd get through it. Then he'd bid farewell and join Ryan in the gym or for a game of chess or to visit Tucker in his man cave or do whatever it is that guys do to kill time.

Looking back, she realized she had been selfish and pigheaded. The girl tried to kill Ryan. She would have disintegrated had Audrey not irreparably destroyed that part of her brain that caused her body to self-destruct.

Dr. Wickman was a kind and empathetic person. A good soul. He would have treated the girl's body and all the secrets she held with utmost respect. He lost the opportunity to gain significant scientific knowledge that could have provided vital information necessary to the Larkians for protecting and defending themselves in the event of another attack. They all knew the significance of that opportunity; one she chose to ignore. She violated the first and most significant Code of Conduct as a full-fledged Larkian given the honor to serve as a crew member on the ship: to protect nation first and foremost, to protect fellow team or ship mates, and to protect the families of those who serve and all the other civilians who were part of the Larkian nation. Nowhere did it list the individual. She screwed up royally and lost all respect for it.

On top of the humiliation and guilt, she deeply mourned for Sinto. If he was alive she was certain he could help make up for what she took away from Dr. Wickman.

Thinking of that possibility opened that box where she had locked up her memories and feelings for Sinto. Opening it brought festering grief to the surface. She traced the lines of the Mark. Steely hard as the day she summoned it. Hardened, but cold and dormant. She wondered if it would ever fade or if it was there as a painful reminder of what could have been if only she had been strong enough to stop it.

She accepted she was cursed; a soul carved hollow and meant to be alone.

Sleep came begrudgingly.

63

Eyes Opened

Audrey had been assigned to spend her last day assisting Dr. Wickman. She had not seen him since the trial, nor talked with him since her misguided decision to dump the girl's body into the sea. She was frightened and unsure how he would react to her presence.

Dr. Wickman was in the inner lab studying something under a microscope. He looked up when she entered.

He didn't say anything. Not even his usual, "How are you today?" inquiry.

The inner lab felt chilly even though it was a comfortable seventy-two degrees. Audrey glanced at the gurney stowed and secured against the wall exactly where she saw it the first day she set foot on the ship. It looked as if it had never held a dead body. The floor was squeaky clean. A faint smell of disinfectant lingered. The large tank remained dry and empty.

"I owe you an apology."

He sat back, crossed his arms, and fixed her with chilly gaze.

She took a deep breath. Readied all the things she needed to say to quell the angst troubling her heart and soul. A confession.

"It was wrong of me to question your motivations. I realize I have set back important research that could have led to new insights on how to protect the crew should another encounter occur. It was selfish and shortsighted of me to consider only my feelings and beliefs in the matter. I violated the number one Code of Conduct. I am part of a team. A nation. A community. A family. It is something I am struggling to accept. I've been alone half of my life."

She swallowed down the knot growing in her throat. "You know how cold my father can be—how cold he was—how much he has changed since the accident. The day Mom died, I lost him. And because of my selfish and unforgivable actions, I fear I've lost you too."

Dr. Wickman uncrossed his arms and gestured her to sit on a stool next to him. She did.

"Your father's coming around and I'm helping him to see what he's done to you. The way he raised you—and he *did* raise you by the way—was atypical and lacking in finesse, to put it mildly. But he loves you more than you will ever know. He just has a difficult time expressing it. A big part of who he was died when he lost your mother. He may or may not ever get that part of himself back. As I've said, he is coming around and committed to understanding how to better express his true feelings. Especially to you."

"So where does that leave *us*?"

He frowned. "I am disappointed." A long pause. "Not just in you, but in myself. I was insensitive to your objections. I did an end-run with Alvarez. I got to him first. Because of that, you didn't have a chance of changing his mind, no matter what you said. It was sneaky and manipulative on my part. For that, I am sorry."

"And all this time I thought you were perfect."

He laughed. "I'm human, like you, and very capable of making mistakes. I'm just more experienced in covering them up."

"Clearly, I made the mistake here. I was insensitive to the potential danger we face. I was blinded by emotion, not thinking rationally. My eyes are now opened."

He smiled, and her heart felt a little lighter. "Good." He tapped the microscope. "Now that you can see clearly, you should take a look at this."

Audrey bent to look at the sample he had been studying.

"A sample of her blood," he said. "Looks normal; red blood cells one would expect to see from a healthy young person. But look in between." He increased the magnification on the microscope. "There is an anomaly. Something else present."

Between the healthy red blood cells were tiny worm-like cells. In one case one was boring into a healthy red blood cell.

"What is it?" she asked.

"I don't know. I suspect it might have something to do with that orange fungus. I need to run more tests to be sure. I did get a sample of brain tissue I've yet to study." He paused. "There was no need to cut so I figured it was fair game."

Audrey nodded. "Of course." She leaned back. "Her eyes were orange, like the one that grabbed Ryan and pulled him under."

"A potential side effect of consuming the fungus based on what we observed with that crab."

"I wonder what those Terrakai were doing in the Pacific?"

"I've wondered the same. Maybe we can learn more from a sample of her hair."

Dr. Wickman pulled a single strand from the sample of the dead girl's hair. It was about twelve inches long. "With this, we can learn a great deal about where she was from."

"I've never studied human hair before."

"A strand of hair can tell you a lot about a person. As you know, our bodies release hydrogen and oxygen and other chemicals. These compounds are incorporated into proteins the body produces."

"Keratin's one of those proteins. It's an essential component of our hair and nails."

"Correct. The food you eat, the type of water you drink, the quality of air you breathe, whether you've ingested drugs or been exposed to heavy metals—all are recorded as isotope signatures in your hair. The longer the strand, the older it is, and the more history we can learn."

Audrey scanned the cabinets and countertops encircling the lab. "You have the equipment to run isotope tests?"

He smiled proudly. "This lab is set up to test for everything." He led her into the dry lab where banks of electronic equipment hummed with life.

He showed her a white boxy machine that looked like a copier.

"This is a mass spectrometer for recording various isotopes. We'll start with oxygen and find out the source of water she frequently drank, whether from a lake or stream or filtered through the ground, such as from a well." He placed the sample inside, pressed a few buttons on the front panel. It hummed to life. "This shouldn't take long." He leaned back against the counter, crossed his legs.

"Your birthday's coming up soon."

She laughed. "I guess it is. With all that's been happening I completely forgot."

"Twenty-one—a full-fledged grownup in all respects."

She winked. "Finally, I can sip rum, legally."

The machine beeped, followed by a quiet whirring sound. It spit out a small piece of paper. Dr. Wickman picked it up and read the results.

"Interesting. She lived an abnormally squeaky-clean life up till the last six months." He crinkled his brow. "Every living thing on earth has been exposed to something toxic from our food and the air we breathe and the water we drink."

"She might have come from Merluma."

He dragged his finger down the list as he read further. "Then as of six months ago she shows a typical exposure to man-made toxins." He flicked his finger against the paper. "Ah, this is what I wanted. Looks like her oxygen count is high. She drank lake water."

"The Terrakai prefer fresh lakes."

"Let's narrow down which fresh water source."

They returned to his workspace in the back lab. He sat and flipped open his laptop.

"So how exactly can you find out what fresh water source she comes from?" Audrey peered over his shoulder.

"Isotope maps available on the Internet."

He ran a quick search and opened up a website displaying several geographical maps of the United States. He began with the West Coast; first, Lake Washington near her home in Seattle, then Lake Tahoe in Nevada. Then the Great Lakes. His fingers were a blur as he flipped through several tables with rows upon rows of numbers.

He pointed at the screen. "There, the closest match, one of the Great Lakes. Lake Superior."

"What would a pregnant Terrakai female, barely past puberty, from Lake Superior be doing in the North Pacific Gyre?"

"I don't know. But I suspect it might have something to do with Orange."

64

Going Home... For Real

THE ALL-BLACK SIKORSKY S-76X parked on the helipad gleamed in the early morning sunshine. It was a specialized model of the S-76. Manufactured with modifications made by Grey Industries—wholly owned and managed by the Larkians—thus the reason for the designation X.

She also learned that Grey Industries did that sort of thing: picking up existing technology and making it better. Especially in situations where the original owner of the technology fell upon hard times or experienced a dip in market demand and was seeking new partnerships or investment. Grey Industries would swoop in and negotiate for a big piece of the technology, if not all of it. It was much more efficient, cost-effective, and quick to build advancements on top of established technologies, at least in many cases. Like what Tucker did with the sonobuoy.

Her duffel sat at her feet. Her shadow stretched into a long-legged thing across the steel deck from the low angle of the early morning sun.

Ryan was inside the helicopter's garage bidding farewell to his new friends, bear hugs all around. The humiliation they put him through was a form of initiation. Apparently, he passed the test by taking the whole situation in stride.

Blake was also departing with Ryan and Audrey, though Stokes told him that he could stay with the ship. He declined the offer, saying he came with his friends, and he'd depart with his friends. She looked around; he was nowhere to be seen at the moment.

Audrey felt a little sad and lonely. No one ran up to bid her goodbye. Still a pariah. She figured it was part of the punishment. Voted off the ship, no hugs and kisses, no lingering goodbyes. More like good riddance. She hoped it wasn't permanent, that she would be given a second chance. There would be another mission, of that she was certain, based on the percolating unrest among the Merahvu and the discovery of Orange. If her interaction with Dr. Wickman yesterday was any indication, then she was hopeful she'd be welcomed back into the Larkian family, eventually.

Her long shadow was joined by another. She turned to see whose. Tucker.

"Look a little lonely over 'ere," he said.

She looked back at the mob of guys surrounding Ryan, yucking it up. "They love him."

"What's not to love?"

"True. Everyone loves Ryan."

She gazed down, frowning.

"Ah, don't be goin' all mopey."

She laughed. "I really screwed up."

"Yep, but don't be too hard on yourself. We all have one time or another. Some just more than others."

He pulled something out of his pocket. Held it out in the palm of his hand. A pin. Matte black and round. In the center was the white Larkian logo. Printed below the logo in white, bold letters it said, "BADASS".

"Now it's official. Yer little stunt made it that way. We were waitin' for you to screw up. You shoulda seen the list of possibilities, but no one imagined you'd start by pissin' off senior officers. While it was wrong, it takes guts to stand up for what you believe in." He softly punched her in the shoulder. "You put up a good fight."

"It was a mistake, a big one. One I truly regret. It was a shitty thing to do to Dr. Wickman."

He tapped her forehead. "Ah, good, you're learnin'. Dontcha fret, we all get another chance. Though let me give you a bit of advice."

Then he stuck her with a white-hot gaze that made her heart skip a beat.

"Don't do that again. Ever. Defying direct orders and pissing off the seniors." He tsked. "You broke trust. That's a biggy. We break trust, the whole thing falls apart. You can make mistakes, but never the same one twice. Especially that one. Break trust again and..." He drew his finger slowly across his throat. "You gettin' me?"

"Loud and clear."

His eyes softened. She was amazed at how quickly he went from hot to cold, Dr. Death to Mr. Nice.

"Good. Still got the hat?"

She bent, unzipped her duffel. It was sitting right on top. Her most prized possession. She pulled it out.

Tucker took it and stuck the badass pin on it. "That's better." He put it on her head, covering the halo of loose hair sticking out from the braids and the short pony he had called a "baby boop" the day she challenged and beat him three rounds on the mat. "And that's where it belongs."

Tears welled in her eyes. She was going to miss these guys. He wiped her cheek where one slipped out.

He grinned, scar tugging at his lip. "Don't be gettin all sad. This isn't goodbye. Just a pause. Besides, I want my hat back."

She smiled. "Are you throwing down a challenge?"

"Not yet. Gotta do some homework before I tumble with you again, maybe sign up for a session with Dr. Wickman."

"And I the same."

It was sudden. He wrapped her in his arms and gave her a hug with such strength the air was forced from her lungs. A bear hug. And as quick as it began it ended.

He stepped back. "Now take your friends and get out of here. You're stinkin' up the place."

Ryan came up. Tucker grabbed his hand and pulled him to his chest, wrapped his other arm around his back, gave him a couple of firm pats.

"Keep an eye on her." He released him, then joined the other crew members huddled by the open garage doors.

The pilot finished his preliminary systems check. Jumped into the pilot seat. Started the engine. The blades ramped up, whirling then whipping until she couldn't see them anymore. She clamped her hand on the hat to keep it from flying. Warm air buffeted her face and tugged at her pant legs. A little humid and distinctly tropical. The Hawaiian Islands were less than four hundred miles to the south.

Stokes came up and grabbed her duffel. Ryan's was slung across his shoulder. Together they all stooped and fast-stepped to the helicopter. They tossed their bags in the storage compartment. Ryan climbed in the main cabin, Audrey after him.

Blake came running up, stowed his duffel, and hopped in beside Audrey. He was huffing as if he'd just run the entire length of the ship.

"Sorry I'm late."

Stokes leaned in. "Safe trip." That was all. No hug for Audrey. Ouch.

Ryan shrugged and pulled on his headset. Stokes stepped back, shut the door, and waved to the pilot.

Then they were airborne. The ship dropped away and they were zooming across a deep blue sea speckled with white froth.

The pilot put on some Hawaiian music for the ride. Steel slide and ukulele, with sappy lyrics about waterfalls and majestic cliffs, and the beautiful and gracious way of the Hawaiian people.

She was going home.

Tears slid down her cheeks. Everything let go. The attack, the dead girl, the stupidity of her defiance, the humiliation she put Ryan through, and everything that came before. She missed her life at the Labs, she missed her mother, and deeper than everything that welled from the depths of her soul, she desperately missed Sinto.

They landed at the Honolulu airport a couple hours later, dropping down away from the main terminal gates to the area where private helicopters and planes parked.

Stokes had arranged for a company jet to fly Ryan back to Seattle and a smaller local airline to fly him from Seattle to San Juan Island. He'd be home in less than eight hours and back to his old life. She was torn about not going with him. She missed her studies and her previous life, when she was oblivious to all the things that threatened to up-end it.

Ryan actually thanked her for his humiliating experience. Then he play-punched her in the arm and said he was sorry how it worked out, but that he still valued her friendship and would readily be there to help if she ever needed it again. Of course, he premised it with the fact he would first need full disclosure of the consequences of performing said help and that he had the right to refuse with no questions asked or further groveling or manipulation on her part.

He was especially interested in being a guest on *Requiem Sea II* once again if the opportunity presented itself. If she ever wanted him to come along on a future mission, she should count him in.

"You will be at the top of my list. And I promise, Ryan, what happened will never happen again. I'm wiser now."

Ryan chuckled, rolling his eyes. "I doubt it, kid. You are who you are. Promise me to never change."

"One thing will change. You won't be able to call me a kid anymore. I'm going to be a big girl soon. My birthday's tomorrow. The big two-one."

"I'm sorry to miss it."

"No big deal." She flashed him a toothy grin. "More cake for me."

He wrapped his arm around her shoulders and gave her a knuckle rub across her braided head. Then he kissed her on the cheek. "Don't be a stranger. You know how to find me."

"Of course."

He let her go and turned to Blake.

Ryan and Blake hugged, hands clasped in front with a single-arm embrace.

"Going to miss you," Blake said to Ryan.

"And I you. Take care of our girl."

"Always."

Then he spun on his heel and hitched his duffel over his shoulder, walking like a new man toward the waiting jet.

Once the helicopter was refueled, Audrey and Blake hopped aboard and were on their way to her one true home: Isla Salvación. She boarded with trepidation. Her mother drowned on the island on her tenth birthday. Audrey hadn't been back since she died. Her twenty-first birthday would mark the eleventh anniversary of her death.

Her father warned her that Isla Salvación had seen many changes since she left, except for the south end, where the house she grew up in was located. He assured her the beach where she met Sinto and last saw her mother alive had been preserved and untouched by human influence.

Blake took her hand. "Are you ready for this?"

She had been bracing for it the entire trip to Honolulu. "I hope so."

His gaze grew distant. "Me too."

PART THREE

65

Isla Salvación

IT TOOK LESS THAN an hour for the helicopter to pass by the island of Kauai, the west-most island in the Hawaiian chain and halfway to Isla Salvación. Shortly after, Audrey's birthplace and the island nation of the Larkians, discovered and established by her father and his original pirate crew, rose up from the white-speckled Pacific.

Isla Salvación was roughly the size of Kauai, slightly less populated, but just as wild and shaped like a seahorse. The entire east coast was composed of steep and unnavigable mountains much like Kauai's Na Pali Coast, rising along the entirety of the curved backside of the seahorse-shaped island.

The pilot approached looming mountains, then veered south along the jagged shoreline where knife-edged cliffs dove into the sea and the ravenous waters of the Pacific pounded its rocky shore as it had for millions of years, slowly reclaiming it back to the sea. From the air, it was easy to see how the east side of the island was cut off from the west, with the mountains providing an impenetrable wall from an eastern attack by sea.

The helicopter lowered as it rounded the south end of the island. The tail of the seahorse shape curled around and formed a large cove abundant with sea life. The azure sea brightened, deep blue fading into a rainbow of cerulean blue and turquoise surrounded by the glowing white curve of a coral sand beach where water kissed land. Her mother had dived and hunted in those waters every day while Audrey was growing up.

Audrey's breath caught when the house where she was born and grew up came into view, set back from the shore among a riot of jungle green. Her heart clenched when her gaze followed the curve of the cove to the very tip of the seahorse tail, curling into a smaller protective lagoon with the small beach where she learned to swim, met Sinto, and last saw her mother alive.

The yin-yang of emotions made her belly quiver and breath catch.

Blake squeezed her hand. "You okay?"

Her throat was clamped tight. She squeezed back. It was all she could do at the moment.

Then the cove was behind them and the pilot screamed along the west shore where the soft belly of the seahorse expanded, rippling with grasses and sparkling ponds fed from streams rushing down from the mist-topped mountains. The entire coast was edged by white sandy beaches along the low-lying wetlands where turtles laid eggs and birds migrated to feed and mate.

Further north, beyond the wetlands, was the airport and a well-protected, deep-water harbor cut deeply into the landscape. The harbor had changed significantly. The old wooden dock where a supply ship used to dock once a week was gone. Fingers of massive concrete floats spread from the shore beside the runway. Enough to accommodate several ships as large as the *Requiem Sea II*. At the head of the harbor was the marina. It too had expanded and been given a face lift. Hundreds of yachts, sail and power, filled the slips.

The local village, located along the shore at the very head of the harbor and a few steps from the marina, bustled with activity.

The pilot overshot the harbor and circled around the northern end of the island—the head of the seahorse—home to most of the Larkian population. Residences dotted the green landscape and stretched deep into ravines and up hillsides. Above the village, a large lake provided abundant freshwater fed by daily rain showers brushing across the mountains. Surrounding the lake, the plains and hillsides were patch-worked with fields of reddish loamy soil and abundant vegetation; vegetables, melons, pineapple, sugar cane, fruit and nut trees, and recently, coffee. Crops that sustained the Larkian population. The upper hills were dotted with goat, cattle, and sheep. Wild fowl roamed the entire island.

Solar arrays and wind turbines peppered spaces in between, powering the entire island, backed up by generators and massive battery storage. Most of the vehicles on the island were electric.

The helicopter circled back, dipping low over a sprawling compound across the harbor from the airport. It had been built in the last ten years for housing new recruits and crew on leave from Larkian ships. It included a training facility, a large community center, and a banquet hall for local gatherings.

What she once believed to be a sleepy island home to a few hundred had bloomed into a nation of over twenty-five thousand in ten short years.

They began their descent, touching down on the sand-colored cement of the airport featuring one small and one giant runway. When they settled, Audrey and Blake released their seatbelts and stowed their headsets. The pilot flipped switches and shut down the engine. Silence and rays of intense sunshine filled the sudden void.

The pilot hopped out and opened their door. Blake jumped down first, then Audrey.

She breathed deep the tropical air, salty and moist and scented by plumeria that grew around the original open-sided building that served as the airport terminal. Several four-seater utility task vehicles—UTVs—were parked beside it. A squat man of Polynesian descent, wearing a rust-colored sarong and colorful Hawaiian shirt, waited next to a larger UTV. A smile exploded across his face when he saw her.

"Audrey! How you've grown!"

"Mako?"

"Yes, yes!"

Mako had been the groundskeeper, and his wife the fabulous cook and baker who shared meals with their small family when Audrey was young. Poe was the one who introduced Audrey to croissants.

"How is Poe?"

He patted his belly. "She's doin' what she loves and so excited to see you. Cooking up a storm anticipating your arrival! But first, let's get you settled."

They loaded their things and hopped into the open-air UTV large enough to seat ten. Audrey hopped up front, Blake behind her. She noticed he had grown strangely quiet, or maybe he was just being contemplative as he commonly was, taking in the beauty of the island.

Mako swung the shuttle away from the terminal and veered south. Being electric it quietly whizzed along.

"Your father asked me to open up the house and get it ready for your stay. Been shut up for too long. A house is meant to be lived in. I think you will find it exactly the same as the day you left." He frowned. "No day passes when we don't think about what happened. Very sad. Poe misses Teola every day. We were both sorry to see you go."

"I was too."

Mako confirmed nothing had changed on the south end while the northern part of the island exploded with new growth. The southern part of the island had been claimed by her father long ago and included the entire cove and jungles nestled up against the mountains at the tail end of the island. Most of the changes were happening in the north where new residences were being built to accommodate the rapid influx of newly nationalized Larkian citizens that Alvarez and his team were actively recruiting. Mako and Poe had lived on the island most of their lives, recruited from Oahu before Audrey was born, and lived near the village.

"Population growing. Good for us long-time locals. The village is booming. Everyone is happily employed. Many new artists and tradesmen. New places to eat and gather." He grinned. "Less stress on me. More time to play."

Mako and Poe were a newly married couple when Audrey was born. As far as she knew, they never had children of their own and had made a point of spoiling her every chance they got, much to the chagrin of her mother. She guessed Mako to be in his early fifties at this point. A sprinkle of gray in his hair and a few more facial wrinkles were the only clue. He appeared as fit as ever. Living here kept people active, and without the stress of the big city, happily living the quieter pace of island life.

The shuttle whizzed south down the center of the two-lane sand-colored cement road. Mountains rose to the left, grassy wetlands spread to the right. The road had no lines painted on it. No need. They passed no one else.

"Turtle population's been good but the birds have varied. Some years more pass through than others. A few new species as well. Been hotter than normal, especially this time of year. We've had more tropical storms hit the island in recent years. In fact, we're watching one form off to the southeast. Cross your fingers it stays south, else you'll be having a very wet and windy birthday."

The wetlands fell away and the jungle began. The air cooled and freshened. Bamboo and palm. Kukui and mango. Fern and ginger. Bird of paradise and many more wild and colorful tropical flowers lined the roadway. Her mother had taught her about each one, their names, what time of year they bloomed and how often, and which birds and insects relied upon them.

Mako slowed the shuttle, rounded a bend in the road, and stopped at a closed gate artistically forged of steel with a school of fish welded across the vertical rods; the gate itself was grounded by a pair of volcanic rock pillars. The gate automatically split open when they approached.

"The gate is only for aesthetics and to mark the beginning of the property as private." He pointed to the vast open space beyond the pillars. "You see, no fence, open for wildlife to pass. If we lose power, you might have to open manually." He pointed to a large switch mounted to the driver's side pillar. "Flip it up to disengage the lock. Push it open with muscles." He flexed a bicep and grinned his Mako grin.

He drove through, the gate automatically closing behind them.

The jungled thinned. Enticing glimpses of the southern cove cut through the greenery. The UTV burst into the bright sunshine. White sand and turquoise water edged the road. The cove her father named after her mother stretched before them.

Mako turned and smiled. "Welcome home, Audrey!"

Audrey's heart trilled.

Mako parked where the road ended and walking paths began. Two UTVs and a couple of electric bikes were parked in the double-wide carport. They all hopped out, Audrey and Blake grabbing their bags, Mako grabbing an ice chest.

The house was intentionally hidden from the road and parking area by dense foliage.

She felt as if she was nine years old again, anticipating her tenth birthday.

The path to the front door curved toward the jungle. She raced past Mako. The modest house came into view. She stopped and dropped her bag. She tried to breathe, but her chest was bound by a tightly cinched corset of emotion.

The house was exactly as she remembered. Built by her father exactly the way her mother wanted it. The path from the carport led to the main entrance, opposite from the cove, facing into the jungle. The back side of the house faced the cove. Covered and open lanais wrapped all around. Regardless of the time of day, you could find an outdoor retreat either in the sun or the shade, or a perfect spot for viewing the rising moon and stars. Gardens of fern and colorful flowers surrounded the entire house.

The house had been built for outdoor living and was strong enough to withstand a hurricane. It sat on elevated cement pilings and was constructed from iron wood, cement, and rock. The cement-tiled roof was topped with grass thatching for aesthetic purposes.

Blake and Mako caught up to Audrey. Blake lingered a bit behind, eyes darting around. She wondered if he was worried about their safety being so close to the open sea, especially after the Terrakai attack. Audrey felt a little the same, but tamped that uneasy feeling down. She refused to let fear trample on the moment.

"This is where you two stay," Mako said.

She looked at Blake. He looked as surprised as her. "Just us?"

"That is what your father suggested."

They followed Mako up a set of stairs to the covered lanai and the main entry. He stepped aside for Audrey. The front door was already open, capturing the breeze and scents from the jungle. She kicked off her black leather shoes and stepped barefooted into the foyer. The bamboo floor was cool to her feet. On the left was a nook with a bench and hooks along the wall where various hats hung. On the right was a well-organized storeroom, modified with up-to-date shelving and cabinets. Lining the shelves were lanterns, flashlights, umbrellas, day packs, a small ice chest, beach towels, and canvas bags, each meticulously organized and labeled. Mako said the addition of organized shelving and hooks had been Poe's idea.

He opened a cabinet in the far corner and gestured at what was inside. A selection of crossbows and spear guns, night-vision goggles, and plenty of extra spears in preloaded barrels. High tech like those the crew used on the *Requiem Sea II* to fend off the Terrakai attack. In a cabinet beside it were hooded wet suits, including gloves and booties.

"Your father wanted you to know these were readily available." He shook his head. "Shouldn't be necessary. You are safe. No crime here."

Audrey looked at Blake, raised her brows, then nodded. "Of course."

Her heart beat faster as she moved from the foyer into the main living area. There were two bedrooms, one on each side, each with a private bath. One for Audrey and one for her parents. Simple, just as her mother liked it.

Her knees felt weak; tears welled. The furnishings were exactly the same: a pair of stools tucked under a counter facing a modest kitchen; a small dining table with seating for four. Facing the ocean was a sofa and two easy chairs upholstered in vividly colored floral patterns. The koa coffee table was topped with a tall stack of books waiting to be read. The far wall was lined with bookshelves and stuffed with trinkets and sea shells she had collected with her mother. Hawaiian-themed paintings hung on white walls. Hand-woven mats lovingly selected by her mother were scattered across the bamboo floor. A fan with woven grass blades lazily stirred the air scented with fresh-cut jasmine and gardenia, bursting from a large vase on the kitchen counter. And the one thing her mother absolutely loved—Bob Marley, playing softly on a boom box tucked in the far corner.

Simple living was what her mother preferred. Televisions, computers, and cell phones weren't allowed. *Love, family, land, and the sea is all I need*, her mother used to say. Audrey released a choke-filled laugh, remembering the day her mother bought the boom box on an excursion to the Hawaiian Islands and her father giving her a hard time. It was the only form of electronics she had allowed in "her" house. She had loved Bob Marley. Every CD he had ever recorded sat on the shelf next to it.

Audrey closed her eyes. It was as if time had stopped. She imagined this was what it would feel like if her mother had never died and she had come home to visit, and that at any moment her mother would burst from her room wearing a colorful pāʻū. Audrey squeezed her eyes tight, wishing it was true—that she would open her eyes and her mother would be in the kitchen slicing mangoes, humming along to the music, stopping only to ask Audrey to fetch her father from his morning swim...

Someone touched her shoulder. She opened her eyes. Blake.

"Are you okay?" he asked.

"Yeah, this is just so... surreal. I thought this place didn't exist anymore, but it does and it's exactly the same."

Mako waved them over to her parents' old bedroom. He reached for Blake's duffel. "Blake stay in here."

While everything else was the same, this room was different. Not one piece of art hung on the freshly painted white walls, and the brightly colored quilt her mother loved was gone. Sliding doors opened to the sea. White sheer curtains billowed from the light briny breeze. Musical notes of the sea in motion filled the room. The king-sized bed was covered by crisp white linens. The ensuite bathroom had white fluffy towels. The door to a private outdoor shower was open and ready to hop into. The walk-in closet was empty except for a few items of men's clothing, still tagged, that Mako said were left for Blake by Poe. Everything of her mother's was gone: her jewelry, her shell hair pieces, her vast collection of batiked pāʻū... Except for the wood-lined ceiling, her parent's old bedroom looked like the inside of a milk carton.

Mako frowned. "Your father requested we remove everything, effectively sanitize it. Too painful for him otherwise. Very sad."

"Sanitized is right."

Audrey stood in the doorway looking across to the bedroom on the other side of the living area. Her room. The door was closed. Her name was still painted on it, an afternoon mommy-daughter project, with stickers of fish and turtles circling her name. Her father was upset about the stickers they had attached to the beautiful fruitwood finish. Her mother said it was only sticky paper, but most importantly, it made Audrey happy. She didn't understand why that had upset him.

She crossed the room and opened the door.

Nothing had changed. She held her breath, afraid if she breathed it would disappear.

A drawing of her with her mother on the beach was tacked crookedly on the wall, exactly the way she hung it the day her father drew it. She was eight or so, a couple of years before their world fell apart. The quilt her mother made for her covered the double-sized four-poster bed. At each corner of the bed were netted curtains tied back by teal-green bows—the same bows her mother tied every morning after waking Audrey up. Audrey had loved the way the curtains had made her feel like she was sleeping in a cloud high in the sky with her mother bringing her back to earth with a kiss every morning.

Her ten-year-old clothes still hung in the closet. Including the new dress she never got to wear for her tenth birthday party. Because there wasn't one. She had spent the day hiding under her bed until Dr. Wickman came and found her.

Audrey walked over to a bookshelf and pulled out a ragged-edged book, not a real book you buy in a store, but a picture book she created herself. On the front was a crude drawing of a mermaid and pirate ship. *The Lonely Mermaid*, was the title. It was a story about a lost pirate who meets a mermaid. The mermaid was forbidden by her gods to talk to humans on the surface, but she feels sorry for him and helps him find his way home. Then they fall in love and he doesn't want her to leave. But she can't stay. So she dives into the sea broken hearted. Never to be seen again.

She remembered her mother reading it and asking; *Why is the ending so sad?*

And Audrey replied; *It was not supposed to be sad, except, I guess, for the pirate and the mermaid. She gave up her true love because she was the queen and worried that the pirate would tell his friends and the merpeople would be hunted for their treasure and mystical powers. That was why she left him, and because she did, the merpeople lived happily ever after, at the bottom of the sea.*

She clearly remembered her mother suggesting; *Maybe you should add that part to the end of the story.*

Audrey had been nine years old when she wrote it. The last few pages were still blank, having never had the chance to add the happy ending her mother suggested. She had forgotten about it, until now. A mermaid and a pirate, falling in love, and the mermaid's fear of humans. Irony stabbed her in the heart. Her fingers shook when she tucked it back on the shelf.

She sat down on the bed and stared at her reflection in the mirror hanging above her dresser, staring at the lost girl who used to live in this room. For how long she sat there, she didn't know. Her lap felt damp from crying. Her father was right; this place held so many memories. Memories she had thought were lost forever. Some were painful, as he said, but some were never meant to be forgotten.

Her father had angered her to the point she never wanted to see him again, to cast him out of her life and sever his puppet strings, but this... This he kept after all these years. He could have torn it down, sanitized it, like their bedroom. But he didn't. She wondered if he had planned to bring her here, one day, all along; the best gift he could possibly give her for her birthday: to relive memories of the past when they were a close and loving family. The only thing missing was what he couldn't give her. Her mother.

Someone tapped on the door. Mako's head popped in. "Poe made you grilled fish salads and pineapple cake. I left in the fridge along with some other items you may need. Cupboards are stocked. The phone still works. Numbers are listed beside it. Call me if you need anything. Should Poe and I expect you for dinner?"

The lump in her throat made it difficult to answer so she smiled back and nodded.

He smiled that Mako smile. "Poe will be ecstatic. The UTVs are charged up and ready to go. Come after sunset. I left directions by the phone."

They bid Mako farewell. The crunch of gravel and quiet whine of the shuttle faded. The sliding door from her room was open to the lanai with steps to the beach, where the water in the cove danced like diamonds. She was cocooned in silence, but for rustling palm fronds and the melodic swoosh of waves lapping the shore.

Blake slipped into her room, sat and wrapped an arm around her. She buried her head in his shoulder and sobbed tears of joy and of sorrow. Her world wasn't pitching under her feet, the sky wasn't exploding in a downpour of fury, and orange-eyed monsters weren't leaping from the sea. She was home along with a torrid sea of memories and emotions.

She could no longer ignore that Blake was a big part of her new reality. She knew he cared for her, deeply, and understood her apprehension. He had been patiently waiting to resume where they had left off, with a promise she once made. It was up to her to choose if or when.

He grabbed a tissue from her bathroom. She used it to dry her cheeks and blow her nose.

"You should see what Mako left in the refrigerator."

She sniffed, "Yeah, that good?"

He smiled. "Oh, yeah, and I'm starving."

She smiled back. "Me too."

66

Boundaries

AFTER LUNCH AUDREY AND Blake snorkeled in the sea and walked along the beach. She gushed with childhood memories; catching her first fish, her mother teaching her to weave a hat with wetland grasses, her father teaching her how to draw the creatures she saw in the sea. By the time they showered and changed the sun was readying to set and soon it would be time to leave for dinner with Mako and Poe.

Mako had left a few simple dresses and pāʻūs that Poe had picked up for Audrey to wear. She was grateful since she had packed sport-practical and for the cooler weather of the North Pacific. The dresses were basically wisps of brightly colored fabric, but one stood out the most, a thin-strapped slip-like dress with swirling patterns of blue and specked with white. It reminded her of the ocean gone wild. Anything but orange.

The braids in her hair were still tightly wound with a minor amount of escapees. Those she smoothed down with a little conditioner. She loved how easy the braids made caring for her hair. A gentle pat with shampoo and a good rinse and she was ready to go.

Blake waited on the lanai. The sun hovered low in the sky. He had slipped on a tastefully-patterned coral-colored tropical shirt and cream-colored linen slacks Mako had left for him. Both of them glowed from a day in the sun.

He turned when she stepped out of her sliding door and onto the lanai. He was holding a glass of white wine. He held up his glass. "I found this in the refrigerator. Would you like some?" Her smile said it all and he poured her a glass from a bottle set in a bucket of ice. They settled on a love seat and watched the sun dip lower.

"I could get used to this," he said, taking a sip.

"Me too." She touched the space between them. "I remember sitting right here between my parents, them sipping wine, me sipping guava juice, and together we would watch the sun set. Now I'm sipping wine and—" She sucked a breath. "Not exactly the same." She reached for Blake's hand. "But this is nice. Thank you for being here."

Blake's gaze traced its way from their clasped hands up the line of her bare and sun-blushed arm to her lips. "Yes. This is very nice."

His gazed lingered on her mouth for a beat.

She set down her wine glass. He set down his.

Audrey's heart skipped a beat. The Mark in her arm twitched, another lingering and reminding echo.

His eyes found hers. His brow rose, questioningly. Silence stretched. Blake patiently waited for a sign. Was she ready to open that tiny piece of her heart?

He made the first move, tracing a line where his gaze went before, starting with their clasped hands. Her skin tingled where his fingers grazed her skin, past the dormant Mark, around the bend of her elbow, to the muscled mound of her shoulder. There his finger lingered. He inquired, "Dare I go farther?"

Her heart fluttered, awakening that piece of her heart that once found him mysterious and irresistible. Her lips parting ever so slightly.

Yes.

He continued, tracing his finger across her collarbone, the side of her neck, to her chin. He gently lifted her face till her lips met the same plane as his and pressed his lips to hers. It was like their first kiss on *Annabelle*, tentative at first, then more urgent and exploratory. Audrey surrendered and Blake fulfilled a need she'd been suppressing: for tenderness and warmth and someone who would love her in return. The sun set. They missed it, enthralled in a fiery kiss.

Blake ended it, but the sunset kept going, a stunning display of orange and gold and green along the edges. They sipped their wine. Neither said anything, pretending to be awestruck by the beauty unfolding in the sky, and not from the awkward aftermath of their impassioned kiss.

Audrey was at war with emotion. Guilt for doing it, desire for more. Blake patiently waiting for her to make up her mind. The fact they were staying together in her childhood house, alone, added an element of confusion and complication.

The awkward silence between them stretched. Blake broke it. "Should I be sorry for that? I can be if you want."

She smiled. "I'm not sorry—it was rather nice, but…"

"Ah. But." He nodded. "I understand and respect boundaries as long as I know what they are."

She said nothing. She honestly struggled with what they might or should be. She found it difficult to look at him. Whatever boundaries she did declare might just evaporate the second she met his gaze.

He added, "Barring no input, I will set my own; that is, if you agree. I think we should agree it's premature to take things in a direction that we can't claw back from, until we're both certain we're ready."

She finally met his gaze. And from what he just said she found herself wanting more, to just let go and flow with it…

But.

There was that itch in her arm and now it was burning, hot and painfully. As if jealousy was an emotion embedded in the Mark as a curse for what happened to Sinto and her role in it.

Why is the Mark still active and alive?

She decided it was a sign. A very loud and obnoxious one, not to be ignored.

"I agree, honestly, as nice as that kiss felt, I—I'm just not ready."

"It's okay, I understand. I care for you, very much, and have no desire to hurt or pressure you." He squeezed her hand. "And I'm not one to run away with a wounded ego. I learned to be patient long ago."

"Thank you. You're my rock, always there steady and sure. That will never change, no matter what."

They finished their wine, buttoned up the house, and turned on a few lights. Audrey grabbed a pā'ū to wrap around her shoulders and Mako's hand-written directions to the compound. It would be dark and cooler when they returned later in the evening.

Audrey slipped her fingers through Blake's. "Should we agree holding hands is okay?"

"Of course, friends hold hands." Then he kissed her knuckles and laughed. "And kiss them once in a while."

She kissed his knuckles back. "Okay."

They hopped into one of the UTVs. Blake drove and Audrey navigated, which simply involved reading Mako's brief instructions: "Follow road to the harbor. Take second left past the village."

Several hours later, Audrey and Blake returned to the house in darkness with full bellies and tipsy from too much wine. The headlights of the UTV bounced along the pale road, lighting a small circle of blinding light in a nocturnal world. Disturbed critters skittered out of their way.

They reflected back to a time at the Labs after they went kayaking and Ryan was taking their picture and Blake coaxed him to step back a little farther, then farther still, and he stepped right off the dock into the water. Blake and Audrey howled with laughter.

Ryan was not amused. He lost his phone and Blake had to buy him another.

"The look on his face was priceless!" Audrey burst out in snorting laughter, which brought on more howls of laughter, mostly from her. "I miss him already!"

It had been a long day, reeling from the emotional spectrum that motivated her overconsumption of wine. Blake had not indulged as much, being the responsible one. Audrey ripped out a loud burp. More snickers and giggles, mostly from her.

Once the UTV was safely parked, Audrey profusely thanked Blake for getting them back in one piece. Audrey clung to Blake as he helped her navigate the path lit by mushroom-shaped lights, voices raised, singing a silly made-up shanty, one she would surely forget in the morning.

Blake helped her up the steps to the front door. She stumbled her way into the little house and collapsed on the sofa. Blake tried to pull her to her feet, but she pulled him down atop her. He respectfully extracted himself from a leg she'd hooked around one of his. Then he pulled her to her feet and guided her to her room.

She plopped face down on her bed, "No! Another shanty! You know that one about drinking too much rum?"

He slipped off her sandals and tucked her under the colorful quilt lying on her bed. He left her in her lovely new dress.

The last thing she remembered before passing out was a tender kiss on the cheek, and a silky voice saying, "Sweet dreams, my sweet Audrey."

67

Seeking A Friend

THE LANDSCAPE WAS A blur of white, brown, gray, and green. Rachel had picked the fastest and most direct route along the interstate heading due west toward the Pacific, cutting through North Dakota, Montana, a sliver of Idaho, and into Washington State.

The landscapes were beautiful and had Sinto not been frantic to warn his mother and to get word to Audrey he would have begged Rachel to stop frequently. Rachel promised she would bring him back, "Once this business of the Orankai is resolved."

Sinto loved her enthusiasm but didn't have the heart to tell her: that might be never. Or worse. He might not survive to take her up on her offer.

They stopped twice to rest. Once in Glendive, Montana, where the Yellowstone River cut through. Rachel was exhausted from driving hours on end, from worrying about Sinto's state of health, from the stress of their rapid and violent escape, and even more distressing, reeling from the fact she killed two Orankai by intentionally running them down, though Sinto explained they more than deserved it. It would have been Rachel and Sinto lying dead if she hadn't acted decisively.

Rachel needed time to process what had happened. Sinto needed a source of water to revive and heal. They chose a quiet hotel close to the river, though Rachel wasn't keen on Sinto taking a swim.

"You don't know what kinda pollution or bacteria's in that water. You might get an infection."

Sinto assured her the wound was cauterized and the redeeming qualities of river water would help him heal faster.

Still, she was afraid to be alone and reluctant to let Sinto out of her sight. He reminded her about the locket and would let her know if he needed help. She finally relented and waited in the cold and the dark, locket in hand with the car engine running, while Sinto took a brief dip.

The second stop was in Coeur d' Alene, Idaho, with a giant lake of the same name. Sinto was still weak from his wound and the taxing abuse his merlux endured while imprisoned by Arkis, but he convinced Rachel he would be better off resting in the lake instead of in a stuffy hotel room. He stayed close to shore and settled into a soft silty spot and slept for many hours.

On the third day of their journey they crossed the vast rolling hills of eastern Washington, where wheat and barley fields lay dormant under a fresh dusting of snow.

Sinto was slowly regaining his strength. Sleeping less during the day and feeling restless and uneasy. He concentrated on self-healing the damaged fibers of muscle along the side of his torso, his mind visualizing them stitching back together. The fatty layer would take weeks if not months to build up naturally. Not a problem, as it was more for insulation. He would have a rounded indent where the fat was missing for several months. The skin he worked on regenerating whenever he had a moment of privacy. It was an unpleasant task of tearing it apart and putting it back together, a sight he didn't think Rachel would handle very well.

He missed Wantemo's finesse. Plus healing one's self was difficult. The end result would be functional but not necessarily pretty. He would forever have a circular scar the size of his hand that would reflect irregularly whenever he camouflaged his skin.

Sinto whiled away the hours, reflecting what he learned about his father's role with Arkis and the Orankai. He returned to that brief conversation they had on Merluma, before his father went missing. He had asked Sinto if the future of the Merahvu lie on Merluma or Earth. Sinto now realized it was a test: did Sinto believe in The Eradication Arkis had spoken of? Sinto had been clear he did not.

He wondered, *If I had stated indifference would he have tried to recruit me right there and then?*

What confused Sinto was the fact that his father had made an earnest effort to aid his mother's attempt to contact Culliford in an effort to reconcile. Was it just a ruse? Not that knowing the truth mattered, at least not now. Ramasis had clearly chosen his side. But what made little sense was the fact Arkis was in charge. What was it that Arkis held over their father? Arkis claimed he had saved Ramasis' life. Had Arkis threatened to let Ramasis die if he didn't support him as the Orankai leader? What other reason could there be?

Rachel interrupted his thoughts. "So how do you plan to find Audrey?"

"Same way I track you with your locket. Through the Mark. We each have a piece of the other."

"And she's not where you expect her, meaning this island where she supposedly lives?"

"No. Wherever she is, it's far from the coast. I can sense the direction, much more west, and south. That's all I can tell right now."

"More west is the Pacific Ocean."

"Yes. Somewhere in the Pacific."

"That's a big place to find someone. Maybe she's on a ship or an island."

Sinto suddenly remembered something. "I think there's someone who might know where she is."

During her attempt to kidnap him a couple months ago, Audrey had babbled on about her close friend while Sinto fell into a drugged stupor. He closed his eyes and searched for the memory. It was fuzzy but eventually her friend's name came to mind.

"His name is Ryan. She met him through school. He's studying to be a marine biologist, same as her. The school's in Friday Harbor on San Juan Island."

Rachel waved her cell phone. "We might have a way to find him."

She pulled over at a rest stop just before the pass crossing over the Cascade mountains that divided Washington State, east from west. "Be sure to dim your eyes and use the stall. You made quite a commotion at that last stop."

Sinto cloaked his eyes, unfolded his body from the car, and stretched. The skies were heavily clouded. It felt like snow was coming. The wound in his side felt the shock of it more than the rest of him. Their breath fogged as they made their way to the small building. He wore the same clothes he found in Santa Monica and the t-shirt she bought for him in Boulder City, growing a bit ripe, but better than nothing.

When he came out, Rachel was pacing beside the car working over her cell phone. She looked up.

"I think I might have found a place that teaches marine biology on San Juan Island. It's called the Friday Harbor Labs. Sound familiar?"

He nodded.

She tapped the screen, put the phone to her ear, and slipped into that syrupy way she talked. She was gracious and complementary, enthusiastic and super appreciative, and when she hung up she gave him a deep-dimpled smile.

"His name is Ryan Wood. He just returned from a short leave."

She got back to work on her phone. She tapped around on the tiny screen, stopped. Her brows shot up.

"Good news! Next ferry to the island is in four hours. We can make it if we hurry."

Sinto's mood lifted with Rachel's enthusiasm. If it had not been for her, he would most likely be dead or an orange-eyed Orankai monster. One day he was going to make it up to her.

Sinto folded himself back into Rachel's car and pointed to her phone. "Can I see that?"

She handed him the cell phone, told him the secret code. He tapped in the number and gazed at the shiny screen with tiny pictures scattered across its surface, fascinated by all the things Rachel was able to do with it.

"Dontcha be doin' any of your electronic mind-meld stuff and mess it up. I got it all set up how I like it. That there's my brain and we need it to get to Ryan."

68

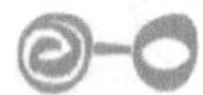

Team

Once Sinto and Rachel boarded the ferry, she declared the need to pee and jumped out of the car, promising to be right back. Sinto stayed in the car afraid if he got out he would run and dive off the back of the ferry and aimlessly wander the Pacific in search of Audrey. He was anxious to learn where she might be, if she was safe and somewhere that Arkis' Scouts couldn't find her.

He was also anxious to return to his mother and sister. Wantemo had told Sinto before leaving him on Merluma that many of the displaced had joined the Arctakai in their small city located in the frigid southern waters and carved within the glacial ice of Antarctica. Once he found Audrey and confirmed that she was safe from Arkis' reach, he planned to seek out his mother.

The ferry's engine droned and the landscape of the San Juan Islands passed by. The water of the Salish Sea was a bluish green and full of intelligent life; orca, porpoise, seal.

Rachel hopped into the driver's seat grinning. "What did I miss?"

His fingers were a blur, tapping his thighs. "Me thinking of diving in and going on my own."

"Really? We're so close to learning where she is and you're thinking random and crazy like?"

"That's what I'm worried about. We're so close. So many potential near-misses or almosts. I can't afford one mistake. The stakes are too high, and right now, only I can protect her."

"Bah humbug!" She slapped his knee. "Honey, you ain't alone! And after what I just witnessed, she's gonna need a lot more than just you to protect her. Look at the odds, so far we're winnin'. And I mean *we*. It took both of us to escape that mess in Duluth. We just need to grow the team beyond you and me. Maybe this Ryan will join us once he learns what's at stake. So get your shit together!" She dug in her oversized purse. "Here, eat this." She handed him a plastic-wrapped sandwich and a candy bar. "Start with the protein. End with the candy. Should help lift your mood."

They nibbled on their plastic-tasting sandwiches and deliciously sweet candy bars. Sinto had to marvel at Rachel's enthusiasm and determination after everything he told her and what she witnessed in Duluth. After ridding the world of two of Arkis' guards she was upset, but after much discussion and spilling of regret, she came around. This was war. A war she readily chose to help Sinto fight. One Sinto was afraid to spell out for her completely. He was afraid to believe it himself. She was more than just a friend, and he was lucky he found her. He reached over and gave her hand a squeeze.

"Thank you for the sandwich—for everything, my gold nugget." That made her smile.

"Just you wait 'til you see me shine."

Sinto looked forward to it and added "shiny" to the list of things she had been for him; funny and sweet, resourceful and life-saving, and her recently demonstrated skill as a true warrior.

The sun had set and it was dark by the time the ferry reached the dock on San Juan Island. Rachel punched in Ryan's address on her phone, then gave it to Sinto to hold. The ferry had passed the Friday Harbor Labs at the mouth of Friday Harbor, so once they got off the ferry, they had to backtrack, but not far.

Ryan had no idea they were coming as Rachel was unable to convince the nice lady she talked to to give her his phone number. But Rachel, forever optimistic, declared that would not be a problem. While the nice lady didn't reveal his number, she did tell Rachel he lived in one of the school's cabins on the small campus. Rachel said she was good at knocking on doors. Sinto had no doubt.

And knock they did. Most were empty and Ryan was not in any that were occupied. They did learn which one was Ryan's, but it was dark and no one answered. A woman passing by suggested they might find him in the cafeteria because dinner was being served, and she offered to show them where it was.

Sinto followed behind, dimming his eyes. Towering above Rachel and the other woman, he hoped not to intimidate. Rachel chatted it up with the young woman, asking things like how to get into the program and what previous education was required and would a GED suffice. She was exceptionally good at extracting information in a way that the person providing it had no idea what was happening.

Once they reached the cafeteria Rachel suggested Sinto wait outside. He agreed. Rachel would have much better luck convincing Ryan to come outside. The last thing Sinto needed was to create a commotion in front of prying eyes and phones with cameras.

Sinto watched Rachel work the room through the window. Her asking someone if they knew Ryan, them pointing to a table across the room to a group, bantering between bites. Rachel crossed the room. Before she made it the table, a man at the table noticed her, dropped his fork.

She went straight to Ryan, the man who dropped his fork. Ryan appeared surprised when he realized she was looking for him. Sinto couldn't decipher what they were saying through the walls and the ambient noise of many voices and dishes clanking inside. What he could surmise was Rachel introducing herself, holding out a hand. Ryan standing, smiling, shaking it a little too vigorously.

Rachel stunning him with her dimpled smile. Ryan offering her a seat at the table, her declining. Rachel leaning closer and talking in Ryan's ear. Ryan nodding, Rachel telling him more. Then Ryan's face grew serious and his gaze shifted to the window where Sinto was watching. Ryan picked up his dishes, bid his table mates goodbye, and followed Rachel out the door.

The door swung open. Rachel stepped out. Then Ryan. Ryan locked eyes with Sinto.

He huffed and blinked. "So you're him? Sinto? Holy shit—I mean, wow—" he stuck out his hand. Sinto reached for it but Ryan pulled back. "Wait... You're not, you know—charged-up, are you?"

Sinto smiled. "No."

Ryan reached out and they shook hands. Ryan didn't release it right away. He rubbed his thumb across the meaty part of his thumb, Ryan's thumb slipping effortlessly across Sinto's slick rubbery skin. "Remarkable. I—I have so many questions. And Audrey—Audrey's going to freak! Not like, freak out in a bad way, I mean, in a very good way. She's been pretty messed up, believing you died."

Rachel looked at Sinto and smiled. "I like him."

Ryan swung his gaze to Rachel. He looked like he had been mildly shocked. "What?" Then he gave her quite the charming smile. "And I like you too."

"Got somewhere we can talk?"

"Um, yeah, my cabin." He started walking, Rachel picking up her step to keep up. Sinto took up the rear. "I've been trying to reach her, but she's not answering her phone. I'm not surprised really because of where she is." They had reached Ryan's cabin. He dug in his pocket, pulled out a metal key.

Sinto felt a wave of relief. "Where is she?"

Ryan unlocked his door, invited them inside. "Uh, sorry about the mess, wasn't expecting company."

Ryan was picking up things and tossing them into a corner. Smoothed out his bed covers and offered them a seat. He sat in the chair by his desk.

Sinto asked again, more urgently. "Where is Audrey?"

"Right, she's in Hawaii, I mean, not really Hawaii—she's on an island west of Kauai. Apparently it's an independent nation. Larkian. Really long story if you—

Sinto stood up, "I know where that is."

"Slow down, cowboy." Rachel tugged his hand. "We're not done yet. We need to talk to Ryan, remember what we talked about earlier?"

Sinto reluctantly sat. He could feel adrenaline flow, the roil of anxiety. His merlux buzzed and fingers twitched, ready to launch a one-way tunnel to the island where he first met Audrey. Sinto's eyes glowed, casting a green tint across Ryan's face. Ryan shifted uncomfortably in his chair.

"Audrey's in danger," Sinto said.

Rachel sighed. "Sinto, calm down a sec. Now that that little fact is out, let's get down to business."

Sinto was too worked up to organize his thoughts, breathing erratically and fidgeting, fighting the urge to flee. Rachel picked up on it, held his hand, and laid out everything to Ryan, succinctly and getting right to the meat of the situation. Ryan was quick to understand the magnitude of the situation. He told them he had more than one personal encounter with the orange-eyed Terrakai they called Orankai.

Rachel told him what happened in Duluth, with Sinto filling in details about the Orankai, what he witnessed in the caves on Merluma, the alarming number of Orankai roaming free in the Sapien world.

Ryan described the mission on the *Requiem Sea II*, the missing ships, the discovery of Orange and the attack by Orankai, and Ryan's near fatal encounter with a young female. How Audrey killed her. Of the two of them dumping the body in the sea and being booted off the ship because of it.

"Where is the ship?" Sinto asked.

"Sailing to Isla Salvación."

Sinto stood and paced. "They can track it. The ship will lead them right to her. I have to go, *now*."

Rachel and Ryan looked at each other. "What about us?"

"Warn her, tell her I'm coming."

Rachel said, "Let's try right now."

Ryan got to work with his phone. He shook his head, "She still hasn't returned a single text." Been trying all day." He tapped the screen, put the phone to his ear. "Aud, call me, it's urgent." He hung up. "Rings straight to voice mail. She's got no connection."

Sinto turned to Rachel. "I can't wait."

"What about me?" Rachel asked.

Sinto turned to Ryan but before he could say anything, Ryan piped up, "I'm happy to help, whatever you need. Rachel can stay here, with me. We'll keep trying to reach Audrey."

Rachel beamed at Sinto. "Team. It's growing."

69

Beach Of Dreams And Nightmares

AUDREY WOKE WITH A dry mouth and pounding head. She had kicked off her covers sometime in the night and lay sprawled in the same dress she wore last night. The quilt her mother made for her lay on the floor in a tangled heap.

She tried to piece last night together. The singing and laughing and her clinging to Blake because her legs stopped working by the time they got to the house. Her grabbing him and pulling him down on the sofa, thinking... what was she thinking? Then, of him respectfully tucking her into her bed with a simple kiss to the cheek and softly spoken goodnight. No regretful, oh-shit-what-have-we-done, awkward morning-after where both woke fuzzy headed with naked limbs tangled together. Blake respectfully kept his word and their agreed-upon boundaries. Because of that, her heart bloomed with a deeper level of respect and love for him.

Excessively bright sunlight bled through the sheer white curtains pulled across the windows and sliding glass door of her room. She wondered why she had bothered to close them. She remembered her mother saying the sun was her clock. Thus the reason for sheer curtains in the bedrooms. When it rose then so should she. This morning Audrey wanted to do anything but.

Her door was opened to the living area and she could hear Blake rummaging around in the kitchen. The smell of brewing coffee and the buttery scent of baking croissants wafted into her room. The sound and scent of a knife slicing something sweet and fragrant followed.

A tall glass of water sat on the table beside her bed along with a couple of aspirin. She gulped down the pills and the entire glass of water. She was unsure if she felt better or worse. She sat up. Her head went *thumpa-thump-thump*.

Oh, boy. Wine is bad, very bad.

She willed the aspirin to do its job, and quickly.

She pushed herself to stand up, then headed to the bathroom, then pawed through her duffel lying on the floor. She really had all the wrong clothes for tropical weather. She decided to stay in the dress and worked her way to the door.

Blake was bright-eyed and bushy-tailed as if the wine he drank last night was merely tinted water. Just watching him bustling around the kitchen was exhausting.

"Happy Birthday, Sunshine!"

Uff da. Right. "I almost forgot, that's today?" She peeked at him with one opened eye. "Twenty-one and I already have a hangover."

"Take a dip, you'll feel better. Sure helped me. You've got time. The croissants need time to rest."

She had no swimsuit so stripped to her underwear and slipped on a tank top she found in her bag. She padded down the steps outside her bedroom door to the beach and dove in. Blake was right, the water was rejuvenating. After about fifteen minutes of floating on her back and staring at a sky streaked with thin clouds the aspirin kicked in. She rinsed off in the outdoor shower next to the lanai and walled off for privacy. It was stocked with plenty of shampoo and soap. Dry towels were tucked inside a protected cupboard. She hung her wet things to dry and put on the dress she wore the night before.

Blake served breakfast on the lanai with lots of coffee and fresh squeezed orange juice. Her plate was artfully presented with fresh sliced mango, croissant, and scrambled eggs. A tiny origami rose was nestled next to the mango. Ravishingly hungry, she ate. She had the kind of hangover where food and orange juice were the best remedy. Slowly, she began to feel human again.

"Ship arrived early this morning. I was thinking of joining some of the guys for a day trip to Honolulu. Poe was planning to go too and offered to pick up some things you might need. Will you be okay by yourself all day?"

Audrey was curious why she hadn't been invited. Then it hit her. It was her birthday; maybe they didn't want her tagging along. She smiled at the sly way Blake presented the question.

"A day here by myself would be heaven. A perfect way to spend my birthday. Tell Poe I need shorts and warm weather tops, and a swimsuit. Oh, I wear a size six, small to medium, as long as the shoulders are wide enough. Maybe some sandals, size ten."

"I'll let Poe know. Anything else you might want?"

She winked. "Surprise me."

They shared grins and memories of the night before. She thanked him for his discretion and respect once they returned to the house. He blushed and confessed that leaving her alone in her bed wasn't easy. Then he wolfed down his breakfast and apologized for leaving dirty dishes.

"Festivities start at six sharp. I should be back by four. We can get ready together."

He pinched her chin, then he was off. A whizzing sound of the departing UTV faded like a distant dream.

Audrey was alone with the sea and a stiffening breeze. She slowly sipped the rest of her coffee. The thought of having the day to herself was exactly the birthday gift she needed. She needed to visit the beach where she met Sinto and where her father dragged her mother to shore after she drowned. Something she had to do alone. There were other places she wished to revisit as well, like the jungle trails behind the house, near where the mountains sprang up, where she had collected bugs and climbed trees with Sinto.

After cleaning up the breakfast dishes, she decided to cut off a pair of her full-length leggings. She put on her only short-sleeved T-shirt. Knowing she had a time line for the day, she slipped on her Larkian-issued dive-capable watch.

She packed a hat, sunglasses, towel, sweatshirt, a folding knife, a snack, and a couple bottles of water in one of the day packs hanging in the entry nook. At the last minute she decided to grab her phone and tossed it in her bag without bothering to switch it on since reception was sketchy around this part of the island. She felt a twinge of guilt knowing her mother wouldn't have approved. But Audrey was raised with twenty-first-century technology. If she got in trouble, she felt safer having it. Plus it doubled as a camera.

On her way out the door she picked several tropical flowers from the garden, using the knife to cut through their fibrous stocks. She tied the bouquet together with one of the teal ribbons she stole from the curtain tied around her bed post.

She planned to recon her old haunts. When she was younger, she rode her bike. She planned to take the remaining UTV. It would cover more ground in the short time she had. She hoped the paths she once traveled were free and clear. This UTV was the smaller of the two, outfitted with dual seats and a small cargo area. Perfect for navigating tight paths. She grabbed a chair and beach umbrella from a locker tucked along the back of the carport. There was a machete; she grabbed that too in case she needed to hack back vegetation ever-growing along the paths. She stowed the bulky things in the back, the machete and day pack on the passenger floor, laid the flowers on the passenger seat, and started it up.

She was off!

The gravel path to the small cove on the southernmost point of the island was wide enough for the UTV and well used from what she could tell. Mako and Poe had taken excellent care of the property; so much so that Audrey felt like she was ten all over again. Only now she was driving a modern sport vehicle, where before she rode her bike powered by boundless energy.

The path wound around upheavals of volcanic rock deposited millions of years ago and through part of the cool jungle, before bursting into bright sunshine. The path ended at the lagoon on the far side of the cove.

She shut down the UTV and stared in disbelief at the crystalline waters where she had spent many days of her childhood. Half her life had passed since she'd been here, and she sometimes wondered if this place still existed. It did, exactly as she remembered. The beach was a salt-and-pepper mix of sand ground down from coral in the sea and lava rock spewed from the mountains. Palm and kukai offered cool shade and refuge for nesting birds. The sign her mother had carved and painted hung on the sloped trunk of a palm tree whose fronds hung above water. It was faded and splintered by time and hostile weather, but the name remained: "Beach of Dreams." It was here, on the beach of dreams, that Audrey realized she wanted to be a marine biologist and where she first met Sinto.

The lagoon was enclosed by a curl of black volcanic rock on the left and a coral reef on the right. They did not quite meet in the middle where the ebb and flow of the sea passed through to replenish the calm waters and provided access to the outer cove, where her mother once hunted fish.

The lagoon had been a safe place for a young Audrey to learn to swim without fear of riptide or current. It had also been a private escape for her parents to watch the sunset and stars awaken. It was here, her mother confided shortly before her death, that Audrey had been conceived.

And ten years and nine months later, her mother would die just outside the lagoon, tangled in a fishnet stuck to the other side of the coral reef.

And it was here that two souls from different worlds forged the seed of the Mark gently vibrating in her arm, screaming to finish the thing they had started but never had the chance, because Sinto was dead.

A beach not just of dreams, but of nightmares.

She grabbed the bouquet of flowers and hopped out of the UTV. She kicked off her black leather shoes and took that first step. The sand was silky and coarse, light and dark, the blending of soft coral and hard rock, of salt and earth. She crossed over the dry to the wet where waves rolled into the narrow opening and connected the land to the sea.

Toes to water, then ankles, then knees.

She conjured a memory. Her mother standing beside her, spear gun in one hand, a pair of fins in the other, goggles propped atop her head, a netted bag clipped around her tiny waist, a thick braid of black hair trailing down her spine.

Water's clear and sea calm, a good day for fish! she had exclaimed. Then she leaned over and kissed Audrey as she always did before she went hunting in the sea. Did she kiss Audrey goodbye because she knew that maybe one day she might not come back?

That was the last time Audrey saw her alive.

A tear slipped down her cheek and the bouquet of flowers shook in her hand. She raised it to her lips and kissed the bound stalks as her mother had kissed her for the last time. She bent to put the bouquet in the sea but stopped upon seeing the ribbon. A man-made thing that didn't belong in the ocean world. She untied it and freed the flowers. They floated together at first but, like all things in nature, they separated and chose a path of their own. Scattering in random directions from a sudden gust blowing in from the southeast.

Audrey tied the ribbon around the ponytail on the crown of her head.

She whispered a silent goodbye to her mother who was robbed from her eleven years ago to the day.

70

Follow The Ancient Stone Road

AUDREY WAS UNSURE WHAT to do next. She had hoped to linger longer on the beach. The sun bore down from above but clouds were gathering to the southeast. The stiff breeze gave way to periodic, angry gusts. Flying sand erased her footprints and fronds whipped and clacked loudly. A rain of coconuts littered the beach. The sea beyond the lagoon was frothy and a mild current tugged at her ankles even in the protection of the lagoon.

The jungle would offer better shelter from the wind. The tropical storm Mako warned of was threatening landfall. She guessed she had several hours before the rains would come and pose a danger of flash flooding. To the jungle, she decided.

She dried her feet and put on her shoes. She hoped to find a path she frequented when she was younger that ran through the jungle toward the mountains. A path of flat volcanic stone laid thousands of years ago by Polynesians who once inhabited the island. Hands to hip she surveyed the ground, kicking wind-whipped low-lying vegetation at the edge of the jungle. It took several minutes of searching, but she found it; the stone path had been hidden by a thin layer of sand. Her gaze followed the cut in vegetation, winding east toward the mountains. The path was wide enough for the small UTV to traverse.

Feeling adventurous she hopped into the UTV and veered onto the old stone path.

The jungle was thick and wild and the wind settled to a gentle breeze the deeper she ventured. At first it was slow going. She had to stop frequently and use the machete to clear the old stone path. It was a tight squeeze for the UTV. So at this point, she was committed with no obvious way to turn around. After nearly an hour of slowly grinding her way forward and upward, she broke out of the thick greenery into a clearing where the stone path intersected with an old dirt road. Deep ruts from a larger vehicle were carved in the dried mud where it had made a tight turnaround. The road was wide enough for a full-sized truck and ran parallel to the mountains.

She stopped for a drink of water. By the state of foliage creeping along the edges, it appeared the road hadn't been used in a long time. She tried to remember back to her childhood, but couldn't recall ever stumbling upon this road cut so deeply into the jungle.

When she was younger, her mother made her promise not to wander too far from the beach. *Only as far as you can still hear waves crashing along the rocky shore,* she told Audrey. She was way beyond that point now. The only roar she heard were the occasional gusts grazing the tops of the trees.

Mountainous cliffs rose beyond the tree tops to the east. She was closer to the mountains then she expected. The air was much cooler, so she slipped on her sweatshirt.

She followed the road, avoiding the ruts, and stopped when she came to a fork. On the dash was a compass, one she wondered if she could trust. She had noted it would spin wildly, then stop and appear to work as expected, during her journey along the old stone path. It appeared to be working at the moment, clearly indicating the cliffs were east as she would expect.

The more-used fork in the road veered north toward the beach house, while the other headed due east, toward the mountains.

Her watch indicated she had been gone more than two hours. She had less than six hours till the time she agreed to meet Blake back at the house. She was certain the old dirt road would be faster than retracing her tracks, banking on the hope it intercepted with the main road running north and south across the island.

Curious, she decided to venture farther and veered east taking the less-used fork towards the mountains.

Hundreds of birds sang in the canopy above, safe from the wind along the shore. She marveled at the variety of sounds they made, a language of very few sounds, yet complicated enough for mates to find one another, or to announce a bounty of food.

The road grew steeper and the wind began to pick up the higher in elevation she climbed, whipping treetops above. Dead leaves rained.

The road flattened and the walls of the cliffs drew in like a big C around her. The wind subsided within the protection of soaring rock walls. The trees in this part of the jungle were bigger and more widely spaced, with the ground open and accessible in between. An old-growth tropical forest unmolested by a chain saw.

The road came to an abrupt end at an old wrought-iron gate bolted to high, rock-laid walls smothered by jungle vine. The rusty gate sagged heavily to the ground on one side from years of neglect. Oddly, a modern-day galvanized chain and shiny new Master padlock was wrapped around the rusted center.

Audrey shut down the UTV and hopped out. She pressed her face to the rusted uprights and peered beyond. The road continued through the gate and curved to the right, a thick row of broad-leaf bushes blocking any view of what lay beyond the curve.

At one time the land beyond the gate must have been beautifully landscaped. Exotic flowers fought with overbearing ferns for sunlight. Dead branches and palm leaves littered the ground and weeds grew in the gravel roadway thicker than on the road that led her here.

Audrey grabbed the gate and shook it. The chain and lock held firm. She moved along the wall, pulled back the thick foliage, looked for a break in the rock-laid wall, batting away bugs and dead leaves jostled loose from her disruption. The wall was solid and stretched as far as she could see, her efforts useless. She retraced her steps back to the gate.

She itched with curiosity and bug bites, stole a peek at her watch. Ten-forty-five. She figured it would take an hour or more to get back to the house with plenty of time to spare before Blake returned. She figured she had over three hours before she had to be back.

She was here. She was curious. The rusty gate taunted.

Move in harmony with force of life, flow as water, like stream around rock.

"So it is decided," she said to herself, scanning every inch of the gate.

Find the weak link. A grin spread across her face. *Rusty hinges.*

She dug around in the back of the UTV looking for something strong she could use to break through the weakened metal. She found a spare tire and a jack and grabbed the eighteen-inch-long metal jack handle from its compartment in the cargo storage area.

She approached the gate and looked for the weakest hinges. She picked at the top hinge on the sagging side of the gate. Chunks of rust crumbled in her fingers. The hinge was barely attached to the rock wall with rusty spikes. She drove the end of the jack arm between the hinge and rock and used all her strength to pry them apart. Bits of rust and rock broke away. She continued to work at it. Sweat dripped from her brow; the hinges were much stronger than she first thought. After working at it from different angles for fifteen minutes, the gate suddenly shifted. The top portion fell forward a couple feet, askew, then came to a shuddering stop.

She could tell it was heavy and wondered if it would buck unpredictably if she tried to loosen the lower hinge. Plus, all the weight was balanced at that point. Plus, she was wasting precious time. There was a gap big enough for her to slip through at the top, requiring only a bit of climbing and staying atop the gate instead of risking it falling on top of her. The safer and less time-consuming option.

She put the jack handle back in the UTV. Grabbed the day pack and the machete. She tossed them both to the other side of the gate.

Committed.

She easily scaled the rock pillar with toe and finger holds, then tested her weight on the angled gate. Stuck as she had hoped. She wedged herself between the pillar and the gate and inched toward the other side until she was clear enough to jump.

Success.

She slung the day pack over her shoulder and picked up the machete.

The effort made her heart pound and brow sweat. She stole another drink of water, finishing off one of her bottles. Then she set off down the grass-shot gravel driveway meandering through the overgrown garden.

The road split and curved into a large circular driveway. In the center was an old pond, bright green with algae and surrounded by water-loving plants and the soft sound of frogs croaking. They silenced as she drew closer.

On the other side of the pond, barely visible through a tangle of vines growing up its dark green walls, was a two-story plantation-style house with a large covered lanai framing the front door.

The house was as old as the wrought-iron gate and appeared not to be in any better shape. The paint was cracked and peeling with neglect, revealing gray weathered wood underneath. One end of a gutter sloped from the roof and disappeared into the overgrown garden. A corner of the rusty metal roof was curled up and flapped noisily with each gust of wind screaming through the treetops above.

The sun was blotted out by thickening clouds. She sensed a change in barometric pressure. The storm was moving closer. She made a note to keep watch on the weather.

She approached the front steps with caution, testing each before fully committing her weight, then the same across the wooden decking of the covered porch. The front door was a solid hunk of wood, four feet wide with leaded-glass paned windows running across the upper quarter. Huge windows fronted the house, darkened by thick curtains inside. She stood up on her tip-toes and peeked inside the door's upper windows. It was too dark to see anything inside.

She had never heard of this house when she was child. Surely she would have known if someone had been living in it, possibly having to pass by their beach house to reach the port or the village. Something a curious nine-year-old would have observed.

The house appeared old and rickety and must have been here when her father built the beach house for her mother. But her mother never mentioned this house either. Maybe it housed hired help. Maybe it had been deemed unsafe to occupy long ago, thus the reason for the chained gate. She wondered who may have installed the new chain and lock. Maybe Mako would know.

Her father had been very protective of his privacy as long as Audrey could remember. The entire southern portion of the island was part of his estate. No other houses or residences had been built on this part of the island. The cove and access to it belong to her father. The house, its location... it made no sense.

She stomped her foot. The wood beneath her feet rang solid, as were the steps leading to the deck and front door as well as the protective rails enclosing the deck. The wood siding beneath the peeling paint was hard and solid when she tapped it. Ironwood. The south end of the island was prolific with it. An entire house built from it would last a long time. The front door was solid, the bronze hardware and hinges sound.

She stole a glance at her watch, less than three hours to go...

She reached out and turned the knob on the front door.

71

Mystery House

THE DOOR MOVED AN inch and stopped. She pushed a little harder. It didn't budge. She stepped back, shifting her weight to her back foot, then lunged forward, driving her shoulder into the door. Hinges screamed in protest as it swung inward. Her shoulder throbbed from the effort. Light flooded the foyer and particles of dust swirled and danced, as if ecstatic to see the light of day.

Audrey stepped inside, blinking to adjust her eyes to the dark interior. Cobwebs clung to a chandelier hanging from the two-story-high open ceiling. The floors were covered in a thick blanket of undisturbed dust.

A stairway on the left led to the second floor, ringed by handrails open to the foyer below. A hallway extended past the stairway and disappeared into the darkness deeper inside the house.

To the left and the right were arched doorways leading to darkened rooms; living areas, she guessed. Once her eyes adjusted to the darkness, she stepped inside the one on the right, where a crack of light bled from between closed curtains. She grabbed the edge of the heavy drapery and yanked it open.

Dust exploded. She jumped back and sneezed.

Light flooded a large living area fully furnished with dual sofas and arm chairs covered with very dusty dust covers. A game table with an old chess set was coated in a layer of gray dust. The rock fireplace was stained with soot. A painting of a sailing ship hung above, the colors dreary and muted as was typical of old paintings. A poker and a small shovel hung next to the fireplace from hooks pounded into mortar between the rock. Toward the back of the house, the outline of a dining table faded into darkness.

She crossed the foyer to the other room, slowly creeping toward the window in the darkness. Took a big breath before yanking the drapery aside. Dust danced in the light flooding the room; an office.

Old books and trinkets filled shelves on two walls. A large desk prominently faced the foyer. A massive wooden carving hung on the wall above it. It was a voluptuous mermaid, bare chest thrust forward, hair thick with waves like those in the sea, eyes gazing forward determinedly, tail wrapped around a stunted fore-stay once attached to a sailing ship of old. Above the masthead was another wood carving, flat with jagged edges as if torn from the transom of a rotten ship. Carved in large capital letters was the name: SEA LARK.

The *Sea Lark* was the first of five of the Larkians' pirate ships during the eighteenth century. Audrey knew this based on old drawings of her father's that she had seen, and were since lost, on the *Requiem Sea*.

She crossed the room, leaving footprints in the dust, to the shelves of old leather-bound books. She ran her finger down the spine of one of them. The leather was cracked and very old, the first of several of similar size and color beside it. She carefully pulled it off the shelf. It was surprisingly heavy.

Hammered into the thick leather cover: "Sea Lark Log 1700". She read through some of the entries, which mostly recorded ship location, headings and celestial readings, destination details, who was ill or sick and how they were remedied. Nothing of much interest. She put the book back and grabbed the last in what appeared to be a collection of sailing logs. The last logbook of the *Sea Lark* was dated twenty-two years later. Most of the pages were blank.

The last log entry was dated 14 December 1722 and was brief and to the point: *Storm approaching. Rough seas upon entering Pacific archipelago. Reducing sail. Mountains looming in distance.* Nothing more was recorded.

She found another series of leather-bound books. These were not ship logs but her father's private journals. She pulled the first in a series covering the year seventeen twenty-two. Someone had added an additional stamped description below the date on the front cover. The letters were smaller and of a different font and simply said: AFTER.

She turned to the first entry:

21 December 1722

With heavy heart we put to rest the last of the dead we were able to reclaim from the sea following the attack of Ianthe's people.

Nineteen souls lost with only six survivors: Leonard (Cook), Marcus Wickman (Doctor), Salvo Alvarez (Quartermaster), Francesca La Roche (Gunner, Carpenter), Thomas Below (Second Sailmaker), and myself, Robert Culliford (Captain).

Thomas is inconsolable. Wickman has given him oil of the poppy to calm him. He refuses to eat. I fear he may die and the ache in my heart is unbearable.

Thomas is my only child, not of my seed, but adopted after his mother, who along with Francesca posing as men joined our crew unknowingly pregnant, died giving birth. I pray Wickman can help him. I cannot bear to lose another. Our family is broken.

Alvarez suffers from his wounds and we are unsure if he will fall victim to infection. The local natives we have befriended have provided herbal remedies they chew and mix with spit and press onto his open wounds. Only time will give us an answer of whether he will live or die.

Francesca suggests we find a more permanent place to settle far from the unprotected and open beach where the locals have erected shelters for us to live. She has surveyed a possible location tucked up against the mountains with plenty of fresh water, rich soil ready for planting, and wood for building a strong residence and a new ship. I agreed. We need distraction and time to heal from the tragedy that has befallen us.

Robert Culliford

Adrenaline coursed through her veins, recalling Sinto's story about a sister he never met who had Marked one of her father's original crew mates. After Leela died, her father's pirate crew fled but were attacked by the Merahvu in the Pacific. The ship was lost and many in the crew died, except the six listed in her father's entry. This must be the house Francesca suggested building in this protected and hidden location. The mermaid carving hanging above the desk was all that was left of their original ship.

Audrey closed the journal and slipped it back into its original slot on the bookshelf filled with dozens more. Before her was the complete history of her father's life. She felt guilty for wanting to read them, for intruding on his most intimate thoughts without his permission.

She itched to learn more, but tingling fear held her back. Especially about this son he had adopted. Thomas. The one who had been bound to Leela.

Thomas, her adopted brother...

She backed out of the room full of so many secrets, stunned by the wealth of knowledge pressed between cracked leather. She was an intruder, trespassing in the house built by her father's original crew. Four she knew, two she had yet to meet: Francesca and Thomas. Why was that? Where were they now? Was there a falling-out at some point?

Her gaze wandered to the dark hallway leading to the back of the house.

She swung her pack from her back and dug out a flashlight. She followed its beam down the dusty hall. A door to the left was open; she swung a beam of light inside. A bath room, literally, containing a large claw-foot tub and beside it a porcelain bowl atop a wooden pillar.

A pair of bronze spigots with flipper-like handles were attached to the wall above both the sink and the tub. Bronze pipes dropped down from the ceiling, each forming a T, and were connected to the knobs. As if one pipe was for hot and one for cold. Bronze pipes ran from the drains of both the sink and the tub and disappeared into the floor. There was no toilet.

Curious, she spun one of the knobs. There was a whoosh of air. Dust and shriveled spider bodies were spit out, then a trickle of gritty water. She turned it off and looked up at the elevated pipes along the ceiling. Gravity fed, but from where?

She checked her watch. Two hours till she had to leave.

She continued down the hall, toward the back of the house, flashlight beam scanning the planked wooden floor, white plaster walls, and ceiling. At the end of the hall was a kitchen.

Light bled through dusty glass windows. A thick wooden table with four chairs stood in the center of the room. A wood-burning stove stood in the corner. A wall of cabinets with open shelves and drawers were topped with a slab of thick oiled wood. A hammered-copper sink big enough to bathe a small child was propped on wooden legs. Just like the bathroom, bronze pipes from the ceiling were connected to a pair of handles and spigot.

Rusty cast iron pans hung from hooks next to the potbelly stove. Utensils, worn and dull, lay haphazardly in a partially opened drawer. Chipped and heavily used porcelain plates and bowls were neatly stacked on shelves below the counter, blanketed with dust like everything else.

A back door led to a patio. Weeds grew through the cracks between irregular pieces of flat rock puzzle-pieced together. The trellis above was rotten and sagging under the weight of dead vines and fallen fronds and broken tree branches. It swayed dangerously in the wind, threatening to collapse suddenly.

She stepped out from under it and looked up.

A pair of elevated, metal-sided tanks were perched on rock pillars against the upper story of the house. Gutters from the roof ran into what seemed to be a long-ago rotted filtration system, then into both tanks. One of the tanks, the smaller of the two, sat above a potbelly stove. Pipes ran from the tanks into the side of the house at ceiling height. Larger pipes ran from the top of the tanks and snaked into the jungle. Overflows to prevent flooding. The design was simple for catching water, filtered and heated and gravity fed. She pictured her father unfolding his long limbs and taking a nice hot soak in the tub. Shipwrecked, but comforts not compromised.

She checked her watch. Time was slipping by faster than she thought possible.

She went back inside the kitchen, through a pantry, leading to the dining room. Cupboards held fine china plates and bowls, a wooden box of tarnished silver utensils, clouded crystal glasses, and a porcelain vase that had been broken once and glued back together.

The dining room had a rectangular wood table with six equally solid wood chairs. She stopped in the arched opening of the foyer separating the dining and living spaces, taking it all in. The furniture was masculine and made of old timber. She peeked under the sofa's dust cover. Roughly woven fabric filled with down.

Comfortable, but sturdy. Oil lamps hung on the walls. Chandeliers in both rooms held the stubs of old candles. Raised and lowered by ropes tied off around wooden cleats attached to the wall. No wiring, light switches, or electrical outlets.

Audrey gazed up the stairway in the foyer to the second level, ringed by a balcony hallway. She grabbed the railing and gave it a hardy shake. It felt solid. She tested each step. The wood under her feet was dark with a tight grain. When she rapped it with her knuckles it sounded thick and solid, no softness or rot. There was no evidence of a leaky roof. The house may be old but was still in remarkably good shape.

She climbed the stairs. There were six rooms total. Three on each side; one in each corner with another sandwiched between. All the doors were open except the one in the back corner of the house. The balcony hallway wrapped all the way around, offering a full view to the foyer below.

She moved quickly, ever aware of the time, and poked her head inside the bedroom in the front right corner. A sliver of light peeked through dark curtains. A four-poster bed stood against the wall, a dresser opposite. No mattress. A painting of a sunset with a square-rigged ship floating at anchor hung on the wall above the bed. She returned to the hall and crossed by the front of the house past a window overlooking the covered front deck.

The room in the left front corner was more completely furnished with bookshelves, long emptied, and a chair and desk along with a narrow bed. Seeing it made her think of Dr. Wickman.

The remaining rooms were pretty much the same as the first, sparsely furnished. Merely a place to sleep, nothing else.

She stopped in front of the closed door. She reached out but paused when a chill rippled down her spine. She withdrew her hand. Why was this one closed? What if the occupant of this house was still inside, a shriveled body entombed in its final resting place?

She reached out again, turned the nob, opened it an inch and stopped. No foul smell emerged. She pushed it open completely and gasped.

72

Pandora's Box

THE BEDROOM WAS LIKE a prison cell. Slanted beams of sunlight bled through metal bars spaced at two-inch intervals in the windows on two walls. A metal-framed bed was bolted to the wall. There was no other furniture. At first she thought the walls were covered in dirty white wallpaper but when she looked closer what she thought was grime were words written in charcoal. Some words written so small she could barely read them, others bold and all capped. The messages desperate and confusing:

wobble wobble wobble

MUST STOP THE WOBBLE.

HATE DARKNESS *dark means death I need light.*

GIVE ME A CANDLE!

I hate the dark.

BAD THINGS HAVE EYES THAT GLOW IN THE DARK.

give me a candle!

ARE YOU LISTENING?

hollow empty hollow empty. which one is it? hollow or empty. does it matter? what am I, if hollow? what am I, if empty? does it matter? what is life if there is nothing inside? can I be alive if there is nothing inside? I am a shell. rotting. I died she lived! that is it. I am dead. this is hell. she looks for me.

NoT *crazy* otHers *craZy* I AM NOT CRAZY!

let me die. is she dead? is it a lie? wickman lies. father lies.

THEY ALL LIE!

she lives! truth lives in dreams. my escape.

I try to sleep I cannot. sleep evades. please let me sleep. please!

no more oil of poppy. OIL OF POPPY STEALS DREAMS. *she lives in my dreams.*

leelaleelaleelaleelaleelaleelaleelaleelaleelaleelaleela

leeeelaaa...

THE END IS COMING!

WOBBLE WOBBLE WOBBLE!

MUST STOP IT!

YOU BROKE IT!

YOU FIX IT!

ALL WILL BE LOST!

WORLDS BROKEN!

WHY WON'T YOU LISTEN TO ME!

These were words of madness. She approached the bed. Deep scratches marred the metal headboard and along the side of the frame as if someone had been cuffed to it with something metal and fought to break free.

Stop the wobble.

She imagined the screaming. A man afraid of the dark, the sleepless nights, a gutted soul, fear of an imagined wobble, of the end of the world. The torment of losing the one he loved. She guessed these were the rambles of Thomas, the young crewmen who had been bound to Sinto's older sister Leela. The one who could not be consoled. The one who went mad.

What did he mean by "stop the wobble"? Were there answers in the journals written by her father?

She went down the stairs and into the room with the desk and her father's private journals. She pulled different ones from the shelves, studying the dates. While she could spend a week or more reading them all, she sorted through looking for one that could possibly answer her questions about Thomas. As she found with the first journal she read, they were organized by date, then categorized by events at some point after they were written, with Ianthe clearly playing a key role in her father's life. There were four events into which they were organized: BEFORE, IANTHE, AFTER. Only one was stamped as THOMAS. And like the first journal she read, those words were added after the dates had been stamped in the leather covers, as evidenced by the slightly different size and font style of the lettering that was otherwise the same over the many decades covered.

She looked at her watch. She still had thirty minutes. The wind began to howl. The storm had made landfall. She knew she should go but found it impossible to tear herself away. She was in too deep to stop. She pulled the THOMAS journal from the shelf, flipped it open.

"Tell me your story, Thomas," she whispered as she sank to the dust-covered floor.

She scanned through the entries, seeking more about Thomas' affliction.

I took Thomas to the beach today, although I could not coax him in for a swim. He merely watched as I swam back and forth. Several times he stepped to the water's edge but turned back. He never joined me.

She flipped through several pages.

Marcus suggested we sail to the village for supplies and take Thomas with us. The chief was sympathetic to Thomas's loss. He invited us to a celebration and to meet more of his people. He offered to introduce Thomas to his daughter.

Next page...

Thomas had a relapse last night. I found him in the kitchen sobbing and holding a knife to his chest. It pained me when Marcus chained him to his bed for his own good. I lay unable to sleep as he screamed all night, repeating her name over and over. Claiming something about a wobble, as he does almost nightly.

All Marcus can decipher is that the persistent wobble he speaks of is entirely fabricated in his mind. There is no premise or source of such "wobble" that we have found, neither here nor afar. Thomas himself knows not where it comes from. He only insists that it "is." With no grounding or proof, we can only believe it the ravings of a madman.

Marcus and I struggle to placate or calm him, which merely exacerbates his distress. He claims the wobble will end us all, yet claims he does not know what it means, only that we must stop it as it grows more persistent every passing day. A wobble we neither sense nor feel.

Please give me the strength to see him through.

Another entry...

A year has passed and Thomas is no better. Would I be cursed if I let him kill himself and end his misery?

Audrey closed her eyes and imagined the screams that must have echoed through the halls of this house. She flipped to the last several entries, dated many years later.

Thomas smiled today and told me he wanted to go to the beach. Expecting him to pace the sandy shore as he normally did, it shocked me when stepped into the sea up to his knees. That was all he could manage, but it was the start of a new beginning. We celebrated with a fine bottle of rum I had been saving for this occasion.

Then she turned to the last entry...

Fifteen years has passed since we were attacked by Ianthe and shipwrecked on our lovely island home and finally feel ready to lay to rest Thomas' tragic story. Today we sealed shut his bedroom door. It feels as if time on Isla Salvación has not passed at all. With Ianthe's shared knowledge of sucuvita we have all frozen our bodies in time. I still feel my thirty-nine-year-old self as I did on that true birthday. I am not alone. All of us feel and look the same as we were in 1704. The year I met Ianthe.

Thomas was the only one who had continued to mature, though he appeared to stop aging as a young man in his mid-twenties. I may recall Ianthe saying something like that would happen, that his aging would stop once he reached full adulthood.

I am immensely proud of my adopted son who overcame the darkest of demons and tragic grief that would have crushed most men—and women, as Francesca frequently reminds me—so long ago. He no longer requires constant supervision and has begun to express interest in some of the native girls. Marcus believes it was a miracle, but I know the truth: it was due to Marcus's diligence and patience and ever-growing wisdom of the human condition. Marcus as well as Thomas have been a gift to us all.

Thomas shows promise with his hands, becoming head carpenter on construction of Sea Lark II. He is so creative; an artist at heart. The natives love his artistic creations, with grasses or rope or anything pliable he can shape with his fingers or hands.

Thomas has grown into a capable young man with a promising future.

As I write this last entry into Thomas' journal, he announced that he has decided to change his name to reflect his new life. His "rebirth" he tells us. Thomas Below is no longer who he is and reminds me how he hates this given surname of "Below." I am embarrassed that not much thought went into it; in fact, none at all. It just naturally stuck after I and the others would yell "Thomas, below," whenever foul weather struck, or when approaching another ship or the many strange peoples we have encountered on our journeys. That "below" being behind the sealed hatch and below the main deck in a secret hiding spot we made for him. There he would ride out whatever danger struck.

So after much thought he has decided on his new name. A surname that describes what he is and because it is bold and true. His first name he chose because it is new, and in the meager reports we have received from British colonies, it has become quite the popular choice. Perfect for a new man facing a new future. We all like the ring of it: Blake Goodfellow.

The journal slipped from her fingers to the floor. She couldn't breathe. Her whole body shook.

Blake Goodfellow. Thomas Below. Leela's mate. She remembered snippets of the story Blake told her at the aquarium, one of truth, heavily edited.

Sinto's dead... I know what you're feeling.

You do?

I lost my first love, when I was seventeen... It was so unexpected. It came from nowhere. It was a—a bolt of lightning that struck us both.

A bolt of lightning. Ianthe severing their bond.

Audrey managed to get to her knees, then to her feet. Gray dust clung to her legs. She stumbled from the den into the foyer and grabbed the pack she left by the front door. She stood gasping. Forgot what she was after, reeling from the fact of who Blake really was.

So many confusing *it can't be's* and *what ifs* and *is that whys* running through her mind. Her father's role in it. The pretending. Blake and her father. A secret hidden after all she and Blake had been through.

This is where you two stay, Mako said.

Just us?

That is what your father suggested.

Was that why Blake conveniently came into her life the moment her father agreed to let her go away to the U-Dub? Did he... did *they*, plan for a relationship to blossom beyond a mere friendship?

Shock turned to fear turned to rage.

She opened the pack and pulled out her cell phone, switched it on.

No signal.

Rain began to drum on the roof. Gusts rattled windows.

She slung the pack on her shoulder and ran into the storm.

73

Wobbly Confrontation

AUDREY SQUIRMED HER WAY through the gate's narrow gap and landed on her knees. She wasted no time hopping into the UTV. The rain was coming down in bucketloads and she feared getting stuck by flash floods. She knew it would take her too long to retrace her tracks and backtrack to the Beach of Dreams so she turned right at the fork in the old road and followed it north, hoping she made the right decision.

The road quickly became muddy. Puddles formed and she swung the wheel around the worst of them. She skirted the foothills of the mountains, but had not yet dropped in elevation, rising well-above the main road.

She stopped once to check her cell phone for a connection. Still nothing. She forged on realizing how much she depended on the technology, how vulnerable and alone she felt without that connection.

The compass on the dash was still acting randomly. Holding its course then spinning around ninety degrees, then back again. Based on the amount of time she had been running north she could only guess she was well past the house and somewhere above the grassy wetlands. She had no other choice and continued, bouncing along the mud-slicked road.

The gusts had become constant, whipping the trees into a frenzy. Leaves, twigs, and small branches battered the roof and the windshield of the UTV. The clouds were low and dark, blocking most of the light from a sun shining somewhere high above. It was well past four o' clock and already growing darker.

The road started a slow determined curve to the left, dropping in elevation. That brought new challenges as the UTV's mud-caked tires began to slip and slide. She eased up on the throttle and whipped the wheel back and forth to combat fishtailing. Her shoulders cramped and burned from the constant fight.

The road curved hard to the left, then to the right, a series of switchbacks. She pumped the breaks carefully and worked her way down the steep grade. She was glad she was buckled in, in case she missed a turn and rolled the UTV. Better to be strapped into a rolling cage than flung out and crushed.

She finally took a breath when she reached the bottom and the dirt road intersected the main road between the house and the village. The old road had passed the house from above a fair way back. The wetlands spread before her. She turned left and hightailed it to the house, the wipers barely keeping up with the rain. Lightning ripped across the sky. Thunder boomed, rattling her nerves and the wheel in her hands.

With the thick cloud cover, it was near full dark by the time she reached the decorative gate. She impatiently waited for it to swing open. Rain bounced off the road and glistened in the headlamps. She checked her watch. Five-fifteen. Over an hour late. She inched forward and slipped through the gate once the opening was wide enough for the small UTV to pass through.

Her headlights danced across the rain-slicked road as she raced for the house.

She pulled around the corner and skidded to a stop. Rain water poured off the UTV's roof, puddling inside at her feet. Parked in the carport was the other UTV. The one Blake took earlier to catch the flight off the island. Her heart pounded. Was she ready to confront Blake?

So many emotions swirled. Blake was a good person she cared for deeply. He had endured immense trauma and a hellish recovery from what she gleaned from her father's journal and the writings on the walls of the room where he had been locked up for his own safety.

But.

Had he lied? Or was it a truth never revealed? Was it a lie to hide the truth? Which was it? She remembered all the little things he had said which she blew off. Clues he dropped. Her never fully comprehending the hidden meanings. But had he told her an outright lie? How can you blame someone for lying when you never asked the right question?

Her stomach churned with this impossible dilemma when she pulled the UTV into the carport next to the other one. She hopped out, picked up her day pack, and ran through thundering rain along the path and up the stairs to the front door.

It swung open. Blake was already dressed for her party. "Thank God! I was so worried. Where were you?"

Audrey was breathing hard, from running, from Blake's sudden appearance. She dropped the day pack and slipped off her muddy shoes, avoiding his eyes.

"Was out exploring and got stuck after the rain started. You should see all the mud on the UTV. What a mess!" She pushed her way past him into the living area, hoping he didn't notice her shaking hands or hear her heart thundering in her chest.

He smiled, oblivious, as if his world hadn't just been upended. "I left some things for you in your room." He wiped something from her cheek. Mud. He grinned. "The UTV's not the only thing a mess."

She stiffened from his touch.

"Is something wrong?"

"No." She forced a smile. "I lost track of time."

He regarded her with questioning eyes. "Are you sure?" He took her hand. "You're shaking. What happened?"

She said nothing.

"Audrey, talk to me."

She shook off his grip, stepped back. "I found the house."

His face paled.

"*Thomas.*"

A look she'd never seen before rippled across his face, the look of someone facing a long-buried ghost suddenly coming to life. The ghost of Thomas he had buried centuries ago.

"No." He shook his head and began hyperventilating. "No. No. No."

He brushed by her, collapsed on the sofa, head grasped between his hands, rocking and murmuring, "Should have burned it down, should have burned it down."

Her heart throbbed not in fear but in his reaction to the truth, how small and vulnerable he suddenly became. The torment that still lingered after all these years. She sat next to him.

"Come back to me, Blake."

He looked up, tears welled his eyes. "I told them to burn it down!"

"All I want is the truth."

"I wish I had been the one to die."

"I don't mean with Leela. I need to know the truth about *us*. Was this planned between you and—and *our* father?"

He said nothing, looked away.

"Tell me."

He stifled a sob.

"All I want is the truth." She took his hand. It was hot and sweaty. "I need to know if indeed you are truly the Blake I've come to know and love, not someone else hiding behind a mask, someone whose life is built on lies and deception."

He was breathing heavily. "I've always been the same, Thomas or Blake; it's me, deeply damaged and broken. You are correct about a mask—not to deceive, but to protect myself from my past. I became very good at masking that truth, and work hard to stay whole, every single day. That is the truth." He paused, composed himself, looking more like the quiet confident Blake she first met. "I have cared for you since the day you were born. You've been the only one who I—I came to love in the same way I loved Leela. I know it seems sick, some would say disgusting because of our age difference, but is it? How do we control our heart, who we fall in love with? Why should love be cast aside if it doesn't align with what others think. It's me and Leela all over again, Sapien and Merahvu. Forbidden.

"I was gifted with near immortality. Physically you and I are the same age. I've merely accumulated more memories. How is my loving you wrong?"

"You're my *brother*."

"Am I? I was born an orphan on a pirate ship in seventeen-o-three. Your father took me under his wing and raised me. You are the result of his marriage to Teola. How does that make you my sister and I your brother?"

"His journals, he said he adopted you, that you are a son to him."

"I was a son to them *all*. Alvarez, Leonard, Wickman. They *all* took care of me."

"And Francesca?"

"Yes, even Francesca, eventually. My mother had been her lover and close confidant, and had been a victim of a brutal rape. At the time, Francesca struggled to accept me because of that."

He sucked a breath. "I confess. I conspired with your father that I should be the one to watch over you, like a guardian. I'm the reason he let you go out into the world once you turned eighteen, knowing I was there to protect you. I followed you to the university and then to the Labs, becoming your friend along with Ryan. I always respectfully kept my distance until that day on *Annabelle*. I had to ask, and after we kissed, I knew. I knew I loved you! Then you agreed to be my girlfriend. After everything that had happened to me, the grief, the suffering, the patience, I believed it was meant to be. Karma.

"Your father never pushed me on you. He'd had decades of meaningless relationships. Then he met your mother. Other than Ianthe, he never truly loved anyone else, though he had many mistresses. He once told me he hoped you would find love on your own terms, as he had. Is that not what happened?"

Audrey sat back. Rain drummed on the roof and wind rattled the windows. The roar of waves crashing ashore grew louder, eating away at the beach, and drawing closer to the house. The Mark in her arm tuned into the violence of the storm, undulating in waves as if the storm had awakened it. Goosebumps rippled up her arms. The Mark felt alive, as if participating in her struggle.

Tell him the truth.

She studied his face. Had her father or Dr. Wickman told Blake her secret? Both had promised not say anything to the others, especially once Sinto died. The consequence of it meaningless at that point, only to cause her more pain should the truth come out.

"I—" her voice caught, "have a secret to confess." She pulled her arm to her chest. The Mark pulsed to the rhythm of her rapidly beating heart. It was burning now from the sudden focus of her attention. Hotter than ever before. "Before Sinto died, I Marked him. He had no idea how it was possible. I had no idea what I had done. But it happened." She held out her arm, inviting Blake to feel it.

Her confession hit him hard by the shocked look in his eyes. And by the look of his reaction, this was the first he'd heard of it. Kudos to her father and Dr. Wickman for keeping their word.

He pressed his fingers along the thick coils in her arm, tracing the symbol forged inside, then suddenly let go as if he had touched a hot stove. He looked her in the eyes, then held out his right forearm with a tattoo of two seals curled up like a yin-yang symbol. One was white, the other black. The tattoo concealed a patch of irregular skin Audrey had felt once. She never questioned its significance or the placement on the inside of his right forearm. The tattoo covered an unsightly scar where the Mark he shared with Leela once lived.

"Your Mark is exactly like the one I shared with Leela: a swirl, a line, and a circle. It disintegrated after she died."

"The writings on your bedroom walls... what did you mean by 'stop the wobble'?"

He sucked a sudden breath. Gazed at his fingers. "I still don't know what it meant, or rather *means*. I still feel it at times, the wobble, while no else does. I believe it means something important is unfinished. Our worlds. Earth and Merluma. I think they're—"

He never finished his sentence. The sky boomed, a bolt of lightning flashed. The lights went out and they were cast into utter darkness.

74

Code Red

SINTO WAS SPIT FROM his tunnel offshore of Isla Salvación where he first met Audrey. The Mark vibrated, announcing its mate was near. His heart pounded with anticipation. A war between need and caution raged.

The Orankai knew of the ship, and Sinto had no doubt they would have followed it. And the island was no secret. It was in these very waters that Ramasis and a handful of his companions had attacked Culliford's crew, killing most and stranding the remaining on the island, hundreds of years ago.

The surface of the ocean was frantic, currents from the storm's fury reaching deep into the sea, tugging at his body. Sinto only knew of the beach where he first met Audrey. Navigating through the narrow channel into the lagoon skirting the beach would be suicide. He decided to move farther north and find a safer place to go ashore.

He swam along the sandy bottom, camouflaged, searching for movement besides his own, sensing for any other sea life, working his way north along the shore. As Sinto had expected the surrounding sea was void of the local sea mammals he came to expect here, turtle and monk seal. Having sensed the storm, these sea mammals would have moved on to calmer seas until the danger passed. Any other nearby sea mammals could mean only one thing. The Orankai had followed the ship to the island and were preparing to attack.

Sinto sensed the movement of warm-blooded bodies. But exactly how many and how far away was unclear. The water was dark from nightfall and murky from runoff coming from the land. He secured his camouflage and shut down the glow emitted from his eyes, pretending to be one of them.

Blinded by darkness, he sensed the rhythm of the waves, feeling his way across the sandy bottom toward shore, hoping for a soft sandy landing. His odds were uncertain, but so were the odds for the others.

The water took him, a strong current racing toward the shore only to whip him back out to sea. The movement was violent and stripped him of his protective lorica. Grit filled the filters of his gills. It was a struggle to siphon oxygen from the sandy water. He melded with the motion, linking his mind to the movement, body tumbling with each passing wave. He listened to how the sea pounded the shore. A smooth punch, gentle vibration, and swift rushing *whoosh* meant sand. Random slaps and crashing meant rock. Once he was certain he was near sand not rock he let the current take him ashore.

His body was cast onto a sandy beach by a cresting wave. He jumped to his feet and ran, fighting the roiling waters swirling around his legs trying to suck him back into the sea.

Once clear of the water, he ran blind into the night, tripped, and landed in a thorny bush. He was assaulted by the roar of wind and the snap of sharp foliage. He flushed sand from his gills and sucked briny air deeply into his lungs.

He rolled to his feet. Hunkered low as he shuffled until he found better cover. Crouched among whipping grasses, he tamped down his senses under full assault from the raging storm. He hoped the fury of it would slow and hinder the Orankai he had sensed lying in wait in the shallow waters.

He had to find Audrey, and soon, to warn her.

The Mark thrummed in his arm. He sensed she was on the island as Ryan claimed, but he couldn't tell which direction, nor how far.

The phone in the kitchen rang. Audrey felt her way around in the dark, from the sofa, to the counter, to the phone mounted on the wall. Blake moved with her, his hand on her shoulder. Audrey answered it. "Hello?"

"Code Red!" Stokes yelled through the handset. "The compound is under attack." Blake leaned in and Audrey held the phone between their ears. The sound of men yelling, things breaking, the *ping, ping, ping* of weapons firing in the background. "Same orange-eyed bastards! Take cover! Will send a team to help if we—" There was a loud crash, with the tinkle of breaking glass and howling wind suddenly filling the void.

Then the line went dead.

Blake and Audrey sprang into action, clinging to each other as they shuffled in the darkness, down the hall, to the storeroom carefully organized by Poe. Audrey peeked out the front door window. Individual, solar-powered lights dimly dotted the path.

Blake found a lantern and turned it on. He opened the weapons cabinet, retrieved crossbows, extra barrels of ammo, and night-vision goggles.

Audrey opened the other cabinet, grabbed the neoprene suits, gloves, and booties. She passed a suit to Blake. He passed her a crossbow, goggles, and extra ammo. Then she stripped to her underwear and shimmed into her suit. He did the same. They helped each other zip them up in the back. They sat side-by-side squirming bare feet into booties. It was odd witnessing Blake handling these things he claimed to know nothing about when they were on the ship.

"What's the plan?" Audrey said, pulling up her hood, then putting on her gloves.

"We do as Stokes instructed. We take cover." Then he pulled up a woven mat at their feet, revealing a trap door, and swung it up and open. A ladder disappeared into the darkness. Audrey never knew the space below the floor existed. Blake did. After her recent discovery, she wondered what other surprises Blake might reveal.

She looped the goggles around her neck then picked up her crossbow and extra ammo. "I assume you know how to use one of these."

"Of course. Down you go." His voice had taken on a sharp edge she'd never heard before.

She did as he asked.

Blake slammed the trap door shut, locking Audrey below the ironwood floorboards and into the crawlspace of the house. Blake had the lantern. She was cast into total darkness.

She rattled the door, "Hey! What are you doing? Let me out!" The whistle of wind stealing past the crawlspace vents was the only response.

"Blake!" She climbed up and pressed her shoulder against the door. It was solid as rock. Nothing. No response, no movement. "Damn you!"

Sinto moved fast through whipping grasses toward the center of the island and away from the beach.

The north end of the island twinkled with lights scattered throughout valleys and hillsides, along a long runway to his left, and the docks in the harbor where a Larkian ship was moored, as well as the ship itself. He saw no lights to the south.

One minute he was marveling at the lights, the next the island was cast into total darkness, except for the ship in the harbor.

Shadows emerged from the sea and slithered across the ship's decks. Strange looking things cast by camouflaged bodies. *Orankai.* Arkis keeping his promise.

As Sinto feared, they had followed the ship in search of Audrey.

Explosions filled the night, followed by blinding flashes of light and screaming voices.

The Mark pulled him to the south and away from the most populous part of the island now under attack. South toward the beach where he met her long ago. She had told him she lived in a house not far from where they met. Was that where she was hiding?

Sinto pushed through the grass until his feet landed on a hard surface. He guessed it to be a road running north and south. He ran through the darkness, keeping to the hardened ground. After sprinting for what felt like an eternity, he ran into something solid. He lit up his eyes. A metal gate with vertical rods and cutouts of fish. He surveyed for a way around. It was mounted to stone pillars with no other barrier to the other side. He wound his way around and kept running.

He saw faint lights in the distance, evenly spaced, marking a path beside a covered open-sided structure where two small truck-like vehicles were parked. Water poured off the roof and pooled below.

As he drew closer, the lights along the path went out, one by one, as if extinguished by someone aware of an imminent attack. The path and the open-sided structure were suddenly cast in darkness.

Wind tore at the trees and roared in his ears, making it impossible to hear anything other than the violence of the storm. He ran into a wide-trunked tree surrounded by bushes, and crouched.

Arriving unannounced was risky. With the attack happening on the north end, whoever extinguished the lights may be on high alert and have twitchy trigger fingers. He was all too well aware of how deadly the Larkian weapons could be.

The mayhem of the storm jostled his senses. A major handicap. Without the aid of light or hearing, it was nearly impossible to detect the approach of another body. His only other option was to sense the presence of another by their heat signature. Orankai may or may not mask their heat signature with a layer of lorica. He hoped the Larkians were unaware of his ability to sense them this way.

The Mark was on fire. Audrey was near, of that he was certain. But where and in what state of alarm was unclear. He assumed she was not alone and wasn't the one who extinguished the lights. But how many Larkians were with her? Had she received Ryan's messages that he was coming to find her? What if he was mistaken for an attacking Orankai?

Rumbling came from the north end—a full-blown attack underway and the Larkians fighting back with deadly force. Whoever was hunkered down here would surely be expecting an unfriendly encounter. He sensed others approaching, coming from the north. Orankai or Larkian he was unsure. Both would see him as an enemy.

Adrenaline screamed through his veins. He came for one purpose and one purpose only.

Find her.

He reached out for her mind but found another.

Audrey slung the crossbow she had carried down the ladder across her shoulder, pressed her hands to the ceiling of the crawlspace, and felt her way across to where she thought the front door would be, hard-packed gravel at her feet. She ran into shelving, knocking things over. She felt around at different objects, feeling for anything that might project light. A match, a candle, a flashlight. In the darkness it was difficult to know for sure what she was grabbing. With neoprene gloves it was impossible.

She tried the night-vision goggles hanging around her neck. Nothing. Too dark. They need a sliver of light to work. There was none.

She whipped off her gloves, clamped them between her teeth, and continued feeling around the confines of the space, panic growing with each different object lifted and felt with her hands. Nothing remotely useful.

Peachy.

She felt a flat surface, a workbench with a vice mounted at one end. Hopeful, she rummaged for tools hanging on walls above, a crowbar or a hammer or anything she could use to open the trapdoor. She yanked open drawers below. The top drawer had coils of wiring and electrical cords. In the next drawer she found tools. She pawed a battery-operated drill, a jig saw, hammer, and... a flashlight!

She switched it on. It winked a few times before emitting a weak light that threatened to die any second. She searched for extra batteries, found a shelf on the other side of the small crawlspace full of them. She bumbled in darkness removing the old batteries and putting in new ones.

Click.

A strong beam of light swept across the gravel floor.

She wasted no time and surveyed the trapdoor; hinges with Phillips head screws. She grabbed the battery-operated drill, checked it. Power was good. She rummaged for the right Phillips bit, put it in.

She climbed the ladder and got to work on the trapdoor hinges, cursing Blake for locking her inside, growing more and more agitated by the insane itch and unbearable fire spreading from the Mark to the rest of her body.

Hinges fell to the floor. She pressed her shoulder to the trapdoor and pushed it aside.

75

Deadly Close Encounter

SINTO FROZE. HE SENSED movement other than his own. Near the house he saw a blip of thermal heat, not of a full body, but the circle of a face with eyes masked. He guessed it was a Larkian outfitted in a protective suit to ward off electrocution. A suit that also masked body heat, stealing Sinto's innate advantage of identifying prey in the darkest of dark. He had no doubt the Larkians had the technology to mimic that advantage which all Merahvu were given at birth. It was then he realized his own exposure, naked and radiating thermal heat. He bled lorica to cool the surface of his skin and mute most of his heat signature.

He reached out with his mind, queried the Mark. The heat signature he registered was not from Audrey. He reached further. She was near, somewhere in the house; her mind was closed or masked by something solid.

He dropped to the ground and crawled back from where he came, hoping to find a safe place to hide perhaps near the vehicles he passed on his way to the house.

Something fast and small whizzed past his head, another grazed his shoulder. Thin and metallic with a sharp tip and steel wings.

He rolled into the bushes at the base of a tree, stood and pressed his back against its trunk. He readied his merlux, standing tall and rigid, body pressed sideways behind the tree's trunk, acting as a shield. He stole a glance around the tree where he was hiding. The glowing ball of thermal heat was swiftly moving closer, carefully picking their way along the path.

His best defense was to hide. His goal, to get to the house undetected and find Audrey.

More spears whizzed past. A volley of shots sweeping in a semi-circle. One struck something close behind him. A body, whose eyes flashed orange before exploding into ash. Ash brushed his face before it was swiftly picked up by the roaring wind.

Orankai!

Sandwiched between mutual enemies, he froze, camouflaged and cloaked by his lorica, melding to the tree. He sensed more bodies winding their way along the path, on a collision course with the armed Larkian.

A faint chant seeded by his brief exposure to Arkis' orange nectar threaded in his mind, the hive-mind connection the Orankai shared. While alarmed he still could hear them, though barely, he was grateful.

It means I can track them.

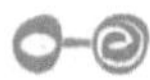

Audrey pulled herself up and out the trapdoor and into the storeroom. She slid the door back in place, not wanting to find an unexpected hole in the darkness. She swung the crossbow from her back to her hands, checked that the safety was set. The last thing she wanted was to accidentally shoot Blake. She laid her trigger finger on the safety switch, ready to release it, just in case.

She had no idea where Blake went and had no way to communicate. An incessant banging came from the foyer. The wind roared and windows howled. In addition, the hood made it impossible to hear clearly, even if someone stood beside her screaming.

All she had were her goggles and even those were useless without the tiniest of light to enhance their night-vision power. Thermal heat was all they could offer; barring that, she was left with intuitive sense which at the moment was yin-yang-ing in rhythm with the Mark; a major distraction. Not because of the physical gyration occurring within her arm but because of the nagging question of why.

Ignore it. It's nothing and no different from before.

She shuffled her feet to the front door, open and banging in the wind. She closed it and put her back to its solidness, the howling wind slightly muted. Blake must have gone out that way, failing to fully latch it shut. As much as she wanted to seek him out, she was acutely aware of how stupid that would be. Friendly fire was the cause of many wartime deaths.

She padded deeper into the house, toward the lanai door. She skidded to a stop and froze. Beyond the glass, she saw movement. Three bodies with weak heat signatures, wavering near the water. So slight, she lost sight of them. She was baffled at first, then it hit her.

Their lorica, she thought, *masks body heat!*

Her heart pounded. She crouched with her back pressed against the wall next to the sliding door, debating. Stay here or attack? She decided to stay put, for the moment. She needed to gather her thoughts, to come up with a plan. She was blind and deaf and may be more of a liability than helpful.

She cursed the fact she and Blake had no way to communicate.

Voices whispered in Sinto's mind. Orankai coming from the north. Four, then six. Then another, totaling seven, headed in their direction. The armed Larkian launched another volley of shots. He struck two Orankai. More ash. Five left. The Larkian was holding his own.

Sinto weighed his options. He had the power to out-shock even the most capable of his kind. He also had the element of surprise. Nowhere in the whispers had he heard a warning of his presence. The wild card was the Larkian, creeping ever closer.

The lanai door rattled, whether from the wind or something else Audrey was uncertain. She pushed up to her feet with her back pressed to the wall. She clicked off the safety on the crossbow and laid her finger beside the trigger, ready to engage once she was certain of the target. She pressed a hand to the sliding door's glass.

It started to open...

Flueox flooded Sinto's bloodstream. He needed to see and there was only one way to make that possible. It was risky and he mapped out in his mind the sequence in which he needed to act.

He used the voices in his head to visualize the approaching Orankai's exact location. Which at this point was on a collision course with the armed Larkian, who was firing with surprisingly good precision.

Time for a distraction.

Sinto wound up a fist and launched a bolt of electrical fire that whizzed across the path, lighting a bush in the jungle on fire.

He could see! Camouflaged, with lorica masking his heat signature in place, he rolled from around the back side of the tree and sprinted toward the house. He dove under the stairs that led to the front door and crouched in the darkness. They were open backed, so he could see between them.

Even though the Orankai were camouflaged with lorica masking their heat, Sinto could see them in the flickering light as shiny rippling shadows. A fault whenever they moved with both in place.

The Larkian must have been aware of this phenomenon. He fired without hesitation, a rapid volley targeting the rippling shadows, striking vital organs. Five voices in his head were forever silenced when their bodies burst into ash.

Three other voices screamed in reaction from somewhere on the other side of the house.

The Larkian spun on his feet, tracking the path where Sinto had run toward the house. He crouched as he approached the stairs, the tip of the crossbow pointed toward him between treads.

Sinto got a good look at the lower half of the Larkian's face, half-lit by the dwindling fire. A face he would never forget, one he gazed upon many times while he was held captive in the catacombs carved deep below the Great Tower in Tallamure. The face of a man Audrey once called her boyfriend. Someone she deeply cared about. Sinto had been curious as to what about the man had captured her heart and drove her to risk her life to save him.

Blake!

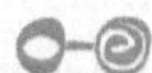

Audrey held her breath, afraid that whoever was opening the sliding glass door would hear her breathing. A fear response that served no purpose. Over the din of branches raining down on the roof and the howling of the wind, she wouldn't hear herself if she was loudly gasping.

She kept her fingers on the glass door as it slid, gauging how far it was opening. It stopped with a gap wide enough for a body to pass through. Whoever had slipped through was camouflaged.

A sudden burst of light came from the other side of the house, lighting whipping fronds high up on palm trees between the house and the water.

The door rattled as if a fast moving body crashed into the frame. Audrey pulled the trigger, firing a single spear uncertain if they had slipped inside or out. It sailed through the air and lodged itself in a book on the bookshelf. Whoever it was had left, and rather quickly.

The thought of accidentally firing on Blake made her blood run cold. She was protected by neoprene and didn't fear being shocked. She needed a different weapon for more up-close encounters.

She hitched the crossbow across her back and padded to the kitchen for a knife. She slipped one into a sheath sewn to the suit's outer right thigh.

She returned to the front door and peeked out a side window. A bush was on fire near the path. Blake determinedly moved toward the door, weapon aimed and ready to fire at something near the stairs.

In the brief flash of light, Sinto saw the object Blake held in his hands: a crossbow with a barrel of many spears. A silent weapon designed to kill, which Blake had demonstrated quite spectacularly. One shot and Sinto would be nothing but ash in the wind.

He thought it ironic it had come down to this. Blake hunting Sinto. He had no desire to harm Blake but the situation was volatile.

He yelled Blake's name but it was useless. It was ripped from his mouth by the raging wind and was cast out to sea. The fire he had started sputtered and died.

The firelight went out. Audrey swore. She was blind once again. She dared not open the door, startling Blake with his weapon aimed in her direction.

She growled in frustration. Nothing had prepared her for this situation. A camouflaged foe who could see in the dark with the ability to communicate telepathically with others. How many may be out there, she was uncertain. Blake, deaf and blind, whose adrenaline must certainly be pumping as wildly as hers, was armed with a deadly weapon and a twitchy finger.

She paced in the small foyer. She had to do something, to keep moving, but what and to where?

She peeked outside, begging for a glimmer of light to see. The Mark had stopped undulating and was outright on fire. She tried to ignore it but its insistence had her wondering:

What are you trying to tell me?

A bolt of lightning lit up the sky.

Blake stood at the bottom of the stairs with his gaze fixed to something beside the house in the jungle. He was suddenly lifted off his feet and landed on his back. The crossbow flew from his hands. Then it went dark.

Audrey swung open the door. She was struck in the chest. Her night vision goggles flew from her face. She fell backwards, landing atop the crossbow strapped to her back. Air was knocked from her lungs. She struggled to draw a fresh breath.

A pair of glowing orange eyes glowered above her. She felt a sudden weight pinning her down. The crossbow ground into her back. Pain shot through her thorax. She stifled a scream.

Electrified hands clasped her arms. Threads of electricity snaked across her suit to the floor. If not for its protection, she would surely be dead.

The woven mat beneath her caught fire. Heat rose around her.

And from the fire came light and she could finally see.

She stilled. Whoever was trying to kill her was camouflaged. They eased their grip but remained atop her. She played dead, slowly walking her fingers down to the sheath with the knife, strapped to her thigh.

The attacker dropped his camouflage. A Terrakai, male, and orange-eyed, like those who attacked the ship. He dipped lower, brow furrowed, scanning her face. She held an unseeing gaze, pretending to be dead.

A look of surprise and shock came over him and he rolled to his feet. His gaze grew distant as if listening to someone.

Mind-speak with another!

The Terrakai must have believed her dead and turned his back to her. She silently rolled to a crouch, knife in hand, then drove up to her feet, wrapped her arm around his chest and swiftly ran the blade across his neck. Hot blood poured from the deep wound and sizzled when it reached the flames dancing from the mat. He stumbled, crumpled to his knees, then burst into ash. It struck her face and landed like snowflakes on her lashes.

The smell of death followed. Metallic and musty plus something else. Something sweet and fishy, like the smell of Orange.

She grabbed her goggles, slipped them on, cracked open the door. She stole a quick peek, capturing the last of the fire's light at her feet to see what was happening outside.

Sinto held his breath, afraid to risk the slightest ripple in his camouflage. Nothing about Blake's demeanor indicated he had seen Sinto hiding behind the stairs. Nor was he aware of the Orankai Sinto sensed and heard through the fading hive-chant, who had sneaked up the stairs to the front door. Sinto thought he heard the door slam, but couldn't be sure if it was that or branches striking the roof.

A light suddenly flared from inside the house, flickering like a flame, bleeding from a window in the door. Blake rose from his semi-crouch in reaction, then was tackled. The Orankai who took him down didn't bother to camouflage; neither did another one, emerging from the dark. There were only the three of them left, the one who slipped inside the house and the two attacking Blake.

They grabbed Blake by the arms, tried to shock him. Blake lay still but very much alive, a lopsided grin spreading across his face. They rose, baffled as to why he was still alive. One kicked him while the other screamed in frustration, the sound stolen by the wind.

Blake grabbed the leg of the one kicking him, pulled him to the ground, and rolled atop him, straddling his back, with knees planted wide and grinding the Orankai's chest against the ground. He looped his arm around the Orankai's neck and yanked up. His other hand grappled for the crossbow, partially sticking out from beneath a dancing bush. The second Orankai joined the struggle, ringing Blake's neck with his hands.

The flicker of light bleeding from the house faded, then died.

So did another Orankai. The one in the house.

Two left.

Sinto crawled out from under the stairs and blindly lunged where he last saw the Orankai attacking Blake. Sinto's merlux buzzed and electrified flueox flowed. His body connected with the one on top. Together they fell to the ground. Sinto pressed splayed hands to the Orankai's chest and fired. The Orankai's heart sputtered. Sinto shocked him again and again until his hands fell to the ground, grasping nothing but ash.

His heart fluttered from the effort and the aftershock bouncing back through his fingers.

One left...

With her night-vision goggles, Audrey caught the last few seconds of fading light. She tried to make sense of the commotion happening outside. Blake was on the ground, pinning an orange-eyed Terrakai, while another held fast to his neck. There was sudden commotion and the one grabbing his neck was knocked clear and fell to the ground, by who she couldn't tell. But she was certain it was someone camouflaged. The Terrakai's eyes bugged then he burst to ash.

Audrey swung open the door.

A bolt of lightning dropped from the sky and struck a tree beside the house. Bark exploded from the trunk and opened a gaping hole at its base.

Audrey was blinded by amplified light filtered through her night-vision goggles. She ripped them off and retreated back inside the house. She closed the door with her back pinned to it, and slid to the floor.

Tears burst from her burning eyes. White spots marred her vision.

Blake's weapon found the last Orankai pinned beneath him. A sudden bolt of lightning struck a tree followed by a bone-numbing clap of thunder. Ash peppered the sky. Blake ripped off his goggles, and his hands clutched his face. He shook his head a few times, eyes blinking frantically, then looked up. Sinto's eyes were aglow, his cloaking having slipped in the commotion.

Their eyes connected.

Sinto hopped to his feet. Blake reached for the crossbow.

Sinto ran, bleeding lorica from his pores to mask his heat signature. Spears flew past, in random directions. Blake firing blind, hoping to get lucky. Sinto stumbled over a rock, fell to his knees and crawled. He found bushes, then a tree. The one he hid behind previously with several spears buried in its trunk. He stood, pressing against the back side, inching around and putting it between him and Blake.

So he thought.

A spear grazed the scarred flesh where Sinto had been mauled by the lamprey, cutting deep enough to raise blood. Another whizzed past his head. Sinto stole a glance back. By the faint glow from a hole at the base of the tree struck by lightning, he saw that Blake had donned his goggles and was looking in Sinto's direction, weapon in hand.

He didn't want to kill Blake, but didn't want to die either. He was so close to reaching Audrey the Mark burned with intensity. Like everyone else, Blake had no idea Sinto was alive, nor did Audrey. Ryan's messages must not have gotten through.

Sinto held his merlux in check, generating enough electricity to stun but not kill. If only he could explain who he was, then they both might survive this deadly encounter. The noise from the incessant wind, the crashing waves, and trees being shredded in the jungle made it impossible to hear a pleading voice, or even a scream.

Rain fell from the sky; a deluge, bouncing off Sinto's shoulders and pooling at his feet. Spears burrowed into the tree where he was hiding. Sinto shifted his position, rounding a quarter way around the trunk. Blake was close and slowly moving, rounding the tree where Sinto hid. If he ran, Blake would shoot him. If he dropped and crawled, Blake would shoot him. If he screamed, Blake wouldn't hear him.

Stuck without options!

Blake was close enough that Sinto could sense his aura, ever so weak and blocked by the black suit he wore. But what he sensed was fear, naturally, but also a sense of desperation and determination that comes from a warrior's devotion to protect and defend, even if it meant sacrificing his own life.

Sinto knew Audrey was in the house. Sinto would do whatever was necessary if he believed her life was at stake and the roles were reversed. Sinto had no doubt Blake would do the same. Sinto was the enemy, Orankai or not, especially after the attack Ryan told him about.

Blake was hunting to kill. In the dark. And aided by superior technology.

Sinto sensed Blake circling close to the tree. Sinto inched around, matching Blake's movements. He couldn't detect the weapon as it was cold and inanimate and dark as the bottom of the sea, but at this close range, he could sense the hands supporting it.

Sinto's heart thundered. A second passed, then another. He caught a whiff of anxious sweat, sudden and fleeting in the raging wind.

He acted, rolling around the trunk, coming up on Blake from behind, merlux charged, the surface of his skin electrified. Sinto rammed into Blake with full force, blindly reaching for the crossbow. Current raced through metal when his hand made contact. Blake held fast to the weapon, spun and rammed the butt-end into Sinto's jaw. Blood filled his mouth where his teeth clipped his tongue. Blake gave him a second strike to his nose. Pain exploded through his head and blood gushed from his nostrils.

Sinto stumbled, then dodged a third strike. Blake was thrown of balance. Sinto blindly chopped and swung his arms, trying to knock the weapon from his hands. He made contact with something hard and solid.

The crossbow fell to their feet. Blake spun, facing away from Sinto. Sinto wrapped his arms around Blake's chest, pinching his arms to his sides, and squeezed with every ounce of strength he could muster. Sinto was taller with more body mass. Blake was surprisingly fast and slippery. Sinto dare not let go and risk another strike to his head.

Rain crackled and sparked across Sinto's electrified skin. Blake wheezed as Sinto squeezed the air from his lungs.

Suddenly Sinto was falling, something tangled up around his feet—Blake's foot, hooked around his ankle, tripping him. Sinto fell to his back; Blake landed on top of him. Air was knocked from his lungs. His grip loosened.

Blake was a wily and cunning fighter Sinto underestimated. Blake rolled to his feet and hopped back, the shadowy look of rage coloring his face's thermal image. The goggles Blake wore were skewed but he could clearly see. Sinto's lorica had slipped sometime during their fight. His heat signature a bright beacon in the night.

Blake charged. Something sharp and lethal pierced Sinto's upper thigh. The sharp sting of a knife. A feeling Sinto knew well and would never forget. The blade slid through flesh and muscle and nicked his femoral artery. A strategic strike aimed to kill.

Heat trickled down Sinto's leg; blood and electrified flueox glowing faintly green in the dark as it mixed with rainwater snaking down his body. He shuffled backwards, through whipping vegetation, bounced off the tree trunk where he had hidden, and rolled to the protected side.

He had seconds before Blake would round up and strike again.

Blood and flueox spewed with each frantic pump of his heart. He had seconds to stop the nick to the artery before he lost consciousness. He drove his finger inside the wound, cauterized the artery with a jolt of fire. He clenched his teeth to keep from biting his tongue. He gasped for air. The wound stopped leaking.

He rounded the tree, bent at the waist, drove forward, and rammed headlong into Blake with his shoulder.

Blake fell back with Sinto on top of him. Sinto scrambled to find an arm or a wrist to grab hold of, his legs twining around Blake's. Blake's face glowed bright red inches from Sinto's. His goggles were gone, blind but not unarmed. He had Blake's legs and one arm pinned.

Where's the knife!

He found out, painfully. The knife's tip sliced across Sinto's shoulder, punched holes in his upper arm. Vicious repeated strikes, blindly seeking his neck.

Blood and flueox gushed from the cuts. Sinto fumbled in the dark for Blake's knife arm, found it and squeezed with everything he had left. He beat Blake's arm on the ground until the knife slipped from his fingers.

Sinto charged his merlux. Electricity crackled below the surface of his skin. He pressed a cheek to Blake's, making full skin-to-skin contact, and gave him a jolt. Not enough to kill but enough to stun him unconscious. Blake thrashed then stilled, his body melting beneath Sinto's.

Someone slipped atop Sinto's back, yanked his head back by his hair. A blade pressed to his throat, the tip biting skin. Sinto had no doubt who it was by the way the Mark began screaming in his arm, warning its mate.

He choked out her name, "Audrey." But not loud enough for her to hear over the storm's commotion.

The blade lingered against his jugular, crosswise to the delicate and sensitive skin surrounding his gills. Hesitation. Was she listening to the Mark?

Desperate, he pushed a mind-speak message, hoping her mind was open.

"Audrey, it's me, Sinto."

76

Marks Sing

AUDREY'S JAW FELL, THEN the knife she held to Sinto's throat.

"S—Sinto?"

She released the hair tangled in her gloved fingers and rolled aside. He rolled to face her. It was hard to see his face in the darkness but she held his head in her hands, gazing into his eyes, glowing oddly through her night-vision goggles.

Sinto was bleeding, badly, the red glow of its heat snaking down his chest. Rain hammered and puddled where they lay, a mix of water and blood.

She sat up. "You're bleeding!"

A smile graced his face. "*Just a scratch, I'll live. Now.*"

She kissed him, tears bursting from her eyes. The taste of his lips and the Mark's vibrations confirming it was him.

Sinto, alive. ALIVE!

Audrey dared not blink, afraid that if she did, he would be gone again, her mind playing tricks. But the way her heart thrummed and the Mark sang she knew it was true. Every jolt, burst of fire, and tremor the Mark made—the mere presence of it still in her arm—all had been signs. Signs she failed to acknowledge. Signs she failed to *question*. Sinto survived that day in Tallamure and had been alive the entire time. She flashed back to that time when Dr. Wickman asked her if she had actually witnessed Sinto's body disintegrating that fateful day. She hadn't and wrote it off to the fact they had barely escaped the mayhem with their own lives. There wasn't an opportunity to linger, to confirm he was truly gone. How could she have been so blind, so ignorant to the truth?

She snapped back to the immediacy of the moment. Blake lay beside Sinto, unmoving.

"*I merely stunned him; he'll live,*" Sinto shared. "*If I hadn't—he would have killed me, protecting you. Blake's a fighter.*"

"*You only know the half of it.*"

Lightning snaked across the sky.

"*We've got to get inside. Can you help me lift him?*"

Sinto rolled to his hands and knees, lightheaded from loss of blood. From the deep cut in his shoulder, slashes across his arm, and his femoral artery before he cauterized it. Audrey noticed his distress and came around to help him to his feet. When she let go, he wobbled and she grabbed him.

"*Give me a minute, lost some blood.*"

He bent, hands to knees, clearing his head, filling his lungs deeply.

From what he could tell, Audrey had knelt by Blake's side, and was shaking him.

"*He's out cold,*" she shared. "*Let's get you inside. I'll come back and get him.*"

"*We can't leave him, others—Orankai—might still be out there, looking for you,*" Sinto said.

Her brow dipped in confusion, a scrunched-up V rippling yellow and orange. Her lips mouthed, *Orankai.* Then, she shared, "*Help me get him to his feet.*"

Together they lifted Blake, Audrey more than Sinto because of his weakened state. They slung his arms across their shoulders and wound their arms around his torso. Sinto set his eyes aglow so they could see their way to the front door.

They dragged Blake through puddles and thick mud, up the stairs, and pushed through the front door. They stopped only to lock it behind them, then dragged Blake deeper inside the house, to a sofa. They laid him there. Audrey swung his feet up from the floor, pulled the hood from his head, and yanked the gloves off his hands. She grabbed a pillow and shoved it under his head. Blake looked at peace.

Sinto slid to the floor with the sofa and Blake to his back, blinking away spots filling his vision. Maybe he hadn't been forthright with Audrey about bleeding from just a scratch. The cuts Blake inflicted were much more.

When Sinto reached for the wound on his shoulder, Audrey rested her hand on his, gave it a firm squeeze. "Don't touch it. Let me clean it first. I'll be right back."

Audrey disappeared into a nearby room, leaving him alone with Blake, still unconscious but breathing evenly. Sinto reached back with his good arm and checked his vitals. Strong. No serious damage done, but he was sure to have a pounding headache once he woke up. Sinto looked over at the gaping cut in his shoulder, at the series of puncture wounds in his upper arm, the charred hole in his inner thigh. He wished he could say the same for himself. But he'd endured worse. He had no complaints.

Sinto sat back, exhaling a deep sigh of relief. He pulled his injured arm to his chest, the Mark singing within, radiating heat and joy, flowing through his bloodstream. That tension he felt since the day Wantemo convinced him to fake his death unwound from every cell in his body. He sank a little deeper where he sat on the floor.

Tears flowed freely from his eyes. He had endured a journey of impossible odds. He willingly entered evil's den, witnessed and experienced atrocities no human being should have to endure. But he survived. He fought and won. He had renewed hope. Knowing the world was still populated with good-hearted people like Rachel, who saved his life with her unfailing determination and inspiring encouragement. And like Ryan, who unquestioningly jumped at the opportunity to take care of Rachel, and who led him to Audrey.

But bubbling below the relief and joy and renewed hope laid dread. The war was far from over. He had no delusions. Arkis wouldn't stop until Audrey and Sinto were dead and his sister buckled under his heel. And after, Arkis would kill every last Merahvu who didn't join his evil tribe of Orankai and then inflict suffering and death to the Sapien masses. Arkis wouldn't stop until Merluma and Earth were his.

But mostly, Sinto was dismayed and angered and disgusted by his father who encouraged Arkis, who stood by his side as the lampreys had their way with Sinto, with an innocent young woman, and the day prior, his supposed friend and Circle representative, Beech. An inconceivable depth of deception to Sinto's mother, to his son, to the Merahvu. And if Arkis has his way, to Sinto's innocent sister, Naiada.

He hung his head as these emotions stewed, along with the hope and joy of finding Audrey safe and alive, of the duty he owed to his mother and sister and his people, of his desire to live a life with the woman who Marked him. His essence torn as to which to embrace, which to follow.

Audrey returned with a lantern that bathed the small living room with a warm light, a stack of towels, and some type of liquid in a brown bottle. She set the lantern on the sofa beside Blake, illuminating Sinto's injured shoulder. She set the towels and the bottle on the table at his knees, then ran off and came back with a couple of tall glasses of water.

Thankful, Sinto gulped one down.

She had pulled her black suit down to her waist with the lifeless sleeves swinging from her hips like limp appendages. She wore nothing on top but a bra. Seeing her that way filled Sinto with a new and quite pleasant emotion, swirling among the others.

He was afraid to speak or blink. Afraid he would break the spell of the moment and wake from a dream and find himself back in a slimy city and a windowless room with a door sucking the life spark out of him.

She gazed back, still and unsure, and he wondered if she was thinking the same thing.

He reached for her and she for him, their fingers clicking together like magnets, sure and true. And it was in that moment he realized that while they had shared the Mark and had experienced challenging and adventuresome times together, there was still so much he didn't know about her.

"Is this for real?" she asked.

Sinto smiled. "As real as it can get."

Then he pulled her to the floor beside him. Their Marks sang and lips hovered, then clicked together. She tasted so sweet and felt oh, so real. Lips kneaded with desperation. Tongues danced. Fingers grasping bristled head and braided hair. And when their lips parted they shared tears of relief and joy.

They held each other for what felt an eternity, both unwilling to let go. But reality intervened as it must and sadly always will. Danger lurked and, for Sinto, unfinished business demanded urgent attention; to seek out his mother and sister. To share his important story.

A cherished moment broken but never to be forgotten, by either of them.

Sinto surveyed his wounds. The cuts Blake inflicted were painful but mostly superficial. The wound in his leg ached but had stopped bleeding completely. The bruise on his jaw tingled and his tongue was tender and swollen where his teeth clipped it. His nose ached, but wasn't broken. Physical wounds he could easily live with. The emotional hurts he endured over the past several weeks would take longer, if ever, to heal.

Audrey poured liquid from the brown bottle into his cuts and the hole in his thigh. It bubbled and stung a little. Then she patted them dry with a towel. Sinto watched every twitch and furrow of her brow, roll of lip, blink of eye as she thoughtfully and deftly worked her fingers. A rosy color painted her cheeks as she dabbed that sensitive place on the inside of his thigh. He too blushed.

She laughed. "Look at us. Our roles reversed, me saving you, and thankfully with little chance you'll die."

Once cleaned, the freshly severed flesh danced in shock, open and receptive to grow back together with a little encouragement. Sinto used his finger. Engaged electrical threads that knit the flesh back together followed by fire to seal the surface of his skin.

He pointed to the lantern. "Turn down the light. Orankai may still be out there, searching for you."

"Who are these Orankai and what do they want from me?"

So Sinto told her. He held her in the near darkness, whispering a summary of all he had learned and experienced from the moment the knife entered his chest in Tallamure to the moment she nearly slit his throat. Some parts he heavily edited, especially some of the gritty details from Las Vegas. But he told her of his new friend Rachel, the woman who helped him get to Duluth and back out, killing two Orankai in the process. He didn't hold back when it came to Arkis' threats and determination.

And once he finished Audrey held him, body trembling. "I felt you, through the Mark. Brief surges I didn't understand, but now make sense. I can't imagine how you must have felt, no one knowing you were alive..."

She told him of the missing ships, of what they discovered about Orange, and the attack on the ship by what she now knew were Arkis' Orankai rebels. Of Ryan nearly falling victim. Of her killing the pregnant Orankai girl. And the two of them returning her body to the sea. The deep disappointment by Dr. Wickman for her actions. Her banishment from the ship.

"My father has started a war."

"This war was started long ago, long before my mother met your father. He only helped it thaw, as did she. For that, both share equal blame."

Blake stirred behind them.

Audrey reached for him. "How do you feel?"

"A little shook up. I confess, I've been listening to your story. I'm sorry, Sinto, I had no idea it was you. Audrey told me about your shared Mark."

Audrey said, "I think now might be good time to tell Sinto about your truth."

Blake sat up. Sadness painted his aura blue. "I'm one of the original Larkians. I once was... Thomas, I was..."

"Leela's mate," Sinto finished for him. He was stunned by the revelation. Not because of who Blake once was but because it was another truth his mother had failed to share. Never had Sinto imagined he would come to know the man his sister had fallen in love with. His mother *knew* Blake was Thomas when she asked Sinto to capture him. Fury burned in his essence. If there was anything Sinto learned over the past few weeks, it was never to assume, but to question everything. Even one's own blood.

Sinto gazed at Blake with fresh eyes. Not as a foe fighting for Audrey's heart, but as a brother. Before Sinto could say anything, they were startled by a flash of lights approaching the house.

Blake jumped to his feet and ran to the front door. Audrey rose and helped Sinto to his feet even though he didn't need it. He felt stronger from the rest and unloading everything that he carried on his chest since finding the breeding caves on Merluma.

"It's Stokes," Blake announced.

Audrey turned at Sinto. "Stand behind me, while I explain."

He shook his head. "I have to go. Tell them all I told you. I must find my mother."

"But—"

"I'll return; soon, I promise."

He held her, reluctant to let go. His heart warred and the Mark burned in fury. But he had no choice. Neither of them did. Tears welled in her eyes. Both sharing the same regret. They lived in a world full of turmoil, one they couldn't run away from, only toward.

He bid her farewell with a brief kiss, camouflaged himself, and slipped out the back door.

77

Taken

SINTO TUNNELED THROUGH THE Pacific toward the Arctakai city nestled in the icy waters of Antarctica. He was spit out into an ice-covered sea lit from above by a forever summer sun.

Thousands of glowing blue domes littered the ocean floor like eggs laid by a giant sea creature. Merahvu families cast from their homes in Tallamure were starting anew with underwater structures under varying stages of completion.

A flash of blue light cut through the dark water as two of the small domes merged into one—an organic process constructing a new underwater city. The many would continue to merge as one, like individual cells joining to create a newly formed body. It would take over a year to birth a new city the size of Tallamure.

He swam above the domes, his mind reaching out for his mother and sister, for Wantemo. He found the Keepers of Knowledge, as well as the Healers aiding the sick and weak, younglings training with mentors, and atmospheric engineers toiling to build a mock sun and the systems necessary to bring warmth and light to a new city in the barren waters of the Southern Ocean.

He finally heard Wantemo's voice, desperate and responding to his call.

Sinto traversed amongst the domes, deeper into the center until he came to one of the smallest, surrounded by a ring of larger domes filled with thousands of Merahvu engaged in pseudo-fighting. A long-ago way of life before peace had settled tribal friction. Something he had never witnessed in Tallamure. Warriors were training for battle, confirming his fear. The Merahvu were no longer at peace.

Sinto dropped down to the sea floor where Wantemo greeted him and led him inside the smaller dome nestled among the training warriors.

"Come, hurry." Wantemo looked haggard, as if he hadn't eaten or slept for some time.

He drew back a dark curtain dividing the small space. Lying on a pile of soft bedding was a woman with gold hair, coiled into the fetal position, her back facing him.

Sinto's first thought was of Naiada, fearing she had fallen ill again. He gently rolled her over.

Not Naiada.

Drool ran from the corner of his mother's mouth and her once vivid lavender eyes rolled in their sockets, pale and without spark. Her unseeing gaze reflecting horror and confusion. A string of unrecognizable words spilled from her mouth, a chant such as those she often repeated while journeying through the Timeless Dimension. But this chant was random, disjointed, and desperate. She clawed the moist air, voice rising and fear flashing in her eyes, as if fending off a deadly predator. Her hair was dirty and matted, hunks of it torn from the root, the skin of her scalp exposed. She was terribly gaunt and pale as if she had not eaten in weeks.

"Mother," Sinto said, cradling her face.

Ianthe looked into his eyes and screamed. She recoiled as if he was the monster of her nightmares. A pinched-off scream gurgled in her throat. "Please, stop," she whispered.

Sinto stood up and stepped back in disbelief. That the weak mad woman writhing on the floor was his mother, a once powerful soothsayer and queen of the Merahvu.

"One of our warriors found her abandoned like that in the Winterlands on Merluma." Wantemo noted Sinto's troubled expression when he said the word *warrior*. "We're training the strongest for our defense."

"Has anyone ventured to the City of Green?"

"We sent a couple Scouts."

"Let me guess, they never came back."

"Not yet..."

"Probably never. And what of Naiada?" Sinto asked.

Wantemo looked defeated. "We believe she was taken by whoever did this to Ianthe."

Sinto gazed down on the frail woman clawing at the air, unseeing eyes shifting between imagined horrors, blood-curdling screams gurgling up from her throat.

Something terrible was happening to Sinto's insides. He knew who took his sister. He instinctively scanned the room even though he knew Naiada was not there. He felt a failure, helpless.

"When did this happen?"

Wantemo grimaced. "I am unsure, but believe most recently. Ianthe began training Naiada on Merluma shortly after I left you. When they didn't return, we sent our best warriors to find them." He pointed toward the bed. "Ianthe was found alone, freezing to death and babbling insanely. Only one warrior returned, the one who found her. We assume the rest are dead."

Sinto's heart sank. Arkis must have taken her shortly after Sinto escaped the City of Green.

Wantemo shot Sinto a grave look.

"What else, Wantemo?"

He rolled Ianthe onto her back. Angry red scars cut across his mother's lower torso. "They took your mother's ovaries. Her *eggs,*

Sinto." His gaze hardened. "And rather savagely. I'm surprised she's still alive. I struggle to imagine what has become of your sister."

Wantemo didn't have to say anything more. Sinto already knew. Naiada wasn't dead. Arkis took her. He spelled it out clearly the last time they spoke, and if Naiada didn't cooperate, he had an alternative plan. With his mother's eggs, Arkis could breed the queen he so desired. Sinto grew anxious. He knew his sister and believed she'd fight back. Arkis was impatient. He feared for her safety.

"Did you probe her mind to learn what happened?"

"I tried but—" Wantemo choked. "I have never encountered the madness to which she has fallen. A looping nightmare, planted by whoever did this to her. I fear she may be beyond help. A fate worse than death."

Sinto couldn't believe what Wantemo just said. He was one of the oldest living Merahvu, even older than his mother. He had lived through the Forever War. He had seen and experienced more atrocities in one lifetime than any other human on Earth.

"Do you remember my distant cousin, Arkis?"

"Of course."

"Well, he's not my cousin, he's my bastard half-brother. Ramasis was busy with more than Circle affairs while away in the City of Green. It was Arkis who started the rebellion and is rapidly breeding a new tribe on Merluma called Orankai. He controls them with a special nectar. It connects them, like a hive, acting as one, communicating as one, mindlessly doing as their master commands. It makes them stronger, physically. Arkis rambled on about some new resource on Earth, the source of the nectar. I suspect it's Orange. The Larkians encountered Orankai, harvesting it in the Pacific, while searching for a couple of missing ships. They barely escaped from an Orankai attack."

Wantemo gazed down at Sinto's mother. "She said nothing about foreseeing any of this."

"Arkis is recruiting members from all tribes, especially those with enhanced skills. He was very keen on converting me. I suspect for Ianthe's bloodline, but also for my enhanced ability to shock. He's recruiting elites, not to fight, but for breeding."

Wantemo looked up. "Breeding?"

"It begins with an initiation. They forced this orange nectar down my throat but I fought back and expelled what was left in my stomach. But even that small amount absorbed into my system still lingers, though weakly. I've felt its power and sway; I can hear the hive-voices, chanting, whenever Orankai are near. Anyone under the influence is susceptible, no matter how strong they may be."

Sinto had to stop to catch his breath, to calm his wildly beating heart, to accept the truth of what he must tell Wantemo. "Ramasis is one of them."

Wantemo stood. "And is who I believe did this to Ianthe. By the way she reacted to seeing your eyes—so much like your father's—only confirms my fear."

They looked down at Ianthe. She had silenced but was trembling uncontrollably.

"There are awful things in her mind," Wantemo said. "And I was just teetering on the edge when I tried to enter. Whoever goes there will need help coming back."

Sinto knelt beside his mother. "I'm willing. Will you help me?"

78

Ianthe's Hell

SINTO CLOSED HIS EYES and gently cradled Ianthe's head. At first she jerked away from his grasp, but he held firm and filled her mind with the calming sound of a breeze ruffling the trees in the jungles of Merluma.

Because of her recent trauma he feared he only had a few seconds before her mind discovered his breach and rejected him. He balanced on the narrow ledge of what was left of her sanity, knowing once he crossed over, he might never come back, joining her in her private hell.

Wantemo hovered on the fringes, mindfully hanging back but ever watching and ready to help Sinto return.

Sinto slithered over the edge, vowing not to return until he had answers as to who had confiscated her mind and desecrated her body. Until he learned the whereabouts of Naiada.

The calm vision he had fabricated quickly evaporated and he was suddenly floating in an endless sea of black liquid that clung to his arms and face; the sky was dark and threatening. A foul stench overpowered his senses. Black oil welled below his feet, death spewed from the bowels of earth. He closed his mouth but it didn't stop the foul oil from seeping through his lips, across his tongue, and down his throat, filling his belly and lungs, choking him. He tried to vomit, but that only caused more oil to enter his lungs, drowning him. Drowning but not dying, stuck in an ever-present state of consciousness. The fire of black death spread throughout his body, inside and out, but did not kill him.

He began to sink until the only thing he could sense was darkness and death. Sharp things randomly poked him, what and from where he could not tell.

Then he felt a tug from below and his black world spun as if caught in the whirlpool of a draining tub. He spun faster and faster. A movement he could not control. He felt dizzy and sick.

He landed on his back onto something soft. Bright light blinded his vision. He was coated in something clear and viscous, like a newly birthed child. He retched. Though nothing came out, he felt better, and for a dizzying moment, forgot where he was.

He stood and breathed in the beauty surrounding him. A memory. He was on the beach overlooking the bay of Inception. The same beach where Audrey awoke on Merluma for the first time. But this was a different time and he wasn't himself. He looked down at his hands. Delicate with gently tapered fingers. His mother's.

Her memory took over. He was no longer in control. He was merely an observer.

Ianthe said, "Naiada? Where are you?"

"*Find me*," Naiada answered in mind-speak.

"*So you want to play a game?*" Ianthe replied.

"*Yes, a game! I'm tired of training.*"

"*A game it is.*"

The game Ianthe chose was part of her training. Her final test, only Naiada didn't know it.

Ianthe said, "*You hide, I seek.*"

She busied herself to give Naiada time to hide. She pictured the child-like girl Naiada had been when they came to Merluma to begin her training. In the short time they had spent here, Naiada had grown stronger, surprisingly so, and much healthier than she had been before. Merluma's accelerated time scale gave her the boost to cross over from child to young woman. Ianthe was pleased with her training so far. Naiada demonstrated a maturity she had not expected and was quick to learn for someone so young.

Her thoughts slipped to Sinto and Ramasis, how much she missed them, how much her heart ached.

I've lost my only son and my mate.

She snapped back to the present moment.

I must be strong and not get distracted. Once Naiada is trained, I will mourn Sinto's death and seek the truth about Ramasis myself.

She strolled along a narrow path through the wild jungle that had grown thicker than she had ever seen it before. Sinto had been right. Merluma was exploding with new life, evolving faster with each passing day. A problem that she, as well as what was left of the Circle, needed to address as soon as she and Naiada returned to the Arctakai colony in Earth's Southern Ocean.

She decided to give Naiada a little more time and stopped under a tree laden with ripe fruit, hanging high above. She placed her hand on its trunk.

"That one," she told the tree, gaze fixed on a perfectly ripened mangeleno.

The tree trembled and branch shook. The fruit let go and fell into her outstretched hand. Her teeth sank into the thin skin to the sweet-soft meat inside.

It's time.

She focused her mind and launched telepathic tentacles, seeking out Naiada. The last trick she had taught Naiada, who had yet to perfect it. Ianthe's tentacles slithered around tree trunks, bored into the soil, sailed across the sky, swam through sand and water. Hundreds of tentacles seeking input from every living thing they encountered.

She heard plenty about their concerns regarding the strange things happening among the species on Merluma but got nothing about Naiada's whereabouts. That didn't surprise her. She had taught Naiada well. This was her final test, after all—a fitting end to her training. Afterwards, Naiada would have all the skills necessary to lead the Merahvu as their next queen.

She extracted her mind from the simple living things surrounding her and launched a second set of telepathic probes, tuning their sensors to pin-point and find the electrical firings of more sophisticated life, such as those with a human brain. Ianthe had inherited the ability and precision to root out and sift through intelligent minds all from a safe distance, and in most cases, with the mind unaware of her probing violation.

Could Naiada hide from someone as powerful as herself?

Ianthe's answer came quickly and she frowned, disappointed.

Near the outer reef, she thought to herself. *Too obvious.*

She cast the pit of the mangeleno aside and stepped from the cool jungle. She ran across the hot sandy beach and dove into the waters of Inception Bay.

As she swam toward the outer reef she noticed the bay was empty of the sea creatures she connected with only moments before. Confounded, she stopped swimming and probed deeper. The only living breathing life she found was hiding in a cave cut deep inside the outer reef. Pinpricks of thoughts from a leaking mind. Predictable and smacking of Naiada.

Ianthe approached the reef, camouflaged and mind-locked. She dove down then up a hidden passage to an above-water cave carved within thick coral. Her head broke the surface where air met water.

Slowly she emerged, ever conscious of making a sound. Water snaked from her hair and beaded down her skin as she crawled out of the water. The cave was lit by sunlight bouncing off the sandy bottom and into the mouth of the cave.

She heard a steady heartbeat, beating stronger than she would have expected from Naiada. She brushed off that thought, believing it was merely due to echoes in the confined cavern. She adjusted her vision, capturing meager rays of light reaching deeper into the cave. The deeper she ventured the darker it became.

She nearly stumbled upon the shape of a slumbering Terrakai whose lacy finned tail spread at her feet. A slumbering body much too big to be Naiada's.

Confusion muddled her thoughts. The thought patterns emitting from the mind before her were familiar. She held her breath and stilled her heart, not wanting to alert the slumbering stranger to her presence. Then her gaze settled on an arm splayed away from the body and gasped when she saw the raised Mark. Three dots encircled by a swirling loop.

"Ramasis!" She reached out to wake him.

His eyes opened. He smiled weakly and grabbed for her hand.

"I thought I lost you," Ianthe said.

"I've been sick, weak—not strong enough to pass through the portal."

She hugged him. "Not anymore, let me help you."

"Yes." He smiled brightly. "You certainly will." Then his eyes brightened with an orange glow. "You are going to help a great deal."

She was grabbed from behind and yanked to her feet by brutish hands. A pair of male Terrakai, wearing matching black leather skins. Wraps brushed the tops of their knees and their vests were stamped with a triangular trio of dots and adorned with rows of silver buttons. Their eyes glowed orange like Ramasis'.

How did she not sense them?

The third male stepped forward. He had wild dark hair and his orange glowing eyes were ringed in black. He wore a red silk shirt messily tucked inside his black leather wrap. He was young, not much older than Sinto. His aura carried a strong air of arrogance. Behind the garish display he looked vaguely familiar.

He snapped, "Guard your minds. You don't want her toying with you."

The two guards pinned her against the wall. Sharp coral bit into her back. The garish one unhooked a band from his waist. The guards forced her hands to her sides, and he looped the band around her torso, pinning her arms to her body. The effect was immediate and she gasped. An electrical parasitic draw sucking the life force from her merlux.

"Remember me?" he said. "It has been way too long since you've bothered to visit."

The name attached to the face came to her swift and sure. "Arkis."

"Ah, ha, she speaks! And she remembers." He shivered as if freezing. "Gives me goosebumps just hearing your voice." And in a mocking dramatic voice said, "The mighty and great Queen Ianthe."

Ramasis stepped up to Arkis' side. His eyes glowed intensely orange, not their natural emerald green. His hair was wild and unkempt like the rest of him. He wore fur coverings, unlike the others.

Arkis stepped aside. Ramasis drew closer.

"I missed you, Ianthe."

He pressed his nose to hers, brushed his lips across hers before kissing her, forcefully. His teeth ground on hers and cut into her bottom lip. His breath was foul and tasted of rotting fish. He forced her mouth open with his dirty fingers. Saliva and blood swirled when he thrust his tongue deep inside.

Ianthe struggled to break free, but the guards holding her and the band sucking her reserves were having their effect. She was growing weaker with each passing second. Sparks snapped and burned where the band touched her bare skin.

Ramasis broke off the violating kiss. He gripped her chin. Ragged nails cut into her flesh. "Oh, how I have wanted to see you weak and helpless. Time to reverse our roles. I want to dominate you, control you as you have me, ever since you chose me to be your puppet." He held out his arm with the Mark. "I know you faked this, toyed with my emotions and my mind, weakening my resolve, and once you tired of me, swatted me away as if I was a pesky fly. I will no longer bend my knee to your will, or do your dirty work while you run around bedding whomever you want, scheming and planning your great escape from your duties, from the people who look up to you, from your family, from me!

"I knew you deceived me long ago. I *smelled* him on you, and you pretended as if nothing had happened, then bedded me after. It took a week to rid the smell of him from me.

"We were never equal as you falsely portrayed to the Circle. I was your puppet. Every time I tried to object to a decision you didn't agree with, you brought me to heel, like a dog."

"No, I was just—"

He smothered her mouth with his hand. "Shut up! I am sick of your babbling! You're *my* dog now!"

She felt sick to her stomach. Some of the things he said were true; she did fake their Joining, but not because she didn't love him, but because they were not meant to be together in that true sense. She was ashamed of her affair with Culliford; she had been young and careless and disrespectful. Killing Leela was her biggest mistake, one she struggled with every single day.

But not all he claimed was true. She did respect his opinion, though not always agreeing. She did recall him getting his way, many times.

By the wild and crazed look in his eyes, she realized he had gone mad. Was it from her affair or something else?

He smiled. His front teeth were chipped and plaque filled the cracks between his lower ones. "As you can see I've realigned my priorities. Thanks to Arkis' foresight and support I've become a new man." He licked her cheek. "Care for a little sample of the new me?"

She recoiled. This was not the man who once vowed to be on her side, no matter the challenges. The man who fathered their children. A wave of nausea struck her and her vision swam. Of one thing she was now certain. She was in dire trouble and so was Naiada. Her chin fell to her chest and she gagged.

Ramasis took her by the shoulders and violently shook her. One of the guards grabbed her by the hair and yanked her head back. Ramasis' foul breath brushed her face.

"Not so strong now are you, my love."

"*What happened to you, Ramasis? Why are you doing this?*" she pushed to his mind.

He laughed, turning to the others. "She wants to know why we're doing this." He grabbed her by the chin. "Because it's time for a new queen and new rules. A queen who isn't afraid to do what is necessary."

"What do you think is necessary?"

"Rid Earth of the Sapiens and claim it for ourselves, a necessary re-balancing long overdue. By killing Leela you altered the course of history. The Sapiens were never supposed to proliferate as they have. Did you not foresee it? The Mark chose Leela and her Sapien mate to unite Merluma and Earth by joining Merahvu and Sapien as one and restoring the balance between the warring planets. You were nothing but a selfish, blundering fool, blinded by Culliford's cunning and manipulative attentions!" He pointed his finger at her chest. "You murdered her, Ianthe, and I will never forgive you for that."

Ianthe's heart sank. "How do you know these things?"

"You amaze me, Ianthe. Blind, even to the obvious!" He jammed his finger into her forehead, the ragged edge of his fingernail piercing her thick skin. He jabbed, emphasizing each word. "Think, think, think."

Bile rose in the back of her throat. "Naiada?"

"Very well done. You've passed the first test, my love. Now it's time for round two. Oh, and don't let me forget to thank you for doing an excellent job of training her. She has foreseen so much more than you can imagine." He turned to Arkis, who wagged a brow at her. "Alongside the king of the Orankai she will make a fine queen. I believe our best, ever!" He laughed and the others joined in, their sick cackles echoing throughout the cave.

Ianthe could hold back no longer and heaved. Bits of mangeleno pooled at her feet.

Ramasis made an exaggerated face of disgust. "Not feeling well? Not so nice is it? That's how I felt after Leela died. After I learned of your affair. Sick to my stomach. Every. Living. Moment. Since."

Ianthe's mind reached out, seeking Naiada. "*Naiada, run!*"

His brow furrowed. "What's that? Trying to warn Naiada? Nice try, but you won't find her. She's safe now, under our protection, unlike our dearly departed son." He cocked his head as if someone was whispering in his ear. "What's that I hear?" He glared. "Oh, right, you served him up to Culliford on a golden platter. But don't you worry, I will make sure Naiada is safe. No harm will come to her. As for you, well, that I can't promise."

Ramasis pressed himself against her, forcing her legs apart, pinning her against the wall. Razor-sharp coral dug deeper. Blood threaded down her back.

He grabbed her by the hair, yanked her head back and stared into her eyes. "Look at us. Nice and cozy, just like the old days. What do you say, my love—one last tryst before we let you go? You always liked sneaking off to dark places where no one would hear you scream."

"Please, no—this isn't like you."

"Maybe this was like me all along, only you failed to see."

He smashed his mouth to hers, burying his tongue down her throat with such force she gagged. Each time she fought him, he yanked her head back, deepening the kiss. His fingers slipped beneath the fold of skin covering her groin, then, painfully he thrust them inside her. Tears streamed down her face and she set her thoughts somewhere else whilst Ramasis prepared to have his way with her.

Suddenly, he pulled back. Extracting his ragged fingers and his tongue, he gazed into her eyes. Flickers of green out-shining the odd orangeness as if shocked and disgusted by his actions.

"Don't do this Ramasis," she begged in mind-speak. *"There must be another way to appease your grievances. Do with me what you must but the future of the Merahvu is at stake and must be protected. Naiada deserves to be free, to make her own choices."*

An orange-green war flashed in his eyes, first of their hopeful beginning, then a hatred she had never seen before as years of pent-up rage aimed at her and what she had done bubbled to the surface, the outcome of which led to the destruction of their family, the loss of their first-born, and recently of their only son. The way he looked at her she knew he would never forgive her. He had decided that a long time ago. She could no longer look at him and the ugliness of what he had become. She closed her eyes and wept. For him, not for herself. She was to blame, and Ramasis was broken because of it.

"I have not forgotten what I promised the people. Because of your actions, it has come to this," he replied. *"The future is Orankai, which you are no part of."*

He probed her mind, rifling through memories, but those were of no use to him. He dug deeper, sifting out secrets and fears and the monsters she had locked away. First he buried every good memory she had, then he unlocked every fear, minute or gargantuan, whether an irritating sound, a spider slithering up her neck, or watching someone she loved tortured with her helpless to stop it. He left these grotesque things to run amok in her mind.

And then he planted one last horror.

Being her Joined mate, forced or not, she had given herself freely as he had given himself to her. And with that sacrifice she had given him another much more powerful gift—access to her mind to a degree she'd given no other. An avatar to run freely though her mind. A ringmaster of the circus that would become her private hell. Whatever fear she had, a piece of him would linger in her mind to magnify it and use it to taunt her, weaken her resolve and her sanity, until finally her mind became a useless mass of gray matter and she would shrink and wither away, a failure as a queen, a mother, a mate—becoming only a forgotten memory to a misplaced people. Her name banned from ever being spoken by the new world order of the Orankai.

When he had finished planting his monster in her mind he stepped back and Ianthe fell to the floor of the cave sobbing.

Ramasis waved to Arkis. "You may have her to do with as you must, and after, dump her in the Winterlands for the white bear to feast upon."

Arkis knelt beside her and slipped a knife of jagged steel from a sheath tied to his thigh. The guards grabbed her and pressed her to the ground. She lay on her back with the band sucking the life out of her, helpless to stop what came next.

Arkis flashed a wicked grin. "Before I begin my treasure hunt I will leave you with one last, troubling thought... Should Naiada refuse to join me by my side I have an alternative plan." He lazily ran the tip of the knife across her belly, raising a thin line of blood. He tapped the protective skin, lying between her pelvic bones with its sharp tip. "With these little gems I will breed another."

He gazed up to Ramasis. "You have my promise: I will not harm your precious daughter." Then he gazed back at her, pushing his last words in mind-speak, so only she would hear. "*At least as long as Ramasis lives.*"

"No! Take your grievances out on me!"

He slapped her. "Stop begging! And don't worry, I fully intend to, as Ramasis has suggested!"

His eyes grew wide and manic as he used the tip of the blade to peel back the flesh covering her most vital female organs. "Shall I cut deep once or shallow many times? What if I slip and hit something vital? Will you die slowly and painfully?"

He laughed manically as the knife pierced her flesh, his fingers digging for her gold.

Her screams faded and the horrors Ramasis summoned began. Black oil seeped from the corners of her mind, its rancid fumes assaulting her lungs. She gagged, working her gills uncontrollably, trying to gasp a clean breath. Her eyes could see only what was in her mind, not the hands that grabbed her and pulled her from the cave into the warm tropical waters of Inception Bay, and racing through the Great Ocean to the Winterlands.

They dragged her near-lifeless and bleeding body across snow and ice, deep into the barren and uninhabitable Winterlands, where safe shelter and a meal were scarce and only carnivorous creatures survived. They unwound the band that bound her and left her on the frozen ground. Blood from the cuts Arkis inflicted stained the snow, the cloying scent announcing a fresh meal.

"Have a nice stay, your highness," one of them said mockingly.

Then they were gone.

Ianthe instinctively coiled her tail between her legs and hugged herself into a tight ball. In her mind, a sea of black engulfed her, filling her ears, mouth, and lungs, oblivious to her cold barren surroundings.

She chanted in the ancient tongue of the Wise Ones who were occasionally encountered during her journeys through the Timeless Dimension. Whispers of apology, pleading for forgiveness, begging for a swift death.

But it was not the wise ones or a ravenous creature that found her, but a brave Arctakai warrior who heard her pleas.

79

Curious Proposition

SINTO HELD TIGHT TO his mother's consciousness as he ascended from her private nightmare. He fought to shed the feeling of deceit and helplessness, of the images, smells, and feelings he experienced in the hell-scape where his father had left her; of the wicked smile on Arkis' face as he brutally cut her and ordered his guards to dump her like trash in the frozen wasteland on Merluma.

He clawed his way out of the abyss of black oily death to the precipice of his mother's mind where the horror ended and reality began, where Wantemo waited. Together they reached for her consciousness and extracted her from the grip of Ramasis' hell-scape. Wantemo then set fire to the sea of black oil, an all-consuming explosion eating away Ramasis' demon avatar until there was nothing left but smoldering ash.

Sinto pondered for a moment the timing of Arkis' attack on his mother and the abduction of Naiada. He had stolen his mother's eggs and taken Naiada *before* Sinto arrived in the City of Green. Arkis' talk of Sinto delivering Naiada was merely a test. Arkis had Naiada the entire time he held Sinto captive. He needed Sinto to turn Naiada. That meant there was a chance Naiada had not succumbed to embrace the Orankai, at least not yet.

Wantemo stood by as Sinto held his mother in his arms. Her face turned upward, eyes sparking with surprise upon seeing him. "Sinto? Wantemo told me—"

Sinto hugged her, then said, "Wantemo *saved* me. It was his idea to let everyone believe I died, which enabled me to learn the painful truth. And have I got a story to tell."

Tears welled in her eyes. Joyful to see him. But the joy waned in a fleeting moment.

"They took her," she said.

"I know," Sinto replied. "But we'll get her back. And we will seek vengeance, and soon. They will both pay for what they have done to you, Naiada, and all the others who refused to join them."

She squeezed his hand. "No."

Sinto was taken aback.

She took a deep breath. "You must be patient, my son. That is a warrior's best weapon. Blind vengeance is a fool's game, a distraction, the road to senseless destruction. Look at what it's done to your father, where it has lead us. Our people are scattered, the Circle is weakened. We have not seen war for hundreds of years. We need to consider and prepare. We must seek help to gain any hope of defeating them."

Sinto pondered her wise words, smiled and nodded. "I know who can helps us."

She looked at him questioningly.

"Our once sworn enemy, the Larkians."

80

Overdue Union

SINTO AND WANTEMO LAUNCHED dual vortexes through the Southern Ocean and raced at unfathomable speed toward the island shaped like a seahorse in the middle of the Pacific. Wantemo carried Ianthe, for Sinto was still recovering from his long and challenging journey.

Soon after Sinto and Wantemo pulled Ianthe from the hell-scape where Ramasis had imprisoned her within her mind, the three of them forged a rudimentary plan armed with information Sinto gleaned both from Audrey and from his own arduous journey.

The sun bore down on the now-calm but murky waters surrounding Isla Salvación. Floodwaters had dumped dirt and sand and other things loosened from mountainsides into the sea. Sludgy water crippled their ability to see beyond their noses.

Sinto worried about possible Larkian defenses and reached out to Audrey to warn her that they had arrived, seeking peace. She was near and responded immediately, promising safe passage. He shared with her their plan and she readily agreed to help.

They came ashore on the same beach Sinto had used before, where sand met grass near the island's only airport. Not long after they emerged from the water, he heard the whizzing sound of a quiet vehicle race down the runway, Audrey at the wheel. As she suggested, they met at the far end of the landing strip where it butted up next to the sea. She jumped from the driver's seat and ran to greet them.

She stopped an arm's length away, lungs laboring, eyes wide with disbelief.

She grinned. "I can't believe this is really happening."

Sinto officially presented his mother and Wantemo, though she had met them both before in Tallamure. But this time was different. Today there were no pretenses, no secrets or prisoners to exchange, only a lost people seeking help.

Audrey struggled to hide her shock at Ianthe's physical condition and the way she favored her scarred belly. Dark circles ringed her eyes, bruises colored her arms and torso, and the dull and knotted hair Sinto tried to bundle atop her head hung limply. But regardless of her physical condition, she gazed back at Audrey with a determined set of mouth and a lively spark in her lavender eyes. A fighter through and through.

Audrey reached out, stopping short of actually touching Ianthe's matted hair. "May I?"

Ianthe nodded and bowed her head. Audrey untangled the knot of hair Sinto tried to tame and combed it out with her fingers, pulling it back from her face and smoothing it as best she could, overlaying dull, golden waves across the bald spots.

Audrey bent, pulled a shoelace from her shoe, then picked a few wildflowers growing among the grasses alongside the runway. She secured Ianthe's hair at the base of her neck with her shoelace. She added the flowers, and finished it with a tidy bow.

Ianthe reached out and brushed Audrey's cheek. "I have nothing to offer to express my gratitude for your sweet and caring gesture, except... to thank you."

Audrey gathered Ianthe's hands in hers. "Seeing you alive is all you need to offer. Your fortitude is an inspiration to us all." Then

Audrey kissed her on the forehead, the nose, each cheek, and finally her lips.

These kind and tender gestures made Sinto's heart swell. Especially when Audrey accepted his mother with the traditional Merahvu greeting of respect and love.

Then Audrey turned to Wantemo. She hesitated at first then threw her arms around him. He seemed pleased to be given such a warm greeting and wasted no time returning the gesture. They had all been through hell of one kind or another.

Audrey grabbed a stack of folded fabric from the front seat of the vehicle she drove.

"Sarongs," she said. "My mom called them *pā'ū*." She held them out. "They're like your skareefs. Call them what you wish, you won't offend. Some people call them wraps or pareos. I guess it depends on where you're from."

Ianthe picked a pale yellow one and Audrey helped Sinto wrap it around her bruised naked body. She had grown much thinner since the last time Audrey saw her. Sinto silently explained to Audrey the trauma she recently experienced, and the reason for the fresh scars on her belly. Hearing what Arkis had done to Ianthe visibly angered and saddened her.

Wrapped in sarongs, they piled into the multi-seated vehicle with Audrey. Sinto sat in front while Wantemo cradled Ianthe in the bench seat behind them.

Sinto and Audrey shared furtive glances. Their Marks' ever-connected antenna, sharing similar sensations; fluttering butterfly-filled bellies and quivering hearts. Both anticipating a quiet moment when they could be alone.

"Soon, *very soon*," Sinto promised. "*But first, we must convince your father and the Larkians of our sincerity with all that we know.*"

They wound around the harbor where the Larkian ship was moored, past a village filled with many shops and businesses. The streets were littered with storm debris. Larkians were opening metal shutters and pulling wooden covers from doors and windows. Some swept, while others cast branches and fronds and other organic refuse into the back of trucks. Steam rose from reddish muddy puddles. The air was humid and smelled of things pleasant and unpleasant recently stirred.

Audrey pulled into a covered grand driveway that fronted a sprawling one-story structure on the other side of the harbor. She brought the vehicle to a stop in front of a pair of ornately carved wooden doors.

Sinto helped his mother from her seat, moving slowly but purposefully.

"My father should be inside," Audrey said. "I've not told him anything other than Sinto's alive, and—I hope I've not overstepped—that you've come seeking peace regardless of what happened in Tallamure." She paused and looked to Ianthe for confirmation.

His mother nodded. "Yes, peace, and more."

Audrey reached out and gently squeezed her hand. "Good. Sinto and I will go first. Ianthe, you follow with Wantemo," Audrey sucked a deep breath, looked at each of them. "A historic first step—are we ready for this?"

Ianthe nodded. "I have sought this moment for a very long time. I am grateful to still be alive to see it through."

Sinto said, "And we will, Mother."

Audrey took Sinto's hand and together they passed through the double doors into a great room filled with Larkians tending to the wounded and cleaning up the mess after the Orankai attack. A once lovely room for gathering and dining had turned into a battleground. Shards of glass littered the floor. Death ash covered everything, the scent of it strong and lingering. Blood splatters covered the walls and floors. Draperies hung in burnt shreds. Furniture was splintered, charred, and toppled.

Silence descended when they entered, every eye turned in their direction.

Audrey's father stood, his once dark hair shot through with more silver than Sinto remembered. He approached, his glacial gaze locked on Sinto, like that fateful day in Tallamure right before he tried to kill him. But Culliford stopped, giving space between them, with his hands loosely hanging by his sides in a non-threatening way. His gaze fell to the puckered scar peeking out from the green sarong Sinto had wrapped across his shoulder. It lingered there for a beat, his skin tingling from the memory of Culliford's knife entering his chest. Then Culliford swung his gaze to his daughter. His face softened and he reached out. She took his hand and moved to stand beside him, facing Sinto.

Sinto turned to his mother. Her gaze was cast to the floor as if she was afraid to look up, to face the man she still deeply loved and who was the sworn enemy of the Merahvu. Sinto pulled her forward, holding her to his side.

Culliford wobbled and gasped at the sight of her. Ianthe looked up and captured his gaze. Something visibly clicked between them. His face softened as he surveyed the dark circles under her eyes and the dark bruises on her arms. A tear slipped from his mother's eye. Their facial expressions became animated. More than a simple gaze passed between them. Sinto was certain Culliford had learned the way of mind-speak from his mother long ago, just as Audrey had recently learned from him.

Three Larkians came forward and Audrey made quick introductions; Dr. Wickman, Captain Stokes, and a twitchy sort of man named Alvarez. Not much was said, other than sharing of names and associations. There was a shuffling of feet and an awkward silence, no one knowing who should start and where to begin.

Audrey stepped up and broke the ice. "We have a common enemy who is intent on destroying all of us and attacking innocent Sapiens of Earth. The same enemy who attacked the *Requiem Sea II* and our island home. The same enemy who attacked the first *Requiem Sea* during our attempt to form a lasting truce and eventual peace. The same enemy who attacked your Larkian crew in these waters surrounding this island long ago. The same enemy who killed my mother, Teola."

Sinto took over. "They call themselves Orankai and they're breeding an army on Merluma. They're controlled by my bastard half-brother, Arkis, along with my father, Ramasis."

He looked down at his mother. "They attacked Ianthe and she would have died had not one of our own found her. They kidnapped my sister, Naiada, who they anticipate will provide foresight into any of our future plans and actions to stop them."

Sinto nodded toward Audrey, and continued, "Arkis discovered Orange in the Pacific—when, we're unsure, but I believe you happened upon Orankai harvesting it, which is why you were attacked."

He acknowledged the men Audrey introduced as Dr. Wickman and Alvarez. "Orange is the primary source for a powerful drug—a nectar Arkis brews to accelerate the breeding process on Merluma and to control, empower, and create a hive-mind connection amongst his followers. He's recruiting Merahvu from all of our three tribes, the strongest and most capable. He desperately wanted to recruit me for my mother's bloodline and my enhanced ability to shock. He calls those recruited his Elites, whose sole purpose is for breeding future generations of Orankai. There are many who follow him, and many more are being born every day on Merluma."

Sinto looked to Audrey. She nodded back, then said, "Sinto and I propose we join forces, Merahvu and Larkian. It is the only way we will have a chance to defeat Arkis and the Orankai. We have more in common than not, with much to share and learn from each other. Together, we can build a power coalition against the Orankai."

Culliford and Ianthe shared a look. Then he turned to the twitchy man named Alvarez.

Alvarez said nothing at first, his eyes shifting between Sinto and Audrey as if measuring up their sincerity. "Everything you said is true?"

Sinto said, "Experienced first-hand."

"Hmm," he said, pausing for another beat. "Impressive."

Audrey said, "So what now? Do we all agree, shall we cast a vote?"

Culliford said, "I agree."

"Aye," said Dr. Wickman.

A voice rose from the back of the room. "So do I." Blake.

A third came from the kitchen from a jolly-looking white-bearded man with a colorful scarf tied around his head. "Aye, and 'bout bloody time if yer ask me."

Audrey was squeezing Sinto's hand so hard he couldn't feel it any longer. She turned to Alvarez and asked, "What about you, Alvarez?"

He gave her a rare smile. "Well done, Culliford. I too agree."

A dam burst open and a rousting round of "Ayes" rippled across the room. Those who wanted to learn more crowded around Sinto and Audrey. Each told their stories, interweaving what they had learned and experienced from their independent journeys, drawing a crowd of the curious and the weary.

Wantemo offered to help Dr. Wickman tend the wounded. Each gaining mutual respect for their uniquely different knowledge and skills, realizing what each could offer the other by working together.

Sinto shared his observation with Audrey. *"Dr. Wickman will learn what he seeks from Wantemo. Far more than he would have gained from studying the body of a dead Orankai. You did a noble thing, respecting her like that. She was one of many innocents, born to fight in a war in which she had no choice."*

Sinto noticed Ianthe and Culliford settled on a torn and slightly burned sofa, engaged in a quiet discussion. He pointed them out to Audrey. A surge of hope swirled through their shared connection.

Audrey and Sinto sought out Blake, who had lingered on the fringes, quietly helping others while observing. Audrey grabbed Blake's hand and led him to meet Sinto's mother, whom he had not seen since that day when she severed the bond between him and Leela.

It was a tension-filled moment at first; a brief flash of anger, then regret followed by a deep apology, tears, and finally, acceptance and forgiveness. A fate cast long ago that could never be undone. Both agreed that forging a new path forward was best for all.

Then Blake excused himself and emerged shortly after from the kitchen, carrying an elaborately decorated cake ablaze with twenty-one candles, Mako and Poe in tow with bottles of champagne and glasses.

Larkians and Merahvu shared a moment of reprieve from the senseless violence that passed before. Past grievances were buried. Together they wished Audrey a happy birthday and toasted to a prosperous future; for the Merahvu, Larkians, and the innocent people and creatures of Earth and Merluma.

As the cake disappeared and champagne kept flowing, Sinto and Audrey stole away for a well-earned moment of privacy. They walked in silence, holding hands, toward a nearby beach where the sea lay quiet and reflective. Stars burned bright in the night sky, scrubbed clean from the recent storm.

Once they reached sand, Audrey kicked off her shoes. Sinto led her to the sea's edge and spun her around to face him, their toes immersed in the warm shallow water.

Audrey combed her fingers through his shortened hair. "Where do we go from here?"

Sinto took her fingers and twined them through his. "We go wherever the swift wind takes us; stealthy as a lion, fierce as a wildfire."

"And into the storm?"

"Is there any other possibility?"

Audrey fell silent. Her chin quivered. "As much as I try, I see no other way forward."

"So we must embrace it, go forth, boldly like lightning, and strike."

"Together?"

"Yes, together."

"And after?"

Sinto cradled her chin. "After we will finish what we started at Club Ballo."

"And until then?"

"Until then we'll push against boundaries."

She gave him a sly smile. "And what might these *boundaries* be?"

He grinned back. "Perhaps we should experiment and figure that out."

Their lips connected. Sinto dragged her deeper into the water, wrapping his lorica around them in a warm embrace. Their essences fevered, hearts sang, and minds and bodies twined.

The Mark lay quiet and dormant, patiently allowing this moment of peace and togetherness without its distraction, for their arduous and dangerous journey was far from over and Sinto and Audrey would need their combined strength. For Earth and Merluma still wobbled, ever so faintly, beneath their feet. A constant reminder of their fated and noble purpose that one day, very soon, would be revealed.

And once it did, they would act without doubt or hesitation.

EPILOGUE

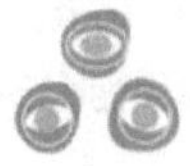

Mole

What luck! he thought excitedly. Having spotted Queen Ianthe and her son leaving the southern waters of the Arctakai, he followed, tightly trailing their dual vortexes through the sea to here—the fortified island the Larkians called home—where he easily slipped through their defenses alongside them, undetected.

Arkis will be most pleased!

Before he ventured to the Arctakai's city as a deeply rooted mole, Arkis' instructions had been quite clear: fully integrate within the ranks of Merahvu, for soon they will embrace the Larkians with Sinto's help. Arkis predicted that he would seek out his mother and the man who watched over her. And he was right.

It was what Arkis asked of him next that made his fingers tingle and heart race. Arkis didn't verbalize this part of his instruction, but shared—quite vividly—what he wanted the mole to do. What he wanted would be challenging, and perhaps, require another round of luck.

But the mole was up to the task. While Orange rage simmered within, he tamped down the urge to lash out with unchecked emotion. He was highly skillful and outwardly patient and had proven nearly one hundred percent successful in his other missions. It was why Arkis chose him for this vital assignment.

The mole dipped lower as the two lovers waded deeper into the water, distracted and oblivious to his presence.

He could do it now, if he wanted, but a quick calculation held him back.

The Larkians had stepped up their defenses. A messy escape at this point would be risky. The mole was lucky he was able to penetrate their sophisticated technology so far. He had achieved a critical first step; to infiltrate Isla Salvación.

Kudos to me!

Acting now raised the possibility of failure. And Arkis had also been vividly clear: the mole must not get caught. Not only that, the timing was wrong.

Integrate, he would, until the right situation presented itself. For he had all the time in the world to prepare. Besides, this was the part he enjoyed the most; the hunt and the setup, even more than the final act.

The mole slipped past the lovers, enthralled in a passionate kiss, to the beach. Then he slipped into the thick jungle, camouflaged and quiet as a ghost.

NOT THE END...

The adventure concludes with Fierce as Fire

~ ~ ~

The final battle to save two worlds will test the bonds of love and destiny...

Audrey and Sinto stand on the front lines of an epic battle against a trio of catastrophic threats.

While the Larkians and the Merahvu maintain a powerful alliance, their mutual enemy—the Orankai—remain one step ahead and descend upon every corner of the globe. A sudden explosion of unexplained deaths confounds Earth's authorities. And Orange, a water-borne fungus, continues its deadly march across Earth's oceans.

Although torn apart by forces Audrey and Sinto cannot control, the mystical Mark binding them makes them stronger. Audrey enlists unlikely allies to join the fight for control of Merluma. Sinto discovers an ancient stone that holds the secret to the Orankai's advantage—and the truth about Merluma's origins.

As war rages, a foreboding reality becomes frighteningly clear. Merluma and Earth embroil in a war of their own. One in which no one can escape.

Fierce As Fire is the epic conclusion to Lisa Cram's *Earth Stones Trilogy*, a breathtaking finale where love transcends worlds, sacrifice defines heroes, and two souls discover the only way to save everything is to unleash the power of the earth stones.

~ ~ ~

Acknowledgments

Some believe writing is a lonely occupation. I believe the opposite. Every friend, family member, and stranger I've met or observed in daily life—in an airport, a restaurant, a store, in the news, frankly everywhere—live vividly in my head and are active participants in my story creation. Bits of me are sprinkled throughout my characters, and so are some of you. So, I thank *you* even though you may not know exactly who you are!

I don't have a mega staff of editors or marketing people, but this book would not have made it to the electronic or bookstore shelves if I didn't have a few, critical people to help me turn my dream of writing and publishing these stories into a reality.

Lynn Nansen-Dale, my sister, artist, and butt-kicking editor extraordinaire. This book would not be the same without her input and insight into the story, especially when I got stuck, or mixed up my science, or used the entirely wrong word for what I was attempting to portray. She also created the maps and images sprinkled throughout. She lent an ear and offered wise advice when I became stymied while navigating the road to publication. She converted these words to e-book and into a beautiful print book layout. She helped me fine-tune the cover. Gettin' the idea she's the super talented one?

Dana Cram, my daughter, whose incredible artwork graces the cover, and for her invaluable professional knowledge of mental health issues, which helped me add a level of depth to my characters I otherwise would not have been able to achieve without her insight and advice. Plus, she doesn't tolerate lazy writing or BS. Show don't tell, Mom! Got it!

My early beta readers: Julie and Rebekka—I wish I could write as fast as you both read. To Lisa, who has an uncanny eye for typos that slipped by many of us. Thank you all for your everlasting enthusiasm that encourages me to keep writing new and exciting stories.

Those who helped me from the beginning, starting with *Flow As Water*, also flow into this addition: David Welker, my marine tech adviser. Gregory Scott Houle, for training me how to seriously hurt someone. These lessons will continue to flow forward. Buckle up for book three, *Fierce As Fire*!

Summer Huntington and the Flowshala staff, plus Mark Wildman, for teaching me the correct way to wield a staff, clubbells, and a steel mace. You've helped me change my body and outlook on life in such a positive way... Which I channeled to make Audrey a badass character!

Thank you Stephanie Cariker, my communications consultant, for your continued expertise in helping me promote and market myself as well as my books. Sometimes I believe you know me better than I know myself!

And finally, Doug, my husband, whose love and support keeps me sane. Every. Single. Day.

May I ask you for a favor?

Reviews serve a dual purpose: to help readers find new authors, and independent authors, such as myself, connect to a community of new readers. I would be forever grateful if you could leave an honest review, if possible, wherever you acquired this book and/or on goodreads.com.

You can learn more of what I'm up to at my website: www.lisacram.com. Subscribe for important announcements and upcoming releases.

May you always find words to bring you joy, entertainment and wisdom!

Lisa

About the Author

RAISED ON A LOUISIANA bayou and the evergreen-cloaked shores of Puget Sound, Lisa Cram spent most of her life on the water, fantasizing about what lay beneath. The Earth Stones Trilogy is her debut as a writer. When not writing, you might find her reading, immersed in the outdoors, swinging a golf club, or her steel mace to raucous music. She divides her time between the Pacific Northwest and the California desert with her musician husband.

For news on upcoming releases from Lisa, visit lisacram.com